I0718720

Secrets

THE BOXED SET

ONNÉ ANDREWS

This is a work of fiction. All characters, organizations and events in this novella are products of the author's imagination and are not to be construed as real. Any resemblance to persons, living or dead, is entirely coincidental.

SECRETS: THE BOXED SET

ISBN-13 - 978-1-938745-82-9

Copyright 2020 by Onné Andrews

Tied By Lust, ©2012 by Onné Andrews
Bound By Desire, ©2012 by Onné Andrews
Taken By Passion, ©2012 by Onné Andrews
Enslaved By Love, ©2013 by Onné Andrews
Captured By Devotion, ©2020 by Onné Andrews

All rights reserved

Published by Angry Sheep Publishing
Findlay, Ohio

Cover Design by Just Write. Creations and Services
Interior Design by QA Production

More books by Onné Andrews
(Each series is in suggested reading order)

Secrets

Tied By Lust
Bound By Desire
Taken By Passion
Enslaved By Love
Captured By Devotion
Secrets: The Boxed Set

Club Noir

Domme
Voil Jeanette (Coming soon!)
Bon Temps (Coming soon!)
Noblisse Oblige (Coming soon!)

Naughty Neighbors

Three's Company
Four of a Kind
The Cherry on Top (Coming Soon)

Dirty Dozen

Eat Me
To Punish and Service
Take Me
Dreams of Anubis
Do Unto Others

Educating Lisa

The Professor's Wife
The New Master
The Final Lesson

Horny Holidays

Santa's Gift
Cupid's Arrow
Son of a Bunny (Coming Soon)

Sex and the Single Monster

Everlasting Hope
Zombie's Night Out
Puppy Love (Coming Soon)

For news, sales, and giveaways, join Onne's mailing list or visit Onne's website at www.onneandrews.com. You can also check her out on Twitter or Facebook.

(Your information will not be sold, leased or otherwise given to a third party.)

Contents

TIED BY LUST

Alicia's Story

Chapter One

Alicia Thomas's thumb rubbed the base of the fourth finger on her left hand. "All he ever wanted with me was vanilla sex. Anytime I suggested anything remotely adventurous he'd get this look." She screwed her face into Hank's pompous expression. "He'd say, 'Just where did you learn about things like that.' But then I catch him."

Her three friends stared at her with rapt expressions. Even the two little old ladies at the table next theirs had stopped their conversation, eavesdropping on her story.

"In his office, a ball gag in his mouth while this *professional* paddles his lily white ass."

Diana's mouthful of iced tea sprayed across the table. Micki laughed, loud and hard. Poor Beth blushed a brilliant red. And the elderly ladies' jaws dropped.

On one hand, her tale wasn't exactly appropriate talk for the little upscale sidewalk bistro. Alicia leaned back in her chair and took a sip of her soda. On the other hand, it felt good to get the real reason for the divorce off her chest. The four of them managed to keep their friendship going since high school despite life taking each of them in radically different directions. She gazed down Connecticut Avenue. In the distance, the Washington Monument spiked into the clear spring sky, mocking her for her failed marriage.

"Y-you would have done—" Beth cleared her throat. "Would you have spanked him if he asked you?"

"I don't know." Alicia stared at the faint line on her finger that still existed even though she'd taken off the damn ring the same day she'd caught Hank. "I've been asking myself that for the last five months."

Micki tossed her napkin on her plate. "Maybe that's what we all need. Something different." She found a sudden interest in the pigeons battling for crumbs along the sidewalk. Today was the first time Alicia had heard Micki laugh since her partner had died in a police raid gone wrong last year. And she hadn't dated in forever.

"Torrid fucks with some hot boytoys are what we all need," Diana grumbled. "Screw this relationship shit."

Alicia closed her eyes. At least she knew the reason for her split. Diana still didn't know what went wrong in hers. Her fiancé had packed up and walked out while she'd been at work. He'd left a note saying he simply didn't love her.

And then there was poor Beth.

The impulse seized Alicia. An idea so crazy it might actually work. She leaned forward. "You're right. Let's make a pact. Before our lunch next month, we each find a stud, use him for some type of raunchy sex we've never done before, then report what we learned." She raised her soda. "Who's with me?"

"Oh, hell, yes!" Micki held up her glass as well.

The expression on Diana's face was dubious at best. "This isn't one of your marketing ideas. You can't just brainstorm a relationship into existence."

Alicia glared at her. "You just said we needed boy*toys*, not boyfriends."

"All right, all right." Diana hoisted her ice tea to meet the other two glasses. "A freaky guy and some freaky sex before next month."

In unison, they looked at Beth.

Pink still flushed her face. "W-we shouldn't treat men as objects."

"C'mon. They do it to us all the time," Alicia scoffed. "Or at least they'd treat you like an object if you'd ditch the glasses, the ponytail and the men's clothes."

Beth had downplayed her looks since that awful night of their junior prom. It drove Alicia crazy. It had been sixteen years, dammit.

Beth finally sucked in her cheeks, then straightened in her chair. "Okay, let's do it."

Four glasses clinked, sealing the deal. Alicia drank a huge mouthful of soda. *Now, how the hell am I going to pull off finding such a man?*

Alicia swore under her breath as another crack of thunder rumbled. The Metro station was a block and a half away and she'd be soaked before she took two steps down the street. And the last thing she wanted to do was to spend a Friday night in D.C. She'd rather be home . . .

No, that wasn't true. Her little colonial in the Maryland suburbs had been cold, empty, since she threw Hank out on his well-paddled ass the day before Thanksgiving. Hell, she didn't even have a dog or cat to go home and feed. Hank had always nixed the idea, saying they were both too busy with their careers to care for pets.

Maybe she should spend the night here. The whole reason the company's annual meeting had been held at the hotel was for the convenience of some of their prominent shareholders. But her auburn-haired reflection gave her a disapproving glare. Not to mention, her next-door-neighbor Mrs. Abercrombie would come over first thing in the morning to check on her. The old lady seemed to have made Alicia her personal project since Hank had been sent packing.

As she debated whether to take a taxi home or wait for the rain to stop, a limo pulled up under the awning of the hotel. How nice would it be for someone else to do the driving?

"Ms. Thomas?" Sheik Abdul's deep voice drew her attention from the waiting vehicle.

"Yes," She turned and smiled. "Your Highness, is there something I can help you with?"

"The offer to join us for the evening is still open." He gestured toward the limo. The sheik's face was inscrutable, but behind him, his brother's held a slightly hopeful look.

One of the executive assistants must have let the little fact of her divorce slip. And Sheik Abdul had made no secret that if she were ever free, he *and* his brother were interested.

Piercing, dark eyes examined her. The Savile Row suits didn't hide either man's trim physique. The sheik's shoulders were a hair wider, his brother a hair taller. Otherwise, they could pass as twins despite the five-year age difference and the different mothers.

The temptation to say yes lay on the tip of her tongue. A weekend ménage with two foreign dignitaries would definitely qualify for the lunchtime boytoy pact. But the pact wasn't worth losing her CFO position by having a fling with the company's two biggest shareholders. Losing her marriage was all she could handle right now.

And having a one-night stand with a married man would make her a hypocrite. A hypocrite four times over considering the sheik's four wives.

Alicia inclined her head. "Your offer is incredibly gracious, Your Highness, but I must decline."

The sheik eyed her, then turned toward the plate glass separating them from the storm. "It is terrible weather. Perhaps we could take you someplace?"

Something in her gut said if she got in that limo, she wouldn't be getting out until the men had their way with her. So why the hell were her panties damp from that thought? She gave the sheik a rueful smile. "I already have plans—"

"Alicia? There you are, sweetheart."

She whirled at the familiar voice. Richard Brand stalked up to her, wrapped his arm around her waist, and planted a kiss on her lips. A kiss that sent tingles south. A kiss that stole her breath. A kiss like she'd never had before.

Richard Brand. A man she'd fantasized about all those nights when Hank had refused to touch her.

Richard Brand. Her ex's boss.

Chapter Two

If it weren't for Richard's firm hold on her waist, Alicia would have fallen over from that kiss. She could barely catch her breath when their lips parted. Sharp, gray eyes twinkled at her. A gray so light, they appeared silver.

Slapping addled brain cells back in place, she looked at the sheik and his brother. Their expressions matched her own confusion. "Sheik Abdul, Prince Mohammed, may I present Richard Brand?"

"*Alsalamo alikom*," Richard said. He held out his huge palm. "A pleasure to see you again, Your Highnesses."

Both the sheik and his brother shook hands with Richard.

"My pleasure as well." The sheik's attention flicked to Alicia, then back to Richard. "I beg your forgiveness, Mr. Brand. I did not know."

Richard made some comment in Arabic that left all three men chuckling.

Alicia wanted to pull away from Richard's possessive grip, but some instinct said she was safer with him. What the hell was going on here?

The conversation continued for a few more seconds before Sheik Abdul said, "Until we meet again, Mr. Brand. Ms. Thomas. *Salaam*." Abdul and his brother gestured their farewells before they headed through the main hotel doors. The limo driver leapt out of his seat and hurried around to open the back door for the two men. Prince Mohammed shot a contemplative look in her direction before he climbed into their limousine. But seconds later, the vehicle pulled into Connecticut Avenue traffic.

"I think you can let go of me, Mr. Brand," Alicia whispered.

"Not yet," Richard whispered back. "Two of their bodyguards are still in the lobby. For your sake, go along with this." Aloud, he said, "Ready for dinner?"

She managed to murmur something that sounded agreeable. As Richard guided her toward the hotel restaurant, she caught sight of the two men in black suits, pretending to read the *Post* while they sat in the hotel lobby. Why on earth would the sheik leave two of his people behind to spy on her? It simply did not make sense.

Neither she nor Richard spoke while they walked toward the restaurant. His hand at the small of her back radiated heat down through her already damp pussy. An evil thought whispered through her mind. Wouldn't a night of wild monkey sex with her ex's boss be the perfect revenge?

No, that was totally ridiculous.

Why? a tiny voice at the back of her mind asked. Richard was handsome, single. She wouldn't be hurting anyone. Her tongue flicked along her lips as she searched for the courage to say what she wanted. What she desired.

The hostess, a girl barely out of braces, smiled at them. "Your usual table, Mr. Brand?"

"Thank you, Bethany."

Bethany shot her an appraising look, one Alicia recognized all too well from high school. She brushed her hair back from her face, then cursed herself for the self-conscious habit she thought she'd broken. Damn it, she was thirty-two with a terrific career. Maybe the invitation from the sheik and his brother shook her more than she wanted to admit.

No, it wasn't the invitation itself. It was how much she had wanted to accept it.

Slight pressure just above her ass urged her to follow the hostess. The girl guided them to a quieter area, one sectioned off from the main dining room by a series of folded wooden partitions and huge lush plants.

Alicia took the two steps, and Richard's hand slipped a few millimeters from the small of her back to the curve of her ass. She couldn't help herself. She paused for the briefest of instances, reveling in that intimate contact. A quick glance over her shoulder told her Richard knew exactly what she was doing. And if the gleam of lust in his eyes weren't enough of a message, his slight squeeze of her left ass cheek was.

A slight smile tilted his full lips. He inclined his head toward the table where a not-so-friendly Bethany waited.

Once they were seated and alone, she leaned forward. "Thanks for your help back there, Mr. Brand, but you don't have to do this."

Candlelight glimmered in the silver that flecked his temples as he matched her body language. "It's Richard, and it's the least I can do."

"Richard." Her tongue savored the taste of his name. "It's just that—" There was nothing in Emily Post's etiquette guide for seducing your ex's boss, and Alicia had no clue of how to start.

His black eyebrow flicked upward. "This is awkward as hell thanks to Hank's little performance in his office."

The wrong kind of heat rushed to her cheeks. "Yes." She watched him from hooded eyelids. "Considering you walked in right after me."

He leaned back. "Mind if I ask you something, Alicia?" A secretive smile curved his lips.

"I suppose it's the least I owe you for getting me out of that lobby situation." So why did it feel like she was about to step into some kind of trap?

"Why did you watch for so long before you said something when you caught Hank?"

She straightened at the memories and the odd flood of emotions came rushing back. It had been after hours. She'd hoped to surprise Hank, drag him to a romantic dinner and then to a little B&B in Virginia for the long weekend.

His office door had been cracked open. First had been shock, then . . .

God help her, she'd been so aroused watching the dominatrix spank him, wishing it were her being punished. Then shame and disgust, an equal mix aimed at her own reaction as much as Hank's betrayal. And from the way Richard watched her, he knew exactly what was going through her head. She couldn't meet his eyes any longer. Her gaze dropped to the pristine white tablecloth.

His knee brushed hers. "There's nothing wrong with liking what you saw."

"Except Hank did it with every other woman but me." Months of bitterness coated her words.

Richard laid his hand on top of hers. "There's nothing wrong with doing certain things, Alicia. But there are rules. Rules Hank violated."

She raised her head. A combination of anger and sympathy shone from his expression.

"Rules?" Her voice squeaked.

"Yes. Rules." His thumb eased under her palm and stroked her hyper-sensitized skin. "The first of which is you never harm your partner."

Alicia licked her lips. He wasn't offering what she thought, was he? "What are the other rules?"

A wicked smile lit his face. "Honesty is a must at all times."

"Honesty about?"

"What you want. What you need." He turned her hand over and began stroking the delicate skin on her wrist.

"And the next rule?" Alicia's mouth was so dry she could barely get the words out. She shifted in the chair, but the movement only made the throb between her legs worse.

"Making sure your partner is satisfied." Richard only touched her wrist, and somehow that, coupled with his words and intense look, was far more erotic than when he had slid his hand down and grabbed her ass.

"May I take your order?"

Richard didn't so much as twitch at the waiter's interruption, simply shifted into CEO mode and ordered for both of them.

Alicia blinked and tried to collect her thoughts as the waiter strode away. Thoughts which seemed to be scattered with the storm crackling outside. She'd never let a man order for her. But then, she'd never had a man seduce her with just a touch either. What the hell was wrong with her?

As if sensing her disquiet, Richard released her wrist. "It's all right to want to let go, to let someone else take care of you once in a while. But I'm not forcing you into something you're uncomfortable with."

She reached for the water the waiter had left and took a quick swallow. "Is that another rule?" She couldn't meet his eyes, afraid she'd be caught in his spell again.

"Yes."

Surprise forced her to look at him. Sincerity sparked in his eyes along with desire.

"What did you say to Abdul and Mohammed in the lobby?"

He exhaled and reached for her hand again, this time twining his fingers through hers. "That you were too innocent for their games."

Out of everything she expected him to say, that assessment of her was not at the top of her list. "Excuse me?" She was more embarrassed by the squeak in her voice than his assumption.

Another smile, this one filled with unadulterated humor. "I've known the brothers for a long time. They'd never intentionally harm you, but their tastes are . . ." He paused. "Probably outside of your experience."

She wasn't sure if she should be offended at his assumption of her naiveté or touched by his protectiveness. "You don't think I could handle a threesome?"

"With their wives watching?"

"Wives? Watching?" Once again, her voice squeaked. Oka-a-ay. Maybe she was that naïve.

The waiter chose that moment to deliver the light supper Richard had ordered. He released her hand and changed the subject to Beltway gossip.

He was giving her space she realized. Space to think about his offer. To come to her own decision. Like after a year and a half with no sex she really needed to debate the issue.

After Richard paid the bill, he stood and offered his arm. Knowing the real offer, she took it. There wasn't the look of triumph in his eyes like most men she'd dated, just simple acknowledgement.

Instead of leading her back to the lobby, he guided her to the bank of elevators. She raised an eyebrow when he slid his keycard into one of the penthouse slots. He caught her look and gave her a rueful grin. "Would you believe earthquake damage on top of last fall's tropical storm?"

She laughed and quickly covered her mouth. "I'm sorry. That's not funny." She stepped into the elevator and he followed. She'd accompanied Hank to Richard's estate on Chesapeake Bay for a company function two years ago. The place was absolutely gorgeous. She could imagine what the early fall storm had done to the buildings and grounds. The storm had barely been downgraded from a category one hurricane before it hit D.C. Then the oddball trembler had shaken the east coast last month.

The elevators slid closed. In the tight confines, she couldn't help but be aware of his body heat, his masculine scent. The combination was a heady rush.

Richard's grin widened. "Actually, it is hilarious. I can sell billions in software before breakfast, but I can't control Mother Nature." He shrugged. "I normally stay over in the city several nights a week anyway, so I moved here until the repairs are completed."

The elevator doors slid open, and new nervousness slammed into Alicia's knees, making them weak. Only two doors stood, one at each end of the short hallway. Once again, hot skin at the small of her back guided her, this time to the door on her right. She paused and looked Richard in the eyes. Her hand rose and rested on his chest.

"I-I need to know the rest of the rules before we go inside." She inclined her head toward the mahogany door.

"You must do exactly what I tell you. No more, no less."

A little ball of fear clenched inside her. She glanced at the dark wood. Could she really go through with this? Was obeying him, letting him spank her, sleeping with him worth a final "screw you" to Hank?

She looked back up at Richard, searching his face. For what though?

"Do you trust me, Alicia?" he whispered.

That's what it came down to, wasn't it? She'd lost trust. Trust in other people. Trust in her own perceptions. She closed her eyes, listening for that little voice. The voice that had told her something was wrong with her marriage. The one that never lied to her.

She opened her eyes and lifted her chin. "Yes."

Chapter Three

Pleasure curled in Alicia's stomach at his smile.

"If you get scared or I go too far, say 'parmesan.'" He unlocked the door and held it open for her.

"Parmesan," she repeated, though she had to bite her lip to keep from giggling at the code word. No way *that* could be mistaken for anything else.

Alicia stepped into a suite that put most palaces to shame. Plush sofas and chairs created an intimate conversation pit. Wood of the same deep mahogany as the doors accented various surfaces. The gigantic plate windows drew her with their fantastic view of the White House and, behind it, the Washington Monument. The rain had stopped while they'd eaten. Below, lights twinkled from traffic meandering up and down Connecticut Avenue.

"Take off your jacket, Alicia."

Of course, he'd want her to undress. The impressive skyline had almost made her forget why she was here.

She laid her attaché on the closest end table and removed her jacket. She folded it and laid it on top of the bag. The folding was only to stop the trembling that threatened to paralyze her. She lifted her foot and reached for her pump.

A sharp smack on her ass made her jump. She whirled and glared at Richard.

"Did I tell you to remove your shoes?"

"No," she whispered.

"No, what?"

"No, sir."

He'd turned on one lamp while she'd been staring at the cityscape. Now, he slid off his suit jacket and laid it overtop hers. A mark of possession. He lowered his massive body into an overstuffed chair. His silvery gaze slid over her body, far more intimate than any touch so far.

Alicia shivered. Anticipation and anxiety battled for control of her nerves. "Should I—"

"Did I give you permission to speak?" His voice was as sharp as the smack he'd given her.

She automatically lowered her eyes. "No, sir." Anticipation won. Would he punish her for this transgression? Part of her hoped he would.

"Unbutton your blouse." He steepled his hands, elbows resting on the arms of the chair. "Slowly."

Her fingers reached for the 'V' at the base of her throat. Counting to three for each button, she undid each one until she reached the waistband of her skirt. She paused and peeked through lowered lashes, waiting for an instruction. When none came, she tugged her blouse free and undid the last two buttons.

"Take it off."

Crisp cotton slid from her shoulders. She folded the blouse and laid it on the couch. Despite the need to fidget, she remained still, waiting for the next command.

Silvery gray eyes swept up, down, then focused on her lace-encased breasts. Her nipples beaded under the intense scrutiny. "Now, your skirt."

Reaching behind her, Alicia unbuttoned the wool blend. She inched the zipper down, the rasp of metal teeth scraping her own nerves taut. Fingers eased the A-line over her hips, down thighs and calves before stepping out of the skirt. She folded it with precision, hyper-aware of Richard's watchful gaze.

"It's good to see a woman who knows how to dress appropriately."

The compliment warmed her cheeks. Hank had rarely paid any attention to how she dressed, and then only to criticize. The white lace bra and panties with the matching garter made her feel feminine, desirable, powerful. That had been the entire reason she'd bought several sets after she'd kicked him out.

But now, her reasons didn't matter. From the erection pressing against Richard's slacks, he approved and appreciated. Very much.

Richard stood and approached her. He paced a methodical circle around her, no doubt examining every inch of her. She didn't dare move, didn't want to disappoint him. At the same time, she wanted to move in the hopes he would discipline her.

He stopped behind her. His body heat radiated across her shoulder blades and down to the backs of her calves. He was so close. She trembled, waiting for him to touch her.

"Take off your panties." Warm breath brushed her ear.

Her shaky fingers reached for the waistband and pushed the lace down to her ankles. As she bent to step out of the wisp, something hard and encased in fabric pressed against her ass. She sucked in a deep breath at the sensation. Now, she understood why the saleswoman insisted the panties were properly worn over the garter.

"Bend over and hold onto the arm of the couch."

She obeyed. And never felt so vulnerable, so exposed, so turned on in her life.

*Tsk*ing sounds came from above and behind her. "Alicia, Alicia, whatever am I going to do with you?"

Fuck me!

She expected the first smack, but the strength of it caught her off guard. She wobbled even though she wore sensible two-inch pumps.

"Spread your legs."

She complied, but another smack followed. The stinging sensation snaked through her pussy, turning the light pain into something far more pleasurable. Cool air caressed heated flesh.

"What are you supposed to say when I give you a command?"

"Yes, sir," she whispered.

Another smack.

"Yes, sir," she said, much louder.

"That's better." Behind her, rustling sounded, like a shirt being removed. "How many commands have I given you tonight that you did not reply to appropriately?"

God, she'd lost count. Muscles in her thighs twitched. She wanted to move, to ease the ache in her pussy, but another part of her wanted the agony to go on.

Another smack. Fire inside and out made it so hard to think.

"I don't know, sir." The words came out in little gasps. The orgasm built inside, that delicious feeling of approaching a cliff. All he had to do was touch her and she'd explode.

"Then let's count, shall we? I already spanked you for trying to take off your shoes before I gave you permission. There's speaking without permission . . ."

As he named each transgression, the flat of his hand landed on her bare ass. She squirmed every time. She couldn't help it. A throbbing began deep in her core.

The spanking stopped. "Alicia?"

"Yes, sir." Damn, she was so close. So, so close.

"I don't hear you counting."

Oops. Her mouth opened, desperate for air. "I'm sorry, sir."

Amusement filled his voice. "If I didn't know better, I'd think you're deliberately disobeying me to prolong your punishment."

He wasn't touching her. She wasn't sure what she wanted more, his hand on her ass or his cock buried deep inside her pussy. Frustration made her want to weep.

"What do you want, Alicia?"

"I want you, sir."

"Where?"

Dammit, Richard was going to draw this out until she went insane. "Inside of me."

"Where inside of you?"

"In m-my—" He was going to make her spell it out, wasn't he? But she'd never used dirty language with any man except Hank. And *that* hadn't turned out well at all. Now, she had a handsome, powerful man willing to do whatever she asked. If she could just tell him what she wanted . . .

"Richard, please—"

"Please what?"

Behind her came the tantalizing sound of a zipper. All she had to do was say the words he wanted to hear. "Please, fuck me. Fuck my pussy. I can't stand this anymore. I need your cock inside of me."

Nothing.

"Please, sir," she added meekly.

He plunged into her. So hard, so long, filling her up. One of his arms wrapped around her waist, helping her to stay balanced as he withdrew and rammed into her again. His other hand reached forward, tracing her soaked slit until he touched her clit.

Explosions lit her nerves and bound every fiber with sheer ecstasy. Her knees would surely have buckled if Richard hadn't been holding her upright. Each contraction brought another wave of pleasure.

He continued entering her and pulling out, a slow, delicious friction. His fingers matched the pace along the swollen flesh surrounding her clit. The tingles didn't die, not like they had after every other orgasm she'd ever had. Instead, she could feel the tug of another one building inside. Her fingers dug into the upholstery of the chair.

"Oh, god, Richard, please . . ." She'd never pleaded with a man before in her life. But when it came to Richard Brand, she couldn't help herself.

"Please, what?" His words came out in a harsh gasp.

"Please make me come again."

"Please, what?" He withdrew from her wetness.

Cold air wafted against her hot flesh. She wanted to cry, couldn't think, needed him. Damn, she was so close again. The words. The words.

"Please, sir!"

He rammed into her, unyielding, as his fingers gave her clit a gentle tug. She shuddered beneath his touch. And inside her pussy, she felt him come. And with every pulse, her muscles contracted in response.

Just when she thought she'd collapse, he cradled her in his arms and settled them both on the couch. As he draped her body over his, a disturbing thought crossed her mind. One night with Richard Brand wouldn't be enough to satisfy her.

Chapter Four

"Alicia."

She opened her eyes. A moment of panic flooded her at the strange setting before everything fell into place. Richard's bedroom in his suite.

"Time to get up." Gray eyes stared into her sleep-gummed ones. He sat next to her, his elegant fingers brushing her hair away from her face. Soap and his scent filled her nose.

She nodded.

Before she could wrap her mind around what was happening, he'd flipped her on her stomach. Two quick smacks on her naked ass followed. Moisture filled her pussy at the stinging blows. Damn, hadn't she gotten enough last night?

"What do you say?"

"Yes, sir."

"Will I need to remind you again?"

She watched him from her peripheral vision. He was already dressed in a polo and jeans. "No, sir."

"Good." He stood. "Breakfast is on the way. You may use the bathroom. Shower, whatever other grooming you need, then join me on the patio."

"Yes, sir."

He left, padding out on bare feet, and pulled the bedroom door closed.

Alicia rolled over and laid on the crisp sheets for a few seconds, trying to yank some semblance of control in place. On one hand, it was nice to know he wasn't shoving her in a cab with a "I had a nice time. I'll call you."

On the other hand, she wasn't sure if she wanted the game to continue, even if it made her hornier than a high school boy caught in the throes of puberty. All she had to do was say the word, right?

No, she had to be honest with herself. The queasy feeling wasn't about Richard's sex games. It was the fact she'd used him to get back at Hank. Not that Hank would ever know, but it spawned guilt all the same. And one of Richard's cardinal rules was being honest with each other.

She climbed out of the king-size bed and walked to the bathroom. The sumptuous, over-the-top bathroom with all the works, including a bidet. She pivoted slowly in front of the full-length mirror. Other than a bright red spot on her left cheek from this morning's discipline, there wasn't a mark on her. In fact, her skin practically glowed.

Amazing. Getting spanked and laid is better than any anti-wrinkle cream.

She didn't dawdle in the shower. Her clothing and purse were on top of Richard's dresser when she came out of the bathroom, but the last thing she wanted was to put her business suit back on. Opening his closet, she found his navy robe on a hook, fluffy, comfortable and way too big. It took a couple of rolls to get the sleeve past her fingertips.

A few of swipes with her brush and she felt presentable. She followed her nose to the patio. Under a glorious spring morning, Richard sat at the table, the *Post* spread out over half the surface. The rest was covered in a multitude of dishes along with carafes of coffee and orange juice. It was almost like last night's storm hadn't just scrubbed the sky clean, but her life as well.

Richard looked up at her. One of his eyebrows lifted. "Did I give permission for you to dress?"

Why didn't his criticism bother her? She shoved her hands in the pockets of the robe and returned his look. "Parmesan. I'm sorry, Richard, but we need to discuss things between us before we continue."

"All right." He folded the business section and set it aside. The smile he gave her stroked her depths. "Can we have this serious discussion on a full stomach?" He rose and pulled out the chair next to him.

It would be so easy to get lost in Richard's world. Hank had rarely shown the little niceties, and then he mainly did only when he was trying to impress someone else. Damn it, why hadn't she seen these things before she wasted ten years of her life with the bastard?

Richard filled her plate, then his. He resumed his seat, and as he spread his napkin on his lap, he said, "Did I read things incorrectly last night?"

"Things were wonderful." Alicia reached for the orange juice to cover her discomfiture. "It's just that—" She downed a huge swallow to wet her suddenly dry throat. "I wasn't exactly honest with you before we—" Warmth flooded her cheeks. She couldn't meet his gaze.

His huge hand engulfed hers. "You weren't honest about what?"

She swallowed the lump in her throat. Richard's gentleness, not his disciplines, would be her downfall. "I wasn't honest about why I—" Her free fingers fiddled with the robe's belt. "Why I slept with you," she finished in a whisper.

His thumb stroked her palm. "So it wasn't because you were already aroused by Abdul and Mohammed's offer, and I'm your ex-husband's boss? The same ex-husband who cheated on you?"

The heat in her face built to an inferno. Her head lifted, and she stared at him. "Y-you knew?"

The expression on his face couldn't exactly be called sheepish, but it wasn't exactly the confident look that plastered the covers of so many business magazines. "You weren't the only one who did it for revenge."

His admission jolted her out of her own embarrassment. "You? For what?"

He looked out over the city. "For Hank hurting you. For him cheating on you in my building." The disgust in Richard's voice didn't match his actions. His thumb traced slow, lazy circles on her palm. His silver gray eyes met her gaze again. "I've wanted you since the first time I saw you. The idiot didn't realize what he had."

He leaned forward, his expression as intense as his voice. "We both started this for the wrong reasons, but I want you to stay tonight."

"I-I—" It was her turn to stare at the Mall in the distance. Part of her wanted a repeat performance. Richard's domination set something loose in her. A desire to give in to pleasure. A release from the pressure of her job, the emptiness of her life. The feeling was so damn tempting.

Almost like an addiction.

And that was the part that scared her most. Maybe she didn't have the alcohol problem her mother had, but Richard could easily become a different kind of intoxication.

But maybe the overly-cautious part of her was the reason her marriage failed. If she and Hank had been more blunt about their respective needs . . .

Before she could change her mind again, she said, "Yes."

A hungry look that had nothing to do with breakfast filled Richard's face.

She held up a hand. "One condition—I have to go home tomorrow morning. I've got to deal with the wrap-up of the shareholders' meeting."

Another smile of his turned her knees to jelly. "I'm flying to California tomorrow afternoon. I'll be back late Friday night. Midnight supper when I return perhaps?"

"Okay." She giggled, something she hadn't done since high school. "If our safe word's 'parmesan,' what's our start word? 'Mozzarella'?"

He shrugged. "'Mozzarella' works for me."

Alicia took a bite of scrambled eggs and chewed slowly. It was so worth the look of surprise and anticipation on his face. She snatched a strip of bacon and nibbled it. He stared at her mouth, mesmerized.

She took another sip of juice, and still he hadn't touched his own plate. From the tenting of his napkin, he was like a race car driver waiting for the green light, all revved up and a hair-trigger from exploding.

"Mozzarella," she whispered.

Instantly, his expression switched to stern contempt. "Did I say you could dress?"

She lowered her eyes. "No, sir."

"Take off that robe."

Outside? With so many other high rises around them? Anyone could be watching. That simple acknowledgement dampened her pussy. She untied the belt with deliberateness and shrugged the heavy velvet from her shoulders. The morning breeze caressed her breasts and thighs.

His eyes raked across her nakedness, leaving feverish heat in their wake. Her nipples tightened in anticipation of what he'd demand next.

"Since you're so desperate to put something in your mouth this morning, kneel in front of me." He scooted his chair back from the table.

Alicia stood. For a split second, she debated about grabbing the robe. Surely, he wouldn't object to using it to cushion her knees instead of kneeling on the hard balcony tiles. Dragging the navy velvet with her, she walked around the table.

As she positioned herself between his legs, she peeked through her lashes. Richard kept the stern look on his face, but his eyes gave him away.

She picked up the napkin, carefully folded it and laid it next to his plate. Then came the button to his jeans, the long, slow slide of the zipper. His cock strained against his cotton shorts, but the elastic couldn't contain the pink tip poking out at the top.

The memory of that cock inside her last night clenched her pussy. She licked her lips and bent forward. The flick of her tongue across the tip drew a groan from deep inside Richard. She rolled down his jeans and underwear, and he lifted his hips to help her get the clothing out of her way.

When she gave his cock a languid swirl around the head, she could feel his thigh muscles tighten under her hands. Another stroke along the sensitive underside, then she took him inside her mouth.

Thankfully, he let her set the pace. And god, how she enjoyed exploring him, gauging his reactions to each motion. Quick flutters with her tongue between the indentation of the head of his cock and the shaft brought him to the edge. The slide of her lips down the length brought him back from the brink. And when she hummed while he was deep in her throat, he jerked and threaded his fingers through her hair.

"Alicia . . ." Her name was both a moan and a plea when it came from his lips.

Taking pity on him, she decided it was time to end the torture. She cupped his balls with one hand and squeezed gently. With her other hand, she wrapped her fingers around his shaft. Her mouth followed her hand up and down his cock. She felt the tightening of his sac, and he exploded.

The taste of him was rich, salty. As Richard gasped for breath, she carefully licked the come from him. He grabbed the back of her head, rough but not enough to hurt, and pulled her away from him.

"Go back inside. Lie down on the bed and stay there." His words, even his tone, was harsh.

She looked up in surprise, searching for an answer in his face. All she'd done was to try and please him.

"Now."

There was no mistaking the tone. She scrambled to her feet and retreated to the suite. A quick look over her shoulder revealed Richard, his pants still undone, as he leaned back with his eyes closed. His expression was one of . . .

Oh hell, she had no clue. Some combination of lust and worry as best she could tell. What had she done wrong?

His eyes opened. His attention darted in the direction of the patio doors. She raced for the bedroom.

Chapter Five

Alicia wasn't sure how long she lay in Richard's bed. When he finally came in, his clothes were gone. Instead, he wore the navy robe she'd left on the patio. She searched his face, looking for some sign of what exactly she'd done wrong.

He might as well have been made of stone. There was no clue, no hint, not even in his eyes. She held perfectly still, not sure of what to expect. Her breath caught. The uncertainty of what he'd do next sent a trill of excitement through her. What sort of punishment would he use?

Richard pulled something out of the robe's pocket. A light-blocking sleep mask, similar to the one she used on business trips. "Lift your head."

She complied, and he slipped it over her hair. No, it wasn't like hers. Something soft lay against her eyelids. Fur? Fingers pressed her forehead until she relaxed back onto the pillow.

The mattress dipped. He grasped both of her hands and raised them above her head. In seconds, fabric similar to the mask encircled her wrists. She couldn't move her arms.

The mattress shifted under her again. From the rustling of the robe, he was leaving. Her breath caught in her throat. He wouldn't just leave her like this, would he?

Warm skin grasped her ankles and pulled them apart. Again, she was bound. Vulnerable wasn't even close to the sensation she was feeling. With her legs spread, she was exposed. He'd see how swollen her pussy was. How wet.

More rustling of fabric, then a soft *thud*. Something heavy had landed on the carpet.

"I'll be right back."

"Richard?" She couldn't keep the tremor of fear from her voice.

The bed dipped again, and heat radiated next to her. Fingers stroked her cheek. "Do you trust me, Alicia?"

"I-I—" Did she? All she had to do was say the word, and she'd know for sure. But saying the word when he'd barely touched her seemed so childish. She licked her lips. "Yes." She sucked in a calming breath before she added, "Sir."

"Good girl." Satisfaction lay thick in his voice. Warmth covered her left breast. Fingers tweaked her nipple, and she cried out.

The mattress swayed and air rushed in his wake. Gone. At least, she was fairly sure he wasn't in the room. For all she knew, he could be standing there watching her.

God, her pussy ached. She'd gotten so turned on giving him that blow job. If she wasn't tied up, she could at least relieve the tension driving her insane.

Metallic rattling distracted her.

"Open your mouth."

She obeyed, half-expecting his cock. Instead, metal touched her lower lip. Her tongue explored the object. A spoon. With a cool, creamy substance. Chocolate. She accepted the mouthful and swirled it around her tongue. Chocolate pudding.

Cold touch her right breast, and she shrieked.

Hot, wet roughness stroked her nipple. His tongue. Licking pudding off. He drew the bud into his mouth, sucking hard, the pleasure on the edge of pain. Her back arched, her body demanding more.

Laughter filled Richard's voice. "Greedy little slave, aren't we?"

"Yes, sir."

"Open your mouth."

She accepted the bite, doing her best to lick the dessert off the spoon.

When he spread pudding on her other breast, she expected it, but the icy sensation still drew a gasp from her. Heated sucking replaced the cold. A moan filled her throat.

A spoonful of chocolaty goodness for her. Then one for him served on her body. Her neck. Her belly. The inside of her thighs.

Her body trembled, just on the edge, but he wouldn't allow her to fall over. It was like he knew how close she was. Then he'd wait forever before applying the next spoonful of pudding to her skin.

Dabs of cool met her lips, but when her tongue darted out for the pudding, it met his. The tangle devolved into a passionate kiss.

Cold hit her clit. Alicia jerked and cried out.

"Oops." There was laughter in Richard's voice, then a sigh of resignation. "I suppose I need to clean that up."

Something chilled entered her, and she bucked. Fingers, she realized after a moment. Fingers that were cold from holding the pudding container. His tongue stroked her inner lips, carefully cleaning out pudding from every nook.

The feel of him eating her drove her into a frenzy. She couldn't keep still, even tied down as she was. Her hips rose to meet his mouth, demanding more.

The contact disappeared, and she whimpered in frustration. How could he do this to her?

"Uh-uh-uh. I don't reward greedy slaves."

Evil bastard. "Please."

Another exhale. She could imagine the look of disappointment in his eyes. "Do we need to start over, Alicia?" His warm breath tickled her ear. "I'd turn you over to spank you, but you'd just rub yourself against my sheets, wouldn't you? Grind yourself against them until you came?"

"Yes, sir."

Fingertips traced a line between her breasts and circled her belly button. "Good. You're honest about your intentions. But I can't reward bad behavior, can I?"

"No, sir," she whispered.

The bed shifted. He was leaving her.

A sob caught in her throat. She couldn't release it. She didn't dare. If she did, he'd untie her and call a cab. Cool air from the A/C wafted across her soaked pussy, across her nipples damp from the pudding and his mouth. She shivered.

God help her, she was going insane here! Every nerve was alight, wanting, needing a release he wouldn't give until he was damn good and ready. Had there ever been a time when she hadn't been one big raging hormone begging for orgasms?

Yeah, yesterday afternoon at the shareholders meeting.

She giggled at the thought. Maybe she had gone over the edge.

"What's so amusing, Alicia?" Richard's deep voice would have made her jump if she wasn't so thoroughly tied down. He hadn't left the room.

She ran her tongue across her bottom lip. "I wondered when you would come back to fuck me."

"And that's funny?"

"No. I was trying to remember the last time I wasn't horny."

The mattress dipped. Relief washed through her.

"And when was that?"

She giggled again. Dammit, she wasn't a giggler! "When the chairman of the board gave his opening remarks at yesterday's meeting."

Masculine laughter filled her ears. "Let me guess. That put you to sleep?"

She smiled. "Obviously you've heard our chairman speak."

Something warm and very wet entered her. She gasped. It wasn't Richard's fabulous cock. What the hell was he doing to her?

It slid out and back in. No, it definitely wasn't human. Solid, long, a slight give when she clenched her internal muscles around it.

"Tell me what you do to masturbate."

Her breath caught again, somewhere between the desire for him to keep doing whatever he was doing and sheer embarrassment.

The object slid out. "Alicia . . ."

No mistaking his warning. Forcing herself to breathe, she swallowed her unease. She'd let the man spank her. What was a little game of Truth-and-Fucking?

"I use the showerhead," she blurted.

"The showerhead?" Whatever he held slid back into her. "Tell me how."

It was so hard to think when he was torturing her like this. "I-I—" The fullness slid out. "I turn the setting to 'pulse.'" Back in. She almost cried with relief.

"And?" he prompted. Out when she didn't answer fast enough.

"I-I brace myself against the wall tile with one hand." She moaned as it slid into her. "Then I spread my legs. I hold the showerhead a few inches from my pussy."

Out. She whimpered.

"You're not telling me everything. What are you hiding?"

Oh god, she couldn't tell him. It was embarrassing. It was almost as bad as actually cheating. The lump in her throat was back, and no amount of swallowing made it go away.

"Do I need to leave you alone to think about your answer?"

"No. Please don't." Every muscle in her body quivered. "Sir," she hastily added.

"Tell me."

She couldn't. She shouldn't. This was far, far worse than the spanking.

The mattress moved under her. He was leaving.

"You." The word came out somewhere between a curse and a prayer.

"I beg your pardon?"

"You," she forced out through her clenched jaw. "I fantasize about you while I masturbate."

Silence filled the room, Silence except for his harsh breath.

He pulled off the blindfold. Despite the closed blinds, she blinked at the light.

His hands wound through her hair and forced her to face him. "What do you want from me, Alicia?" Richard's voice was gentler than his touch.

"I want you to fuck me." She desperately sucked in air. "Please, sir."

He climbed between her legs and knelt, not bothering to untie her. His cock proudly waved. He hoisted her hips to meet the tip.

Silvery gray eyes bore into hers. "Say it," he commanded, his voice hoarse.

"Fuck me."

A dark eyebrow rose.

"Please, sir," she added meekly.

He drove into her, hard, almost brutal, but she was so stretched, so wet, it felt . . .

Her mind seized, along with her body, as the first orgasm ripped through her. She screamed, but Richard didn't stop. His cock pumped again and again. He reached for her clit, and another orgasm rippled through her.

She couldn't breathe, couldn't think.

With a roar, Richard stiffened. His come spurted deep inside, and the pulsing of his cock sent her pussy into throes one more time. He collapsed on top of her, his weight comforting.

An emotion she didn't want to examine too closely made her kiss his neck and nuzzle against him.

He didn't move, said nothing for the longest time. Then finally, he reached above her head. The distinctive rip of Velcro filled the room. Next, he leaned toward the foot of the bed and freed each of her ankles. Then he lay down and pulled her against his chest. He flicked the sheet over them.

Alicia didn't speak, didn't want to ruin this moment. But her little voice said, *Girl, you are in deep, deep trouble.*

Chapter Six

Late Friday night, Alicia charged through the hotel lobby, shopping bags in hand and an overnight case slung over her shoulder. Richard had given her a keycard to his suite before taking her home last Sunday. She just hoped he'd appreciate her efforts. The pierced clerk at the adult store had assured her that this outfit would drive him crazy.

She glanced at her watch. 10:48 pm. Damn, nothing had gone right today. First, she was late leaving the office because of the glitch in a payroll software. She'd had to kick some IT butt to get them to find and fix the problem. Then the subway stalled on the way home due to some electrical problem. Finally, Richard called to say he'd caught an earlier flight.

Letting go of her own issues, having him make all the decisions for the next day and a half filled her with a sense of complete relaxation. Something she hadn't felt since she, Micki, Diana and Beth had been juniors in high school.

She leaned against the elevator wall. Was that the attraction to Richard and his games? That she didn't have to think? That it had nothing to do with planning the next move in her career? That all she had to do was feel?

The door dinged open. 10:50 pm. This late at night, the limo would make good time from National Airport. He'd be here any minute.

She ran for the bedroom and stripped, not bothering to fold her clothes. Richard would punish her for leaving a mess. That thought made more liquid seep from her pussy.

In the mirror, she held up the outfit. If it weren't for the anticipation of tonight, she'd check herself into St. Elizabeth's for a psych evaluation. This thing was nothing more than leather straps.

She discovered the girl at the adult store was right when she slipped it on. Despite not covering anything that normally would be covered, the one-piece gave her a sense of power. In quick order, she rolled the black stockings over her legs and fastened them to the garters. Then came the highest black heels she owned.

Auburn hair went up into a high ponytail. She slicked on deep rose lipstick, the darkest color her pale skin could accommodate without her looking like a corpse. And last the three-quarters-length black gloves.

She grabbed her watch from the nightstand and checked it one more time. 10:56 pm. She strode into the living area and lit the two dozen votives she'd brought with her. A subsonic *clunk* said the elevator stopped on this floor.

Alicia clicked off the lighter and knelt on the carpet a few feet from the door. Her heart raced as the muted footsteps in the hallway approached. The hum of the electronic lock.

Richard stepped inside the door. She watched him through lowered lashes. Surprise gleamed in his eyes for an instant as he took in the tableau. And her.

Then the stern mask fell into place.

"Welcome home, sir," she said. Her gloved hands trembled where they rested on her stocking-covered thighs.

"Stand."

She rose as gracefully as she could manage. Kneeling wasn't something she normally did in these shoes, but all the practice at home helped.

Richard closed the door and set his carry-on and laptop case on the floor next to the entryway table. The brown paper bag he also carried landed on top of the table. His tie was loosened and his hair ruffled, but he still looked every inch the high-powered executive he was.

He circled her. She could feel his eyes taking in the studded halter collar, the black leather that surrounded and lifted her breasts while keeping them completely bare, and the flared waist that ended at the middle of her hips. Nothing covered her ass or her pussy.

Heat flared in her cheeks when he said nothing. Did he think she looked totally ridiculous? She'd done her research. Had she gotten something wrong?

Richard started another circle.

Shit. She *had* gotten something wrong.

"Spread your legs."

Alicia stepped out carefully with her right foot, putting a yard between the heels.

He stopped behind her, his breath warm on her neck. His fingertips traced the crevice of her ass. "Bend over and grab your ankles."

She swallowed a smile. For once, those damn five a.m. yoga classes paid off. She complied with his command and peeked up between her knees. Yep, he was mesmerized by her exposed pussy. The bulge in his suit trousers didn't lie. It made the torture session called waxing worth it.

He completed the second circuit. "Stand up. Legs together."

Once she was upright, she kept her hand folded demurely in front of her. His gaze was so intense that she wasn't sure she could meet it even if she dared.

"There's something missing from your outfit, Alicia."

She blinked, desperately going over the store clerk's recommendations in her head. What had she forgotten in the race to Richard's suite?

He reached in his coat pocket and withdrew a small jewelry box.

Confusion clouded her thoughts. They'd only spent one weekend together. Granted the sex games had been mind-blowing, but they hardly qualified for this level of gift.

"Take it, Alicia." Richard held the box out to her.

She took it and gave him a quizzical look.

An amused smile tilted his lips. "You may open it."

Alicia carefully lifted the lid. Inside lay two tiny silver loops. No, not silver. Platinum from the look. Two streamers of crystal gems hung off each loop. She ran a fingertip over them. They couldn't possibly be real diamonds. Each set would total over two carats if they were real.

But what the hell were these things? Not earrings. There was no post, no wire to slip through her own lobe piercings. And Richard still watched her with that amused expression.

She gathered her courage around her curiosity. "May I ask what these are, sir?"

"Would you like me to show you?"

At her nod, he stepped so close that she felt heat radiate off him. He plucked one of the odd loops from the velvet and fitted it around her left nipple.

A gasp left her throat before she could stop it. The metal was snug, not quite uncomfortable. But the weight of the crystals tugged the bud tighter, sending exquisite sensations along her nerves.

Richard attached the other piece to her right nipple. The crystals swung with every breath, shooting a sharp current across her nerves. He stepped back to examine his handiwork. "Do you like them?"

"Yes, sir." The words came out in a breathy whisper.

With his index finger, he flicked each set. She cried out. The little bits of jewelry seemed to bore through her skin and yank at her pussy. Every nerve pulsed in time to the swing of the crystals. Her fingers curved, the need for relief so bad—

The flat of Richard's hand landed on her ass with a loud *smack*. "Did I say you could touch yourself?"

"No, sir." She sucked in a deep breath that sent the jewels rocking.

He retrieved the brown paper bag. The smell of Chinese drifted through the air. He crossed the room and sat on the couch. "Go to the refrigerator and get two bottles of water."

Alicia headed for the full-sized unit in the mini-kitchen/wet bar. Every step was torture between the swinging crystals and the damp skin between her legs. She retrieved the bottles and returned to the couch.

Richard had taken off his jacket. Two cartons were open and sitting on the coffee table. CNN flickered on the widescreen. He glanced at her and accepted the bottles. "Kneel."

She eased herself down to the carpet and placed her gloved hands on her thighs once again. That seemed to be the safest place for them. He opened a package of disposable chopsticks and dug into one of the containers.

The smell was heavenly. Unfortunately, it reminded her she hadn't eaten anything since lunch. Her stomach growled a demand as Richard took a bite.

He chewed, taking his dear, sweet time, ignoring her. Then he shot her a dismissive glance. "Open your mouth."

She did. With the precision of a surgeon, he used the chopsticks to place morsels of food on her tongue. Sweet and sour pork, her taste buds reported. She chewed and swallowed, trying to focus on the food rather than the weight pulling on her nipples or the pulsing between her thighs.

He patiently fed them both, alternating bites of cashew chicken with the sweet and sour pork, while he pretended to watch the news channel. But she caught him looking at her from the corner of his eye. His erection remained through the entire meal. Surely, he must be as desperate for release, any release, as she was.

Finally, he set the chopsticks in one of the boxes and nudged the cartons aside. He reached for his belt. She watched, mesmerized, as he unbuckled and removed it.

The faintest of smiles touched his face. He slowed his motions as he unbuttoned his pants. The even slower *zzzzz* of the zipper.

Tension crawled along her skin. What would he do tonight? Take her from behind again? Tie her to his bed?

To her shock, he reached for his cock. In the light of the candles and the TV screen, pre-come glistened at the tip. He continued his act of ignoring her while his hand slid up and down the shaft.

The whine at the back of her throat was totally involuntary.

He stopped and glared at her. "Did you say something, Alicia?"

Eyes wide at her slip, she shook her head so vigorously that her ponytail whipped across her face.

"Do you think you should be pleasuring me?"

Oh, damn. A logic trap. What was she supposed to say?

"Answer me." His voice was so low it was almost a growl.

He wanted honesty, didn't he? "Yes, sir."

"That's a little presumptuous, isn't it?" His hand slid down his cock.

She licked her lips, the memory of his taste oh-so-vivid on her tongue. "Yes, sir."

"You should be punished for such a presumption."

"Yes, sir." The words practically purred out of her throat.

Richard laughed. "You disobey me on purpose because you like your punishments."

"Yes, sir."

He shook his head, amusement still in his voice when he said, "Lay face down on the couch, your ass on my lap."

She obeyed, careful to position herself on his thighs. As much as she wanted to touch his cock, she knew he'd delay longer if she did. And she definitely couldn't wait much longer.

The loops dug into her breasts as she settled herself, a delightful pain that shot her arousal into overdrive. God help her, if he waited too long, she just may come anyway. Fingers brushed her exposed pussy, and she shivered.

The first swat on her ass nearly jerked her out of her skin. The second had her panting. The third burned. The next six had her clenching her gloved hands to keep from rubbing her soaked pussy against his pant legs to relieve her need. He paused. She could sense his hand hovering above her stinging ass as he judged how close she was.

The *smack* echoed through the suite, and she cried out.

"What was that, Alicia?"

"Please." The words choked her throat between the pain on her breasts and ass. "Please, sir."

"Please what, Alicia?" The stern tone told her how close he was as well.

"Please fuck me."

Fingers thrust into her pussy, and she squirmed. "No."

"No?" Another smack on her ass left her whimpering. "You're an educated woman. Say what you mean, Alicia."

"Please fuck me with your cock, sir."

He stroked around her clit, not touching it. Yes, he definitely knew how close she was. "Was that so hard to say?"

"No, sir," she whispered.

"Sit on my lap."

She rose and swung her leg around so she straddled him. His hand grabbed her wrist when she reached for that gorgeous cock of his. A glance down said how close he was. His sac pulled tight against his body.

He simply stared at her, like he was memorizing her features. Their breathing synchronized, and she started counting each one to slow her own reaction.

She reached twenty-five before he released her and nodded.

Rising on her knees, she positioned his cock. She wanted to weep as she slid down his shaft. An answering groan started deep in his chest. He leaned his head back and closed his eyes. His arms rested along the back of the couch, but his fists clenched.

She laid her gloved hands on his shoulders for balance. Surprisingly, he let her set the pace. As she rose, she squeezed with her internal muscles. Another groan vibrated from his throat. Slide down again. Squeeze and up. Somehow, she managed to stay on that agonizing pace.

Slide down. Up and squeeze.

Diamonds swung from the rhythm. The sweet tug of them on her breasts broke her concentration. Her tempo picked up. Slide and squeeze.

Richard's hand grabbed her hips, encouraging her to ride harder, faster. Slide and squeeze. Whimpering filled her ears. Her voice. The sound of want, of need. She couldn't let go. Not yet. But she was so damn close. *Need to focus.*

Beneath her, his muscles stiffened. A hoarse cry preceded the spasms as he pumped his come inside of her. The feel of his orgasm was too much. Spots exploded in her eyesight as every nerve ignited at once. Her pussy jerked the rest of her body along the rollercoaster ride. The delicious pulsations seemed to go on forever.

Her body collapsed against his chest. He pulled her even closer, and his fingers stroked the bare skin along her spine. The low voice of the CNN announcer was the only sound in the room for the longest time.

"I swear you'll be the death of me, Alicia Thomas," he whispered.

A jolt of fear shot through her. She straightened, cupped his head in her gloved hands, and stared intently into his eyes. "Don't say that. Don't ever say that again."

His eyes widened at her sharp tone. "Are you ordering me?"

"I-I—" She dropped her hands from his face. What the hell had come over her? They were in the middle of a weekend of sex games. What had triggered her outburst? She swallowed the uncomfortable lump in her throat, and lowered her eyes. "I'm sorry, sir."

"Parmesan."

She jerked her head up. Was he sending her home already for breaking the rules? The lump of fear she had forced down threatened to come right back up.

Richard reached up and stroked her cheek. "What's wrong?"

"I—" He wanted honesty, and she wanted to comply, but she didn't even know what had hit her or why.

"Alicia?" he whispered.

She sucked back a threatening sob. The truth. "I'm sorry. I'm not even sure where that came from. Please don't send me home." Any other time she would have smacked herself, or had Micki pistol-whip her, for begging a man. Any man. What the hell was wrong with her?

He watched her, his expression analytical. Then he gave her a sexy smile. "Mozarella. It's late. Go to the bedroom. Remove everything and wait for me."

"Yes, sir." She stood and turned for the bedroom.

"And Alicia?"

"Yes, sir?" She looked down at him lounging on the couch. Damn if his cock wasn't already stirring.

"No touching yourself before I come in."

"Yes, sir." She pivoted. There were so many other things she could do.

A light swat landed on her tender ass and she squealed. "No using anything else either."

She glanced over her shoulder and shot him a naughty grin. "Yes, sir."

Chapter Seven

Alicia woke to someone playing with her hair. And with her breast. She gasped at the erotic charge that filled her body. Richard rolled her right nipple between his fingers. His cock poked her ass.

"Good morning." His breath tickled her ear.

She lay on her side, Richard's body spooning hers. Before she could answer, he released the hot bud and slid his hand along the backs of her thighs. At his urging, she shifted the top leg forward. Then he entered her.

Her body shuddered at the shallow penetration of his cock into her pussy. Richard made no move to deepen the contact. Instead he rocked her body against his, the motion both subtle and more erotic than last night's games.

"Touch yourself." Sleep hoarsened his voice, but it made the command even more compelling. Except it wasn't really an order, more like encouragement.

She reached for her pussy, probing delicately with one finger. Damn. Soaking wet seemed to be her permanent state around Richard Brand, even in her sleep. She stroked herself, keeping her clit between her index and middle finger. Not touching directly, but applying the gentlest of pressure against that little bundle of nerves.

His cock was right there. She lengthened her strokes, including him in her touch.

Richard's hand returned to her breast, cupping the weight. He alternated between tweaking the hard bud and teasing the tender skin. His teeth nipped that lovely sensitive area under her ear.

Alicia could feel muscles tightening, the electricity building along her pussy. "Richard?"

"Let it go," he whispered in her ear. "I want to feel you come."

She ran her slick fingers over her clit. Everything shattered in her. Her body spasmed violently, and Richard slipped out of her. Behind her, she could feel him clench. A groan, and hot, sticky come shot over her thigh. It didn't matter. Nothing mattered except this feeling of bliss. Once his cock stopped throbbing against her skin, he pulled her closer to him.

Every muscle in her body relaxed, content even. Maybe too content. Something in her chest broke loose, and tears filmed her vision. Everything felt so good, so gentle. Except . . .

This time hadn't been sex games. It was almost like making lo—

No, she couldn't think it. Wouldn't think it, dammit!

The harsh vibration of an object on the nightstand broke her mood. Richard muttered an oath, rolled over and grabbed his smart phone.

Alicia blinked a few times to clear her vision before she shifted to face him. A frown tugged the corners of his mouth as he read the screen.

"Do you need to leave?" Part of her hoped it was business so she could go home and deal with what just happened. The rest pouted over the fact their day might be cut short.

"No, but I need to make a call. Go take your shower and get dressed."

"Yes, sir." She tried to smile, but his eyes didn't meet hers. From his motions on the tiny screen, he was scrolling through a text message.

When she returned from the bathroom fifteen minutes later, he gave her a quick peck and told her to order breakfast for them. Then he dove into the bathroom and shut the door.

She smoothed her hair away from her face. *Crap.* She was doing it again. Yanking on capris and a t-shirt, she glared at the damn phone. The text was his business, not hers. Why the hell did she care? Fingers itched to snatch up the phone and find out what was going on.

She drew her hand away from the phone. Hank really had done a number on her. She had no excuse for acting like a jealous girlfriend. This was adult fun for a couple of weekends, not a relationship. She forced herself to walk into the living room and dial room service.

But her little voice asked, *So what's he hiding?*

Chapter Eight

Alicia had arranged the plates on the table when Richard walked out onto the balcony. Like last Saturday, he wore jeans and a polo, but these looked more worn. Comfy clothes, as Beth would say.

She started to kneel when he clutched her hand. "No. Parmesan."

Her breath caught in her chest as she straightened. Did he need to leave? She couldn't read his expression.

He gave her a wry smile. "We received an invitation. One we need to discuss as us."

Her eyes widened and she breathed again. "What kind of invitation?" She wanted to wince at the excitement in her voice. This wasn't a relationship.

He chuckled and pulled out a chair for her. "The kind you need to think very carefully about before you accept."

She clutched the arms of the wrought iron chair as he scooted her to the table. "You said the invitation was for both of us."

He sat down and spread his napkin across his lap. "Sort of." His gaze swept across the city, but his attention seemed a thousand miles away. Finally, he turned to her. "What I'm about to tell you needs to remain between us." At her nod, he continued, "Do you know who Katarina Henderson is?"

No one needed a feather to knock Alicia over. A butterfly would have done the job. "The super model?"

"Yes." Richard started forking waffles onto both plates while she poured orange juice for them. "The invitation was from her."

Intrigued, Alicia leaned her elbows on the table. "She supposedly retired six months ago and disappeared off the face of the earth." She reached for her glass and took a sip.

"Retired, yes. Disappeared? Not exactly. She married Prince Mohammed."

Alicia choked on her orange juice. Richard leaned over and patted her on the back while she coughed and wiped away the tears. Holy crap. She'd almost fucked *two* married men. How the hell could she face Katarina Henderson?

Richard rested his chin on his fist. "Her invitation was the text I received this morning. Apparently, Mohammed has raved about you since—"

"Wait a minute!" Alicia stared at Richard. "He actually *told* his wife he wants to screw me six ways to Sunday?"

Richard grasped her hand in his. "Not everyone has conventional views of marriage. The brothers have an agreement with their wives—"

"Stop right there." She pulled her hand from his and held it up for emphasis. An ugly green monster swam in her vision. "I'm not swapping so you can play harem."

"I wouldn't be sleeping with their wives." Silver eyes gleamed in the morning sun.

"Oh." Her hand dropped to her lap.

One of Richard's eyebrows rose. "Will you let me finish? Or do we have to go back to mozzarella mode for you to be quiet."

"I'm sorry." She reached for the dish of whipped butter to keep busy. "Please continue."

Richard sucked in and released a deep breath. "Abdul's fourth wife Azira and Katarina were lovers in college. Azira's family pressured her into marrying Abdul for political reasons, but the two of them came to their own agreement. Abdul is allowed to indulge his appetites at a private club in London in return for Azira spending time with Katarina."

Alicia contemplated the revelation as she drizzled syrup over the waffles on her plate. "And Mohammed has the same agreement with Katarina."

Richard eyed her. "Yes."

"So where do you fit into this scenario?"

He smiled. "I introduced Katarina and Mohammed. Also, my company has enough of a relationship with their business interests they don't want to piss me off, but I also owe them for a favor they did for me a few months ago. Mohammed wondered if your nether hair is the same color as the hair on your head. I refused to answer him the other night and said he'd have to ask Katarina for permission to inspect you. So . . ."

Well, that explained the joking between the three men in Arabic. She laughed. "Guess I'm going to have to let it grow back in to make him happy. Let me guess, since they think we're dating—" She made bunny ears with her index fingers. "—they want your permission as well?"

"Essentially, yes. But the decision is really yours."

"The rules you mentioned?"

"Yes."

Alicia took a bite of waffle and chewed it carefully. She couldn't deny that two men going to such extremes to fuck her was a turn-on. "If I agreed to this, what exactly do the brothers expect?" She swallowed the mouthful. "I mean, spanking, chains, whips? I suck them off? They take turns playing 'stuff the sausage'? What?"

"They'd both take you at once."

The idea should have scared the shit out of her. Instead, a shiver of excitement rippled across her skin. She took a sip of juice. "Give me more details."

A gleam lit Richard's eyes. "If you give them permission, Azira and Katarina will be in the room with you. They will undress you and place you in specially designed manacles." He chuckled. "The manacles are awkward as hell, but they don't hurt."

Alicia's mouth suddenly went dry, but her pussy was a different story. "Then what?"

"They play with you for a while, make sure you're ready for them. You'll want to wear the jewelry I gave you."

Her nipples pressed against her bra, hard and needy at Richard's suggestion and her own memory of last night.

"Then they'll both take you. Mohammed prefers your mouth. Abdul will—" Richard watched her, his gaze intense. "Have you ever been ass-fucked, Alicia?"

She shook her head. Her hole tightened at the thought. "W-wouldn't it hurt?"

"Not if you're relaxed." He leaned toward her. "Would you like to practice before we go to London?"

Her pulse pounded. "You're assuming I'll say 'yes' to this invitation."

Another chuckle. "Alicia, honey, you're about to come just from imagining their dicks in you."

God help her, he was right. Her fingers twisted the napkin in her lap. "How do I know you and the brothers won't use this against me?"

"That's the reason Katarina suggested we meet at Club Noir. They cater to people in our positions, with our needs and desires. We'll have the utmost privacy and the staff ensures the participants' safety. Any mention of private activities outside of the club results in revocation of membership."

A nervous laugh escaped from her throat. "But what will you be doing if I'm busy?"

In a low voice, Richard said, "What would you like me to do?"

She peeked at him from beneath her lashes. "Would you watch if I asked you to?"

"Yes."

Two men fucking her while Richard watched? Her juices soaked her panties. He pushed away from the table and stood. Once again, his cock pressed against the front of his jeans. She rose and took his outstretched hand.

In silence, they walked to his bedroom. Once inside, he tugged her t-shirt up over her head, her arms. The bra flew across the room. He unsnapped her capris and pushed them and her lace undies to her ankles. The need to have him inside her had muscles contracting in anticipation.

"Sit."

She perched on the edge of the bed. He yanked the clothes past her feet and tossed them over his shoulder.

Richard shoved her knees apart and examined her pussy, then met her eyes. "Definitely on the edge just from the idea of two men fucking you." He hiked her legs over his shoulders and buried his face against her.

The first rasp of his tongue had her bucking her hips. He clutched them and licked her clit again and again. The orgasm built so hard and fast, she screamed when it convulsed her body.

Before she could recover, he flipped her on her stomach. Once again, he shoved her legs wide. Fingers probed her ass, finding her tight little hole. She shuddered as one digit then two slipped inside. His zipper sounded like an angry bee.

"Richard." His name came out in a gasp, but he didn't give her time to protest. Deep down, she didn't want to. The fingers disappeared. Something much bigger nudged her hole.

Oh god. The memory of the way he stretched and filled her pussy made her squirm. "Richard."

"Relax, honey." His cock pushed against the tightening sphincter, then rubbed along the crevice of her ass cheeks.

His other hand slid between her body and the duvet, arrowing in on her slick folds. His fingers probed, explored, kept her on the edge, but refused to let her fall over again.

A chuckle rumbled behind her. "Don't move."

Alicia wasn't sure she could if she wanted to. Every muscle was frozen in anticipation of what he planned. A small smile curved her lips. Anticipation, not fear. Damn, she was getting an education with this man.

She heard a drawer open and close. Cool wetness touched her ass and she bucked, only to have fingers slide into both her cunt and ass. Pure electricity ricocheted between the nerve endings. The thin wall of her flesh between his fingers only heightened the need building inside her. A moan filled her throat as Richard worked her into a frenzy.

Then his fingers withdrew, and the head of his cock pushed inside her ass. Soft mewling tore the air. Hers. Fear of the unknown and the tsunami of desire clashed. Desire won. She thrust back, taking a few millimeters more of him. The slight pain stretched into intense pleasure.

"Easy, easy," he whispered in her ear. "I don't want to hurt you."

"Need you." Her voice sounded primitive, guttural.

He pinned her to the bed, one hand bracing himself near her shoulder. His cock continued its slow slide. Her body spread for him. The uncomfortable sensation totally disappeared to be replaced by a feeling of completeness. The rough hairs of his sac brushed her swollen pussy.

With the same exquisite pace, he withdrew until only the head remained in her ass. In. His fingers inside her pussy pressed against his erection. The movement was torrid, erotic. Out. Her own hands curled in the fabric of the duvet. Her hips rocked underneath his.

In.

Her climax hit her hard. Internal muscles grabbed his cock and fingers, squeezing them until she felt his sac tightened and pull away. A gruff shout followed as Richard pumped into her. His chest collapsed on her, his weight as snug as his cock still in her ass.

For the second time, they'd had sex without games, without roles, without the safety word. Something had changed between them, and for the life of her, Alicia couldn't figure out what.

Instead, she looked over her shoulder at him and shot him a wicked smile. "When do we leave for London?"

Chapter Nine

A week later, Alicia couldn't take her eyes off the flight attendant as she accepted the glass of club soda. While the basic cut of material looked like the business attire of any other airline's uniform, the woman's outfit left nothing to the imagination. The sheer gauze blouse displayed her dark brown areolas and the gold hoops that pierced her nipples. The black leather skirt was slit high enough that Alicia knew the woman didn't wear any underwear.

"Now that we're at cruising altitude, you can unbuckle your belts. Is there anything else I can do for you?" The attendant's smile flashed white against her sienna complexion. It was warm, genuine. Her erotic invitation floated on the air despite her crisp British accent.

Alicia tried to keep her wits, but it was hard when those perfect breasts danced at her eye level. Despite the mix of discomfort and desire, she returned the attendant's smile. "Not right now."

Disappointment flashed in the other woman's eyes though she kept her professional demeanor. "Just buzz me if you change your mind."

Alicia turned to watch the attendant's tight ass as it swayed beneath her skirt. How she strode to the back of the private plane in those four-inch heels Alicia would never figure out.

Richard leaned close to her ear. "Are you sure you wouldn't like to try Rashida? You couldn't keep your eyes off of her."

"I've never…" Heat warmed Alicia's cheeks as she looked everywhere but Richard's face. It was like someone had turned up her hormones. She'd never thought about kissing another woman before now, much less wondering what her breasts tasted like.

He threaded his fingers through hers and lifted her hand to his lips. His kiss on the inside of her wrist sent her racing pulse into overdrive. "Never been with a woman?"

Alicia shook her head, not trusting her dry mouth to work. From the look on Richard's face, he already guessed the answer to his question

"For what it's worth, I think the two of you together would be a beautiful sight." The smile he gave her, along with the thick ridge pressing against his slacks, almost made her hit the call button. He ran his other hand down her arm, deliberately brushing her full, aching breast. "What do we need to do to take the edge off your nervousness?"

Damn, how did he read her so well? Of course, she was on edge. Between anxiety over what might happen at this private club and Richard working her into a sensual haze in that VIP suite bathroom at the airport, then abruptly stopping, her emotions hopped all over the place.

She glared at him. "You could finish what you started."

"You mean this?" He pulled her hand back to his mouth. He took her little finger between his lips, sucked on it oh-so-gently. A slight nip of the pad, then a lick to smooth the bite before he moved to the next digit.

She closed her eyes, letting the sensual motions lull her. Wetness tickled her inner thigh, and she squeezed her legs together. Oh god, that didn't help at all.

His mouth moved from her fingers to her ear lobe. Lips and teeth nibbled along her jaw, down her neck. "Stand up," he murmured against her skin.

Her eyes opened, but everything seemed fuzzy with the seductive spell he wove. She unbuckled the seat belt and stood. Alicia turned to face him.

"Unbutton your blouse."

Her fingers undid each pearl button. The silk fluttered to the cabin floor. Despite the air conditioning of the private plane, her skin felt hot, tight. Without waiting for his next command, she unhooked the front clasp of her bra. Her nipples tightened to hard points as his gaze raked across her exposed flesh. The lace bra slid off her shoulder and down her arms. It joined her blouse.

Richard reached for his seatbelt. She licked her lips, but he drew out his movements, deliberately stalling.

Should she protest? He'd surely spank her if she did. That thought sent a tremor through her body. What would she do if Rashida came back to check on them? It wasn't like other women hadn't seen her bare torso in the shower room at the gym. But the thought of another woman watching as Richard smacked her ass, her glistening pussy exposed for anyone to see . . .

Almost as if Richard read her mind, he grinned and unzipped his slacks. That sure, knowing smile of his was pure temptation. It would be her undoing. "Turn around."

She pivoted, waiting breathlessly for his next order.

"Pull up you skirt."

Her fingers guided the flowing broomstick skirt to her waist, showing him what he'd already discovered with his fingers at the airport. She hadn't bothered with panties. Richard grabbed her hips and thrust his knees between her legs. Then he guided her down to his lap. His cock slid into her seeping pussy as if it was made solely for her pleasure. A small sob of relief escaped her throat.

"Close your eyes, Alicia."

Her eyelids fluttered shut. She wanted to rock on his thick rod, but his hands kept a firm grip on her hips. Besides, he hadn't commanded her yet.

"Are your eyes closed?"

"Yes, sir."

The warm palms on her hips disappeared. "You can't do anything until I tell you. Do you understand?"

"Yes," she hissed.

A light pinch on her nipple made her jerk, and a whimper escaped her throat.

"Yes, what?"

"Yes, sir."

Skin slid over her ass, traced her crevice. Another fingertip drew circles around her clit. The nail delicately scraped the sensitive flesh. She squeezed her internal muscles, anything to get Richard to fuck her properly.

"Bad girl." The fingertip caressing her slick folds disappeared. "Did I say you could do that?"

She couldn't suppress the cry of disappointment. It took precious seconds to collect enough thoughts to say, "No, sir."

"Open your eyes."

She complied. Embarrassment and excitement twisted in a weird dance through her nerves. Oh, no, he didn't. She blinked. Then blinked again.

The flight attendant Rashida sat in the seat across from them. Like Alicia, her blouse had been removed. The gold nipple rings glinted in the sunlight streaming through the private jet's window.

Alicia glanced down. The blue gauze of her skirt covered her own pussy with Richard's cock buried inside.

His hands reached up and covered her breasts, molding and caressing the tender flesh. "Alicia's never had anyone watch before. A little practice would do her good."

Rashida's teeth gleamed against her dark skin. "I understand, sir. Would you like me to assist?"

Alicia shivered as Richard rolled her nipples between his thumbs and fore-fingers, not sure if her reaction was to Richard's ministrations or the thought of Rashida touching her.

"Not this time." He pulled on Alicia's tips, making them harder than she thought possible. "But please feel free to pleasure yourself if you so desire."

"Yes, sir." Rashida practically purred the words. She slung one leg over the arm of her seat and flipped the leather back.

Now, Alicia understood why the slit on the flight attendant's skirt was so high. Simple convenience. Short black curls framed a pussy nearly the color of black raspberries. Rashida's folds lay open. Moisture coated the delicate flesh, like dew on a morning flower.

Alicia couldn't stop watching the other woman. To be that comfortable dis-playing herself? Showering in a locker room was one thing, but this view was far too intimate. Her mind had trouble wrapping itself around the concept. Her body on the other hand . . .

Rashida smiled as if she knew the battle waged in Alicia's psyche. She slowly slid two fingers inside her passage, her thumb making lazy circles around her swol-len clit.

Alicia's internal muscles spasmed. She dug her nails into the tops of her thighs to tame her reaction, but it was too late.

"Stand up."

She whimpered a protest at Richard's command. It meant the loss of his cock, but she obeyed. Did she really have a choice? Her pussy felt so empty without him inside. The skirt flowed down to cover some of her nakedness.

He yanked on the gauzy material. The elastic waist roughly passed over her thighs, knees, calves, leaving her exposed. Totally vulnerable.

"Kneel. Hands on the floor," Richard ordered.

When she didn't move fast enough, his sharp slap on her ass reminded her who was master. Scrambling, she assumed the correct position in the tight confines. It meant her head was only inches from Rashida's lovely pussy.

Two more swats quickly followed. "What do you say, Alicia?"

"Sir. Yes, sir." She gasped out the words.

"Are her eyes still on yours, Rashida?"

"Oh, yes, sir." The flight attendant's eyes glimmered with excitement. "And her cheeks are a lovely shade of pink, I might add."

A low rumble of laughter behind Alicia only made her face hotter. How could he do this to her? Yet, this is exactly how she imagined herself with the dominatrix Hank had hired. Humiliated and taken at the same time. She wanted to die of shame. She wanted Richard to order her to lick Rashida's swollen lower lips. Most of all she wanted Richard's cock thrusting inside of her.

"Are you embarrassed to be punished in front of someone?"

He wanted honesty. "Yes, sir," she whispered.

His hand stroked her soaked slit. "But you like it as well."

"Yes, sir," she whispered again.

"What would you do if I left you like this and fucked Rashida instead?" His fingers played with her, sliding in and out.

"I-I wouldn't like it, sir." This time fear made her words much louder. Not fear of watching him take someone else, but that he really would leave her this aroused and in sexual agony for the rest of the long flight.

"Why, Alicia?" His fingers traveled up, played with her tight hole.

"Because—" More shame ignited her skin. God, it felt like she was on fire.

"Because why?" His fingertip penetrated, sending waves of anticipation through her.

"Because I need you," she ground out.

"Need me how?"

"I need—" She watched Rashida lick her lips, anticipation that she would get Richard's cock instead of Alicia. The bitch actually laughed. Anger fired in Alicia. "I need you to fuck me. Fuck me hard."

Richard's cock slammed into her. So fast, she nearly fell face first into Rashida's exposed crotch. This was a rough, furious claiming. No control games, no gentleness. Just a man pumping into a woman with undeniable lust.

And Alicia couldn't help delivering her own smile of triumph to the flight attendant.

Rashida tilted her head in acknowledgment, her fingers trying to match their rhythm.

With a groan, Richard stiffened behind Alicia. That was all the permission she needed. Nerve endings exploded in time with the pulsing of his cock. She shuddered and gasped as the exquisite tremors ricocheted along taut muscles.

With her own little cry, Rashida jerked, joining her private ecstasy with theirs.

Alicia closed her eyes, trying to calm her pounding heart. Collapsing into a puddle and sleeping for a century seemed like a terrific idea right now.

Her eyes popped open at the gentle touch to her chin.

Rashida bent over her, leather skirt back in place and brown eyes warm and friendly once again. "Perhaps next time, you'll allow me to join you, dear." She leaned forward and placed a kiss on Alicia's lips.

Alicia's mouth opened involuntarily, and Rashida took advantage. Her tongue slipped forward in a gentle exploration. She tasted of peppermint and spice and something totally exotic. And Alicia found herself kissing back.

Rashida broke the contact and straightened. She quickly donned her blouse and strode to the back of the plane. And despite the lingering discomfort, Alicia wished she had the courage to accept Rashida's offer.

Chapter Ten

Club Noir was opulent. Magnificent. Old World and decadent.

Alicia wished she was exploring the historic building and admiring the architecture instead of suffering through a physical exam. Richard had assured her that a check-up was required of all participants at the club for everyone's health, but she felt like a total dork in the paper gown. Why couldn't they accept her e-mailed medical records? The whole thing made her feel like she was a prize brood mare being checked out by the buyers' vet.

The doctor patted her knee. "All right, dear. Why don't you get dressed and we'll discuss things in my office?"

Talk about what Alicia would be doing later tonight. Who she would be doing it with. And discussing everything with a woman she'd met less than an hour ago.

The muscles in her neck tightened. It didn't help that the sixty-something doctor looked way too much like her next-door neighbor. The thought of elderly Mrs. Abercrombie working in an exclusive sex club made her giggle.

Dammit! She was not a giggler!

The doctor eyed her with a puzzled look. "Something wrong, dear."

Alicia swallowed the nervous laughter. "I'm sorry it's just that, um . . ." Now the situation didn't seem quite so funny. "You look a lot like someone I know."

Understanding smoothed the furrow between the doctor's eyebrows. "Someone you wouldn't normally discuss your proclivities with?"

"Oh, hell, no!"

The doctor laughed hard. Then she shook her head and fixed her with an earnest look. "Think of me as one of your girlfriends. One who accepts you as you are." She reached for the ornate doorknob. "My office is two doors to your left when you're ready."

As soon as the doctor left, Alicia ditched the paper exam gown and donned her clothes and shoes. Within two minutes, she faced an ancient oak door. A gold plaque bolted to the wood was stenciled with "Dr. Johanna Paine."

She raised her hand to knock, but hesitated. This all seemed like so much drama for such a . . .

Such a what? Was she really having second thoughts about fucking Abdul and Mohammed?

No. Besides Richard would be there, right? She gave the door a firm rap.

"Come in," came a muffled voice.

When she opened the door, Dr. Paine had removed her lab coat. She wore a simple white blouse and a conservative skirt, but damn, her ass looked like it could crack walnuts.

The doctor turned from the sideboard and set down a round, dark bottle. "Please." She gestured toward to comfortable-looking chairs next to an unlit fireplace.

Alicia crossed the room and gingerly lowered herself onto the floral upholstery covering the chair. Dr. Paine followed with two small glasses. She held one out to Alicia.

Alicia accepted it, but eyed the dark liquid instead of drinking it.

The doctor gave a reassuring smile. "I thought we might have some Chambord while we talk."

"Thank you." Alicia gripped her glass, more to keep from playing with her hair than anything else. This felt like a shrink talk, and she hated psychiatrists with a passion. Hated every single one her mother had dragged her to after one stupid incident in high school.

The doctor took a sip of the raspberry liquor. "You love him, don't you?"

The tiny glass should have shattered in Alicia's tightening grip. "Who?"

Dr. Paine's smile could only be called secretive. "Let's dispense with the coyness, dear. You're terrified of your attraction to certain men. You're worried about your desires being used against you. And you're scared of your feelings for Richard. Have I left anything out?"

"What about my Electra complex?" Sarcasm coated Alicia's words.

"There's nothing wrong with you, my dear. I don't know if it was your ex-husband, another lover or your family who put those thoughts in your head. But I can tell you that you will be miserable tonight if you don't deal with them." She held up her hand when Alicia opened her mouth. "I'm not your priest, and I'm not asking for your confession."

Dr. Paine took another sip from her glass. "The brothers can be very good friends to have, and trust me, they are very good to their friends."

Alicia blinked. This wasn't what she expected. "You sound like you have experience being a good friend."

"To their grandfather, yes." She rolled the now-empty glass between her palms. "How do you think a common girl like myself got into medical school?"

Alicia fiddled with her own glass. "You make it sound like prostitution."

The doctor waved a dismissive hand. "Hardly. He expected me to maintain my scores in the ninetieth percentile in return for his recommendations and financial assistance. Then he expected me to make my own path. However, my intimate needs and his meshed. This was the only place he could release his burdens. This was the one place I felt powerful for a very long time."

What Dr. Paine was admitting sunk through Alicia's foggy brain. "You were his domme."

The doctor nodded. "Sometimes a person is in a position of so much responsibility, they need a break. And they need people like me to provide that release." She smiled. "There's nothing wrong with you needing a break, my dear. Richard and the boys won't do anything without your permission, but you have to give yourself permission to enjoy the experience first."

A nervous chuckle tore through Alicia. "If only it were that easy. But I—" She downed the liquor in one gulp. "Our games have been fun. And relaxing, I admit, but I can't live like this twenty-four-seven."

"What makes you think Richard expects you to?"

Alicia's finger circled the rim of her glass. This time she wouldn't find her answers on a spreadsheet. And she wasn't sure what she would do if she couldn't meet his expectations.

The female staff member came for Alicia promptly at midnight London time. Richard had disappeared two hours earlier, saying the brothers had invited him to dinner. His absence gave her plenty of time to prepare for the evening.

Maybe too much. Jitters set in full force as the young woman escorted Alicia through the building and into a section she didn't recognize. What had she done by agreeing to let two men, two shareholders of her company, fuck her? She should march right out of the club and catch a flight home.

Alicia half-expected disapproval from her guide, but the staff member was as professional as any masseuse or spa employee Alicia had ever met. It almost would have made her feel better if the staff woman did judge her. Instead, it was far too easy to get carried along in this game.

At the end of the third hallway, two women in black robes and veils stood in front of a large ornate door. The young lady stopped, smiled at Alicia and wished them all a pleasant evening.

The urge to run after the staff member made Alicia's heart race. Instead, she studied the two robed figures. Both of them bowed to her. When they rose, the taller one with blue eyes gave Alicia a wink.

Somehow Katarina's small gesture released some of the tension threatening to overwhelm her. The shorter woman's brown eyes twinkled. Alicia had the distinct impression Azira grinned underneath her veil. Not laughing at her, but as if this were some grand adventure.

Each woman grasped one of Alicia's hands. Azira opened the door and led their little group inside.

The interior took Alicia's breath away. Deep red fabrics hung from the walls giving the appearance of a tent. Rich Persian rugs covered the floor, adding to the illusion. Thick woody incense hung in the air along with hints of coffee and roasted meat. A handful of Arabian-style lamps glowed on tables scattered around the room, but the main lighting came from recesses at the edges of the ceiling.

In the middle of the room, a platform rose from the floor, high enough that a standing man would have ready access to a woman kneeling on the top. A thick sable fabric covered the surface except for where the manacles were bolted. Another tremor of apprehension grabbed Alicia. These weren't the Velcro straps Richard had used, but real honest-to-goodness steel shackles. Once they were locked around her wrists and ankles, she would be trapped.

The three men sitting on one of the two couches drew her attention from the platform. Richard still wore the slacks and oxford he had changed into when they'd arrived at the club. Both Abdul and Mohammed wore loose, light pants and shirts. All three stared at her with rapt attention. While the brothers' eyes appeared black, Richard's eyes glittered silver in the lamplight. His smile loosened the knot of anxiety that twisted her nerves.

Anticipation and lust flickered in the men's gazes. The atmosphere in the room dripped with dream-like decadence. Alicia's nipples ached in response to the emotions running thick. Her fear seemed to drive more lust-filled adrenaline into her blood.

Katarina reached for the belt of the simple wrap dress Alicia wore. Mohammed said something in Arabic, and his wife paused. He rose and approached the three women. The change in the script brought Alicia's nerves back in full force.

"May I have the honor?" He made a slight bow, but his eyes remained locked with hers.

Permission. Like Dr. Paine and Richard had stressed, nothing would be done without her permission. She nodded, afraid anything she might say would ruin the mood.

Mohammed waved the women away, and Katarina and Azira retreated to the other couch. As they walked, their black robes shifted with the lamp light. With a start, Alicia realized not only was the material incredibly sheer, neither woman wore anything under their robes. Just like her.

Like the gauzy blouse of the flight attendant, the sight sent a wave of sensuality through Alicia. She trembled as Mohammed slowly pulled the belt of her dress loose. His hand parted the folds and nudged the fabric from her shoulders. The cotton drifted down and pooled at her feet.

His eyes widened when the jewels hanging from her nipples caught the light. He brushed one dangling end, the motion tugging her nerves all the way to her pussy. "Beautiful," he whispered.

Mohammed stepped back, his gaze frankly appraising. He circled her. Each step slow and calculating, designed to drive her crazy from the wait.

He started a second circuit. His bare feet padded until he was behind her. Then came a soft rustling. His sun-kissed arm snaked around her waist and pulled her against his chest. His naked, smooth chest from the sensation across her back. She shuddered at the pressure of his still-covered cock against the cleft of the ass. Her eyelids fluttered in anticipation of what he would do next.

"You must watch my brother," he whispered in her ear. "He wants to see your eyes."

Another shiver stole over Alicia, and she forced her eyes open. Both Abdul and Richard stared as Mohammed brushed her hair to the side and laid a kiss on one shoulder. Neither man bothered to hide the erections they sported. The sight sent a thrill of feminine power through her. On the other couch, Katarina held Azira close, one hand tracing lazy circles around her lover's cloaked breast, while they watched.

Alicia gave in to the desire swirling through the room. A subtle swivel of her hips drew a chuckle from Mohammed.

He nipped her ear. "Eager minx, aren't we?"

She didn't bother with a reply. Reaching behind her, she slid her hand over the material cupping his erection.

Mohammed grabbed her wrist and yanked it away from his cock. His warmth disappeared from her back, and a sharp slap landed on her ass. "Forward and disobedient as well, I see."

Her punishment prompted giggles from the other two women. The humiliation should have bothered her. It would have a month ago. It would have even twelve hours ago. Tonight, she merely looked over her shoulder at Mohammed and gave him an insolent smile. "Yes, sir."

His other hand grasped her chin roughly and pulled her back for a brutal kiss. Except the melding of his lips to hers turned into something completely different as her mouth opened and sank into his. She explored him thoroughly. The rich and slightly bitter taste of coffee lay on his tongue. The incense mixed with his own clean scent, a heady musk that added to the sensual cloud.

Mohammed's hands released her wrist and chin. They tweaked her tight nipples until the pleasure-pain drew a gasp from her throat, breaking their kiss.

Triumph glittered in his eyes. Rough palms drifted down, stroking her belly, her thighs. They reached the soft, short fuzz.

In an instant, understanding passed between them over the question he'd asked Richard at the hotel a mere two weeks ago. "Please, let it grow in completely for the next time," he murmured in her ear.

She started at his comment. They'd barely begun, and he already assumed this encounter would be a recurring event.

Even as she contemplated his statement, his fingers parted her folds and delved deep inside her pussy. They hit a concentration of nerves. Her knees would have crumpled if not for his arm back around her waist, holding her upright.

"Eyes open," he commanded.

She leaned back against him once again and forced her attention to his brother and Richard. Mohammed's fingers danced across her slick folds and brushed her clit before sliding deep into her pussy again. This time she couldn't stop the motion of her hips. Her ass rubbed against his covered cock. Desire raced across her skin.

And she managed to keep her eyes on Abdul the entire time. He licked his lips as he watched his brother play her body like a master instrument, making her moan and pant.

Abdul's fingers reached for his own cock. A small smile tilted her lips when he forced his hand to lie on his thigh. She recognized the tingles beginning to ripple along her internal muscles. His loss of control only fed the beginning of what would be a powerful explosion.

He barked something in Arabic.

Mohammed removed his magical fingers. The lack of his attention ripped a cry of protest from her. In her erotic haze and disappointment, he had to half-guide and half-carry her to the platform.

"On your hands and knees," he said. Despite the harshness in his voice, his hands were gentle as he helped her into the proper position. The odd manacles were steel, but the inside surface was coated with black felt. The material beneath her knees and palms was spongy and cushioned her. Soft clicks filled the room as Mohammed locked each limb into the appropriate restraint.

As Richard had promised, the position was awkward. Her legs were spread wide, her arms providing stability.

From the corner of her eye, she could see the women's couch. Azira now sat in Katarina's lap. One of her tan legs had escaped through a slit in her black robe. Katarina's sleeve met the part in the sheer material. From the motions and Azira's rapidly moving chest, Katarina was finger-fucking her just as Mohammed had been doing to Alicia. Instead of making her uncomfortable, their actions only heightened the erotic need inside her.

The platform started to swivel. Fear replaced lust for an instant until the pivot stopped at ninety degrees with her back to the couches.

All the better for everyone to view her ass and pussy.

Mohammed moved in front of her and bent to meet her eyes. His right eyebrow rose a fraction. She gave a slight nod at his unspoken question. He flicked the crystals dangling from her breasts. The swing renewed the tightness of the buds, and she whimpered. Then he pulled the drawstring on his loose pants. The silky material slithered down his hips.

His cock jutted proudly. He stepped forward, out of the cloth surrounding his ankles. The slow, deliberate motions gave Alicia a chance to examine him. The dark pink tip rising from the foreskin. The glistening pre-come. The throb of the vein lining his ridge. Mohammed ran his hands through her hair, and she opened her mouth to welcome him.

A rich, exotic taste filled her, and she ran her tongue around the crest. His shiver was her reward. She tilted her head to take as much of him as she could. A moan that she felt more than heard answered her efforts.

Something tickled her ass, and she wiggled, trying to bend to see behind her. Mohammed's fingers clamped in her strands, not hurting her, but definitely limiting her movement unless she wanted him to yank her hair out by the roots. She surrendered, and turned her attention back to pleasuring him.

Her effort didn't distract her enough. Fingers stroked lightly at first, and then plunged inside her pussy. Abdul, no doubt. He took up where Mohammed had left off. She shuddered at the onslaught. With her tongue, she mimicked each move of Abdul's touch on Mohammed's cock in her mouth. A long, easy glide. A swirl around the tip. The lightest of pressures along the most sensitive of areas.

Something pressed against the crevice of her ass, probed her hole. Something hot and slick. Even though she couldn't see him, her mind painted Abdul and his cock. Wanting her. Wanting to be inside her.

Fear rose again. Would Abdul be as gentle as Richard had been? She was locked in place, couldn't move, couldn't resist, if Abdul started to hurt her.

Something much smaller slid into her hole, gentle, coaxing her to relax. Abdul continued to stroke the folds around her clit. If Mohammed had been magic, then Abdul was power. Teasing both pussy and ass, drawing her to the brink, then retreating. Between the two of them, she was insane with lust.

She rocked back ever so slightly in invitation, pulling on Mohammed gently with her lips. Nothing else mattered than having both of them inside her.

Pressure against her tight hole, then Abdul was in her. But when she leaned back a little more, he withdrew.

Damn, that was the game he was going to play. If her mouth wasn't full, she surely would have protested.

Mohammed tugged her hair lightly, forcing her attention back to him. She sucked his cock, eliciting another groan from him. His hips started a rhythm that demanded her full concentration.

Pressure against her hole again. Millimeter by millimeter, Abdul penetrated her ass. Stretching to the point of not-quite-pain as her body accommodated him.

Then he totally filled her, and his fingers sought and played with her clit once more.

Electricity arched along nerves. The push-pull motion of two men taking her, using her for their pleasure heightened her arousal. The sway of the crystals that dangled from her hard buds added to the rhythm.

Mohammed stiffened, his fingertips dug in her scalp. Then his cock pulsed and come shot into her mouth. A soft groan rumbled through him, and he stroked her hair as she licked him clean. He pulled free, bent and kissed her lightly on the lips.

Behind her, Azira cried out her release. Damn, Alicia was so close herself. She leaned back ever so slightly, trying to edge Abdul's fingers across her clit one more time.

Except his hands grabbed her ass cheeks instead. He pumped into her hard. So hard her teeth rattled. Twice. On the third thrust, he shouted something she didn't understand. But she definitely felt the results. His cock throbbed deep in her ass.

She shuddered, needing relief herself so bad that she wanted to cry. Scream. Anything to vent her frustration at being this close to the edge.

Abdul chuckled and withdrew, the inexorable motion driving her insane. A sob of dismay filled her throat. Surely they wouldn't leave her all wound up, would they?

Azira and Katarina walked over to the platform, each carrying a robe. Katarina helped Mohammed into his while Azira disappeared behind her. Then in a flurry of motion, both couples kissed her cheeks and left the room.

Seriously? They were going to leave her chained?

Katarina paused in the doorway and gave Alicia a wave and wink before she pulled the door shut behind her.

What the fuck!

The platform rotated until Alicia faced Richard. If her hands weren't in manacles, she'd slap that sly grin off his face. A grin that left no doubt he was the instigator of getting her worked up and no way to get off.

"Unlock these things!"

His eyebrow lifted. "Excuse me?"

Oh, crap. The brothers had her so aroused she wasn't thinking straight. Hell, she couldn't even press her thighs together. She sucked in a deep breath. "I'm sorry, sir. May I please be released?"

He rose and began unbuttoning his shirt while he strolled toward the platform. "What am I going to do with you, Alicia?"

Oh, god, he wasn't even remotely finished with this game yet. "Please," she whispered. "I can't take any more."

"Really?" His hand cupped her soaked pussy. "Shall we put your tolerances to the test?"

Before she could answer, a flat palm landed on her ass with a resounding *smack*. "That was for being insolent with Mohammed."

Another spank left her skin hot and her nipples painful with need. "And you made him come far too soon. Your mouth is more talented than that."

A third smack and she whimpered. Richard simply continued his dissection of the evening. "And since the brothers match their rhythms, Abdul came far too soon as well." *Smack!*

Pain mixed with need. She gasped when his fingers stroked her slick folds, but stayed well away from her clit.

"Is that what you'd do with me? Try to make me come hard and fast?" His finger edged closer. All he had to do was touch that magic bundle of nerves.

"No, sir." The orgasm was building. She wiggled her hips, but Richard removed his hand and traced damp trails along her ass.

Another smack. "Liar." There was humor in his voice, not accusation.

Soft clicks behind her said he was releasing the manacles. "Do you know why they didn't let you come?"

"No, sir."

He released the catches on her hands. Then he flipped her on her back. His clothes were gone. He was on top of her, inside of her, filling her. She wanted to weep in relief.

But Richard didn't move. He just stared into her eyes. "Because you're mine."

"Yes, sir." She smiled up at him. "Now please fuck me."

Silver eyes gleamed in the lamplight, and his delicious cock began thrusting. It took less than four pumps before she was screaming and boneless from the first orgasm.

Chapter Eleven

The next afternoon, a different young woman led Alicia through the club. Honestly, she wasn't sure how to handle lunch with Katarina and Azira, but Richard had encouraged her to socialize, saying he had business to deal with.

A familiar voice made her glance down a hallway. The man's back was to her, but the bald spot on the thinning blond hair was in the right place. She shook her head and increased her pace to catch up with her escort. She was definitely imagining things if she thought that was Hank.

When she reached their suite, both Katarina and Azira welcomed her with hugs and kisses. Like friends, not like women who'd watched their husbands fuck Alicia's brains out the night before. Lunch was a pleasant affair. The women stuck to small talk until the servants disappeared after delivering coffee and dessert.

"Did you have fun last night?" Azira watched Alicia carefully.

Heat flamed in her cheeks at the memory. "Well, um . . ."

Katarina giggled. "I think that's all the answer we need. What she's really asking is did you have enough fun to join us again?"

"I'm . . . not sure." Alicia took a sip of the strong Turkish coffee to cover her discomfort. "This is all new to me. Can I ask you a personal question?"

Both women nodded. "Please," Azira added.

"Doesn't it bother you to see your husband fuck another woman?"

Her question prompted gales of laughter.

Katarina took a healthy swig of her coffee before she answered. "Everything's not as cut and dried as you Americans would like to think." She shrugged. "Quite frankly, we like you. And we'd much prefer our husbands play with a friend than a stranger. It's more comfortable. But to answer your question, our arrangement—" She waved between herself and Azira. "—gives all of us exactly what we need."

"Almost," Azira muttered. Katarina laid her hand over her sister-in-law's.

Her lover's, Alicia amended silently. "What do you mean?"

"With our country's culture, no one can know I'm the one actually running some of my husband's business interests. A few months ago, Abdul hired a male puppet for me. He's a—" She glanced at Katarina. "What was the English word you used?"

Katarina met Alicia's eyes. "A total dweeb."

Alicia laughed at the description. Beth had used the same term for Hank after they'd met. Damn, she should have listened to both Beth and her inner voice. "I take it the total dweeb irritates you?"

A wave of Azira's hand dismissed her annoyance. "He doesn't have much intelligence, but I deal with him for my poor Abdul's sake. One of his business associates needed a favor. How this man found such a generous friend is beyond me. Apparently, the dweeb is working off some debt and desperately needs the job." A sunny smile lit her face. "Now, let's talk about our next trip to London . . ."

An hour later, Alicia chuckled to herself as she approached the suite she and Richard shared. Azira and Katarina were fun to be with, much like her girlfriends back in D.C. Would Micki, Diana and Beth even believe her story when they all confessed at lunch next Friday? Not that she would name names or anything.

Her analysis stopped when angry male voices penetrated into the hallway. Angry male voices coming from her suite. She twisted the knob and walked into a scene she'd never dreamed.

Her ex-husband stood in front of Richard, shaking so hard it was a wonder he didn't shatter. "How dare you bring her here! She's an innocent—"

"Hank? What the hell is going on?"

He whirled and faced her. Red suffused his cheeks. He hadn't been this angry when she'd caught him with the dominatrix in his old office. "Good. You're here. Pack your bags."

Richard stood behind him and glowered. "She's not going anywhere."

Alicia eased the door shut and folded her arms over her chest. "And I'm not doing anything until you two calm down and explain what's going on."

"Pack your bags," Hank repeated. Then he whirled to face Richard again. "How dare you use her!"

"I am not using Alicia, and our relationship is none of your business." Richard's voice was hard, cold and utterly contemptuous of the man in front of him.

"I'm paying you back, dammit! You don't have to whore her out to pay my debt!"

Alicia stepped between the men. "Whoa, whoa and whoa." There must have been something murderous in her face because Hank took a tentative step away. "What debt are you talking about? You weren't in debt when we divorced." She jabbed a finger in his direction. "Speaking of our divorce, *that* means you can't tell me what to do."

Hank fidgeted. He actually fidgeted. "You need to leave on the next plane, Alicia. You're too good to be here."

At least, he wasn't shouting any more, but his implication sent a knife through her. "I'm too good? What is that supposed to mean?"

He stepped closer, pleading in his hazel eyes. "You don't understand what kind of club this is."

Pieces started to click into place. Her eyes closed in disgust. Hank was Azira's dweeb with a debt. "How much do you owe Richard?"

When the silence continued for several seconds, she opened her eyes.

Raw fear flickered in Hank's face. Richard appeared on the verge of punching her ex if he said a word.

Another piece dropped into place. "Oh, my god, Hank. You stole from your boss?"

Hank couldn't meet her eyes anymore. "Please leave, Alicia. You don't understand what he'll make you do. What he'll let his friends do to you."

All the rage at catching him with a dominatrix came roaring back up. "And maybe if you'd been honest about your needs, we'd still be married. Maybe I've already fucked a couple of his friends. Maybe I liked it!"

Hank visibly paled. "Alicia . . ."

The volcanic anger disappeared as fast as it had spilled. She swallowed the lump at the back of her throat. "Maybe if we'd both been honest, things would have been different."

Hank reached for her hand, and she stepped back. "No, you need to leave."

He hesitated.

"Now, or I'll call security."

Hank fled, the door slamming shut in his wake.

A large warm hand touched her shoulder. She jerked away. Damn, she'd been so mad she'd forgotten Richard was in the room.

She pivoted to face him. "How much does Hank owe you?"

"Alicia, sit down." An agonized look filled his face.

"Is that a command?" She couldn't repress the sneer at the end. What was all his bullshit about honesty?

"No." He wiped a palm down his face. "You don't understand."

"Then enlighten me."

Richard thrust his hands in his pockets. "Yes, he stole from my company. But there was another victim. I gave Hank a choice. I'd cover the reimbursement for the other person, and Hank would work off the entire amount through Abdul."

"Or?" she prompted.

"Or I'd file charges. As I pointed out to him, a theft record and the resulting scandal would harm your career as well as destroy his."

None of this made sense. She shook her head, not wanting to believe Richard. "But who else could he possibly steal from? What was he spending the money—?"

The realization made her nauseous. The prostitutes. And with his parents dead and no siblings, she would be the only other one whose accounts he'd have access to. She raced for the bathroom and bent over the toilet. The lovely lunch wasn't so lovely in its reappearance.

Alicia collapsed on the bathroom floor, trying and failing to control the shakes.

Richard knelt next to her. He tried to hold her, wipe her mouth with a washcloth, but she batted his hands away.

"Is that what last night was about? The money Hank owes you for paying me back?"

"No! God, no!" If Richard's anger at Hank earlier had been cold, this time it was molten steel. "I didn't know Abdul had brought him to London until this afternoon." He grabbed her hand. "I swear Abdul did not even know he was your ex-husband until today. Katarina, the brothers, me—none of us did this to hurt you."

He brought her hand to his lips. For the first time, his touch didn't ignite the spark of desire in her.

She pulled away. "Don't, Richard. Just don't." Climbing to her feet took more effort than she would have thought. "I'll catch a commercial flight."

He stood near, but held back from touching her. "Alicia, don't leave."

She looked at him through her blurry vision. "Don't call me."

Chapter Twelve

On Wednesday around noon, Alicia finally crawled out of bed. Finding the energy to do laundry was out of the question, so she pulled out a sundress that had seen better days. Then she gathered a glass of ice tea, a trash can and the mail and headed to the patio. Dealing with the crap that had piled up while she'd spent the last three weekends with Richard was all she could . . .

Damn. She managed to make it a whole hour without thinking about him. Without thinking about what a fool she'd been. No one did anything in this world without payment. And that's all their relationship had been. Payback for Hank's screw-up.

She settled on the chaise. Through the open window, she could hear the phone ringing again. It rolled over to voice-mail. She couldn't deal with them. Not yet. But even Abdul had called twice.

Alicia forced down a sip of tea and focused on sorting the mound of mail. Bills went in one stack. Magazines in another. Ads got file-thirteen'd. Then a slim cream envelope with exquisite black penmanship appeared under the electric bill.

The name of a Georgetown gallery was on the return address. Alicia snorted. *They probably want a donation.* The invitation nearly slipped out of her fingers when she read the name of the artist.

"So it's alive after all."

The voice did make her drop the heavy card. Alicia looked up to where Beth leaned against the open sliding glass door. "Why didn't you tell me you'd gotten a showing?"

Beth folded her arms over her chest. "You mean the invite you haven't responded to and all my phone calls weren't clues?" Irritation colored her words. Beth never raised her voice to anyone. Ever.

"I'm sorry." Alicia bent over to pick up the invitation. "I've been . . . a little under the weather."

"Oh, so that's why you've called in sick the last three days."

Sarcasm was Micki's forte, but coming from Beth, it triggered something in Alicia. The tears started and she couldn't stop.

Beth said nothing. She simply walked over, sat beside Alicia on the chaise and hugged her tight while all the emotion of the last few days came pouring out. After some time, the sobs trickled down to wet hiccups.

"I-I'm sorry about that."

Beth chuckled and continued stroking Alicia's hair. "For what? Being human?" After a pause, she said, "It backfired, didn't it?"

"What?" Alicia swiped at her runny nose with the back of her hand.

"You fell for your boytoy."

What could she say to Beth? The whole challenge had been her idea, and look where it'd left her. Just another man's arm candy. Okay, maybe more like fuck candy. But still . . .

Beth leaned back to examine her. "Or should I say boytoys? Mrs. Abercrombie called me. She was worried because she hadn't seen you since last Thursday. Then delivery men kept bringing flowers and packages to her to sign for since you wouldn't answer the door. Flowers and packages from three different guys." Her eyebrow cocked in a question.

Heat flooded Alicia's face. Beth was so . . . well, innocent wasn't the right word. And how the hell did she explain something she promised to keep secret? She plucked at her dress, trying to formulate an explanation.

A sigh whistled past Beth's lips. "Not every guy is going to leave you. You need to stop comparing them to your father and Hank."

"This isn't about—"

"Yeah, it *is* about your dad dying, and you know it." Beth reached over and squeezed Alicia's hand. "And I told you Hank was a dweeb from the beginning."

Alicia couldn't help it. She started laughing.

Beth patted Alicia's knee and stood up. "It's safe for you to come out now."

Alicia jerked. Beth wasn't talking to her. She was speaking to the man standing in her family room, watching them.

Richard.

He took a couple of steps onto the patio flagstones and hesitated.

Beth approached him and shot him an arch look. "I have to put up with your buggy software on a daily basis. You make my girl cry again, and I'll tie you down and electrocute your gonads. Capice?"

"Capice."

She turned back to Alicia. "As for you, I expect you at the gallery tomorrow night at eight for my showing. Do I put you down for two?" A mischievous grin lit her face. "Or four?"

The heat in Alicia's face rose a couple hundred degrees. "Can I get back to you?"

"Okay, two it is." Beth waggled her fingers and disappeared into the house.

Alicia stared at Richard. "How'd you talk Beth into letting you in? For that matter how'd you even meet her?"

A sheepish look filled his face. "Your neighbor confronted me when I came to your door. She threatened to call a friend of yours who's a cop. I waited because any officer, especially a friend, would check on you to make sure you were okay."

"Oh."

"Your neighbor lied, didn't she?"

Alicia couldn't help the giggle that slipped out. "No, she called the wrong friend. Beth's a computer consultant."

He ran a hand over his hair. "That explains the software comment. So she's not an artist?"

"Oh, she paints." She smiled at the curl of happiness that Beth finally took a chance on her talent. "We've been trying to get her to show her work for years."

Richard said nothing, just watched her. The silence stretched to an uncomfortable length.

A length she had to break. "Why are you here?"

He took another step closer, like he wanted to join her on the chaise. "I was worried about you."

"I'm fine." *You broke my heart.* "You know the way out."

"Dammit, Alicia. Hank had nothing to do with us wanting to be with you. With me wanting to be with you."

"You lied to me."

"I—" He raked his hand through his hair again. "I was trying to protect you. What Hank did was inexcusable. He cleaned out your accounts. You were about to lose your house. You didn't deserve any of this shit."

"Tell me something I don't know," she snapped. "But you were the one spouting the rules about honesty."

Richard sucked in a deep breath and blew it out. "You're right. I should have told you. I'm sorry I didn't, and that I hurt you. But I think we have something special here, Alicia, and I don't want to lose you."

"You mean you don't want to lose a willing sub." There. She'd thrown out the bitter truth.

"No, I mean I've fallen in love with you."

Her heart caught in her throat. He didn't say what she thought she heard. Did he? "Y-you love me?"

"Yeah." He gave her a rueful grin. "The brothers kept me from beating the crap out of Hank after you left London. Then they . . . let's just say they got me to admit it. Then Azira and Katarina put together a plan to win you back."

Alicia couldn't help smiling back. "Let me guess. It involves the pile of crap sitting in Mrs. Abercrombie's foyer."

He chuckled. "I told the girls you wouldn't fall for that type of shit. Beth suggested something else." He dropped to one knee.

Oh, god, he wasn't actually going to be this stupid, was he? *Yes, he is,* said her little voice.

He took her right hand in both of his. "I want us to be a couple, an exclusive couple. I'd like to marry you—"

She shook her head vigorously. "No! God, no. Not yet, anyway."

"Whenever you're ready then."

A warmth filled her and spread. For the first time in years, her future seemed as bright and pleasant as this May afternoon. "So how do we seal this sort of deal?"

His hands released hers. His gray eyes twinkled as his palms slid under the hem of her skirt.

A shiver of desire ran over her skin.

He reached her inner thighs and smiled when he realized she wasn't wearing panties. His fingers stroked her pussy, coaxing her legs apart. "Mozarella?"

BOUND BY DESIRE

Micki's Story

Chapter One

Another bolt of lightning lit the sky as Micki Donovan raced for the gym's front door. She'd parked in a decent spot thanks to the nearly empty lot, but in two seconds, the rain had gone from a handful of spatters to a deluge. *One Mississi—*

The resulting crack of thunder rattled the glass as she pulled on the handle. Despite the few yards from car to gym, she was soaked. So much for changing at the police station before coming to work out.

Actually, the storm signified her entire week since she and her three friends made their pact at the bistro. The insane pact to find a hot guy and have some freaky sex.

What her buddies didn't know is that she hadn't had sex since Lee died.

Hell, they didn't even know she and her patrol partner had been an item.

Oddly, Alicia's crazy idea gave her the permission she needed to move on. Except her target wasn't cooperating any more than the weather.

Micki had come to the gym every night, but the hot guy who'd been flirting with her for the last month hadn't showed at his regular time. Well, he tried to flirt with her before the infamous lunch. Looking back, Micki realized what a bitch she'd been.

Behind the front counter, Elaine grinned at her and shook her head. "You've got dedication, Donovan."

Micki shook the water dripping down her arms. "Yeah, I'm so dedicated I didn't bring extra work out clothes. It's either chafe in the wet stuff, or admit defeat and head home."

Elaine reached under the counter and pulled out a large box. "Borrow something from the lost-and-found. You can return them when you come in tomorrow." She tossed Micki a couple of towels.

"You're a life saver. Thanks." It took a minute to find a royal blue t-shirt and black mesh shorts that would fit. Grabbing her damp bag, Micki headed for the women's changing room.

The dull clank of weights drew her attention to another room. A momentary glance turned to a full-on stare.

Her mystery flirt sat on one of the benches. Veins stood out on his arms as he did bicep curls. With his full concentration on his reps and no one else in the room, she had a chance to really examine him.

His dark hair was short and conservative. Her training already placed him around six-one and one hundred-eighty pounds. What police experience didn't evaluate before was his broad chest narrowing into a slim waist. Perfect for wrapping legs around.

All those lean muscles meant he did more endurance sports than a strength regime. Did he have endurance for other things? Like fucking her until she forgot her own name? Warm brown eyes stared into hers.

"I didn't realize you were into watching."

Micki jerked at his comment. She'd been too busy fantasizing to realize he'd stopped lifting. "I—" She licked her lips at his innuendo. "I was wondering if the offer to spot me was still open."

Those eyes went from warm to heated. They swept up and down her body in a frank appraisal and stopped at her breasts. God help her, they perked in response. She'd begun to wonder if she'd feel desire ever again. Liquid pooled in her pussy.

A crooked smile lit his face. "Sure."

Her answering smile felt stiff, like she'd forgotten how to flirt back. No, dammit. She was not backing out. The challenge was to find a boytoy, not a boyfriend, right? "Let me change. I'll be right back."

Nerves rattled Micki as she jogged down the hall and into the women's locker room. The same nerves that shot into overload when she caught sight of herself in the bank of mirrors over the sink.

Even though rain plastered her short bob to her scalp and made her look like a drowned blond rat, that wasn't the problem. Underneath the soaked t-shirt and athletic bra, her nipples announced their presence. Flushed areolas stood out under the white fabrics.

A red-faced woman stared back from the mirrors, mortification stamped on her skin. Thank god, no one was here.

Now, she understood the embarrassment Alicia felt the time she'd accidentally pulled off her shirt along with her sweater during a pep rally in high school. But then, Alicia didn't have her breasts standing at attention and mocking her through a wet t-shirt.

Micki didn't have the excuse of being a stupid kid. Adult seduction was one thing, but her mystery man must think she was a total slut from some bar contest. How the hell could she go back to the weight room now?

The outer door creaked. "Hello?" The masculine voice echoed through the empty room.

Micki dived behind a rack of lockers. "It's occupied!"

She hated the shrill note in her voice. *Please, God, let that be the janitor.*

"Are you okay?"

She peeked around the corner. Her mystery man leaned against the inner door-frame. The crooked grin returned when he caught sight of her. And damn, if her nipples didn't grow harder under her cold, wet clothing.

With the heat in her face, her head should be in flames. "I'm fine."

"I thought you were going to change."

"I am," she squeaked. Mentally, she cursed herself and him.

He lifted the spare clothes Elaine had loaned her. The ones Micki had dropped on the sink counter when she caught sight of herself in the mirrors. "Don't you need these?"

This was worse than the time Vice borrowed her for a prostitution sting. And the outfit they made her wear still gave her nightmares.

Micki sucked in a deep breath. Big mistake. The chafing she originally worried about was nothing compared to damp cotton stretching over her overly sensitive breasts. "Look, I'm sorry. This is a bad idea."

He took a couple of steps closer. Close enough she could see the thick erection pressed against his navy shorts. "Why?"

She shrank back, putting a locker door between them. "Because . . ."

He pressed his lips together, but his laughter sparkled in his eyes. "I see." He tossed the clothes in his hand on a nearby bench. Then he lazily stripped off his own sweat-damp shirt.

His chest was as magnificent as she imagined. Defined, but not too heavily muscled, with a smattering of dark hair that led down his washboard abs to disappear into the waistband of his shorts.

"What are you doing?" She projected her normal authority into her voice. Or she tried to. The last syllable ended with a high-pitched squeak.

"Well, you interrupted my lifting routine." He sat down on the bench next to her borrowed clothes. "And I'm already cooling down, so I might as well forget the rest and hit the whirlpool." As he spoke, he stripped off his socks and shoes.

He wasn't going to do what she thought he was. Was he?

"You're not supposed to be in the women's area."

He looked around the room. "There's just you and me." His grin turned cocky. "I won't tell if you won't."

A familiar electricity sparked deep inside her. Fear rippled through her at the same time, made her shiver. It wasn't fear of him exactly, but something much deeper.

His long fingers slid around the edge of the navy shorts, then eased the cotton knit over his hips. White briefs barely contained his cock. Micki couldn't take her eyes off him.

From the look in his eyes, he knew exactly what she was thinking. "If it'll make you feel better, leave your panties on. But you have to come back here to see the rest." He backed around the corner to the women's whirlpool, keeping eye contact until the block wall hid his face. A couple of seconds later, the familiar *whoosh* of the jets reached her ears.

Micki closed her eyes. She should leave now while she had the chance. This was a bad idea. Not to mention incredibly stupid. She didn't know him. Hell, she didn't even know his name.

Chicken. Who was the first one to second Alicia's hot-guy-hot-sex challenge? Besides, if his ass is as tight naked as it looks under his clothing...

Her inner voice was right. She'd never backed down from a dare before. And that's exactly what her mystery man had laid before her. A dare.

She slipped off her shoes and socks. This was so ridiculous. It wasn't like she didn't know how to take care of herself. Besides, Elaine knew who was in the building, right?

Micki tiptoed to the wall and peeked around the corner. Mystery Man had already climbed into the huge whirlpool and faced the entrance. He leaned back, his arms outstretched along the edge, his eyes closed. She spotted his underwear in the corner, but with the jets going full-blast, the bubbling water hid his package.

"You're going to have to get a lot closer if you want to see anything."

She managed not to jump. How the hell had he heard her with the jets running? "Who says I want to see anything?" she shot back.

The crooked smile was back, even though he kept his eyes closed. "Then why are you standing there?"

"I could turn off the pool if I wanted to see." God help her, she did want to see.

His eyes blinked open. Teasing humor lay in their depths. "So why don't you?"

"Maybe I don't want to."

Liar, her inner voice whispered. More tightness and tingling spread across her breasts to the point that they ached. It'd been too long since a man had touched her.

Something held her back. Not fear, but another emotion. Guilt.

But how could she betray a dead man?

"I think you do." Mystery Man's blatant stare at her chest brought her nipples to the point of pain. "If your tits get any harder, they're going to tear through that shirt." His eyes met hers again. "You might as well take it off. It's not like I don't have an excellent idea of what's underneath."

Her fingers curled, but she resisted the urge to yank wet cotton over her head. "I don't even know your name."

His grin widened. "Ryan."

Her eyebrow rose.

At her unspoken question, he said, "First Lieutenant Ryan Caulfield, United States Army."

The relief at a full name didn't take the edge off her horniness, but it helped ease the anxiety. "I'm Micki."

He gave her the same quizzical eyebrow she'd given him.

"Officer Michaela Donovan, D.C. Metropolitan Police Department."

The cocky version of his grin was back. "So, Officer Donovan, are you going to frisk me?"

Micki rolled her eyes. "Like I haven't heard that one before. Next you'll be asking me to check out your artillery."

Ryan gave her a mocking frown. "I'd be disappointed if you didn't. I've always passed inspection before."

She laughed and shook her head. "Are you always this incorrigible?"

His expression grew serious. "Only when I meet someone I'd like to know better. Join me." He patted the edge of the whirlpool.

This was it. The point of "Put up or shut up." She should turn around and leave. Instead, her fingers hooked the hem of her t-shirt and yanked it over her head.

Chapter Two

Before Micki could think this whole thing through, her hands had already unsnapped her athletic bra. Her body knew what it wanted, even if her brain and her heart still had their doubts. She edged the bra down her arms, waiting until the last possible moment before she let him see her breasts.

They sprang free, nipples tight, hard points under his appreciative gaze. Mimicking his motions from earlier, she slid her thumbs along the waistband of her knit shorts, easing them over her hips. She added an extra wiggle to encourage the material past her thighs. The shorts pooled at her feet and she stepped out of them.

She eyed Ryan. "Do I still get to keep my underwear on?"

He shrugged. "If you want. They won't do you much good."

A shiver raised goosebumps along her skin despite the heat and humidity in the room. Or maybe because of it. Being fucked by a man would ease the burning along her nerves, but she didn't know this guy. Not really.

Yet, something drew her to him. She took a hesitant step closer to the whirlpool. "What if someone comes in?"

Another shrug. "It depends. Would you want them to join us?"

She shook her head, trying to will her embarrassment away.

"Good. I don't like to share."

His statement sent a thrill of excitement through her. There was no doubt about what Ryan wanted, but still she hesitated. What she had with Lee had been hot, exciting, but they never risked exposure of their relationship. Especially not by having sex in public. Now?

What could the higher ups do? Suspend her? That had already happened during the two-month investigation into Lee's death. Turn her into a desk jockey? That was what she'd done for the last ten months and a half thanks to the department shrink.

Dammit, didn't she deserve a little pleasure after the last year and twenty-six days of hell?

Micki dipped a toe into the frothing water. It was warm, inviting. She wanted to get in with him. She grabbed on the first excuse she could think of not to.

"We don't have any condoms." Heat filled her cheeks.

Ryan chuckled. "Who says we need them? You have your panties on, remember?"

Crap. Had she totally misread the situation? No. Why else would he be in the women's whirlpool alone with her?

Carefully, she lowered herself into the tub across from him. He didn't make a move toward her. Not even a twitch. Warmth seeped into her muscles, and she closed her eyes. She didn't realize how chilled she was from the storm's drenching.

"Micki?"

"Hmmm?" Her eyes blinked open. The crooked grin was back, less than an inch away. Before she could think, the softest kiss claimed her lips.

No pressure. The lightest of touches. An invitation to go farther.

God, how she missed kissing. Besides, they weren't having sex, right? No condoms.

She cupped his face in her hands. Stubble tickled her palms. Her lips parted. She closed her eyes again and focused on this simple act.

The kiss deepened. His tongue brushed her upper lip. Not tentative, but simply exploring. He tasted like wintergreen, fresh and male.

Their mouths continued a leisurely examination. His teeth nipped her lower lip, then his tongue stroked and smoothed the flesh. Still, he hadn't touched her anywhere else. And every single inch of her body cried out for more.

Ryan broke the kiss. Micki opened her eyes in confusion. His arms were braced on either side of her. The look on his face was one she knew—raw desire. But he didn't move, just watched her. Like a panther watching his prey.

"A-aren't you going to touch me?" Her voice was nothing more than a whisper.

"Are you sure you want me to, Micki?"

He was giving her one last chance to back out. But back out of what? He said they wouldn't need condoms.

It was that little uncertainty that fed the fear pulsing at the base of her throat. The fear that she couldn't stop bad things from happening. To accept Ryan's invitation, she'd have to accept that fear and give up control.

The last time she gave up control, Lee died.

He must have seen the panic in her eyes. "You sure you want to do this?"

That little reassurance gave power to the lust begging to break the surface of her emotions. "Please. I need you to touch me."

But instead of running his hands through her hair or stroking her nipples begging for attention, he pushed away and reached for the waterproof controls.

"Hey," she protested.

"Trust me." The jets slowed to a less intense level. One where the bubbles no longer hid his erect cock. "Now turn around so you're on your knees."

Her eyes narrowed.

"Either you trust me or you don't."

She searched his face, but hell if she knew what she was looking for. Finding a guy and getting off was supposed to be fun. Normally, she was the first one jumping on an opportunity. So why did she feel she was stepping into emotional quicksand?

The tension grew along her nerves. It was Ryan or home for a session with her vibrator. Assuming the batteries still worked after all this time. And a real cock sounded so much better than a toy.

Micki shifted and turned so she knelt in the bench, hands on the pool's edge for balance.

Ryan wrapped his arms around her waist and hugged her against his chest. The thin layer of her panties did nothing to muffle the feel of his cock nestled against her ass. He planted soft little kisses along her shoulder, kisses that left every inch of skin wanting more.

As if reading her mind, his hands roamed across her stomach, inching upward. Not fast enough. Every cell vibrated with need. A sigh escaped her when he palmed her breasts.

The relief was short–lived. He stroked her sensitive flesh. Tweaked and rolled her nipples until she was ready to explode.

She needed more contact. Raising her hands, she reached for his head.

"No." He released her breasts and grabbed her wrists.

Micki sucked in a harsh breath. Fear stabbed at the contact. Muscles tensed to fight.

"Don't touch me yet. This is about you." His voice was husky with lust. "Relax, Micki. Let me do the work."

Her mouth opened, but nothing came out. Nothing that wouldn't sound like a frightened, helpless victim. Disgust flared at her over-reaction. It'd been months since she had anything resembling a flashback. Not trusting herself, she closed her mouth and nodded.

He guided her trembling hands back to the ledge.

Please let him believe I'm that aroused. Which wasn't necessarily a lie. The combination of lust and fear produced an adrenaline rush she'd never experienced.

"I'm only going to move you a few inches to the left," he whispered in her ear. Like she was an animal that needed coaxing to accept a treat.

Ryan lifted her body and planted her right in front of a jet. A gentle persistent stream of warm water pulsed against her pussy, and she gasped at the exquisite sensation.

"Keep your hands where they are." His own hands, however, reached for her knees and gently tugged them apart. Her new position intensified the excitement coursing through her.

Ryan pressed against her back. He wrapped his arms around her, once again paying close attention to her nipples. She tilted her head, and he immediately responded with kisses and nips along her neck.

One of his palms slid south across her stomach. Her hips arched, wanting, needing his touch. The jet of water massaging her pussy only whetted her appetite for more.

Instead, he teased her. Stroking her thighs, slipping fingers underneath panties, squeezing her ass. Everywhere but where she needed those marvelous hands.

"Touch me." Her words were more plea than command.

She felt the vibration of his chest more than heard his laughter. "I *am* touching you." But this time, his fingers traced a wide circle around her mound.

"I need . . ."

He stroked the edge of her slit through her panties. That motion combined with the jet pulse left her so close, but his fingers traveled away. A sob broke from her out of sheer sexual frustration.

"What do you need?" he murmured in her ear.

"I need you . . ." Once again, he stroked her slit, and she lost the words.

Another rumble of laughter. "Do you want my hand inside your panties?"

She couldn't speak, only nod. Her knuckles turned white from her grip on the tiled edge.

His fingers rimmed the edge of the elastic waistband. "Like this?"

"No." She ground her teeth.

His hand dipped a couple of inches inside and played with her curls. "Like this?"

"No, dammit." Fine. If he was going to be that way . . .

Micki ground her ass against his cock. A gasp of surprise whistled past her ear. The hands teasing her froze in place. "What's the matter?" She gave him an innocent look over her shoulder. "I did what you asked. *My* hands haven't moved."

"Bitch." But his crooked grin was in place. "Paybacks." Two fingers plunged inside her hot pussy. His thumb caressed her clit. She leaned against him, so close to the edge—

Every cell exploded. Ryan held her, stroked inside her, milking every last tremor. Never had she orgasmed that hard, that fast. Not even with Lee . . .

A wave of guilt hit her.

"Hey, you okay?" His expression serious, Ryan tilted her chin, searched her face.

Micki swallowed the lump at the back of her throat. She forced a smile. "Yeah. It's just . . . been a while. Kind of took me by surprise."

This time a self-satisfied smirk appeared on his face. "Then why don't you sit here and rest a minute."

She opened her mouth to protest.

He laid an index finger over her lips. "Close your eyes." When she hesitated, he whispered, "Close them, and meet me outside in five minutes."

This time she obeyed. He cradled her body until she once again sat on the whirlpool's bench. Water splashed, and she heard the wet slap of bare feet moving away.

Micki counted to ten before she blinked her eyes open. What the hell had she been thinking? She had sex in a public place with a total stranger. It was stupid. It was dangerous.

Her pussy spasmed.

And damn, if she didn't want more of this man.

Chapter Three

Micki half-expected Ryan to be gone along with the spring storm when she shoved the main door of the gym open. Instead, he leaned against the building's brick wall when she emerged.

He smiled. "What are we doing for an encore?"

She blinked. An encore? She wanted to kick herself. Of course, he wanted to continue. She'd gotten off. He hadn't. It was that simple. But if spending more time with him meant an opportunity for her to come again, preferably with his cock inside her . . .

"Gee, I usually get dinner and a movie before I'm expected to put out." Micki waved at her old t-shirt and ratty jeans. "This is hardly date apparel."

Ryan stepped closer, so close she could feel his body heat in the post-storm chill. "You look fine, sweetheart."

Laughter burbled out of her at his bad Bogart imitation.

His crooked grin returned. "There's a diner just off of White Rock and a theater two blocks from there. Would that satisfy your criteria?"

She nodded.

"Your carriage, m'lady." He gestured toward a Jeep that had seen its best days before her dad was born.

Micki held up her keys and rattled them. "How about I follow you?"

He bent even closer, his breath hot against her skin. "You let me finger-fuck you, but you won't ride with me?"

"Oh, I'll ride you," she whispered. "But you can't pay me enough to get in that death trap you drive."

His lips dipped toward hers, but she pivoted and marched across the damp asphalt toward her Mustang before he could kiss her.

"Donovan! Long time, no see!"

Micki had stepped into the diner less than a second before Butch Wayne charged from the kitchen and enveloped her in a bear hug.

"Bear" was an accurate description. At six-five and three hundred pounds, Butch could give any Redskins linebacker half his age a bruising. But time was taking its toll. His braids wrapped up in his hair net were now fully gray.

"Good to see you, too." She pounded the owner and chief grill cook on the back. "What're you doing here on a Friday night?"

He broke the hug. "Alonso called in. Emily went into labor."

She frowned. "Isn't she early?"

"Just a couple of weeks." The older man shrugged. "I learned that lesson a long time ago. Mother Nature has her own damn clock."

Butch would know with six of his own. Alonso was just the youngest of the pack.

He turned and gave Ryan a once over, then cocked a hopeful eyebrow. "New partner?"

"Not yet." She gave him a rueful smile. "Butch, this is my friend, Ryan. Ryan, this is Butch. He makes the best cheeseburgers this side of the Potomac."

"Friend, huh?" Butch shook Ryan's hand. White teeth shone against his dark skin as a sly grin spread across Butch's face. "'Bout time, girl." He leaned close. "Has he met the major yet?"

"Butch!" Heat flooded her cheeks.

"Don't worry, girl. I'll put in a good word." He shot Ryan a nasty look. "Provided he doesn't need to die for making you cry."

"Butch, stop it. Now." Micki glared at him. When he opened his mouth, she added, "Don't make me shoot you."

The older man laughed. "You're impossible." He twisted to grab a couple of menus off the counter, then crooked a finger. "This way."

Of course, Butch headed for the same booth where he always sat her. The one that mortified her to no end. Micki just prayed he wouldn't mention the picture. She breathed a sigh of relief when he merely took their drink orders.

Once Butch disappeared into the kitchen, Ryan cocked an eyebrow. "Let me guess. The major is your dad."

She winced. "Sorry about that. Butch is a really good guy. It's just that he served with Dad for a long time." And no doubt he would phone her parents about Ryan as soon as she left.

"It's good to have friends looking out for you."

Micki leaned back against the booth's vinyl. Ryan wasn't freaking out about the mention of her father. In fact, he looked . . . sad.

But he would freak eventually. All guys did when they found out in which division Major Donovan had served. "Yeah, it is."

Ryan's smile was back. "So you played me when I mentioned this place."

She spread her fingers. "You didn't ask if I've been here before."

He chuckled. "True. So, why do you need a new partner?" His eyes had a laser-like intensity.

Thankfully, Letisha, Butch's oldest granddaughter, bustled to the table with drinks and took their orders. The last thing she wanted to discuss was Lee's death and the resulting investigation. Unfortunately, the interruption also gave him time to examine the pictures on the wall. And one picture in particular.

The knowing gleam in his eyes was almost as bad as Butch bringing up her father. He leaned across the table. "I've never done a cheerleader before."

"Shhhh . . ." Micki glanced around, but none of the Wayne family were close enough to hear.

"If I asked you to pull out your old uniform, would you wear it for me?"

"Ryan . . ."

His cocky grin was back. "With no panties on," he whispered.

She glared at him. "Don't make me shoot you, too, Lieutenant Caulfield."

He chuckled. "Sorry, I just can't see you as a cheerleader. Besides all military brats are loners."

"Talk about profiling." Micki fiddled with the napkin-wrapped silverware. His shot was a little too close to reality. "Or are we speaking from experience?"

An expression crossed Ryan's face that was almost wistful. "Envy is closer to the truth. You all look happy. Almost like a family in that picture. I take it your coach—" he leaned closer to read the caption "—LaShaun Wayne, is Butch's wife?"

Micki nodded and looked at the picture. Really looked at it. Ryan was right. Butch had taken it the day they won the state cheerleading title. It was her junior year in high school, and probably the last time any of her friends felt like kids.

The following week Diana and her baby sister Steffi would move in with the Donovans after their parents' kicked them out. Alicia's dad died in a car crash less than a month later, so she spent a lot of nights at Micki's when her mom's drinking got to be too much.

And then there was Beth . . .

Micki took a sip of her Coke to hide her emotions. "Contrary to some popular misconceptions about military families, Butch, LaShaun and my parents were the closest thing to stability some of my civilian friends ever had."

Ryan reached for her hand. "Hey, I'm sorry for dredging up old shit."

For the second time, a Wayne family member interrupted the conversation to her relief. Mike plunked down their plates. "Hey, name of my name, how's it hanging?" Another hug enveloped her.

"Absolutely fine." Once again, introductions were made.

"You know Dad's already on the phone with the major."

Micki wiped a hand over her face. So much for the half-hour reprieve to eat.

Mike grinned. "Don't have too much fun tonight."

He leaned over to give Micki a second hug. "But in case, you do," he whispered. He dropped something into her lap, winked and sauntered away.

She glanced down. Three foil packets lay on her napkin. Heat flooded her face.

Micki looked up to find Ryan staring at her. The same desire he exhibited at the gym flared in his eyes. Embarrassment and lust warred in her head. To distract both, she reached for the ketchup bottle.

Ryan held his hand out for the bottle once she poured some on her plate. "Should I ask what the 'name of my name' thing was about?" That smile of his took any accusation out of his words.

She laughed and shook her head. "Mom and Dad were absolutely sure I would be a boy. Butch and LaShaun were expecting around the same time. Both sides claimed dibs on the name 'Michael'. So you can imagine Dad's expression when I was born, and it turned out it had been my thumb on the sonogram. I really think he insisted on 'Michaela' just to be ornery."

Then Ryan's tactics hit her. She still knew almost nothing about him. Seizing the opening, she asked, "What branch was your dad in?"

"Army." He took a large bite of his cheeseburger.

"Any siblings?"

Ryan shook his head as he chewed. He barely swallowed before he took another bite.

"Your parents still alive?"

A nod this time. No words though, just another bite.

Interesting. He didn't like being on the receiving end of an interrogation. Micki swirled a fry through her ketchup. "You know, I can always run a background check."

Humor lit his eyes, but he still chewed slowly.

She released the fry to swim in the pool of ketchup on her plate. "If you have any hope of using one of these—" She snatched a foil packet from her lap, glanced around to make sure no one was watching them, and slid it across the table. "— you *will* talk to me."

His eyes widened, then narrowed, and he swallowed his bite. "You were holding out on me at the gym."

Micki schooled her expression, reached for the drowning fry and nibbled on it.

Ryan glanced around before he palmed the condom package. "You need to use the ladies room." It was a statement, not a question.

The first fry was gone. Micki reached for another, but Ryan grabbed her wrist.

They stared at each other for what seemed to be an eternity. He wasn't hurting her, and even if he were, she could have broken his hold. Finally, he said, "Please. I'll knock out 'Shave and a Haircut.'"

Excitement hit Micki hard in her pelvis. What the hell was wrong with her?

She would *never* have dared to have sex in public before tonight. There was too much at stake. Her career. Her family's reputation. Hell, even her self-respect.

Yet, she'd done it at the gym. And that fact only added to her arousal.

Micki found herself placing the other two condoms in her jeans pocket, folding her napkin and sliding from the booth.

Thank God, the Waynes were occupied with other customers. She practically ran down the short hallway that led to the restrooms and Butch's office. Already, her spare panties were damp at the thought of what she was about to do. She stepped in and closed the door of the tiny bathroom.

Her hand clenched around the knob. Leaning her forehead against the wood laminate door, she sucked in a deep breath. Industrial-strength orange freshener scented the air. What was she doing? What if she and Ryan were caught? God, she felt like a naughty teenager sneaking around with her boyfriend, not a thirty-two-year-old D.C. cop.

Rap. Rap. Rap-rap. Rap.

Micki edged the door opened. Ryan slipped inside, closed and locked the door. He cupped her face. His kiss was languid, exploratory. The memory of him pressed against her in the whirlpool was enough to push her doubts aside. Her own fluids soaked her panties at her need for him, for his cock inside her. She nudged her shoes off her feet and yanked his shirt from his waistband even as he unbuttoned her jeans.

Ryan broke their kiss. He knelt and tugged her jeans and panties down and off. His fingers stroked her very wet, very open slit. His eyes looked up into hers for an instant, then his tongue traced the same path.

Micki bit her lip to keep from crying out. Unlike the empty gym, people stood just feet from the ladies' room. Yet, Ryan was doing his damnedest to wring a reaction from her. He alternated. First, delicately sucking her clit, then sliding two fingers deep into her pussy.

Her muscles clenched as he worked her into a frenzy. Just as she reached the edge of the cliff, he pulled away.

Ryan stood, undid his jeans, and sheathed his cock in record time. He pressed her body against the wall, lifting her at the same time. She wrapped her arms around his neck. Her legs encircled his waist. Then he plunged his cock into her. Hard. Fast. And the feeling was absolutely glorious.

The doorknob rattled. *Shit!*

They paused for a split second, but instead of interrupting their rhythm, the sound only spurred them on. Faster. Harder. Micki felt the edge coming and let it take her. Ryan muffled her moan with his lips. Then his body stiffened. The pulse of his release triggered another set of contractions in her pussy.

Someone knocked on the door.

Annoyance rippled through Micki. "One moment!"

Ryan buried his head against her shoulder to stifle his chuckles. He withdrew and set her back on her feet. For an instant, Micki wasn't sure her knees would hold after two orgasms. She already missed the feel of his cock filling her.

"Hurry," she whispered as she grabbed her jeans off the floor.

While she dressed, Ryan disposed of the condom and cleaned up.

Another round of knocking. "Come on." A woman. A very irritated and impatient woman from the sound of it.

Checking that both hers and Ryan's clothing were back in order, Micki unlocked and opened the door. A gray-haired woman stood there, her fist raised to knock again. She glared at Micki.

Micki smiled brightly. "Sorry about the wait, ma'am. We're the plumbers. Had to fix a leak. It's all yours now."

The woman's expression grew downright suspicious when Ryan followed Micki out of the bathroom, but she pursed her lips, entered the restroom and slammed the door.

Micki took two steps down the hall when she realized there were no footfalls behind her. She turned to see a wicked grin on Ryan's face.

He shooed her towards the dining area. "Go. You don't want Butch to see us walking out together."

Once again, heat ignited Micki's cheeks. He was right. But it wasn't just the idea of Butch knowing what they'd done in his diner.

It was knowing that less than two hours after learning Ryan Caulfield's name, she'd had three incredible orgasms with him, and she wanted more.

Guilt smacked desire upside the head as Micki slid into the booth. The same booth she shared with Lee for years.

If she didn't get a handle on her feelings for the two men, she'd go crazy. Crazier than the PTSD already made her.

Chapter Four

Micki stepped out of the diner and breathed a sigh of relief. She and Ryan managed to finish dinner. The woman from the bathroom must not have complained because Butch surely would have said something as they waved their good-byes.

"Well, now that I know the owner of this fine establishment is ex-military, it explains why he has obsessively clean bathrooms." Ryan wrapped an arm around her waist. "Want to skip the movie? My apartment isn't far from here."

She hesitated. It would be so easy to give in. And a large part of her really wanted to give in.

He released her. "No pressure here. It's just that . . ." He ran a hand through his short dark locks. "I like you. I know this is crazy, but . . ."

Something about his hesitation touched her. She laid a hand on his chest. "But what?"

His sheepish grin shone under the neon lights of the diner's sign. He leaned close to her ear. "I'd really like to fuck you properly in a bed."

The admission triggered her own laughter. "What? You mean doing it in public, twice, wasn't enough?"

Ryan's expression turned serious. "I'm not sure I'd ever get enough of you, Michaela Donovan."

She swallowed hard. The statement hit her because she was starting to feel the same way. And it only gave the guilt a stronger hold on her emotions.

Micki stepped into an apartment so neat and functional that for a split-second, she expected her dad to pop out of a closet. Her gaze swept the perfectly stacked pile of magazines on the table and the orderly bookshelf. The two pictures on the wall could have been used to calibrate a carpenter's level.

Ryan dropped his gym bag next to a well-used, but clean, couch. "Now, where were we?" He dipped his lips to hers, his kiss all-consuming.

Micki reached up to twine her fingers through his hair. His erection pressed against her stomach, triggering a need deep inside of her. A need to have that magnificent cock. Not a rush job like before, but a slow, sensual invasion.

Without breaking the kiss, his hands encircled her wrists drawing them down and behind her. She tried to pull loose, but he tightened his hold . . .

Micki was back in the warehouse. The knife glinted as one of the slavers yanked Lee's head back, exposing his throat. Arterial blood sprayed in an arc. All over her face, her hair. She screamed and fought, but the assholes had used duct tape on her wrists. Sanchez whispered in her ear how he was going to rape her, let his boys have a turn with her, before they killed her. But all she could see was Lee. His life leaking out on the filthy concrete . . .

"Micki! Micki!"

She stopped thrashing, her right arm extended in mid-punch.

A dark-haired man stood two yards away, his hands in the air. "Micki?"

She sucked in a lungful of air and lowered her arm. Adrenaline made everything jittery.

"Micki? You with me now?"

Ryan. His name was Ryan and they'd been about to . . .

Fuck. She raked fingers through her hair. It'd been months since she'd had a flashback. And never in front of someone. Her lungs reminded her she needed to breathe.

"Micki, what happened?" Ryan's voice was soft, gentle, like he was trying to calm a frightened child.

"I-I'm sorry." She edged toward the door.

He didn't move toward her, but concern filled his eyes. "Micki, I don't think you should drive—"

"I'm sorry." The words ended in a sob, and she raced out the door.

Chapter Five

A few blocks away from Ryan's apartment, Micki pulled into a deserted shopping center parking lot and turned off the engine. Her hands were still shaking. She leaned her head against the steering wheel and let the sobs come.

Slowly, the residual terror somersaulted into anger and embarrassment. The first time she felt any kind of sexual attraction since Lee . . .

And she managed to ruin everything with Ryan. Should she call him? Apologize?

No. She used the hem of her t-shirt to dry her damp eyes and cheeks. Best to just forget tonight ever happened.

She flipped the ignition, put her Mustang into gear and headed for home.

On Monday morning, Micki sat in her usual chair in the department shrink's office, just as she had for the last fifty-two weeks.

Dr. Johnson watched Micki over her wire-rimmed glasses, just as she had for the last forty-one weeks.

Like Micki would ever tell the bitch anything after she'd blabbed about Rodriguez's drinking problem and gotten him fired. Well, technically, Rodriguez resigned, but everyone suspected the truth. Someone with his dedication didn't just voluntarily resign.

"What happened this weekend?"

The sound of the doctor's voice jolted Micki out of their usual staring contest. "What do you mean?" If nothing else, she'd learned from the shrink how to respond to a question with another question.

A slight smile tilted Dr. Johnson's severe mouth. "You're not glancing at your watch every few seconds, and you're not tapping your foot."

"Maybe I'm getting used to my sentence."

As usual, the shrink didn't react to her rancor. "This isn't a sentence, Micki. It never was. This is about you being healthy."

"But you're not releasing me for street duty." It wasn't a question. Micki stared at the diploma on the wall to keep her temper in check.

There was a soft sigh. "You know I can't do that. Not until I'm sure you're not a danger to yourself or to the public." The shrink was silent for a moment before she added, "You met someone this weekend."

Fury snapped like the sting of a rubber band. "That's none of your goddamn business." She glared at Dr. Johnson.

The shrink pulled off her glasses and pinched the bridge of her nose. "Officer Donovan, I can't release you for street duty until you talk to me." She looked up and replaced her glasses. "And I can't help you unless you let me."

Micki stood. "Then there's no reason for me to be here." Three quick strides brought her to the shrink's door.

"I'll see you next Monday morning at ten a.m.," the shrink called behind her.

It was all Micki could do not to slam the door. The only thing worse than telling the shrink the truth about Lee would be admitting she'd had sex in public places with a complete stranger.

Neither option would get her back in a squad car.

Maybe she *should* go back to Caulfield's place and screw his brains out. Lord knew she was already fucked by the force.

Instead, she went straight home after work. Going to the gym would be a colossal mistake. Except she wasn't sure what bothered her more; that Ryan might be there or that he might not.

She worked through karate katas in what constituted her townhouse's yard. The chilly air that had followed Friday's rain front put only the slightest of dampers on her libido. And the fact that she was still revved up from Friday night only reinforced her decision not to go to the gym.

After a shower and a phone call to the pizzeria across the street, she curled up on her couch. The cop show she flipped to was a joke when it came to real procedure, but the actors and the Hawaiian scenery were gorgeous.

Five minutes into the show and a half slice of pepperoni and mushroom, someone knocked.

Micki stared at the door, then stared at the rest of her slice. Cookie season was over, and she was pretty sure she'd bought out the entire supply of Thin Mints from Molly next door. Mrs. Krenski from the condo on the other side wasn't back from wintering in Florida. Besides, it was after ten p.m.

Whoever it was knocked again.

She set down the slice, crossed to the door and checked the peephole.

Familiar shoulders encased in a brown leather jacket darkened her front step. Ryan reached up to knock a third time.

She jerked the door open before he could connect. "What the hell are you doing here?"

He raised an eyebrow as he lowered his fist. "I'm doing fine, thank you. And you?"

She glanced at her service revolver in its holster hanging on her coat tree, then decided it wasn't worth the paperwork. Her vibrator was a better idea for dealing with her pent-up sexual frustration. She'd bought fresh batteries yesterday. "I'm eating. Good night."

She started to shut the door, but somehow he was faster, sliding inside and hanging up his coat before she could react.

He grinned over his shoulder at her. "Great! I'm starved."

Micki couldn't help staring at his waist where the forest green polo was neatly tucked in his jeans. The memory of her legs wrapped around him as his cock rammed into her raised goose bumps along her skin. She closed the door and tried to yank her body back under control.

"You know it's illegal for Elaine to give you my personal information," she said as she strode after him to the couch. The bastard had already flopped on the cushions, grabbed a slice of *her* pizza and munched with a blissful expression.

"Elaine didn't give it to me." He took another bite.

She crossed her arms over her chest, all too aware she hadn't bothered with a bra after her shower. "How did you get my address?"

Another cocky grin shone on his face. "You're not the only one who can do a background check." He finished the slice and stood. "Do you want another soda while I'm in the kitchen?"

Was this guy mental? She stared in disbelief as he sauntered over to her refrigerator and pulled out two cans. He didn't meet her eyes as he returned, just sat a soda next to her plate before sprawling on the couch once more and grabbing another piece of pizza.

Should she call 9-1-1? No, that was ridiculous. What would she tell the dispatcher? That the guy she had sex with in public showed up on her doorstep and was now inhaling her large pizza and watching her TV?

After a couple of bites, he looked up at her. "Seriously? You watch this crap?"

"What's wrong with what I watch?"

"Besides an alleged active-duty SEAL answering to a civilian governor?" He took another bite before he added, "You can't tell me this is a realistic representation of *your* job."

She rubbed her forehead, but it didn't alleviate the growing headache. "I'm not debating the merits of a TV show with you. Why are you here?"

Ryan looked down at the growing erection pressing against the fly of his jeans. "You mean it's not obvious? Man, that's cruel."

Micki tugged at her t-shirt, more to keep her own physical reactions from becoming obvious. Her breasts ached at the very thought of him touching her, plucking her nipples until they were hard, needy—

"Leave."

"No." He calmly finished the slice of pizza as they stared at each other.

"This is breaking and entering."

"Nope. I knocked and you answered the door. That constitutes an invitation."

"Does not."

"Does too." His expression was serious, but the twinkle in his eyes gave him away.

"Look," she started. She ran a hand over her hair and yanked her ponytail for good measure. This was going to hurt his feelings, but it needed to be said. She blew out a deep breath. "I'm sorry for Friday night. It was a mistake. This—" She waved a hand between them. "—isn't going to work."

The humor in his eyes disappeared. "And what is 'this,' Micki?"

Tears collected in her eyes and she blinked them back. "I just can't." She couldn't meet his steady gaze any longer. Staring at the floor, she hugged herself.

"I get that part."

Rustling came from the couch. A whisper of air as Ryan walked past her. Muffled footsteps on the carpet as he headed for the front door.

The rattle of metal-on-metal made her look at him.

He held up a pair of handcuffs. "That's why I brought these. In fact—" He snatched her pair off her utility belt. "I'll borrow yours as well."

Anxiety flickered along her nerves as he took two steps toward the living room. Then he turned and jogged up the stairs.

"Hey, where do you think you're going?" She crossed to the foot of the staircase. Steel dug into her palm from her tight grip on the black metal railing.

He didn't answer. She peered up the stairwell. He didn't stop on the second floor, but kept his pace up to the third. To the master suite.

To her bedroom.

He disappeared from view. What the hell was he doing up there?

No sound filtered down except the faint *tink* of metal on metal.

What the hell should she do? Call for backup? Grab her purse and drive to Alicia's or Diana's? They both owed her for all the nights they spent at her parents' or here. And she sure as hell didn't want to explain any of this crap to Beth. The girl would positively freak over Micki's stupidity, especially after what had happened to Beth in high school.

Her eyes flicked over to the coat stand. If Ryan wanted to do anything to her, he could have grabbed her gun.

I'd really like to fuck you properly in a bed.

His words from Friday night echoed in her head. Was he simply waiting for her to join him? Micki buried her face in her hands. God, she'd been the first one to jump on the hot-guy-hot-sex bandwagon, she had a gorgeous man waiting for her in her bedroom, and she stood here paralyzed.

Chicken, her inner voice whispered.

Old terror crept in so silently it seized her before she realized what was happening.

Duct tape had stripped the top layer of skin, yanked out the fine hairs on her wrists. The rankness of old cologne and even older sweat clogged her nose in that freezing warehouse. Silvery shards of Lee's transmitter lay scattered across dull concrete. The team had calculated sixty seconds as the best-case scenario to reach them if something went wrong. But thirty seconds in and Lee lay on the floor. Crimson spread under him. His lips moved, telling her . . .

Cold sweat dampened her tee. Micki clung to the railing to stay upright. She couldn't go through that helpless feeling. Not again.

Forcing her spine straight, she glared up the stairwell. No one was going to make her feel vulnerable again. Determined to get rid of her unwanted guest, she marched up the stairs.

When she reached the third floor, her will faltered. Under the light of the bedside lamp, Ryan lay on her pale blue sheets and pillows, clad only in a white t-shirt. His cock stood at attention, as if waiting for inspection. His eyes were closed, long dark lashes brushing his skin. One pair of handcuffs looped through the black iron railing of the headboard, firmly securing his hands above his head.

And damn, if her panties weren't already soaked by the sight of him waiting for her.

Chapter Six

Micki stared, unsure of what to do. However, her body definitely knew what it wanted. The ache in her pussy spread through the rest of her pelvis. Her breasts perked at the sight of his full lips. But her sanity threatened to desert her completely if she let him stay.

She cleared her throat. "What do you think you're doing?"

"Waiting for you, Ma'am."

"Ma'am?" The emphasis in his voice enforced his title for her.

"Would you prefer I address you by something else, Ma'am?"

The abrupt change from self-assured soldier to sex slave threw her off. She was so used to guys trying to prove they were more powerful. They sure as hell never submitted to her, made themselves helpless, let her do whatever she wanted with them. The terror that overwhelmed her downstairs a moment ago seemed like something that happened to another woman in another lifetime.

This type of power over someone else, over Ryan in particular, was … different. Part of her liked it. *Really* liked it. "'Ma'am' is fine.

"Yes, Ma'am." He still hadn't opened his eyes.

For some strange reason, the switch added a level of comfort with him. With herself. She padded over to the bed. The other pair of cuffs sat on her nightstand along with the keys to both. And beside them lay the last two condoms Mike had slipped her Friday night.

Micki had meant to toss them in the trash. What had Ryan thought when he saw the foil packets sitting there? Incriminating evidence or an invitation?

She sat on the edge of the mattress and ran her fingers along his leg. His skin prickled at her touch. His cock jerked.

Never before had Micki had a chance to truly explore a man's body. Her gaze ran over him. Her fingers tested everything. The wiry hair covering his arms and legs. The weight of his balls. The velvety hardness of his cock.

Wanting more, she tugged his t-shirt up a little to see his abdomen and belly button. His muscles tensed under her hands. Interesting. Definitely hiding something.

"Why did you leave your t-shirt on, Ryan?"

Crimson edged along his neck. "I—" He swallowed hard. His eyelashes fluttered, a quick glance at her before staring at the ceiling. "Please, don't—"

Sympathy spread through her heart. He hadn't asked about her freak-out at his place when he got here tonight. She could allow a little compassion for whatever he was hiding.

Micki ran a hand over his abdomen, feeling his muscles tremble beneath her palm. "Next time, I want you completely naked."

"Yes, Ma'am," he whispered.

What to do with him now though? Her mind ran through all kinds of delicious possibilities with a few suggestions from other body parts. Part of her couldn't believe he was doing this, allowing himself to be in such a vulnerable position. Yet, she was honored by his gift.

And that's exactly what it was. A gift. Letting her take control, set the parameters. She needed him to know how much she appreciated his thoughtfulness.

"Ryan?"

"Yes, Ma'am."

"I want you to look at me."

His dark eyes met hers. Micki hooked her thumbs in the hem of her t-shirt. With a slowness that tantalized her, she slid the cotton up and over her head.

Yep, she definitely had his full attention now. That erection had to be painful from the way it appeared to want to leap from his body. She reached behind her head and pulled the band from her ponytail. Her fingers ran across her scalp, shaking out her hair.

His tongue darted out and licked his lips. Did he realize how much he gave away? Or were his motions a calculated move?

Did it really matter? Want trilled along her nerves. Despite what she'd told the girls, she hadn't bothered with her vibrator for the last year and twenty-nine days. Now . . .

She shimmied out of her sweatpants. Shedding her clothes released all that tension buried under grief. She'd been naked Friday night, but this was something else altogether. This new aspect of herself reveled in its freedom. Free from her parents' expectations. Free from society's view of her. First as a cheerleader. Then as a woman. As a police officer. Free from everything she thought had defined her.

This was just her. Michaela.

She climbed onto the bed and straddled Ryan. Her hands rested on his cotton-clad chest. His cock throbbed against her slick folds, in time to the beat of his heart beneath her fingertips. God, how she wanted him inside her again, but not yet.

"Why did you come here tonight?"

He was silent for a second. From the flickering in his eyes, he weighed the consequences of his possible answers. "I want you. I want to be with you."

"Why?"

He hesitated.

"The truth, Ryan."

"I can't tell you."

That took her aback. "Are you sassing me?"

His face hardened. "You say you want honesty, but you're not ready for it. If I give you the truth, you'll use it as an excuse to run away. Again." He closed his eyes for an instant before resuming his intense gaze. "Then neither of us gets what they want. Ma'am."

He bit the last part out, like a rookie daring her to do something about his disrespect.

And just like some rookie snot, she needed to teach him a lesson. Not out of ego or anger, but so he understood that trust and respect needed to go both ways.

Then it hit her. In every encounter, Ryan kept his back away from her. Or kept his shirt on, like now. He had no problem exposing much more vulnerable areas of his body. Time to push the issue.

She climbed off Ryan. His sharp gasp filled her ears, but she didn't look back as she headed for the stairs. Nor did he say anything more.

Micki hit the second floor landing and entered the room she'd converted to an office. Reaching into the closet by the door, she retrieved her sewing box. Dad had drummed keeping her knives and scissors sharpened since elementary school. Her sewing shears would make quick work of that t-shirt.

She padded back up the stairs. Ryan noticeably relaxed at her appearance.

Until he saw the shears in her hand. Wariness filled his features.

She climbed onto the mattress and straddled him once more. Her pussy tingled, throbbed, wanting that huge cock inside. Not yet.

Micki rested the shears against his flat abdomen. His muscles jumped underneath her thighs. "I don't appreciate being sassed, Lieutenant." *Slice.* He wanted to protest. She could see it in his eyes.

"You chose this game." *Slice.* Damn, he didn't have a six-pack. He had a freaking case.

She waited a second to see what he'd do. A muscle ticked along his jaw.

"If you want me to play this game, then you have to obey my instructions." *Slice.* Anger shimmered in his eyes, but still he said nothing.

"Or you will be punished." *Slice.* She spread the cotton aside to reveal his chest. It was a delectable as it had been Friday night. Dark, hard nipples against tanned skin.

She trailed the point of the shears across his pecs, and damn, if his nipples didn't get even harder.

A couple of inches of material remained, and she slid the edge of the shears around it. "Do we understand each other?"

His eyes smoldered with his pent-up ire. "Yes, Ma'am."

Slice.

Micki made quick work of the sleeves and smiled. A seething Ryan lay in the shreds of his t-shirt. And she couldn't even remember the question she'd originally asked him. Not with his cock twitching against her pussy.

She set the shears on the nightstand, next to the extra handcuffs, and snagged a packet.

With deliberate movements, she unwrapped the condom and sheathed him. But her efforts to torture him only drove her libido into fourth gear. She rose up on her knees and slid down over his cock.

Despite how wet she was, he stretched her, filled her. Lust didn't replace the ire in his face, but it covered a good chunk of it. His hips thrust against her.

She rose until only the head of his cock remained in her passage. "Uh-uh-uh." She wagged a finger. "My bedroom. My rules." Power and passion thrummed through her veins. It had been too long since she'd felt either. God, how she missed this.

"Yes, Ma'am." This time a wicked grin accompanied the words.

Alarms went off in her head. What was he planning?

His legs and hips relaxed under her and she slid back down.

With a slow rolling of her hips, she made a figure-eight motion. It wouldn't give his cock enough friction, but the pressure of her clit against his pelvis more than made up. For her, anyway.

His brows knitted in want and frustration, but he kept his mouth shut.

"Why do you have such a hard time showing your back to people?"

He tensed underneath her. Something else flared in his eyes. Definitely not anger this time. A look she'd seen in the mirror for the last year and twenty-nine days. Guilt.

Ryan refused to meet her eyes anymore. Instead, he stared at the ceiling.

She reached behind her. His sac was warm and comfortable in her hand. Ryan closed his eyes. Expectation lay on his features.

Understanding clicked in Micki's brain. He was deliberately disobeying her. Wanting, needing to be punished for whatever fed his guilt.

She stroked his balls. "That's why you came here. You think I'm strong enough to punish you."

He said nothing, kept his eyes shut.

Her hand stilled. She shifted and started to rise when he gave a sharp, curt nod.

What could he possibly have done that he felt such a need? Had he killed someone overseas? There was a war going on even if no one in the freaking country wanted to acknowledge that fact.

Blowing someone's brains out is inevitable, part of the job, Dad had said once when she'd gotten the nerve to ask him. *If killing someone meant I survived to come home, see you, your mom, your brother, then I did it. No question.*

"Ryan, look at me."

Not even an eyelash fluttered.

"Lieutenant Caulfield, I order you to look me in the eye."

His eyes snapped open.

"I'm not punishing you for something when I have no clue of why." She rose up on her knees. She wanted to whimper when his delectable cock slipped out of her.

Ryan made a protesting sound low in his throat. She glanced at him as she reached for the key. This time his fear was all-too-obvious.

She couldn't be mad at him. She'd pulled some dumbass moves over the last year until Alicia threatened to smack her upside the head for acting like a bitch. Micki knew how bad it'd become when quiet, little Beth offered to hold her down for Alicia.

Now? Now, she no longer felt aroused. Just bone-tired.

It took a second to unlock the handcuffs. She lay them on Ryan's chest and climbed off his lap. To the right to give him a clear path to the stairs. "You should go home."

"Micki . . ."

She barely knew this man, but pleading didn't seem to be in his repertoire. "Show me your back or leave." His weird defensive quirk could be something as simple as Army training and too much experience on the battlefield. But her gut said something else was going on.

Slowly, he sat up.

She wanted to stroke the bleak expression from his face, tell him never mind. But doing so wouldn't help him. What he needed was some tough—?

Well, she couldn't exactly call her weird attraction to him "love." But he needed firmness to face whatever was haunting him.

Ryan placed the handcuffs on the nightstand, then swung his legs over the side of the mattress.

The sight of his back made her gasp in horror. She'd seen such awfulness before on crime victims.

Thick ropey burn scars covered him from his shoulder blades to just above his waist.

Chapter Seven

Micki's fingers drifted along the mixture of scar tissue and new skin on Ryan's back. A domestic call she and Lee had responded to a few years ago rose, unbidden, in her mind.

Enduring such pain said something about Ryan Caulfield's own strength.

As much as she wanted to see Ryan's eyes, something told her he'd clam up if he faced her. "Tell me what happened."

He tensed under her touch. "Don't . . ."

She recognized the mixture of grief and guilt in that one word all too well. "Tell me." Oddly, her stern tone seemed to release something in him.

"I can't tell you where we were. What we were doing."

"I'm not asking you to betray any military secrets, Ryan." And she could guess. The scars were too new to have been earned in Iraq. Afghanistan, then. "Tell me."

"Our vehicle hit an IED." His tone flattened, like he was reciting his official report. "The captain was killed instantly. Instead of shrapnel, the device was filled with flammable chemicals. Wol—"

His muscles stiffened under the damaged skin. "Our comm officer pulled me out. My uniform was on fire."

His ribs expanded, then he blew out the air. "He was trying to extinguish the flames when a sniper nailed him. Our explosives expert tried to pull both of us to cover and paid for it as well."

Micki closed her eyes to keep in the tears. Dad, Butch and the surviving men from their unit still got together once a year to toast the friends they lost in Vietnam. The rawness in Ryan's voice sounded too much like Dad's.

She continued to stroke Ryan's back. "The incident wasn't your fault."

"I planned the route we took." Bitterness didn't just drip from his words. It ran with the blood of his friends.

Micki crawled closer and hugged her breasts against him, against those awful scars. "The mission's only as good as the intelligence. You telling me that you col-lected all the info? Flew the drones yourself?"

He looked over his shoulder, his eyes meeting hers finally. "Your dad?"

She shrugged and rested her chin on his shoulder. "You listen to Dad and Butch get drunk and gossip enough times you start to put two and two together. Why didn't the sniper take potshots at you?"

He shrugged as well. "I passed out. He probably thought I was dead. Once dark fell, Jimmy and Dylan booby-trapped what was left of the vehicle and dragged my ass to cover." Ryan turned away. The tightness along his neck and shoulders was back. "When the docs were sure I wasn't going to die, they shipped me back here. I ended up at Walter Reed."

"How much longer for the skin grafts and PT?" Damn, how she envied him. All he had to show was that he was physically fit for duty.

"They're not doing anymore." Disgust filled his voice.

"No more grafts? Why?"

Ryan's muscles were rock hard once again under her touch. "I had a bad reac-tion to the anesthesia during the last two surgeries. The docs think it's too risky for more grafts. That only leaves PT."

"And what does the physical therapist say?"

Ryan's silence told her volumes. No wonder he pushed so hard at the gym, both on the weights and flirting with her. Everything he believed about himself had been destroyed. At least it wasn't his own stupidity that put him in this position, unlike her.

She laid her head against his scars and held him for a long time. Neither of them said a word.

After a while, his breathing slowed. The staccato beat of his heart became a steady rhythm. Micki shifted and placed a kiss on Ryan's neck.

His sharp intake of air said she surprised him. Good. He needed some pleasant surprises in his world. Maybe she couldn't help herself, but she could help Ryan by accepting him as he was.

She trailed butterfly kisses along his neck, his back, his shoulders. Her fingers reached around him and stroked his chest, his stomach, his thighs.

"Micki . . ." Hesitancy filled his voice.

"Shhh . . ." She nibbled his earlobe and kissed his jaw before she said, "Lay down on your back." She scooched back to give him room, but kept one palm on his shoulder.

For an instant, she thought he'd get up and leave.

He laid down on the mattress, his cock already erect, waiting. The first condom was missing. It must have slid off.

An odd light shone in his eyes. Not quite his usual cockiness, but almost like . . . gratitude. Or acceptance. And damn, if she wasn't wet all over again at the sight of him ready and willing to be ridden.

She eyed the two sets of handcuffs on the nightstand. No. Some instinct said he wasn't going to test her any more. At least not tonight.

"Hold on to the iron bars and do not let go until I give you permission."

"Is that an order?" His lips twitched, but those dark eyes gave away his hidden smile.

She raised an eyebrow.

He obeyed, wrapping long fingers around the latticework. His position defined the lines of muscle along his arms and chest.

Micki picked up the last foil pack and held it an inch from his nose. "Waste this one and I will most definitely punish you. Understand?"

"Yes, Ma'am." The sly smile was back.

Why did she have the eerie feeling that she wasn't as in control as it appeared?

Ignoring the question dancing around her head, she let her body take the lead. Trembling fingers ripped open the foil package. She rolled the condom over his cock.

Instead of straddling him once again, she lay next to him, her feet on the pillows. Her head propped on her elbow, she traced patterns on his skin with her index finger. His balls contracted as she followed the line, but she didn't touch his cock. His muscles quivered under her fingertip. Once again, he closed his eyes.

The power was intoxicating. Arousing. She wanted, no, needed to touch herself. Anything to relieve the tension in her own body. Instead, she focused on that one finger drifting over his skin. Feeling the curl of each hair, the heat of each skin cell, the twitch of hard muscle underneath.

His Adam's apple bobbed and his knuckles whitened. Each breath came out in a harsh gasp as she continued to play with him. From his tight, wrinkled sac, he was so close.

But she wasn't quite finished with him yet.

Micki sat up and bent over his chest. A swirl of her tongue dampened his hard, dark nipple. Puckering her lips, she blew air over the moist skin. Repeating the process on the other nipple drew a soft moan from Ryan.

The wait was too much for her. She crawled into his lap and straddled his abdomen. His cock danced against her ass. Her lips met his. The kiss started as a wrestling match between their tongues, each seeking to claim the other.

Micki broke the contact. That wasn't going to work. Time for another tactic. She rose on her knees.

Ryan's eyelids fluttered open.

"Keep your eyes closed." Her words came out in the same tone she used to order a suspect to keep his hands in sight.

It worked. His eyes closed again.

Two of her fingers slid into her pussy. The motion didn't relieve the tension as she hoped. Instead, her touch intensified the desire to have Ryan Caulfield buried inside of her again.

She withdrew her fingers and traced the wet tips over his lips. His tongue darted out and brushed the pads, sending a tremor through her body.

"What do you taste?"

His tongue swept his lips before he said, "You." After a heartbeat, he added, "Ma'am." The sensual tone of his voice made her shudder.

Inching back, she positioned herself over that magnificent cock and slid down. Not so tight this time. She was too aroused. But it filled her all the same.

Under her thighs, his body twitched. Other than the involuntary motions, he didn't move, kept his grip on her head rail.

She placed her hands on his chest for balance. Once again, she rolled her hips in a slow figure-eight motion. Each time she hit the center, she squeezed her internal muscles. The slow friction made her clit throb.

"God, Micki, please let me touch you."

"No." How could she sound so normal while she rubbed her body against his?

Ryan's jaw line tightened.

She couldn't help the smile that curved her mouth. This kind of power went beyond intoxicating. She added a slight rise of her hips with the squeeze.

A strangled sound came from Ryan. He panted with the effort not to move as she played with him.

Micki sped the rhythm. The familiar tightening began in her pussy. She couldn't have stopped if she wanted to. She needed to feel Ryan come. She . . .

Beneath her, he stiffened. A hoarse cry, the buck of his hips, then the pulse and jerk of his cock sent her over the edge.

Rainbow spots danced in her vision as wave after wave of sensation ripped through her nerves. Her nails dug into his skin as everything rippled and contract-ed. She couldn't breathe, couldn't think. Only feel.

She didn't realize she'd closed her eyes until his palm cupped her cheek.

"Hey, you okay?"

She opened her eyes and nodded. Dark brown eyes stared into hers, and in that moment, Micki Donovan knew she was in deep, deep trouble.

Chapter Eight

"I don't know about you, but after all that sex, I'm hungry again."

Ryan's wry comment pulled Micki out of the darkness threatening to bury her. He wasn't Lee, dammit. But she didn't need a framed psychiatry degree to know that's why guilt poured through her. Food was a good distraction. She forced a smile. "Me, too."

"Good." He grinned. "Up." When she didn't move, he slapped her ass.

"Hey!" The urge to shoot him returned.

"If you're going to shoot me, you still need to get off me."

"I wasn't—"

"You eyed your service piece when you answered the door. And you had the same look on your face just now."

"You ate my pizza without permission."

His sly grin was back. "May I have some more, please, Ma'am?"

She shook her head and laughed. "After you get cleaned up."

Ryan followed her into the bathroom. When she reached for the washcloth, he took it from her. "Let me."

He rinsed the terrycloth under hot water. His palm against her lower back held her steady. Comfortable heat stroked her thighs, her pussy, as he cleaned her. The rough texture of the washcloth against over-sensitized flesh was enough to set her teeth on edge. She closed her eyes, attempting to corral her libido.

What the hell was wrong with her? Alicia said a boytoy, not a . . .

Familiar warmth tugged at her chest. She ruthlessly squashed the emotion. It felt wrong, like she was cheating on Lee. And that thought led to old pain, as if she were picking at a scab, refusing to let the wound heal.

"Penny for your thoughts?"

Her lids fluttered open at Ryan's words. "I'm sorry?"

Dark eyes stared at her, as if he were examining her soul. "You were in a galaxy far, far away."

"I'm fine." Micki snatched the cooling washcloth out of his hand. "Your turn." She flipped on the hot water and prayed he'd let the subject drop.

"Does this have anything to do with what happened in my apartment?"

"No." Panic stabbed through her. She rolled off the condom and tossed it in the trash to avoid his piercing gaze. With great care, she stroked the warm cloth over and around his cock, his balls.

"Micki—"

"You know, I'm really starving. And I, for one, do not feel like cold pizza." Dammit, she was not a babbler, but she couldn't make herself shut up. God, she sounded like Alicia's mother, trying to pretend everything was normal while drunk off her ass. "There's a little seafood place down the street. Let's get dressed."

She turned to rinse the washcloth one last time and stole a glance in the medicine cabinet mirror. Behind her, Ryan's lips were pursed, but thankfully, he remained silent except for a quiet, "Sure."

Tuesday evening, Micki stood at the mailbox flipping through envelopes when she was attacked from behind.

"Hey, munchkin!" She twisted to give Molly a proper hug. "You going to con me into buying more cookies?"

Molly rolled her big, brown eyes. "Really, Officer Micki, that joke is so-o-o lame. You know cookie season's been over forever."

Abigail Ng appeared behind Molly. The dark circles under her eyes tugged at Micki's heart.

"Molly, why don't you go feed Miss Kitty while I talk to Micki?" Abigail ruffled her daughter's midnight black hair.

"But I haven't asked Officer Micki if she can cat-sit this weekend?"

"Of course, I will." Micki gave the girl another hug. "And I'm sure Miss Kitty is starving."

"See you later." The nine-year-old waved as she darted into the neighboring unit.

Micki faced Abigail. The truth etched itself in the lines around her neighbor's eyes and mouth. "This is more than just your mom."

Abigail stared at the toes of her sensible pumps. "Dad rented a cabin at Shenandoah. We're heading up Friday morning. One last *normal* weekend before Mom goes into hospice." A long sigh. "She called Derek and asked him to join us."

"Oh, boy." Micki tapped the envelopes against her palm. "You want me to pick him up Friday? I can hold him in the drunk tank for twenty-four hours."

Abigail laughed and looked up. "No. He called the other night. He wants to try to work things out."

Micki nearly swallowed her tongue to keep from saying anything bad about Abigail's husband. The bastard had walked out on his family because he couldn't handle the strain of his mother-in-law's breast cancer.

"How do you feel about that?" It was the most neutral thing she could come up with.

What the hell was wrong with people in this world? Everyone expected her family to be fucked up because her dad had been in Army Special Forces during Vietnam, but they were the Cleavers compared to her friends' relatives.

"He's willing to go to couples' therapy." Abigail stared into Micki's eyes. "I still love him, and I don't want Molly to grow apart from him." The surety in Abigail's face said volumes.

Micki grinned. "Well, if you need some private time, Molly and I can have a sleepover."

Pink flared on Abigail's sharp-planed cheeks. "Thanks. We may take you up on that offer."

"And you know Miss Kitty is always welcome. Why don't you bring her over Thursday night so you can get an early start on Friday?"

Relief spread across Abigail's face. "You're such a good neighbor. I don't know what I'd do without you."

"I know I would fit in my uniform better."

Abigail laughed in earnest. "Then don't buy a whole case of Thin Mints."

"I'll see you Thursday." Micki saluted as she headed inside her condo.

She dropped the mail on top of the stereo while she took off her utility belt and hung it on the coat tree. Kicking off her shoes, she grabbed the cream-colored envelope that had caught her attention before Molly came running up.

The return address was a gallery in Georgetown. She held her breath as she ran her index finger under the flap. This couldn't be what she thought it was. Had Beth finally grown a pair and taken a chance on her painting?

Micki let out a shriek as she read the announcement on the card. She grabbed the phone and back-flopped onto the couch. Her feet kicked the air while Beth's cell rang once. Twice.

On the third ring, Beth answered with a breathless "Hello, Micki."

"Why the hell didn't you say you had a showing when we met for lunch, you bitch?"

"The, uh, the details weren't finalized until last week."

"Congratulations! Definitely put me down on your RSVP list."

"Will-will—" A sharp gasp then a sigh came through the receiver.

Concern flared, and Micki sat up. "Are you all right?"

"Yesss." A pause. "Should I put you down for plus one?"

It was Micki's turn for total silence.

"I'm sorry. I thought you had someone lined up already the way you jumped on Alicia's challenge."

More heavy breathing sounded over the receiver. Like there was another person on the line with Beth. "Are you sure you're all right?"

"Just an aerobics video." Beth was lying her ass off. Micki would lay good money on it. In fact, it almost sounded like she was having sex. And for some reason, that just pissed Micki off.

"You know what? Put me down for two. I'll see you in a couple of weeks." She punched the "OFF" button and tossed the phone between her legs. It bounced once on the couch cushion.

This was stupid. If Beth found someone, she should be happy for her. Lord knew the girl needed someone to show her that not every man was an evil son-of-a-bitch.

Micki stared at the ceiling. Why the hell was she jealous? She'd had sex last night, but then she and Ryan had done nothing *but* screw each other's brains out. Butch's diner and the seafood grill didn't count as dates. They were both post-sex munchies.

Would Ryan even be interested in a gallery showing? Why was she thinking about asking him? It wasn't like they were a couple. Maybe she should fall on her stand-by. She and Mike had been each other's mercy date at events for years.

The phone rang at her feet. She sat up, picked up the receiver and glanced at the caller ID. Unknown name, unknown number.

It was probably a sales call, but some instinct made her answer it. "Hello."

"What are you wearing?" Ryan's voice flowed over her like warm caramel.

Micki laid back down. "Just got home. I'm still in my uniform."

A throaty chuckle. "Good thing I love a woman in uniform. Wish I was there to take it off."

"You're not at home?"

"Not right now. I won't be back until Saturday."

Years of experience with her father told her not to ask where he was. "That's too bad. I was hoping you'd show up on my doorstep to steal pizza again."

"Just steal pizza?"

God help her, she liked his teasing. "What else were you planning on taking?"

"Your clothes . . . off." He sounded like a cat the way he purred the last word. A big cat. The kind where you weren't sure if he'd rub his whiskers against your skin or eat you alive.

His voice sent her pussy throbbing. Her nipples tightened, her bra rubbing them with each breath. "Too bad you aren't here to help me undress."

"Unbutton your pants."

Micki's breath caught. She'd had phone sex before, but this time was . . .

Too intimate.

Nerves raced and she searched for something, anything, to stall. "Are you sure you're in a safe place to do this?"

Another chuckle. "I'm alone. You're home. No one's there, right?"

"No." God, she hated the quiver in her voice. "You first."

"Scared?"

"No."

"Yes, you are." His voice was no longer teasing. "Micki, there's nothing but my voice and your imagination. No one's going to hurt you."

"Like anyone could," she scoffed. But his remark hit too close to the truth. Black spots danced in her eyes.

"Unbutton your pants," he repeated.

Ryan was totally right. No one else was in the condo. She'd locked the front door when she came in after talking to Abigail. The windows and patio door were also closed and locked. The adrenaline rush was from hearing his voice.

Right?

She switched the receiver from her right ear to her left. Her free fingers crept down to her waistband. With a flick, the button was free.

"Okay. Now what?"

"Slide your zipper down."

She did as she was told, and held the receiver close to the metal teeth so he could hear. She placed the handset back to her ear.

"Good girl. Lay down."

"Already am."

"It's a good thing I'm not there. I'd have to spank you for being a smart ass."

Instead of the coppery taste of fear in her mouth at his words, her own liquid dampened her panties. "I was already lying on the couch when you called."

"Thinking of me?"

The eensy hint of wistful hope in his deep voice made her change her mind about lying. "Yes."

"Tell me what you were thinking."

She hesitated. The desire to ask him on a real date lay on the tip of her tongue. She'd never had a problem stating what she wanted to a man before. Why did she get so tied up in knots when it came to Ryan Caulfield?

"I was wondering—" She sucked in a deep breath. "Would you like to go to a friend's painting exhibit with me? It's two weeks from Thursday."

Static filled the connection. God, had she been totally stupid proposing they make this, whatever it was between them, formal?

"Are you asking me on a date?"

"Yes."

"On one condition."

Her internal voice screamed a warning, but her body shut it down. She wanted him inside of her again, and no doubt, sex would be his condition. She could live with that.

Couldn't she?

"What's your condition?" she choked out.

"Well, I did what you told me to last night, so you do everything I say between now and your friend's show."

She snorted. "One night versus two weeks isn't exactly a fair deal."

"I promise you'll enjoy what we do."

His offer sounded tempting, but she couldn't give in so easily.

"Like what?" Desire and suspicion laced her voice. She couldn't help it.

"Like what we're doing now." There was an edge of humor to his tone.

"Then I have a few conditions of my own."

"All right. What are they?"

"One night only. No extra people involved, either participating or watching.

Just you and me at all times. And no recordings of us." Her internal voice breathed a sigh of relief.

Ryan laughed. "Don't worry, Micki. Like I said before, I don't share. Anything else?"

He capitulated too fast. There had to be something she was missing. But she couldn't for the life of her figure out what.

"Micki?"

She released the air she'd been holding. At least, she wouldn't be going to Beth's showing alone. "No."

"Good. Now where were we?"

She gritted her teeth against his mocking tone. *Just wait until I have you hand-cuffed to my bed again, Lieutenant Caulfield. You'll pay.* "Seriously? You can't remember?"

More laughter. "Slide your hand inside your pants, Micki." His voice roughened with his deep, seductive words.

She obeyed. Anything to ease the ache between her legs from hearing his voice. Her fingers brushed over her cotton underwear. Part of her wished she'd worn something sexier even if Ryan couldn't see them.

"Are your panties damp?"

"Yes," she hissed. Touching herself through the cotton sent electricity sparking through her pussy.

"Slip your hand inside your panties. Think about me stroking you."

Her fingers eased under the elastic waistband. Goosebumps rose on her skin. Soft curls met her touch, then slick flesh. Her inner lips were already parted, wanting Ryan, ready for him simply from the sound of his voice.

"Talk to me, Micki. Tell me how you feel."

"I—" She gasped when she ran her index finger over her swollen clit. "I'm wet. Open." Her knees spread as she traced her hot flesh. "I can feel your head between my legs. Your hair tickles my thighs." A soft sigh. "Your tongue on my pussy, licking me . . ."

"You taste so good. You're shivering under my touch. I slide two fingers into you."

A small cry escaped her lips as she did exactly what Ryan described. Internal muscles clenched around her fingers. The friction as she pulled them out was so exquisite that she plunged them back into her pussy and twisted them slightly.

There. Her body quivered from touching her sweet spot.

"Talk to me, baby," Ryan whispered.

"You're finger-fucking me. You're tongue swirls around my clit." She forced each word past her gasps. Her thumb grazed the swollen nub. A whimper built in the back of her throat.

"I want you naked. Take off your clothes."

Damn, his command meant she'd have to remove her fingers from her pussy or put down the phone. Decision made she pulled her damp fingers from her pants. She lifted each ankle and pulled off her socks. God, even her toes tingled with desire.

"Micki?"

"Yeah?"

"You're not talking."

Her laugh was self-deprecating. "Sorry." She sat up and stood. "You're pulling down my slacks. I step out of them. My panties—"

She looked down. They were cotton. Sturdy. Utilitarian. Hardly sexy.

"Tell me about your panties."

"They—" Why the hell was she embarrassed? Her underwear had never mattered with any other guy. They hadn't mattered the last couple of times with Ryan either.

"Are they the blue ones with the little white daisies you had on Friday?" She shivered at the passion in his voice. He remembered her underwear?

"No." She swallowed hard. "They're pink with green stripes."

A groan sounded through the receiver. What was Ryan doing at his end? His voice was hoarse when he spoke again. "I slide them down over your hips, inch by inch, and kiss your thighs, your knees, your calves as they pass."

Her skin prickled as she pushed her panties down her legs. She closed her eyes, savoring the feel of ghostly lips on her body. Cool air caressed her exposed pussy.

"Now, unbutton your shirt." He didn't question whether she had obeyed his last direction.

She juggled the phone as she slipped her arms out of her uniform shirt. Soft rustling as it slid down her back. A flick of the clasp, and her bra followed the rest of her clothes to the floor.

"You already have your bra off, don't you?"

"Yes." Micki lay back down on the couch. "I needed you to touch me." Her free hand cupped her right breast. Fingers tweaked her nipple. In her mind, Ryan's mouth gently bit the hard bead.

"You have the most beautiful breasts, mounds of cream topped with the most luscious strawberries. I tug on them—"

Her fingers sought her left breast as he talked, and they plucked the sensitive nub. The whimper finally escaped. Her back arched. "Ryan, I . . ."

"I need to be inside you."

Micki trailed her free hand down her stomach and cupped her mound. She circled her slick folds before inserting her fingers. The picture of Ryan's cock firmly in her mind, she thrust and withdrew.

"You're so hot, so wet." His words came between sharp breaths.

"I love the feel of you fucking me." It almost felt like he was there, thrusting into her. Her legs wrapped around his waist as he pumped. "Your huge cock filling my pussy until . . ."

She pressed the heel of her hand against the hood of her clit. The sensation was too much. Fireworks exploded in her vision. Every muscle seized and waves of ecstasy flooded her nerves. She gently stroked herself, determined to wring every last contraction from her body.

"Do you have any idea what you sound like when you come?"

Micki laughed. "No. Was it good for you?"

Ryan chuckled. "From the mess on my hand and stomach, I'd say yes."

She sighed. "I wish you were here."

"So do I. Saturday night. I'll be at your place at nine."

"I'll see you then." Micki thumbed the "End Call" button and considered what Ryan said. She had a sneaking suspicion she sounded exactly like Beth had earlier on the phone.

The real question was how would she survive with no sex until Saturday night. No. It wasn't just the sex. It was Ryan.

Damn, girl. You're in way too deep, her little voice whispered.

Chapter Nine

Friday night found Micki curled up on the couch with Miss Kitty in her lap. For a cat, she was quite personable. This had to be the first feline in history that actually liked Micki petting her. But Miss Kitty didn't alleviate this feeling of . . . loneliness.

She sighed as she ran her fingers over the cat's black and white fur. This weird melancholy wasn't like her. Normally, she enjoyed her solitude. Mom claimed Micki was far too much like Dad, recharging her batteries in stillness.

When she called each of the girls, no one could come over. Beth was prepping for her art show. Diana had some business dinner. Alicia said she was stuck at work with a payroll issue and wasn't sure how late she'd be there.

Not even an action movie on Netflix could distract her. Resentment reared its ugly head. Micki had always been there for them, no matter what. And now, when she needed someone . . .

She was acting like a totally selfish bitch. God help her. The truth was she sat here mooning over Ryan. Calling girlfriends because a man wasn't available. Totally pathetic.

Disgusted at the turn her thoughts had taken, Micki looked at the cat. "Shall we go to bed and start fresh tomorrow?"

Meow.

That answer was good enough. She set Miss Kitty on the floor and rose. The lights were out, TV off and her foot on the first step when someone knocked.

She should ignore it. Wanted to ignore it. But it might be Abigail if things hadn't gone well with Derek at Shenandoah.

Micki reversed course and flicked on the entryway light. A check of the peephole sent her heart into overdrive, and she flung the door open.

Ryan stood there in fatigues, a duffel bag slung over his shoulder.

She launched herself into his arms. Their kiss went beyond passion. It was a fierce melding of lips and tongue. He tasted of coffee and male, and she simply couldn't get enough.

He broke the kiss and grinned. "I need to breathe sometime."

"Sorry." She returned his wide smile. The press of his erection against her stomach launched electricity through her nerves.

She clasped his hand in hers and tugged him inside. "You said you wouldn't be back until tomorrow."

"I can leave." He turned toward the open door.

Her kick slammed the door shut. "Oh, no, you don't." She flipped the deadbolt.

He laughed as Micki practically dragged him up the two short flights of stairs. Miss Kitty sat at the top of the staircase, her tail twitching. Her eyes widened at the sight of Ryan.

Meow.

The cat dove under the bed.

Okay. That was definitely weird for Miss Kitty.

"I don't remember you having a cat." A bemused smile remained on Ryan's face.

"She's my neighbors'. I'm sitting for the weekend." Micki knelt next to the mattress and flipped up the comforter. Green eyes glowed from the center. She reached for the dark form. Miss Kitty hissed and swiped with her clawless front paw.

"What the hell has gotten into you?"

Ryan knelt next to Micki and ducked his head. "You might want to leave her before she sinks those sharp little teeth into your hand." He turned to Micki and gave her a wry look. "Unless you want to go to the ER tonight for stitches."

"I don't know what's gotten into her. She's the most well-behaved cat I know."

"I'm sure she'll crawl out once we're occupying the bed." He stood and dropped the duffel bag next to the nightstand.

Micki looked up at him. For an instant, her heart stopped. Ryan looked nothing like her father or Lee, but there was something about his stance, his persona, that gave her the same safe feeling. She didn't want to analyze the emotion too closely. It led to other things best forgotten and buried.

She opted for cheerfulness as she climbed to her feet, no matter how fake the emotion might be. "Then maybe we should be occupying it." She stepped closer to him.

His large hands reached behind her, grabbed her ass, and pulled her tight against his erection. "I've needed you since our phone call." He lowered his mouth to hers

If the kiss at the door was hot, this one was positively volcanic. Their bodies ground against each other until Ryan gently pressed her back.

"Not yet, Micki." He tilted her chin and kissed the tip of her nose. "Lay down on the bed."

Her head spun from the switch of near-orgasm to his playful affection. "What?"

"Our deal on the phone. You do everything I say for tonight."

Her hormones made it so damn hard to think. Oh, yeah. Sex games in return for him accompanying her to Beth's show.

She gave a nervous laugh. "You're not going to blindfold me or anything, are you?" The stern expression on his face sent a tiny wiggle of unease through her body.

"No." Ryan tossed his cap on the wicker chair by the window. "I think you'll do better if you can see everything."

"Do better?"

He folded his arms over his chest. "Either do as I say or I'm leaving, Micki."

God help her, she didn't want him to leave. But she couldn't shake her gut feeling either. What was wrong with her? He hadn't given any reason to be concerned before. In fact, he'd handcuffed himself to the bed to get her to relax the last time.

"You promise you won't blindfold me?"

"I promise."

Micki crawled onto the bed and reclined.

Ryan unfolded his arms. "Grab onto the railing and hold on."

So that was his game. A replay of Monday night. Her eyebrow rose, and she smirked. Fine. She could take what she had dished out. Micki reached over her head and gripped the wrought iron.

"I'm going to take off your sweats."

She lifted her hips to help, and he slowly tugged down the jersey knit. The sweatpants flew over his head, and he sat down next to her.

"White with purple paisleys." He examined her underwear. His interest was so intense it made her want to cross her legs and cover herself. With his forefinger, he traced each little design. His exploration traveled south until he reached her mound.

That smug grin was back as Ryan eyed her. His fingers grazed the cotton over her slit. Even with her panties on, his touch sent electricity through her nerves. Her hips twitched at the sensation, her body wanting more.

"Uh-uh-uh." He waggled his free index finger in front of her face. "Don't move, or you won't get your prize."

She could imagine what her reward would be. And she had no doubt he'd walk out if she didn't comply. But it took everything she had to remain still as he touched her.

He leaned over her and captured her mouth. His exploration was slow, sensual. The stroking of her pussy through cotton added to the haze clouding her mind.

His mouth left her lips and travelled along her jaw line, down her neck. The iron railing dug into her palms in her efforts not to move.

His finger slipped under the elastic of her panties and caressed her slick flesh. "So wet already," he murmured against her collarbone. He tugged the cotton down her hips and tossed them over his shoulder.

Ryan planted a kiss between her still covered breasts. "But there's one more thing to make this perfect." The handcuffs were around her wrists and locked before she even realized they were in Ryan's hand.

She had to give him credit. He was fast. And quiet.

"What the hell!" Micki yanked her arms. Steel bit into her skin. She glared at him, tried to ignore the glimmer of fear in her mind.

Ryan's face carried a stoic expression. "Are you backing out on our deal?"

"I—" Black spots danced in her vision. She had never reneged on a bargain, but panic gibbered deep inside her.

Micki closed her eyes and sucked in a desperate breath. *This has nothing to do with Lee. This is just a game. This is just a game. This is just a game.*

So why did it feel like an elephant sat on her chest?

If Ryan could deal with his demons, let himself be vulnerable and powerless, then she could, too.

"No," she gasped.

"Micki, open your eyes." When she didn't, couldn't, his voice grew stern. "That's an order, Officer Donovan."

Her eyelids sprang open.

Ryan stroked the back of her cheek with his hand. "I want you to keep your eyes open. Watch me at all times. Do you understand, Micki?"

She nodded, but couldn't stop the shaking in her limbs. The blackness waited for her on the edge of her vision.

What if he pulls out duct tape? What if he has a knife? Remember what happened the last time you let someone make you helpless.

She tried to shove the memory back into its hole, but the fear oozed and overflowed.

Ryan stood and watched her as he undressed. He neatly folded each garment as he removed it and placed the clothing on top of her dresser. Except for his combat boots. Those stood at attention beside the bureau with their heels to the wall.

His erection bobbed as he returned to the bed. "Spread you legs."

The mixture of desire and dread in her stomach made a strange cocktail that spread through her body. Her senses magnified to the point where she felt each stitch in the comforter. Smell the musk of his body. Heard not just his breathing but Miss Kitty's as well.

Heard . . .

Oh, sweet God! None of her neighbors were home. If something went wrong, if Ryan hurt her, no one would hear her scream.

Her lungs locked. Each breath was a struggle. She couldn't stop the violent shaking of her body. The handcuffs rattled.

Ryan cupped her cheek. "Micki?"

Her eyes darted back and forth while she wildly searched for a way to escape.

"Micki, what's wrong?"

"Nothing." Air froze in her lungs. She couldn't reach the key on the nightstand.

"Micki."

She couldn't meet his eyes. If she did, he'd know it was all her fault. *All that blood on the concrete. On her.*

Ryan held her chin. His grip was firm but not painful. His eyes were inches from hers. "Look at me, Micki. Breathe with me. In." His nostrils flared. "Out."

"I-I—" She gasped the words.

Reassuring brown eyes stared deep into hers. "You're having a panic attack, honey. Breathe with me," he repeated. "In. Out." His coffee-sweet breath caressed her skin.

Under his mantra, her chest muscles loosened. She focused on his gaze, followed his instructions. In. Out.

Their breathing synchronized. In. Out. She blinked cold sweat from her eyes.

"There we go." He smiled and brushed damp locks from her face. "Better?"

Micki nodded. Her heartbeat slowed, not to its normal level, but enough that the pressure in her head eased.

"Haven't you played sex games before?"

"Of course." Despite trying to project surety in her voice, it quivered.

"But not bondage?"

"Yes, I have." *I'm not lying. Exactly.* Lee had used the belt of her bathrobe once, but he hadn't tied it in a knot or anything.

"This has something to do with what happened at my place, doesn't it?"

"No."

Liar, liar, pants on fire. The blackness giggled in its corner.

Ryan's lips pursed, but he didn't question her further. His palm stroked her damp skin. Her neck. Her breasts. Her stomach. The touch comforting, not sensual nor demanding. "We should stop." He reached for the key.

It took a moment to find her tongue. "No."

His expression clearly showed his doubt. "Why?"

She licked her dry lips. *Because I don't want to be alone tonight.* "Because we made a deal."

His expression was still. His eyes gave nothing away. "You said you've played games before, but you just had a panic attack. That is not worth some deal."

"I don't break my word." Fierce anger filled her voice.

"You sure?" Ryan sat upright.

"Please." Red hazed her vision, but her anger was directed at herself, not him. Neediness and desperation in other people pissed her off. To hear it in her own voice . . .

Her body and her emotions batted around the question. It came down to her original dilemma long before Ryan knocked on her door. She didn't want to be alone tonight.

She sucked in a deep breath and loosed it. "Yes, I'm sure."

"Spread your legs for me." His voice was low, seductive again. And it was then Micki realized she'd curled into a semi-fetal position.

She forced her back to unbend, her legs straight and apart. His hand drifted from her stomach, to her hip, down her thigh. Her position left her so damn exposed, vulnerable. Once again, lust and fear mixed a strange cocktail in her.

Black spots threatened. Micki blinked them away. Instead, she focused on the sensation of Ryan's fingers stroking her inner thigh. The light, sensual brushing. His calluses rough on her delicate skin.

Her breathing picked up again, short panting gasps that left no question to her physical state.

He pushed up her t-shirt, bent over her and took a nipple in his mouth. Soft sucking, a nip, then his tongue soothing the sting. The rhythm had her hips twitching despite his earlier admonition not to move.

Ryan turned his attention to her other breast. The tip was already hard, tight. The first graze of his teeth would have shot her off the bed if not for the handcuffs.

Cool air hit her damp nipple. "Micki, your eyes are closed."

She blinked them open. Under his ministrations, she hadn't realized her lids had drifted shut. "Sorry."

"Watch what I do next." Ryan reached for his bag and produced a condom. In less than a second, he tore the foil and rolled the rubber down his huge cock.

He climbed onto the bed and knelt between her thighs. Lust sparkled in his eyes. "You're sure you want me to continue?"

She nodded. Her pussy clenched in anticipation of him filling her.

"Keep your eyes open," he repeated. His hands slid under her ass and lifted her pussy to his mouth.

Those lips molded around her clit. The orgasm hit her. Hard. Fast. Neurons fired like she'd stuck her finger in an electric socket. She screamed and shook and thrashed as he sucked on that little nub.

Finally, he released her clit. Her body still trembled from the powerful waves when he slung her legs over his shoulders.

"That should take the edge off." A Cheshire Cat smile lit his face.

The slow slide of his cock into her set off another round of convulsions. Ryan paused, closed his own eyes as her internal muscles hugged his erection.

When he opened them, he pulled out until only the tip remained. Another deliberate thrust in. The friction sparked her nerve endings. An easy motion out. It was erotic agony.

She bucked her hips. He withdrew totally and raised a dark eyebrow.

Heat flooded her cheeks at his non-verbal reprimand. She could probably strangle him with her knees, but that wouldn't get her what she wanted—that magnificent cock buried deep in her.

Ryan kept that agonizingly slow pace. In this position, she was so open, his thrust so deep. Every time Micki felt the contraction that signaled an imminent explosion, he halted. Hitting the brink and stopping was driving her insane. How the hell could he read her body so well?

After he ceased his rhythm for the fifth time, she broke. "Please, don't. I can't take this anymore." The whininess in her voice would have made her slap another woman, but she couldn't stop her begging. "God, please fuck me."

A wicked grin spread across his face. "Exactly what have we been doing, Micki?"

"You've been torturing me," she shot back.

"Oh, baby, this is nothing." Ryan pulled his cock out and lowered her legs back to the mattress.

She wanted to kick herself for opening her mouth.

He climbed off the bed and headed for the staircase.

"Where are you going?"

He glanced back. "All this work has made me hungry. I'm raiding your kitchen." He disappeared down the stairs.

The blackness didn't come in spots. It came in a tsunami. "Ryan!"

At her shriek, his head bobbed above the top step. "I'll be right back. Start counting, Micki. Breathe with each count."

He disappeared again. Her heart pounded so hard she couldn't hear his footsteps. Another yank on the handcuffs, but all she accomplished was to add more bruises to her wrists. A hard sob convulsed her throat.

Terror replaced all lust. What if he didn't come back? She was trapped in her own bed. Who'd find her?

No, dammit! Breathe! The panic subsided a little as she counted with each intake of air. *Now, think. Abigail and Molly will be back on Monday. They have my extra key. They'll find me when they come over to pick up Miss Kitty.*

Then a worse thought occurred. Little Molly absolutely could not see her like this, handcuffed to the bed with no underwear. The kid would be scarred, and Micki wouldn't be able to look Molly's parents in the eye ever again.

Micki looked around her bedroom. She needed a plan. The phone sat on her nightstand. *And people wonder why I keep a landline.* She could grab the phone with her feet and drop it close to her face and hands then punch 9-1-1 with her nose if she had to.

Movement sounded up the stairwell, along with rattling. Metal against glass or ceramic.

Ryan appeared at the top of the stairs.

Micki swallowed her sigh of relief. Then she realized he carried one of her metal cookie sheets as a tray. On top was a jar of peanut butter, her stash of hot fudge, strawberry jam, a couple of bananas and her emergency carton of Haagen Dazs.

"You weren't joking about the hungry thing."

Again, the cocky grin. "You never joke about food in the army." He crossed the room. Using his foot, he scooted the wicker ottoman closer to her bed and set his makeshift tray on top.

He sat on the edge of the bed, and his expression sobered. With his thumb, he wiped wetness from each of her cheeks. "You okay?"

Heat flooded her face. In her panic, she hadn't even realized the tears had fallen. "I'm fine. You forgot the bread though."

"You don't put bread on a banana split, Officer Donovan," he chided.

"A banana split?" She glanced at the tray. "You don't have any dishes."

"I have the only dish I need." His hand cupped her breast and tweaked the nipple.

The arousal that had died under the suffocating weight of her fear came roaring back to life. "You don't have any whipped cream or cherries."

His head dipped. His mouth latched onto her breast, teasing the nipple to a hard knot. Her throat vibrated with a low moan. Her back arched at the sensation.

Damn, she was so on edge, so close. If he'd just suck on her sensitive bud a little more . . .

Ryan released her, his eyes glittering. "I think we have plenty of cherries." Two fingers slid into her pussy, and she gasped. "And plenty of cream." He withdrew his hand and licked her juices from his fingers.

Micki tried to steady her breathing. Every sensation seemed magnified despite her emotional roller coaster. Or maybe the rush was because of the wild swings. Fear-based adrenaline combined with serotonin from the earlier two orgasms.

Now, curiosity crawled along every nerve ending. She watched him as he contemplated the tray. What would he do next?

He took a spoon from the tray and stirred the jar of hot fudge. Raising the utensil, he dribbled chocolate-y goo on her right breast. The sauce was hot, though short of being uncomfortable. Then came a spoonful of vanilla ice cream on the nipple.

She squirmed at the mix of cold and heat.

"Don't move," he whispered. Micki forced her body to still.

Once again, Ryan's lips surrounded the tip, sucking off the ice cream before licking the hot fudge from the surrounding skin.

God, she wanted to move, *needed* to move. Jump him. Pump her hips. Have something, anything, fucking her. A whimper trilled in her throat.

He moved to the other breast and repeated his anointment of fudge and vanilla. His tongue caught a drop of melted Haagen Dazs that trickled down her ribs before licking the rest of her skin clean. Ryan watched her for a moment, but she managed not to wiggle despite the growing pulse in her pussy and breasts.

Her breath caught as he contemplated the tray. He reached for the jar of peanut butter and twisted off the lid. He didn't bother with a spoon this time. Ryan dug his index finger into the spread and drew a circle around her belly button.

When he was done, he held his finger to her lips. She obeyed his unspoken command. Her mouth wrapped around the digit and sucked the remaining peanut butter from his skin. Then she nipped the pad of his finger before she ran her tongue across it.

His eyes closed, and his erect cock jerked. Good to know she had a similar effect on him.

Micki blinked. The condom was gone. Had he gone down to the kitchen to get his own libido under control?

More ice cream landed on her belly button, and she cried out at the icy sensation. With his tongue, he cleaned every bit of the mix from her abdomen.

Another spoon. This time, he smeared strawberry jam across her nipples, followed by small dabs of ice cream. More suckling the sweetness off her body. She squeezed her thighs together to keep from bucking her hips.

Her body burned in raw sexual frustration. Liquid seeped from her pussy. Every cell felt like it had been dipped in acid.

"Ryan, please . . ."

"You need something inside you." His fingers toyed with her dripping pussy.

"Yesss . . ." The answer was more of a moan than a word.

"Anything?" he whispered in her ear as he petted her damp curls.

Somewhere deep inside her mind, her little voice screamed a warning. Sheer need drowned the stupid bitch. "Yes," she whimpered.

Ryan leaned over the edge of the bed. When he rose, two fingers held a foil packet.

Finally.

But instead of dressing his throbbing cock, he lifted a banana. A thick, long banana.

She stared at the fruit, then at Ryan. "You can't be serious."

His dark eyebrow rose, and a mischievous gleam filled his eyes. He leaned over her until their noses were millimeters apart. "Are you telling me you've never had anything besides a dick in that pretty little cunt before?"

"I-I'm not saying that."

He straightened. "Good. I'd have to call you a liar if you did. I saw your vibrator."

Heat flooded her cheeks.

His cocky smile turned downright evil. "Though I must admit, purple would look good *in* you, too."

Her heart pounded. "You went through my drawers?"

"Correction. I went in your drawers. Several times. With my hands. My tongue. My dick."

"Damn you." She jerked at the handcuffs. Micki wasn't sure what pissed her off more—the violation of her privacy or her overwhelming arousal.

He laid the condom on the bedspread between her thighs. Dark eyes stared into hers as he reached for the tray again.

A paring knife. Her heart stopped. Her lungs stopped. Ryan held one of her kitchen paring knives.

The all-too-familiar black spots swam in front of her eyes, but they didn't block the glittering blade.

"Micki, count with me and take a breath after each number." His voice was commanding, sure, even as he carefully cut off the stem of the banana. "One."

She couldn't do it. A raw scream ripped from her throat. And none of the neighbors were home to hear her.

Chapter Ten

Micki screamed until her throat burned. Screamed until her lungs ached. Screamed until she couldn't make a sound anymore.

Ryan set the knife on the tray. He said nothing the whole time, just waited.

Finally, she couldn't inhale. Her ribs hurt. Her entire chest was on fire.

As she lay there and panted, sadness lay in his expression. Or maybe it was disappointment. "Micki, I'm not going to release the cuffs until I'm sure you've got control of yourself. We both have loaded weapons in the house, and frankly, I'm not letting either of us become a statistic."

She couldn't get enough oxygen to answer him.

He exhaled, a sound she could barely hear over her own pounding pulse. "Are you seeing somebody?"

Her body was frozen. But her mind raced so fast his words didn't make sense.

He looked back at her. "Micki, I need to know if you're still with me. Nod if you understand me."

Ryan's voice seemed to come from far away, like listening to someone while underwater. It took all her willpower to move, but she managed a small dipping of her head.

"Micki, are you seeing a counselor?" His eyes searched her face. "A shrink?"

Shame burned her face. For the third time in her life, she felt . . .

God, there were no words for the intense guilt. She buried her face in the crook of her shoulder and sobbed.

With a metallic clink, her wrists were free. She turned away from Ryan, couldn't face him. The mattress dipped and hot skin pressed against her back. His arm wrapped around her, pulling her tight against his chest, as the tears poured out.

Micki wasn't sure how long she cried before the hiccups started.

"I'm going to the bathroom to get you some water," Ryan whispered in her ear. "I'll be right back."

Numbness cocooned her thoughts, her limbs. Deep down, she welcomed it. Anything to avoid the searing pain he'd managed to dredge out of her soul.

A firm hand raised her head and she took a couple of sips from the cup he held to her lips. The coolness soothed her raw throat.

He set the cup on the nightstand, then he laid down next to her again. His left arm held her snug in the crook of his shoulder while his right hand stroked damp hair away from her face.

They lay like that a long time before he said, "You haven't told your shrink about the flashbacks." It was a statement, not a question.

"No." After all the screaming, her voice was a hoarse whisper.

"Micki, I know it's not my business—"

"Then shut the fuck up." Her rasp mitigated her command.

Ryan rose up on his elbow. "If you don't want to patrol a desk for the rest of your life, then talk to her. You've got a shot of getting your career back on track. Or don't you want that?"

"Of course." She gulped in air. "But I can't."

"Why?"

She said nothing. Couldn't say anything. She'd kept the secret for so long. The concept of releasing it was unthinkable.

"Oh, God," Ryan whispered. "I am such a dumbass."

He hugged her, hard, his face buried against her neck. When he loosened his hold, he said, "Your family and friends don't even know you're in love with him, do they?"

"In love with who?" The buzz in her voice from the screaming fit was the only thing that kept her voice from sounding flat, mechanical.

"With your former partner, Lee Castille."

Her body stiffened. "How—" She swallowed but it felt like broken glass slicing her vocal cords. "How did you—" Her throat hurt too damn much to continue.

A weary chuckle in her ear. "I googled you." His breath ruffled her hair, a sad sound. "I read about his death on the *Post*'s website."

The last thing she wanted was to discuss Lee with Ryan. Even less so while they lay naked in her bed. The same bed she'd shared with Lee.

A dull ache in her heart replaced the numbness. Gradually, her muscles loosened. The silence stretched on between them, but it wasn't the uncomfortable quiet of sitting in the department shrink's office.

Nor was it like the peaceful times she and Dad lay on a blanket in the field behind their house in North Carolina, watching the stars. No, this was more like those endless nights she kept Beth company after the rape. The quiet of empathy and shared pain.

Except this time, it was Micki having the nightmares.

She wasn't sure how many minutes passed with Ryan simply holding her. Maybe it been hours before she heard the inhalation that signaled he was about to say something.

"I know you think I don't understand, but I do. You need to talk to someone. Let this thing out of you before it eats you alive."

She stared at the ceiling and debated. For someone she barely knew, she was far more comfortable with Ryan than her family or her friends. If she spilled her guts, who would Ryan tell about her and Lee? Even better, why?

Micki swallowed again. This time her throat felt like sandpaper, not broken glass. "If I tell the department shrink, she will report me. Relationships between fellow officers aren't permitted."

There was a long quiet moment before he said, "Is it worth living in fear—"

Her body stiffened again.

"Honey, listen to me before you kick me out." His hand stroked her abdomen. "Is this fear that someone will find out about the two of you worth your silence? Or are you punishing yourself for his death? You pointed out I was doing something similar Monday night. It's been a year, Micki."

"One year, one month, three days," she intoned.

"What's the worst that would happen?"

"They could demote me for fraternization. Or fire me."

"Maybe. But then you'll know for sure where you stand instead of constantly looking over your shoulder."

He was right. Damn, she hated to admit it, but she could already sense relief from the burden on her psyche.

"I'll think about it."

Ryan placed a light kiss on her forehead.

Quiet descended on her bedroom once more. He continued to rub her stomach, the touch no doubt meant to be comforting.

Except the gentle stroking affected her body now that the emotional meltdown was over. Electricity darted from her abdomen and settled in her pelvis.

"Ryan?"

"Hmmm . . ."

"What exactly were you planning to do with the banana?"

"Eat it." The way he purred the words stirred her curiosity and her libido.

"How—" She coughed. "How were you going to eat it?"

"Want me to show you?" Humor and desire thickened his voice.

"Yes," she whispered.

Ryan pulled his arm from around her shoulders and leaned on it. His dark brown eyes stared deep into hers, all humor gone. "Are you sure, Micki?"

"Yeah." Heat bloomed in her cheeks again, and she had to look away for a moment. Embarrassment over losing control of herself coated her emotions. Dammit, she was not letting the past rule her anymore.

When she could face him again, concern flickered in his gaze. She reached up and cupped his cheek. "I was enjoying things until you pulled out the knife while I was handcuffed."

Understanding dawned on his face. "The warehouse."

She nodded.

He closed his eyes, disgust flitting across his features. "I'm sorry. I didn't realize—the paper—" He sucked in a harsh breath and blew it out. "The article didn't go into detail. I assumed he had been shot." He laid his hand over hers. "I know this is difficult for you, but tell me what happened so I don't hit another trigger accidentally."

Her hand started to drop from his face, but his fingers wrapped tight around hers. She couldn't repeat the story. Not while looking at him. She stared at the ceiling.

"There was a sex trafficking ring, but they filled specific orders. I matched the request for a blue-eyed blonde, so . . . we volunteered."

Old pain sliced through her.

"I was tied up, but the traffickers wrapped duct tape around my wrists once we were inside the warehouse they were using. Someone had tipped them off. They didn't even pretend to search him. They knew exactly where to find Lee's wire. He didn't have a chance. They—"

A hard knot stopped the words for a moment, but she pushed them past the lump. "They slit his throat. Our backup busted in before they could do anything more than threaten me. But—" Her vision blurred. "He bled to death in my arms."

"Jesus," he muttered. "No wonder you have panic attacks whenever I hold your wrists."

He shifted and terror smacked her in the gut.

"It's okay," Ryan whispered. "I'm not leaving." He reached down to the foot of the bed and shook out the blue, white and gold block quilt she'd made last year. At the time, it seemed reasonable to put her insomnia to good use.

"How about I turn the lights out?"

Micki rolled over to look at him. "Leave the bathroom light on, please." When he climbed out of bed, she considered hopping in the shower to rinse off. Instead, she yanked off the sticky t-shirt and threw it in the general direction of the hamper.

It took him a couple of seconds to flip off the bedroom lamps and flick the switch for the globe bulbs over the sink. He pulled the door partly closed and climbed back under the quilt with her.

Warmth crept over Micki. His solidness felt so damn good. "I thought you were going to show me your trick with the banana."

"I will." He nuzzled her neck. "After we both get some sleep."

Micki laughed. Ryan juggled jam and fudge and peanut butter faster and faster. Except he miscalculated and the jar of peanut butter splashed all over her stomach.

"Don't worry. I'll clean it up." He proceeded to lick her clean and purred.

Micki jerked awake from the odd dream. A rough tongue lapped her skin just north of her belly button. She lay on her left side with the quilt wrapped around her hips. Ryan's arm covered her breasts possessively. She glanced down to find Miss Kitty crouched next to her, enthusiastically cleaning her stomach.

It could have been worse, but Ryan's arm protected the other places he'd smeared food on her body.

"Shoo," she whispered and tried to scoot the purring feline away from her.

"I think she's trying to steal my job." Ryan's voice held a sleepy husk.

Micki couldn't help her laugh. "Don't worry. I'm not into pussy."

He laughed. "That's good. I'm pretty sure I told you twice before that I don't share."

Miss Kitty hissed and jumped from the bed.

The mattress shifted. Butterfly kisses peppered their way across her shoulder and up her neck. When Ryan's lips hit the sweet spot just below her ear, she shuddered.

His fingers rolled her nipple, adding to the electric shivers. His growing erection pressed against the cleft of her ass cheeks.

"Feeling better?" he murmured against her skin. His hand switched to her right breast, gently kneading it until it was hot and swollen.

"Yes." Her answer was more of a gasp than a word. Liquid dampened her pussy. "Still going to show me that banana trick?"

His chuckle vibrated beneath her ear. "The first part involves double penetration."

She sucked in a breath. Anticipation raced through her. Was he serious?

The one boyfriend in college she'd convinced to try anal sex hadn't been that enthusiastic, and he'd broken up with her shortly afterward. She'd been reluctant to suggest it with a partner since then.

His hand left her breast. A single finger parted her folds and tested her wetness. Everything flew out of her head when he teased her clit.

"Micki?"

Instead of replying, a moan reverberated through her body. Her ass ground against his cock. In retaliation, Ryan slid two fingers into her passage.

"Micki?"

"God, yes, please . . ."

His damp fingers slipped out, and a tiny whimper escaped her. What was it about Ryan that sent her body insane? He gently pushed her top thigh forward.

She twisted and looked over her shoulder. Sure enough, he was dressing the banana in a condom. Now, she understood why he trimmed the ends. Scratches from stems or bottoms of the fruit would not be fun. Once the fruit was covered, he donned a condom as well. Then he reached down into his bag of tricks and produced a bottle of edible lube. Liberal amounts were spread over his cock and the banana.

He glanced at her. "You sure?"

She glared at him. "Caulfield, either fuck me or get out of my bed."

A wicked smile stretched his lips. "Yes, Ma'am."

Micki gasped at cool, latex-covered fruit sliding into her pussy. Her fingernails dug into the mattress while he slowly withdrew it and plunged it back in. She faced away from him, enjoying the ripples of pleasure.

"Grab the banana, Micki."

She lifted her knee, braced her foot on the mattress and reached between her legs.

"Play with it, honey."

She did as she was told, fucking herself with the fruit. Behind her, fingers traced her puckered hole before penetrating her. The thick liquid on his skin warmed with their body heat. She thrust back, wanting him deeper in her ass. His fingers withdrew.

Something bigger, rounder tested her opening. She cried out at the quick shove into the tight juncture. The brief instant of pleasure-pain shot through her. A few deep breaths gave her body the time it needed to adjust. Slowly, Ryan pushed into her.

Once her body sheathed his cock, he reached for the banana. "Let go," he whispered.

She complied, feeling vulnerable and more aroused than she thought possible. The rhythm of his cock and the banana were leisurely, gentle, intense all at once.

And totally mind-numbing.

She moaned at the pressure through the thin layer of tissue separating the two. Electricity danced and popped along her nerves at the erotic sensation. The feeling of fullness, completeness had her rocking her hips in time to his tempo.

"Touch yourself, Micki," he whispered.

Only then did she realize her fists were twisted in the comforter. One hand released the fabric and eased between her thighs. Rubbing the slippery bud, touching the banana shoved deep in her pussy left her panting. She was so close.

The dam of pleasure broke, and all she could do was ride the waves. Ryan continued his motions. He seemed determined to wring every iota of bliss from her.

When her tremors subsided, he withdrew his cock but left the fruit. She grabbed the banana, but he said, "Not yet. There's a part two."

It took some effort to look at him over her shoulder. None of her muscles wanted to work. "You can top that?"

"Oh, yeah." His answer sounded like Miss Kitty while her tummy was rubbed. Totally self-satisfied.

Ryan stripped off the condom and put on another. "Roll over on your back."

"With my legs spread." She giggled, but she did as he commanded.

He knelt between her spread calves, leaned on his elbows and started peeling the end of the banana.

Micki propped herself up on her elbows. "You're eating it from that position?"

He gave her a mock frown. "I told you to lie down. Or do I have to leave?"

After the orgasmic intensity of his last trick and not wanting to miss the next one, she obeyed.

The sensation inside of her was odd . . . and arousing.

Despite the stories in women's magazines, she never believed in double or triple orgasms. Now . . .

Now, excitement claimed her again. Her internal muscles hugged the fruit while Ryan tried to nibble it free. Every few attempts, he'd swirl his tongue around her clit. Her fingers and heels dug into the mattress. When he pulled the banana free, she cried out at the loss.

"Need something else in there?" He hovered above her.

"God, yes!" Micki reached for his cock, but he grabbed both arms and pinned her wrists above her head. Only a twinge of fear jerked her emotions.

"Let me take care of you." He watched her for a moment, looking for signs of another freak-out.

She smiled. "I'm okay." Then she frowned. "But I won't be if you don't fuck me now."

"Your wish . . ." He sank into her pussy, his dick as thick and full as the banana. His lips claimed hers in a sweet, fruity kiss. He withdrew until the tip threatened to pop loose, then plunged deep into her again.

Micki wrapped her legs around his waist and tightened her hold enough to raise her hips. "Enough of this slow, gentle shit."

A lopsided grin. "Yes, Ma'am." He picked up the pace, ramming his cock into her over and over again. His expression turn serious as those dark brown eyes stared into hers. Watching, analyzing, and something else she couldn't quite figure out.

Not that he gave her any time to. There was no turtle-paced build-up this time. Stars nova'd behind her retinas. She screamed. Her pussy contracted around his cock, not willing to let the source of all that pleasure go.

Underneath her calves, his back muscles stiffened. With his shout, she felt his cock pulse inside her. Ryan collapsed on top of her, the weight reassuring instead of stifling.

She stroked his scarred back, his arms, his hair as they both caught their breath.

This time, there were no sarcastic comments, no one-upmanship. After a couple of minutes, he rolled off her. Once he tossed the condom, adding to the growing collection in her little wastebasket by the bed, he gathered her in his arms and pulled the comforter over them.

Something had changed. Not just inside her, but between them as well. His soft snores filled her ears. Micki still hadn't figured it out before sleep took her.

Chapter Eleven

Tension plucked at Micki's nerves when she entered the department shrink's office for their Monday morning appointment. Deep down, she knew Ryan was right, but the idea of confessing her affair still tore at her. It was one thing telling him. Somehow, she felt even more naked here than she had been in bed with him.

Dr. Johnson gestured for her to sit down in one of the damn comfy chairs. She smoothed her skirt and sat across from Micki. A slight smile tilted the corners of her mouth.

"Did you have a good weekend?"

"Lee Castille and I were lovers," Micki blurted. She hadn't planned to vomit the information. The words sounded tawdry the way she spit them out, but her feelings for him had been so much more. And his last words . . .

One eyebrow rose, but the shrink didn't look surprised. "Go on."

"I know you have to report violations of the code of conduct."

Dr. Johnson leaned back against her chair. "Why?"

Micki shrugged. "I wish I could tell you it was proximity or some other shit—"

"No." Dr. Johnson shook her head. "Why do you think I'll report you?"

"Because . . ." Calling any member of the department a narc was the equivalent of the old-fashioned gesture of slapping someone's face with gloves and challenging them to twenty paces at dawn with pistols. When you depended on each other for your life, you didn't question the other person's honor. Even if that person was the department shrink.

"Detective Rodriguez," Micki finished lamely.

"Ahh . . ." the shrink breathed. "That explains quite a bit of behavior from the staff over the last couple of years." She folded her hands over her notebook. "Did you speak to the detective directly?"

"No." God, this felt like a reprimand from Dad. The same steel hidden behind a quiet voice. It was all she could do not to squirm in the chair.

"Have you ever played the child's game 'Telephone', Officer?"

Micki shook her head.

"Well, one person tells the second a story. The second person passes it on to the third, and so on. With each telling, the story becomes distorted until the final product no longer resembles the original except in the most superficial of ways."

A sad smile played across Dr. Johnson's features. "It takes a strong person to admit she did something she knew was against the rules. Just like it took Rodriguez a hell of a lot of strength to realize his addictive personality was a detriment to being a narcotics detective. He resigned of his own volition."

"Oh." This was embarrassing as hell but it needed to be said. "I owe you an apology."

This time, a surprised look appeared on the shrink's face. "Apology accepted, Officer. For the record, the only time I'm required to report a patient is if she is a danger to herself or to someone else. Understand?"

"Yes, ma'am."

Another smile from the shrink. "Can I ask what prompted your confession?"

Micki rubbed her damp palms across her thighs. "Someone told me I was letting the past rule me, and I needed to decide whether I really wanted my career back."

"Would this be the young gentleman you recently began seeing?"

Micki's jaw dropped open. It took a couple of tries to make it work. "H-how did you know?"

"Body language. There's a certain look to a woman who's met someone she's attracted to." She unclasped her hands and picked up her pen. "He's not a fellow cop, is he?"

Micki shook her head.

"Good." Dr. Johnson leaned forward again. "Micki, would you mind if I gave you some personal advice?"

The shrink's look was so earnest that it reminded her of Beth. She nodded.

"You've learned the hard way why the non-fraternization policy is in place. I think you've punished yourself more thoroughly over Lee's death than anything the force could inflict. And we both know you've been officially cleared of any wrong doing in the incident. It would be best if we keep our discussions between the two of us."

For the first time in one year, one month, and six days, a sliver of hope sprang to life in Micki's heart. "Does this mean you'll recommend that I can return to duty?"

"Are you willing to come in and see me a couple of times a week and do the exercises I give you?"

"Yes—" Micki's promise to Ryan made her falter. "There's something else."

Dr. Johnson gestured for her to continue.

"I—" She swallowed hard. "I've been having flashbacks and anxiety attacks."

"That's not unusual with post-traumatic stress. Tell me about them."

Micki spent the next hour and a half spilling her guts.

On Friday night, a solid yank confirmed the handcuffs were locked. Micki looked up at Ryan and licked her lips. Anticipation made her hungry.

"They aren't too tight, are they?" he asked.

"No."

He looked deep in her eyes, his nose an inch from hers. "You okay?"

"I'm fine." She smiled to reassure him. And for once, she wasn't lying. She still didn't find her bondage that thrilling, but no black spots encroached on her vision. The desensitization practices Dr. Johnson gave her over the past week seemed to be working. In fact, the shrink had enthusiastically endorsed bondage games with someone Micki trusted.

"Tell me about your day." Ryan lay down beside her, head propped on his elbow, and lightly stroked her skin.

Goose bumps rose at his touch. It took her a second to remember her good news. "They're returning me to street duty, and I've been assigned a new partner."

"That's great, honey." Ryan pecked her forehead.

She rolled her eyes. "It's just a presence duty at a Northeast high school. The sergeant's starting us out with something light."

"The school year's almost over," Ryan pointed out.

"Yep." She grinned. "I can be back in a patrol in six weeks if the shrink signs off."

"I'd rather face Taliban insurgents again than high school kids." He gave a mock shudder.

"It's progress," she protested.

"I can think of other progress I'd rather make." His head dipped and his lips latched onto a nipple.

Her back arched as his tongue played with the tight bud. He teased the point until the ache traveled from her breast to her pussy. He shifted his attention to the other nipple. Wetness slicked her folds. Her thighs shifted to ease the neediness of her body.

Ryan's knee pressed between hers, forcing them apart. She thrust her hips up and ground against his leg.

He released her nipple and grinned at her. "A little horny tonight?"

"No." She grinned back. "Very horny tonight."

"Then maybe you've earned a little time off for good behavior." Ryan rolled away long enough to grab the handcuff key. In a second, her arms were free to pull his head down for a tonsil-searing kiss. Her mind registered the muffled jingle of the cuffs landing on the floor.

When he broke the contact, he held up a foil packet. "You want to do the honors?"

Micki snatched it from his hand. "Lie on your back," she ordered.

He obeyed, but his hands constantly roamed, touching her arms, cupping her breasts. His cock already stood at attention, her personal amusement park ride.

She straddled his hips and ripped open the package. He reached for her pussy, and she slapped his hand away. "Not yet."

"Tease."

She raised an eyebrow. "Takes one to know one." She took her time sheathing his cock, stroked the velvet-covered steel until his jaw line hardened with the effort to contain himself.

Once the condom was in place, she rose on her knees, centered herself and guided his erection to her hot, wet core. Sliding down on his shaft gave new meaning to bliss.

He grabbed her hips, and once again, she slapped his hands away. "I said not yet. If you can't listen to my instructions, I'll stop."

Ryan groaned in frustration, but he wound his fists in the sheets to keep from touching her.

Micki rode his cock like a carousel. Up. Down. Up. Down. She reached behind her, massaged his sac in time to her motions. His knuckles tightened until the bones shone white through the thin layer of skin.

He's so close. But she wasn't ready for the fun to stop yet. Her hands sought her breasts, kneaded the swollen flesh. His eyes rounded as she plucked her nipples.

"Like what you see, baby?" she purred.

He nodded.

"Do you want to touch them?" She rocked her hips against his, relished the feel of his cock filling her pussy.

Again, he nodded.

She released her right nipple and waggled her index finger in his face. "You didn't say the magic words."

Ryan licked his lips. "Please, may I touch you, Ma'am?"

The power of a man begging her sent a charge through Micki. She clenched her internal muscles. The result was plain in the brief closing of his eyes.

"You may," she whispered

Ryan pulled himself into a sitting position, Micki still firmly impaled on his cock. He bent his head and grabbed a ripe nipple in his mouth. He sucked until the point of pain, then released it and gently bit the other one.

Her cry elicited a gleam in his eyes, something that smoldered. Their bodies locked into a rhythm neither wanted to break. Beneath her thighs, her arms around his neck, his muscles stiffened. With a guttural moan, his cock jumped and pulsed inside her. Liquid warmth filled her pussy.

She came in the waves of his orgasm. Ryan held her as she shook and trembled in pleasure. He nuzzled her neck while her breathing settled back into a regular rhythm.

His cock slipped from her as they lay down, limbs still entwined. She didn't want to do anything to mar this perfect moment.

"I love you, Micki," he whispered.

Time stopped.

When time started again, Micki sat huddled in the corner between the tub and the wall. At least, she thought it was the tub from the smooth ceramic against her right arm and ass cheek. The room was totally dark, and she shook from cold.

She felt her way across the carpet until she found the door. Somehow, she managed to get her cramped legs underneath her and rose. Her hand felt along the wall until it met the light switch. She blinked at the shock to her retinas and unlocked the door.

It was still dark outside. Or dark again. She wasn't sure.

The bedside lamp was still on. And she was very cold because . . .

Naked.

She was naked because . . .

Ryan.

She and Ryan had been in her bed. Vague images flitted through her mind. The anxiety attacks and flashbacks were one thing. She'd never had a total blackout before.

They'd been making l—

The L-word was an alien parasite in her brain, and she ruthlessly squashed it. It didn't stop the scents though. Of his male spice. Of sex.

Micki dug in a drawer until she found sweatpants and a sweatshirt by touch. It took a lot of effort to dress herself. So much, she had to sit in her wicker chair for a few moments to catch her breath. The clock silently winked off five minutes before she found the energy to go downstairs.

Ryan sat on the couch, dressed in his t-shirt and jeans that he'd arrived in. He held her home phone. The look he gave her scared her more than her inability to remember what happened.

"You okay, honey?"

Was she okay? She wasn't sure of anything anymore. The comforting numbness since Lee's death was gone. It left her raw, aching.

"I don't know."

He stood. Her self-preservation ignited. Ryan felt . . . dangerous. She skittered up a couple of steps.

His expression consisted of agony and worry. "I found Dr. Johnson's card and called her. I'm sorry, Micki, but I didn't know what else to do." He held out the handset. When she made no move to take it, he set it on the couch. "She's waiting on a call from you. No matter how late it is."

The silence stretched. She couldn't decide what to do. Something deep in her said Ryan was a threat, but she couldn't remember why.

He shoved his hands in his back pockets. "I think it's best that I leave." Dark brown eyes bore into hers. "I meant what I said, Micki. I hope someday you can accept that."

What had happened? As much as she wanted him to stay, she needed him to leave. She couldn't think with him there.

Sadness filled his eyes. Four quick strides later, the front door closed behind him with a soft click.

The memory flooded her head, and she collapsed on the bottom step in sobs.

Lee on the cold concrete, trying to talk. His lips formed the same three words over and over again until the light in his eyes faded. "I love you."

Chapter Twelve

On Sunday morning, the fuzz on her teeth pried Micki from the couch. She couldn't bear to face the rumpled sheets on her bed. Didn't trust herself not to fling her body on them and sniff them for a trace of Ryan's scent.

Instead, she went to the second floor bathroom and pulled out one of the new toothbrushes she kept on hand for overnight guests. She opened the medicine cabinet door all the way so she wouldn't have to look at herself in its mirror.

A whiff of her sweatshirt as she spit out toothpaste made her turn on the shower next. After soap and shampoo she needed something clean to wear. A load of folded laundry sat in its basket inside the utility closet. She pulled on a pair of ripped jeans and a gray t-shirt. The clothing matched her mood.

Eventually though, she'd have to go upstairs. Her uniforms hung in the master bedroom closet. If only she could buy more before tomorrow morning, then she could avoid her bedroom forever.

She needed to talk to someone. Dr. Johnson expressed her concern when Micki called late Friday night, but by then, the memories of what had happened were clearer. She'd screwed up with Ryan. Big time. In a way, that wasn't exactly a I-need-psychiatric-help situation, though her PTSD hadn't helped the resulting mess any.

As hard as it was to admit, she would have freaked if Ryan said he loved her without the PTSD. Hell, she would have freaked if Lee had said he loved her before he lay dying in that damn warehouse.

No. This was definitely a girlfriend and ice cream emergency.

No one answered their phones. Not Alicia. Not Diana. Not even Beth. Everyone had a life it seemed except her. She stared at the handset beside her on the couch.

Maybe she should call Mike about going with her to Beth's showing on Friday. It would avoid a lot of awkwardness.

Her legs and back were stiff by the time she decided to drive up to Germantown.

Only Dad's pick-up was in the driveway when Micki pulled up to her parents' little ranch-style house. Good. Mom would try to coddle her, insist she stay with them for a week or two. And as good as that sounded, there was too much career stuff at stake with Micki starting her new assignment in the morning.

The main door was open, but the screen door was locked when she tried it. "Dad?"

"On the deck" came the muffled shout.

Micki circled the house.

Dad set his e-reader down and stood when she climbed the redwood steps. "Hey, baby." Comforting arms enveloped her in a hug. "Didn't expect you until Mother's Day. Want some lemonade or a soda?"

"Lemonade sounds great." She injected some fake cheerfulness into her reply. Not that it fooled Dad from the odd look he gave her.

She followed him into the kitchen. Only the shock of white hair indicated he was pushing seventy. Then she took a closer look. He moved a little slower, favoring his left leg as he strode to the refrigerator and pulled out the pitcher.

He poured a large glass and waved her back to the deck. When they were both seated, he fixed her with a hard stare. "Gonna tell me what's really going on?"

Micki sipped her drink. The tartness indicated Dad still squeezed his own lemons. No kiddie mixes for him.

"Well," she started when the feeling returned to her tongue. "I've got some good news. I'm back on street duty." She told him about the new assignment and her new partner.

"That's good." He stared at the orchard on the hill across from them. "What about this new fella?"

"Daniel seems all right."

"I don't mean him. I mean the guy you've started dating."

Her heart lurched. "Butch tattled."

"Yeah. A couple of weeks ago. But that's not what I'm talking about." Dad's finger brushed the condensation on his own glass. "I got a call from Mike yesterday morning. He and your fella were worried about you."

Micki swallowed hard. "Ryan went to Mike?"

Dad shrugged. "The kid didn't know who else to talk to. Why didn't you tell us the head shit was that bad?"

Her vision blurred. "I didn't want to worry you and Mom. She's already jumping at every news report out of Afghanistan because of Seth." It was her turn to stare at the orchard. Her brother could take care of himself. Much better than she could obviously. "I thought I could handle it," she finished in a whisper.

"Baby, losing someone you love is bad. Lee dying the way he did . . ." Dad reached over the chaise arm to hold her hand. "Something like that's even tougher. You think I don't get it?"

Understanding dawned on Micki. She turned to face Dad. "You knew?"

He smiled, a sad, heartbroken expression. "Your mom and I aren't as dumb as you think." He squeezed her hand. "You don't grieve for someone like that if you don't love them. Now, your mom wasn't real happy about the sex without marriage thing . . ."

"Da-a-ad!"

He gave her hand another squeeze. "This Ryan loves you, you know."

"I—" She swallowed the lump threatening to become real tears. "I know. It's just . . ."

"You think you're betraying Lee?"

She nodded, not trusting herself to speak.

"Honey, the last thing Lee would want is for you to stop living. It's good to remember the people in your life and what they meant to you after they're gone. No one's asking you to forget him. But you can't give up on love because of one terrible thing."

Dad's words echoed in Micki's head during the drive home. Maybe he and Dr. Johnson were wrong. Maybe she used the regs to avoid a commitment. Her relationship with Lee was fun, easy and required virtually no effort. But since she thought no one knew about them, there was no pressure.

And now, here she was—using Lee's death to push away Ryan. Alicia's challenge fed a physical itch, but the connection with Ryan was so much more.

As soon as she opened the front door of her condo, she headed straight for the phone, still laying on the couch where she left it.

Four rings later, the call rolled to voice-mail. "Caulfield here. You know the drill."

At the harsh beep, the words rushed out of her. "Ryan, I'm calling to apologize about the other night. We need to talk, and I'd like to do this in person."

She couldn't think of anything else to say that wouldn't sound totally stupid, so she ended with "Call me."

Monday passed in a blur. Her new partner Daniel was a breeze to work with, and he seemed to have a natural talent when dealing with the hormone-addled teens. The blond hair, piercing blue eyes and rugged good looks probably helped.

In fact, she'd overheard more than one female student comment on how much he resembled the most recent actor to play a popular secret agent in the movies. From the way the female staff found excuses to talk to him, the teens weren't the only ones nursing crushes.

On the other hand, Micki had learned her lesson, even if she wasn't waiting for a return call from a certain Army officer. Though when she discovered her new partner was divorced, she toyed with the idea of setting him up with Diana.

No. Get your own house in order first.

And that meant a heart-to-heart, no-sex, real discussion with Ryan.

Micki opened the front door of her condo and charged over to the phone. The message light blinked.

She sucked in a deep breath and released it before she hit the 'Play' button. One message from Mom, checking on her. Another from Mike, asking the same thing.

The voice on the third message had her shaking, and she sat on the arm of the couch.

"Hey, honey. I got your message. I want to talk to you too, but this will be the only chance I have to call. Something came up Saturday afternoon, and I'm not sure when I'll be home." A pause, and she could hear an airplane engine in the background. "I've never reneged on a deal, but I don't know if I'll be back before your friend's gallery show. I hope you'll forgive me if I don't, and let me make it up to you." Another pause. The sound of someone shouting his name. "I won't say the other thing, but I'm thinking it. Maybe, someday, you can accept it. Bye, Micki."

She let herself fall back on the couch, and she stared at the ceiling. *You'd better survive long enough to let me say that I love you, too. Otherwise, Ryan Caulfield, I'll go to hell and personally kick your ass.*

Chapter Thirteen

Two days later, Micki walked with Daniel out to the teacher's parking now that the last student had left for the day. At the chirp from her waist, she pulled out her smart phone from its holster. She frowned when she checked the time and the message.

"What's wrong?" Daniel asked, concern in his sharp blue eyes.

"A friend who never calls while I'm on duty." She tapped the icon for Beth's cell number.

"Hi, Micki."

"What's going on with Alicia? And why'd Mrs. Abercrombie call you about a strange man lurking around the house instead of me?"

"Slow down, girl. First of all, Mrs. Abercrombie *thought* she called you." In the background, Micki could hear computer keys clicking. "When you didn't call me back right away, I drove over."

"That was stupid, Beth!"

"Not as stupid as the shitty Asteroid phone you bought. Lemme guess, my message just now popped up, didn't it?"

"Beth . . ."

A laugh came through the receiver. "Speaking of the Asteroid brand, you'll never guess who Alicia's lurker was."

Micki closed her eyes in exasperation. "So help me, get to the point, or I'm coming to your office and shooting you."

"Richard Brand."

Micki's eyes popped open. "The tech billionaire? As in Hank's ex-boss?"

"Yep. When Alicia decided on a boytoy, she set her sights high."

"But she's okay?"

"Yeah. They had a fight, which is why Brand was sitting on her doorstep. When

I left, they were working things out. Do me a favor though and swing by once you're off duty. Just to make sure."

Micki covered the mike on her phone and smiled at Daniel. "Things are fine. Why don't you go on home?"

He grinned. "No way. I want to hear about the billionaire lurker."

"Who are you talking to?" Beth demanded.

Micki returned her attention to her friend. "My partner."

"Partner? You're back on street duty? You bitch! This is payback for me not telling you about the showing, isn't it?"

"Serves you right. I'll swing by Alicia's on my way home. If everything's okay, I'll see you at the Winston's tomorrow night." She thumbed the icon to end the call.

Daniel had a puzzled expression on his face. "Winston's art gallery?"

Micki slid her phone back in its holster. "Yeah. My friend Beth has a show there tomorrow night."

"You want to ride together?" At her hesitation, Daniel waved a hand. "No, not like that. An old friend couldn't go so he gave me his invitation." He raked a hand through his hair. "I admit I have an ulterior reason."

Micki folded her arms. "Which is?"

"The woman I've been seeing will be there."

"And she's not going with you because . . ."

Daniel stared across the asphalt lot. "She has a bad case of relationship jitters. When I confronted her, she told me to go fuck myself."

A little bit of empathy and a healthy dose of guilt hit Micki. "A lot of that going around."

Where was Ryan right now? Was he okay? She didn't give a shit about him honoring his bargain. Just as long as he got home in one piece, nothing else mattered. Now, she understood why her mother never got weird about petty husband things the way the other moms did.

She cleared her throat. "I'm glad you're giving her another chance."

Daniel glanced at Micki. "So you'll be my wingman?"

Micki shook her head and laughed. "What are partners for? But if you hook up and I have to catch a ride home with someone else, you owe me double."

"Of course." He grinned back. "Thanks, Donovan."

The street in Chevy Chase was quiet when Micki parked behind the latest model of Porsche in front of Alicia's house. She strode up to the front and lifted her fist to knock when the door opened.

Alicia and the guy whose throat she was examining with her tongue didn't even realize Micki stood there.

"Ahem."

Alicia jerked away from her tonsil-hockey partner. Her pale face flamed as red as her very mussed hair. "Uh, Micki . . . uh, hi." She pulled the bathrobe tighter around her waist and clutched the neck with her other hand.

God, it was hard to keep a straight face. "We received a report of a neighborhood disturbance." Micki eyed the tall, dark-haired man with Alicia. Even if Beth hadn't told her, she would have recognized Richard Brand from the zillion magazine covers he'd graced. No question now about whether his face had been photoshoppped. He was a hunk of Grade A prime rib.

"Everything's fine, Officer . . ." His eyes flipped to her nametag for a split second. "Donovan."

Micki lifted an eyebrow. "There was a report of screaming."

Alicia slapped a hand over her mouth. Since it was the one holding the collar, she now flashed her ample cleavage to the entire neighborhood. Her muffled words sounded like "Oh, God, Mrs. Abercrombie—"

Micki couldn't hold her humor any longer. She burst out laughing at Alicia's horrified expression.

Alicia's eyes narrowed and her hand dropped. "Beth. So help me, I'm gonna kill that bitch."

"Well, you haven't answered any of my phone calls for the last couple of weeks either." Micki gave Brand a blatant appraisal. "I can see why, too."

"And on that note, I must leave." Brand kissed Alicia, an embrace that left no doubt about their relationship. "See you tomorrow."

He took three steps down the walk when Micki called, "Brand."

He pivoted, his expression wary. "Yes?"

Micki deliberately placed her palm on the butt of her service pistol. "Don't give me a reason to use this."

Acknowledgement appeared in his expression. "I understand. I heard what you did to the high school quarterback."

Both women watched as he drove off.

Micki turned to Alicia. "You could've returned one of our calls to let us know you were okay."

"It's . . . complicated."

Micki gestured at the bathrobe. "Doesn't look that complicated to me." She smirked. "Would you like to clean up while I order dinner, or are you sticking with the freshly fucked look?"

Alicia stuck out her tongue.

Micki followed her into the house, laughing all the way to the kitchen.

After they both changed and ate their Thai food, Micki settled at the other end of the couch with her glass of wine. "Are you regretting your insane idea?"

Alicia leaned back against the arm. "No. I needed to get on with my life. You—" Her lips clamped shut, and she stared at her merlot.

"Shit." Micki closed her eyes. "Was I that obvious?" When Alicia remained silent, she opened them.

"No, neither of you were. We figured you'd talk if you needed to." Alicia traced the rim of her glass. "You've been so strong since Lee's death. You always have been the strong one. I hated you because I couldn't keep my shit together after Hank betrayed me."

Micki leaned forward. "Is that what you think? That I'm strong?" She shook her head and took a sip of wine. "I'm more fucked up than the three of you put together. I met a guy. A perfect guy told me he loved me, and you know what I did? Instead of telling him I loved him, I had a nervous breakdown in my bathroom. Literally."

Alicia's mouth formed a perfect "O". It took a few seconds before she said, "It's not too late. You need to tell him how you really feel."

"I wish I could." Micki slumped against the couch, and her vision blurred. "How I wish I could. He's Special Forces though. On a mission right now, God knows where doing God knows what. I don't know what I'll do if he gets himself killed."

Alicia set down her wine, crawled across the couch and hugged Micki. They sat quietly for a very long time.

It was close to midnight when Micki pulled into her parking spot. The hair along the back of her neck rose. Someone sat on her front step, his face in shadows. While the department protected officers' personal information, it didn't mean someone she'd arrested hadn't tracked her down. She reached into her gym bag and drew her service pistol.

The figure stood and stepped under the security light.

Ryan.

Her heart skipped a beat. She slid her gun back into its holster, grabbed her bag and ran for her front door.

Micki leapt into his arms and peppered him with kisses. In between, she said, "I'm so sorry, I love you too." Over and over again.

Ryan laughed. "Slow down. Slow down. Let's go inside and talk."

The emotion hit Micki hard, like someone punched her in the gut, but she felt so free at the same time. "No. You don't need to say anything. I was the asshole."

He cupped her face. "Let's go inside. We'll have plenty of time. For everything." He kissed her, a deep, passionate melding that held a wealth of promise.

When they both came up for breath, she nodded. "Inside. Yes. Inside is good."

Once the door was locked, Micki set down her gym bag and hung up her utility belt on the coat tree. A wicked idea flared. She pulled out her baton and whirled to face Ryan.

Micki slapped the black stick against her open palm. "But first, there's a discipline issue."

He grinned, a lopsided cocky one. "Yes, Ma'am."

She didn't return his smile, but her nipples tightened under her t-shirt, and liquid heat filled her pussy. "Strip, soldier."

"Yes, Ma'am." And he preceded to do just that.

TAKEN BY PASSION

Diana's Story

Chapter One

Diana Traynor poured wine for her and Kat, then sparkling grape juice for Steffi. The boom and growl of thunder rattled the art deco fixtures. The first drops of rain splattered against the windows of her sister's apartment. Definitely a good night for a cozy dinner with family.

"So how is my nephew doing?" Diana handed the glass of juice to Steffi sitting at the kitchen table.

"Playing soccer with his momma's bladder." She grinned and patted her huge belly. "And frankly I'm sick of talking about the damn pregnancy. I swear every woman at the grocery has to give me advice. Tell me something, anything, that has nothing to do with diapers or hemorrhoids."

Diana handed a glass of wine to Kat before she took a chair next to Steffi. She relayed the latest gossip, including their friend Alicia's revelation at last week's lunch about why she divorced her husband.

Kat joined them and set three full plates on the table. "She caught Hank with a dominatrix? No shit?" She was a lobbyist now, but Kat hadn't lost her waitressing skills. "Always knew that bastard was a pussy."

Steffi speared a forkful of fettuccine. "Is Alicia dating yet?"

"Well, we made a, um, pact." Diana toyed with the condensation on her wine glass.

"What kind of pact?" Steffi's fork hovered in the air, and a suspicious look filled her dark eyes.

Diana had never been able to lie to her baby sister. "We would find boytoys for some kinky sex before our next lunch."

Kat chuckled, but covered her mouth at Steffi's nasty glare.

Steffi turned back to Diana. "What the hell are you thinking, girl? A one-night stand? Do you want to catch some STD?"

"That's not—"

Steffi ignored her protest. "Not to mention assholes just looking to rob you. You're supposed to be the sister with common sense—" She winced.

Kat reached for her hand. "You okay, sweetie?"

"No, I'm not." Her laser eyes shot back to Diana. "Now you've got the baby upset, and I have to pee." She climbed awkwardly to her feet and shook a finger at

Diana. "Don't think I'm done with you." As she waddled toward the bathroom, "crazy bitch" filtered through the air in her wake.

Humor still shone in Kat's eyes. "She can't talk. If I'd known she'd be this horny while pregnant, I'd have agreed to the fertilization crap a lot sooner." Her expression turned sober. "Are you serious about a temporary thing that's not vanilla?"

Diana's nerves skittered at Kat's question. She sucked in a deep breath and released it. "Honestly, after the shit that went down with Steve, I just want some fun. I want—" Her voice caught with pain.

She'd swallowed her own desires in order to be the accomplished daughter her parents wanted. Swallowed them in order to take care of herself and Steffi after their parents kicked them out when they discovered Steffi's predilection for women and Diana defended Steffi from Mom's punches. Swallowed them to be the appropriate political girlfriend for Steve.

She was so tired of being what everyone else wanted or needed.

Diana met Kat's intense stare. If anyone would understand her feelings, it would be Kat. "I want to find some passion in life again. Steve never wanted anything but the missionary position." She snorted. "And he had the balls to accuse me of being a cold fish in bed."

"Male or female?"

Diana had never told anyone she was bi other than her friend Beth. Not even Steffi. And the only reason Beth knew . . .

Heat rushed to Diana's cheeks. Even if her dark skin hid her blush, Kat's expression said she read everything on Diana's face. "Either." The mix of emotions racing through her clenched her pelvic muscles. "Both," she whispered.

There was no condemnation in Kat's face. She rose, grabbed a pen and tore off a sheet from the pad by the phone. The paper rustled with her scribbling. She turned and handed the note to Diana.

"Victoria and Merrick are good people. Safe. Discreet."

Diana looked down at the names of one of D.C.'s top political power couples and back up at Kat. Her fingers shook. "I knew they introduced you and Steffi, but you . . . *know* them?"

Kat sat down and rested her chin on her hands. "We were a trio for a couple of years." A small smile curved her lips. "Until your sister. I think Victoria knew I was ready to settle down."

A quiver of fear joined the surge of desire in Diana's body. "And no one will know?"

"One of Victoria's conditions is your utmost silence. I know you value your privacy, but you can't give your girlfriends even a hint of who you're sleeping with. I won't even know for sure unless you three decide to confide in me."

Old pain bled suspicion into Diana's excitement. "But you just told me that you . . ."

"Victoria called the other day. Said she missed me." Kat glanced at the bathroom before she continued. "I'm totally in love with Steffi. When Victoria said she was lonely, you were the first person I thought of. D, there's always been more to you than you let other people see. I want you to know I understand. If you decide not to call Victoria, toss the paper."

Diana shivered. She hated set-ups, but it'd been so damn long since anyone had touched her. And she wanted to be touched by another human. Someone's mouth on her clit, plunging their fingers, their dick, their toys into her pussy, her mouth, her ass until she exploded.

And obviously, pretending to be vanilla in the sex department had not worked at all. Not with that ugly-ass note Steve left on the refrigerator rather than talking to her.

The sound of flushing echoed down the tiny hallway. Diana nodded and slipped the note into her purse slung over the chair back. Both she and Kat painted bright smiles on their faces as Steffi rejoined them.

Kat twined her cream-colored fingers through Steffi's dark ones. "C'mere, sexy." She pulled her girlfriend into her lap and laid a hand on her swollen belly. She kissed Steffi thoroughly until Steffi giggled and pushed away.

"Hey, not in front of my sister."

Kat laughed. "She's a big girl. I'm pretty sure she knows we have sex."

Warmth rushed through Diana. It was good to see Steffi so happy.

But deep down she knew she couldn't settle for her sister's domestic bliss. She needed more. Much, much more.

Chapter Two

Diana sat in her office and picked up Kat's note for the twentieth time. Just staring at the names and phone number, like she had for the last three days. Fingernails tapped a rhythm on her desk as she considered the possibilities.

God knew she needed some distraction. She should be looking for a new apartment because she sure as hell couldn't afford her current one. Not without a roommate that didn't mind sharing a one-bedroom.

She pummeled the pain of Steve's abandonment back into its little corner.

The little piece of paper tempted her. No strings sex. Just to ease her various itches, right?

But would the pleasure be worth getting involved with such a couple? She was under no illusions about her own career. Being an accountant with a non-profit was hardly in the same league as a senior partner in one of the largest law firms in the country like Merrick Davis or a political commentator from a family that had produced senators, ambassadors and a couple of presidents like Victoria Butler. So why would Kat think she could fit in with these people?

By the same token, there wasn't a breath of scandal involving them. Hell, she wouldn't have known about Kat's previous relationship with them if she hadn't told Diana. And she was so tired of going home to her apartment every night alone.

Not giving herself another opportunity to come up with an excuse, Diana pulled out her smart phone and tapped the number. It rang once. Twice.

"Hello?" The throaty voice was familiar from TV. Seductive.

"Ms. Butler? This is Diana Traynor." She pinched her thigh to keep from babbling.

"Steffi's sister? It's a pleasure to meet you finally." A soft laugh. "And really, my dear, I don't think we need to be that formal with each other."

"Then you know Katherine Wendig gave me your number?"

"Yes, and I know why."

Diana closed her eyes as the silence stretched. A booty call to someone she didn't know was a stupid idea. What the hell had she been thinking? "I'm sorry to bother you—"

Victoria laughed, a silvery tinkling sound. "Why don't you come over for dinner tonight? Merrick's out of town on a case, but that doesn't mean the two of us can't get acquainted."

Her eyes popped open. Victoria's voice might as well have been an electric charge. It took a second or two, but she finally forced out something polite. "That sounds good."

When Diana hit the "End Call" icon, the jitters hit her hard. She was so far out of her comfort zone she might as well have been on another continent. But if it was such a bad idea, why were her panties already soaked?

Diana hesitated before the gate to the Georgetown home, checking the address for the third time. Yes, definitely the right place.

Crossing her fingers on one hand, she pressed the buzzer with the other.

"Yes?" The voice oozed sensuality from the intercom.

"It's Diana."

An electronic hum sounded, and the lock clicked open. Her heartbeat sped past the staccato rhythm of her heels. The front door swung open before she reached it. Disappointment made her falter when she saw the Hispanic woman in a housekeeper's gray dress and white apron. Her smooth bun matched the color of her dress.

The woman smiled and bobbed her head. "Good evening, Ms. Traynor. May I take your things?"

Before Diana could answer, the housekeeper had guided her inside and divested her of everything except the long, thin gift bag she carried. She placed Diana's shoulder bag and purse on a shelf in an armoire next to the door before gesturing for Diana to follow her. "Miss Victoria is waiting for you in the kitchen."

Diana tailed the housekeeper down a short hallway. Delicious odors filled the air with hints of rosemary, basil and onion. She surveyed the walls and floor. Hand-hewn planks, trim and side rails. What looked to be the original plaster. Definitely antebellum construction.

What the fuck was she thinking? Accepting Victoria's invitation only stirred the old conflicts within her. How could she long for submission given America's racial history? Yet, she couldn't force her feet to turn back to the front door.

The hall emptied into a brightly lit kitchen. Raw brick set the cozy mood in the room. Maple cupboards added warmth. But it was the woman setting crab cakes in the iron skillet on the gas stove that drew her eye.

The simple white tee and navy capris were a far cry from the tailored suits Victoria Butler wore during her television appearances. Instead of a smart, elegant chiffon, her hair fell in a silver wash down her back.

Diana admired the woman for having the balls not to color her tresses, especially considering society's obsession with youth, but Victoria had turned her premature gray into a trademark. Diana knew she wouldn't have had the same guts at eighteen. When Victoria looked up from the skillet, her eyes were so alive, so blue, they took Diana's breath away.

Victoria flashed a brilliant smile. "Hi, Diana. Let me wash up." An instant later, she stood in front of Diana, her palm out.

Diana took it, and electricity shot across her skin. She couldn't remember the last time she felt such an instant . . . connection with someone. "Pleasure to meet you, too," she managed to force out.

"Will you need anything else tonight, Miss Victoria?"

Diana jumped at the sound of the housekeeper's voice. How had she forgotten the woman was in the kitchen, too? And Victoria Butler still held her hand.

The feeling wasn't uncomfortable. Far from it. Diana sucked in a sharp breath, and Victoria released her. Reluctantly from the look in those brilliant eyes.

"No, thank you, Consuela. Have a good evening."

The housekeeper murmured something pleasant, but the actual words were gibberish. Diana was vaguely aware of the woman leaving the room, but she couldn't break the hold Victoria's gaze seemed to have over her.

"Kat said you loved seafood."

Diana blinked at the words. "Y-yes."

"It's imported since crab isn't in season yet. I don't know about you, but I prefer fresh crab, don't you?" The words came out so fast Diana barely understood them.

She's as nervous as I am. That realization eased the muscles along Diana's neck. "Nothing like it," she agreed. "It's a good thing I brought a decent Sauvignon Blanc."

"Californian?"

"Australian, actually." She handed the gift bag to her hostess.

Victoria pulled out the bottle before she flashed another brilliant smile. "Have a seat." She waved at the stools around the kitchen's island. "You'll have to tell me where you discovered this little gem."

"Not really much of a story." Diana took the proffered seat. "I was in Australia working with an aboriginal rights group one summer. One of the local girls brought this to a party and I fell in love."

"With the wine or the girl?" Victoria smiled as she screwed the bottle opener into the cork.

Diana chuckled. "The wine. The girl was very unavailable."

Victoria's laugh was delicate, musical. "Her loss is my gain, hmmm?" She set the open bottle and two glasses on the table. "Why don't you pour while I dish up the plates?"

Filling the glasses helped calm her nerves. A sip of the tart wine even more so.

A few seconds later, Victoria placed a plate in front of Diana. "I take it this working trip to Australia was after you shepherded Steffi through college?"

Diana's fork paused in mid-air. "What did Kat tell you about me?"

"The better question is what *hasn't* Steffi told me." Victoria smiled over her folded hands. "Or have you forgotten your sister is the assistant producer of *Inside the Beltway*?"

Oh, this was such a bad idea. Diana set the fork down. The last thing she wanted was to jeopardize Steffi's job. Not with the baby due soon. "I'm sorry. I shouldn't have called you."

In the fraction of a second it took for Diana to stand, Victoria's hand folded over hers.

"Don't leave yet." Earnestness lay in her penetrating gaze. "I'm sorry I upset you. Steffi gushes about you, and I admit when Kat suggested we meet I was very curious about the woman who can do everything you have."

Wariness flared at the base of her brain despite the comfort and acceptance Victoria's touch brought. "What do you mean 'the woman who can do everything you have'?"

"I don't think I could have stood up for one of my siblings in the face of my parents' wrath. It takes a certain amount of balls."

The same term for such disparate qualities started a quiver in her gut. Diana laughed hard and loud before she sat again. "And here I thought you had the balls for leaving your hair *au naturel*."

"Oh, yes." Victoria made a show of flipping her silver locks. "I'm such the rebel." Her mocking look became thoughtful. "Do you mind if I ask a more personal question?"

Another spike of wariness. Had Steve done that much of a number on her that she couldn't trust anybody? No, her reticence started long before Steve came into her life. Diana gave a half-smile to take the sting out of her next words. "As long as you don't mind if I choose not to answer it."

"Fair enough. How'd did you manage to take care of yourself and Steffi? She said you were both underage. To be on the streets—"

"And a couple of black girls on the street can only survive by turning tricks?" Old bitterness didn't leak into her words. It gushed.

"That's not what I meant." Victoria played with an asparagus spear. "Steffi said you couldn't go to anyone else in your family. I just can't imagine not having a relative to go to for help."

Diana slid off her stool, and Victoria's eyes widened. Diana held up a finger. "I'll be right back."

She returned to the armoire next to the front door. She pulled the worn photo in its familiar slot of her purse and headed back to the kitchen.

"I learned an important lesson when I was seventeen." She handed the picture to Victoria. "Family isn't what you're born to. Family is the people who love you for you."

Diana stood next to Victoria as she scanned the photo. She blinked away the threatening wetness in her eyes that came every time she looked at this damn picture. The last time she had been truly happy. She pointed to each person. "This is LaShaun Wayne. She was our cheerleading coach in high school. This is her daughter Taneka. Her husband Butch took this photo the day we won the state competition. Except for Micki's mom—" She pointed to Micki's smiling face. "— LaShaun was the closest thing the rest of us had to a mother figure."

"The week—" Emotion lodged in her throat, and she swallowed hard. "The week after Butch took this picture. Mom caught Steffi kissing her girlfriend Crystal at the mall. She dragged Steffi home and started hitting her. I tried to stop her, and . . ."

Victoria reached over and squeezed her hand. "It's okay. You don't have to—"

"No, you need to understand. We were lucky. We had people who gave a shit about us. LaShaun and Butch would have taken us in a heartbeat, but they already had six kids and a granddaughter under their roof."

"So you went to Micki's."

"Yeah, Micki's brother was at West Point, so her parents let Steffi and me have his room. Then the Donovans and the Waynes sat down with me and put together a plan to keep Steffi and me in school." She chuckled. "Butch and Major Donovan treated the whole situation like it was one of their special ops missions."

Victoria smiled. "I wouldn't say you were lucky. I would say you were blessed."

Diana closed her eyes. She'd never told anybody about what happened that night. At least, anybody not directly involved. And she'd never told Steve the story. So what was the difference?

The answer was simple. Victoria's touch felt so right that she wanted to believe in good things again.

She gave her head a little shake and opened her eyes. "No, my bad luck just spread around my friends." She pointed to the redhead next to her in the picture. "Alicia's dad died in a car accident a month later."

"Things happen," Victoria murmured.

Another bitter laugh rippled out of Diana. "Oh, it got better." Her index finger slid to the next girl. "The quarterback raped Beth at our junior prom. Micki nearly ended up in prison for beating the shit out of that asshole. Our principal tried to cover up everything. LaShaun and all of us on the cheerleading squad quit in protest. Taneka nearly died of spinal meningitis the fall of our senior year." Her finger moved to the girl with the bright grin kneeling next to Taneka in the picture. "Sarah was killed in a boating accident over Spring Break a few months later." She stared at the happy faces in the picture. "It still amazes me how fast everything went to shit."

Victoria touched the edge of the picture. "You said they are family?"

"Yeah. We don't see Taneka as much these days. She and her husband live in California. But Alicia, Micki, Beth and I get together for lunch once a month. And Steffi, Kat and I go to the Donovans for the holidays."

"Then yes, I still say you are blessed." Victoria handed the photo back to Diana, her hand lingering a moment. "Let's finish our dinner before it's too cold."

By unspoken agreement, the conversation for the rest of the meal stuck to local gossip and speculation over the Supreme Court's decisions on remaining cases before they broke for the year. Diana found Victoria interesting and amusing. She was nimble enough to argue any side of a dispute, and she often made insightful and rather snarky comments about both political parties. When she suggested they move to the living room, Diana snatched the bottle of wine and her glass before following Victoria.

She lit a fire, then sat next to Diana on the loveseat. Their knees touched when Victoria held out her own glass for a refill. Once the wine was poured, she made no effort to move away.

Again, that brilliant smile made something inside Diana quiver with need. Victoria took a sip before she said, "What made you call me?" She leaned closer. "And what took you so long?"

Diana laughed. "Honestly, I used apartment hunting as an excuse for not calling you all weekend. As for why I called today, I . . . needed a break from my routine before I drove myself crazy."

Victoria propped her elbow on the back of the loveseat and leaned her head against her fist. "What are you expecting from us?"

"Nothing you're not willing to give," Diana said, her voice quiet. "Kat said you expect discretion. I'd appreciate the same."

"What else did Kat tell you?"

"That was it." She lowered her eyes for an instant before she met Victoria's intense gaze. "Other than we may share some interests. I've never confided certain . . . desires to her. I swear the woman is psychic."

"She is very good at knowing what her partner needs, and she isn't a bit shy in telling you what she wants. The question is what do you want? Do you know what you are?"

Diana snorted. "I'm a bisexual, and I like—no, I love being dominated. And yet . . ."

"And yet?"

"And yet, I'm an African-American woman. I look around this place and realize it was built on the backs of slavery."

Victoria didn't acknowledge the statement, which in itself meant she knew this house's history. "Except to you, submission is a game, and you're ashamed of your needs. That when you're done playing, you can go home and live your life."

Her comment struck home. Diana played with the stem of her wine glass. "My biggest problem." She chuckled, irony thick in her throat. "How do I reconcile my needs with the history of this country? My race?"

"I don't know." Victoria's silver hair shifted and sparked as she shook her head. She set her glass on the trunk she used as a coffee table and took Diana's free hand in both of hers. "All I can tell you is that I like you. I'm attracted to you. And I'd love it if you spent the night with me."

Acceptance lay on the tip of her tongue. But as horny as she was, she'd only known this woman for a couple of hours. Her practical side seized the first excuse it could find. "What about your husband?"

"Merrick knows you're here." Victoria trailed her fingertips along Diana's forearm. Her skin prickled under the feathery touch. "He also knows I planned on seducing you tonight if I decided I liked you. He'll be back on Friday if you'd rather have him join us."

Diana had to give Victoria credit. No one, male or female, had ever stated so boldly exactly what they wanted from her. That very forwardness flamed her desire. "No. I don't want to wait."

"Tell me what you like." Victoria's hip and thigh touched Diana's now without her seeming to move. "With a woman." Victoria's fingers played with the short hair at the nape of Diana's neck while her other hand rested on Diana's knee.

She sucked in a deep breath as she sat her wine glass on the trunk. No one had ever asked what she wanted. Not even Beth, but then what did either of them really know at twenty.

"Bondage?" Victoria prompted.

"I tied up a woman I was seeing once," Diana blurted.

"So you prefer to be the bottom only with men?"

"No." Diana's laugh sounded self-conscious to her own ears. "That's part of the reason it didn't work out. I like to play, but her needs were a little more hardcore. And I was . . . an experiment after she'd been raped."

Victoria's breath warmed her cheek. "Your friend Beth?"

Diana nodded. "She attended college up in Vermont. I went to see her one weekend, and . . . I think we were both lonely. It only lasted a year. We're still friends, but she wanted me to do things that . . . made me uncomfortable."

"Spanking?"

"Whipping. Using toys to hurt her." Diana sighed. "I think she was unconsciously looking for a dom even as a kid. I just wasn't what she needed."

"And if someone is doing those things to you?" Victoria's lips were millimeters from hers.

"That's different," she breathed.

The kiss shouldn't have caught her by surprise, but for some reason, it did. Maybe because the touch was so gentle and enticing, not at all like Steve's demanding ones. Victoria tasted of wine and the spices from the crab cakes.

The light touch of her tongue along Diana's bottom lip was a request. Her mouth opened, and the kiss turned from exploration to torrid desire. Her arms wrapped around Victoria's neck as she pressed Diana against the pillows of the loveseat. She couldn't remember someone kissing her so slowly, so thoroughly, for so long.

Victoria finally broke the contact, and a soft sound of protest rose in Diana's throat. "Would you like to see our playroom?"

She nodded, not trusting her voice.

Victoria sat up, her nipples budding under her tee. Good to know that kiss affected her as much as it did Diana. She rose and held out her hand.

Diana wrapped her fingers around Victoria's and stood as well. She followed Victoria up the narrow staircase and down the hallway to the back of the house.

Victoria released her long enough to fish a key from her pocket. "Officially, this is my office, and I don't want anyone messing with my research." She grinned. "It saves other people's conservative sensibilities."

"Does Consuela know?"

Victoria laughed. "Oh, hell, no! The poor woman would have a heart attack. She chides me for not dropping my career and raising children like a proper woman."

"I hope you're not that proper."

"Definitely not now."

Another kiss. This time Diana didn't hesitate. Her lips parted and her tongue met Victoria's. Teasing and tasting.

Once again, they pulled apart, both of them breathing hard. Victoria smiled. "Our safeword for tonight shall be 'pineapple.'"

"Pineapple," Diana repeated. *If there would be a good time to leave, this is it.* Her body ignored her brain. It wanted more of Victoria's mouth, her touch, her laughter.

Victoria opened the door.

Diana gasped at the room. The four-poster bed dominated the space, custom-built mahogany from the sheer size of it. A little step stool stood near the foot, a necessity since the mattress was nearly waist-high. With a start, she realized the height would be perfect for a standing man to fuck someone lying on the bed.

The burgundy and gold wallpaper would have looked garish any place else. Here, it accented the black velvet bedspread. Matching black and burgundy pillows were artistically arranged at the head.

She followed Victoria inside. On the right, two racks on the wall held various equipment. Large feathers. Whips. Paddles. Handcuffs. She stepped closer to the display. A few items she was embarrassed to admit she couldn't identify. A chair with wood and upholstery to compliment the bed sat in the corner.

To the left, a gorgeous antique boudoir rested. Diana had no doubt more accessories lay in the drawers.

"What—" The surety she felt moments ago fled when she faced Victoria. She swallowed the lump of nerves. "What did you have in mind?"

"Let's start with something simple. Would you let me tie you up?"

"What else?"

"Oh, Diana," Victoria whispered. She moved closer, so close Diana could feel the heat radiating from her, but Victoria didn't touch her. "You need, you deserve some pleasure in your life. I'd like to give you that pleasure. If you'll let me."

Damn. Diana closed her eyes. "Kat told you about Steve." The last thing she wanted was a pity fuck.

A hot palm cupped her cheek. "Darling, trust me. No one who kisses like you is anything but a vital, sensual woman. I'd like to take care of you tonight. That's all."

Diana opened her eyes at the raw honesty in Victoria's voice. "Tying me up is fine, but no accessories."

A devious gleam shone in Victoria's eyes. "Maybe a feather or two?"

Laughter burbled out of Diana at the expression on Victoria's face. "All right. A feather or two."

"Good," Victoria stepped closer. She reached for Diana's blouse and undid each fake pearl button. No rushing, like they had all the time in the universe tonight.

Diana reached for the zipper on her skirt, but Victoria intercepted her hands. "No. Let me."

A shiver rippled through Diana. Victoria was so different from any other lover she'd experienced. No one ever wanted to take care of her to this degree.

Victoria brushed the blouse from Diana's shoulders and laid it on the chair. Light kisses danced across her neck as Victoria unzipped her pencil skirt and eased it over her hips.

A small sound of delighted surprise came from Victoria, and she ran fingertips around the lace edge of Diana's thigh-high stockings. "It's such a pleasure to see a woman dress properly."

Diana chuckled while she stepped out of her skirt. "It's been too damn humid to wear anything more."

Once again, Victoria neatly folded the material and laid it on the chair. "You're making me feel so underdressed."

Desire lay thick on Diana's tongue. "Will it matter when we're naked?"

Instead of answering, Victoria stepped behind her. A *click* and Victoria slid the white lace bra from Diana's shoulders.

Her breasts ached from the rush of blood. Victoria's pale hands covered her nipples, molded the flesh. Her touch felt so good. Could someone explode from feeling pleasure? The gentleness made Diana realize how much she had been missing with Steve.

She whimpered when Victoria tugged the hard tips. No, Steve never paid this much attention to her body. Victoria's hands released her breasts and glided over her stomach.

Diana sucked in a sharp breath as Victoria toyed with her panties. "Please . . ."

"Please, what?" The words caressed her ear.

"Please, touch me."

Victoria cupped her panty-covered mound. "Like this."

"No." The need almost made Diana want to cry. It'd been too damn long since she had been touched. "I don't want anything between us."

Victoria's fingers slipped inside the white lace. Diana's knees shook as Victoria explored her open folds, the liquid slickness of her pussy. With her other hand, Victoria rolled the tight bud between her thumb and index finger. Diana thrust her hips against the hand inside her panties.

A low throaty chuckle in her ear. "Not just yet, my dear." The sudden disappearance of Victoria's touch from her body left her off kilter. "Take off your panties and shoes, then lay on the bed."

"What about my stockings?"

"Leave them on."

There was no question of obeying. Diana wiggled out of her underwear. She followed Victoria's example, folded them and laid them on top of her clothing. The shoes she slipped under the chair.

Thick burgundy carpet cushioned her stocking-covered soles, but climbing the steps to the mattress proved to be a little more difficult. Her foot slipped on the varnished wood, and she landed in an awkward heap on the bedspread. Adding to her humiliation, Victoria simply stood there, no expression on her aristocratic features.

When Diana settled on her back, Victoria said, "Spread eagle, dear."

Once her limbs were stretched out, Victoria approached and opened a secret compartment in the left post at the head of the bed. She unrolled a length of black leather and fastened the cuff at the end around Diana's wrist by the means of two small gold buckles. Matching velvet lined the leather. Diana gave an experimental tug. Definitely secure. Her body trembled at the familiar mix of fear and sexual excitement.

Within a minute, Victoria repeated the process for Diana's ankles and her other wrist. Once she was done, she stripped off her own clothing.

Victoria had a dancer's build. Long, lithe, and fine-boned. Her breasts firm and high despite the decade-long age difference.

She strode to the rack and contemplated the array. Her fingertips drifted along a polished wooden paddle and lingered on a particularly wicked-looking black leather whip.

A jolt of panic shot through Diana's nerves. Would Victoria go back on her word? Was she the type of domme who enjoyed pushing her sub too far?

Diana shivered. One bad experience had been enough. She'd trusted Kat's analysis of Victoria. Depended on it. She swallowed her fear. No, Kat wouldn't put her in danger.

Skin on the back of her neck prickled. In dealing with her looming panic, she hadn't realized Victoria had been watching her. Victoria examined her for another long moment. A knowing smile curved her lips. She selected a huge ostrich tail feather, dyed the same deep burgundy color as the wallpaper and carpet.

A test. Nothing but a test. The realization didn't help Diana relax one bit.

Victoria approached the bed in an elegant glide. "Do you know why we're starting with only pleasure?"

"No," Diana whispered. Was this another test?

"If the sub doesn't understand the pleasure, has only experienced the pain, there's no way for the connection to be made."

The feather caressed her cheek, and she closed her eyes, listening to Victoria's crystal voice.

"I think you have experienced more than enough pain. In some ways, too much so. It makes my role as a domme that much more difficult."

Soft strokes covered her forehead, her eyelids, her neck. Not even Beth had been this gentle with her.

"Who was the dominant who hurt you, Diana?"

The words stabbed into her soul. She didn't want to talk about this. Not now. Not with Victoria.

"Was it Beth?" When she didn't answer, Victoria said, "Steve, perhaps?"

A sharp bark of laughter erupted from Diana. "Oh, hell, no." The bed shifted underneath her, and the feather traveled up her right arm.

"Your experience with us will be much more uncomfortable if we don't remove the . . . deadweight, as it were." The feather drifted down her arm, across the delicate dip at the base of her neck and up the other arm.

Her throat constricted. Talking about Jack, even thinking about him, dredged old humiliation. And not the good kind.

The feather paused. "Diana, open your eyes and look at me."

She didn't want to, fought the urge to obey. But in the end, her lids blinked, and she was caught in Victoria's intense gaze.

"You don't have to tell me the person's name if you don't want to, but I need to know what happened so I don't hit any of your triggers."

"He—" Diana tried to swallow past the lump, but her mouth was so damn dry. "I said the safeword."

A long pause followed. Sadness lay in Victoria's eyes. "Oh, dear." She set the feather on the small stand next to the bed. Her lips found Diana's. They didn't taste of sympathy, but of comfort.

Victoria rolled on top of her without breaking the kiss. Her body yielded to Victoria's slight weight. Hands stroked, offering acceptance, soothing her anxiety over the memory of Jack. Diana wanted to reciprocate, wanted to run her fingers along Victoria's back, wanted to wrap her legs around the woman kissing her senseless, but the bonds wouldn't allow it.

A tear leaked from her lids despite her efforts. Victoria brushed away the wetness. "Shhhh, dear, that was then. This is now, and as I said, now is only for pleasure."

Another kiss. Victoria coaxed her mouth open, tasting and teasing. That kiss chased everything away. Betrayal. Loneliness. Grief.

Victoria's lips left hers, nibbling along her throat. The tantalizing trail raised goose bumps, and she shivered. Victoria shifted her weight and surrounded a ripe nipple with her mouth. She sucked and bit until a low moan started deep in Diana's chest.

Switching to the other breast, Victoria continued her sensual assault. Diana arched her back, strained against the straps, offering more.

Victoria lifted her head, a wicked smirk on her face. "That's better, isn't it?" She reached for the ostrich feather before she shifted to kneel between Diana's thighs.

Diana quivered at the wait. Liquid pooled in her wide-open pussy. Surely, Victoria couldn't miss the effect, but she couldn't demand that Victoria continue no matter how bad her clit ached. That wasn't how things worked.

The feather drifted over the damp, straining nipples. It brushed the underside of her breasts, and she twitched.

Victoria knelt there like a cat toying with her mouse. Watched every reaction as she stroked Diana's ribs with the feather.

A giggle burst out of Diana's mouth when Victoria hit the ticklish spot at her waist. The laughter switched to a moan as the feather caressed her inner thighs. Another giggle at the knee. More goose bumps along the calves.

Diana knew what was coming, tried to steel herself. When the feather hit her soles, she screamed. The damn stockings seemed to amplify the electric sensation instead of dulling it. She jerked and thrashed against the restraints, but her nerves sizzled and sparked. Pain, she could handle, but someone tickling her feet was too much overload.

"Pineapple!" she shrieked. "Pineapple!"

Victoria pulled the feather away from her feet and trailed it back up Diana's leg. Thank god, this was a woman who could stop. A feather was a small thing in a domme's arsenal, but listening to her sub's safeword laid a tiny block of trust.

Diana sucked in oxygen, tried to catch her breath while Victoria set the feather aside. She stretched out between Diana's legs.

The first touch of her tongue on Diana's pussy nearly sent her through the ceiling. The second made her cry out. By the third sweep, her hips thrust of their own accord.

Victoria's lips closed around her clit, sucking lightly before her tongue flicked the tiny bundle of nerves. Diana could feel the tension building in her pussy, her muscles. It was too soon. While she loved a woman eating her out, this time was different. All her disappointment and anger gathered amid the lust, ready to be expelled.

The exquisite flicking stopped. She couldn't prevent her tiny mewl of protest. Victoria swept her tongue over Diana in a languid motion.

At the slightest pressure on her clit, Diana exploded. Her body jerked as waves of ecstasy enveloped her. Even with her body convulsing, Victoria didn't stop. Long, leisurely licks that refused to let the blissful contractions of her pussy fade.

Finally, Victoria halted, crawled up beside Diana, stretched out on the bed. "That was a delightful beginning." Her arm encircled Diana's waist as she nuzzled her neck. "I can't wait to call Merrick."

"Call Merrick?" The post-orgasm endorphins muddled Diana's thinking.

"Yes. I need to call him in a few minutes."

Chapter Three

"So, I'm just the appetizer?" Confusion reigned inside Diana. Should she be amused or annoyed at Victoria's tactics?

"Don't look so appalled, dear." Victoria toyed with Diana's nipple, tweaking the tip until it hardened again. "Half the fun of my trysts is narrating the encounter over the phone to Merrick." She chuckled. "Blow-by-blow so to speak."

"You're going to kick me to the curb while you have phone sex with your husband?" Diana closed her eyes. How could she have been so wrong? Again?

"I'm not kicking you anywhere," came the throaty reply. "I hadn't planned on releasing you at all."

Diana's eye's popped open. "What?"

"I planned on video conferencing so he can watch me fuck you again."

The little block of trust exploded. Words clogged in the back of her throat. It took a couple of tries to force them out. "Y-you said discretion."

Victoria arched an eyebrow. "Surely you didn't think Merrick wouldn't join us at some point?"

"Yes, but in person! Not recording us."

Victoria leaned forward and covered the nipple she'd tweaked with her lips. The suckling threatened to derail Diana's train of thought.

"You're not distracting me, dammit! I am not ending up on some internet porn site."

Victoria nipped the tight, hard nub, and Diana cried out. Air cooled the damp skin when Victoria released her. "We're not recording anything."

"You agreed no accessories this time."

"You didn't say no one could watch us. And Merrick is *not* an accessory." A wicked smile appeared on Victoria's face. "Unless you were lying about being bi-sexual. Then I would agree a man could be classed as an accessory."

Shit. Stupid, stupid, stupid.

Victoria stroked Diana's inner thigh. The sensual caress threatened to overwhelm her anger. And yet, the idea of someone watching her being taken and used sent tremors of excitement through her.

Diana clenched her fists. Dammit, she wasn't lying to Victoria. She was lying to herself. Again. About what she wanted. What really turned her on. She might as well be back in Steve's bed, faking it.

"I'm sorry," she whispered. "It's just that . . . I'm scared."

Understanding shone in Victoria's eyes. Her fingers shifted downward, drawing idle circles around Diana's clit. "You've never had a decent dominant put you through your paces before, have you?"

The restraints thwarted the urge to squeeze her legs together. She shook her head.

Victoria kissed her nose. "I'd be honored if you'd trust us enough to train you properly in the bedroom. Steve and that other idiot really screwed up, and you'd be the most beautiful sub with the right enticement. But if you don't feel you can, then it's best if we stop now."

A different kind of terror gripped Diana. Not fear of being alone, but of never finding someone who understood her. Who accepted her needs and acted upon them without judging.

"Please, no." She sucked in a deep breath. "I don't want to stop. Not now."

"All right then." Victoria slid off the mattress. "I'm going to get my phone. I'll be right back."

It wasn't the fear that threatened to consume Diana while Victoria was gone. It was the boredom. And the need to touch herself. To relieve the tension Victoria had aroused. Diana grimaced. She'd never been this horny again in so little time after such a powerful orgasm.

Victoria strode through the doorway, a smart phone in her hand. The phone jingled as she settled on the mattress.

Diana never had a third party watch her before. Her anxiety spiced the arousal Victoria had already engendered.

"Hello, love." She touched an icon and held the phone in front of her face. "Are you receiving us?"

"Yes." A deep, masculine voice issued from the phone's speaker.

Victoria shifted so Diana could see the picture on the screen. Merrick Davis had that indescribable look of most men between thirty and fifty, a sense of maturity but with an amused twinkle in his gray eyes. He cut his dark brown hair very conservatively, but it was tousled. He still wore a red tie, but the knot had been loosened. Behind him, she could make out the edge of a headboard. He could be in any decent hotel room in the country.

Victoria held the phone so its camera would pick up both women. "Merrick, this is Diana. Diana, Merrick."

Diana licked her lips. "A pleasure to meet you."

He chuckled. "I see Victoria has already extended an invitation to you."

"Yes." Diana smiled, but the expression felt foreign. At least, she'd been clothed when she met Victoria. And she couldn't cover herself if she wanted to, not bound like she was.

"Victoria, I'd like to see the rest of her."

Diana tugged at the restraints. Was it possible to die of embarrassment? This was far worse than the time Alicia accidentally stripped off her blouse while removing her sweater during a pep rally. And *her* privates had been covered.

The phone drifted over Diana's shoulders, her breasts, before Victoria paused over the apex of her thighs.

An exhalation hummed through the speaker. "Such a pretty little cunt. It's nice to see a woman with a proper triangle. I'm sorry I'm not there to touch it. Is her ass as adorable?"

"Oh, yes," Victoria breathed. "More than adequate for you to grab as you plunge into her."

Diana's jaw dropped. She wasn't sure if she should be insulted that they were discussing her as if she were an object. Except her hips twitched at the realization they were discussing what they would be doing to her this weekend.

If she came back to the Georgetown home once Merrick returned.

Oh, hell, who was she kidding? Victoria Butler had already licked her pussy into submission. Her internal muscle spasmed in anticipation of a repeat performance.

Merrick chuckled. "If I didn't know you better, Victoria, I'd say you deliberately found someone who was your physical opposite."

With a start, Diana realized he was very close to the truth. Victoria's skin was milk compared to her dark cocoa. She wore her hair in a straight, modified pixie cut while Victoria's hung well past her shoulders. She worked out regularly, but still had pretty generous curves next to her hostess.

Victoria laughed. "All I really wanted was some pussy." She crawled on her knees to the nearest post at the foot of the bed. She connected the smart phone's case to a set of hooks.

Diana stared at the phone's camera. *I guess they aren't just for additional restraints.*

Victoria crawled back to her on her hands and knees, deliberately creating a show of her ass for her husband before sitting next to Diana. "How's the view?'

"Wonderful, my dear. Will you be whipping her tonight?"

Victoria cupped one of Diana's breasts, her thumb massaging the already hard nipple until Diana gasped. "No, Merrick. I told you how cruel her previous lover was. She'll need some gentle training at first."

"Spanking with the flat of my palm this weekend maybe?"

Diana felt Victoria's gaze on her and looked up.

"What do you think, dear? Would you feel up to a good spanking on that gorgeous ass of yours by Friday?" Victoria's eyes twinkled as if she found this whole discussion rather amusing.

"I, uh—" Dread dried Diana's throat. Yet, every ounce of liquid in her body rushed to her pussy at the thought of Merrick and Victoria punishing her. "Yes, please," she finished in a whisper.

"Good girl." Victoria release Diana's nipple and patted her on the arm.

She turned serious. "I know you said no accessories, but the next thing I'll do to you requires a bit of lubricant and a rubber glove for you to enjoy it properly."

Diana wiggled her hips. "Are you sure I need lube?"

Victoria laughed at her lame joke before her eyes widened and her hand flew to her mouth. "Oh, dear! I forgot to ask you about your allergies."

Diana couldn't help grinning at Victoria's mortification. "It's okay. I don't have allergies to latex or anything else." Her ass muscles clenched. She had a suspicion Victoria knew far more about anal play than Steve pretended to know the one time he tried.

"I really wish you would let Victoria play with toys." The mellow voice from the speaker made them both jump.

Victoria glared at the phone hanging from the post. "She's relaxing her rule on accessories. Don't rush her."

Relief flooded through Diana. Victoria would stick to the rules agreed upon before play began. Merrick would be the one to push her. Knowledge of the terms of a play scene was a little comforting.

Once again, Victoria slid from the bed. She crossed to the bureau and rummaged through the top drawer. She trotted back with a bottle of thick lube and a latex glove that she quickly donned. She must have been conscious of the camera angle because she knelt on the opposite side from the post where the camera hung.

Diana took a deep, calming breath. Damn, anticipation and Victoria's teasing already had her body on the edge. Having someone to play with who had a clue was freeing in so many ways.

Victoria squeezed a dollop of lube on her gloved fingers. She rubbed them together for a minute to spread the clear gel and smiled. "Ready?"

Despite Victoria's attempt to wait and warm the gel through body heat, cool liquid touched Diana's puckered hole. She squealed at the sensation.

"Oops." Victoria didn't look a bit sorry though.

Gentle pressure of a finger at the opening felt a little odd. The ring of muscle gave with a slight *pop* sensation. She tensed.

"Relax, dear. Let me do the work."

Diana nodded at the quiet assurance. She tried to keep still as Victoria eased the finger into her ass. The problem was her body had other ideas. Her hips shimmied, wanting more inside.

The same cool wetness drew a lazy circle around her clit. She closed her eyes, rocking to Victoria's slow, even rhythm as her domme finger-fucked her ass.

Her domme. Somehow, that thought reinforced her decision to come here tonight.

A warm, wet finger slipped into her pussy. Her hips bucked, and a soft cry of pleasure tore from her throat.

Victoria picked up the pace. Diana's muscles tightened as the erotic current built along her nerves. *Almost th—*

The hand playing with her stopped. Victoria's touch disappeared. Diana's body danced on the edge of the cliff, but instead of falling over it, her flesh paused. Her eyes snapped open.

Victoria sat on her heels, a Cheshire-like smile on her aristocratic face. "Eager little vixen, aren't we?"

Merrick chuckled. "Now, that's just evil, even by my book. Really, Victoria. The poor girl was about to come."

Diana blinked. She'd totally forgotten he was at the other end of the video conference. Had that been the point of using the phone, to acclimate her to someone watching her without the pressure of him in the room?

Victoria simply looked at Diana as if she expected some kind of reaction. Was this another test?

Diana wetted her lips, unsure of how to play this. "Did I do something wrong?"

"How do you ask for something, dear?" Victoria's eyes glittered, a teacher expecting her prized student to give her the correct answer.

"Please let me come."

Victoria's right eyebrow rose.

"Please let me come, ma'am."

A smile curved Victoria's lips. "Yes, you may."

She started all over again with Diana's ass, but this time it didn't resist Victoria's finger sliding inside. The slow circles of Victoria's thumb around her clit ignited the fire again. Another finger plunged into her pussy and stroked the sensitive bundle of nerves along the wall.

Victoria hadn't even reached the same speed as before. The orgasm took Diana hard, fast. She screamed as her body convulsed around Victoria's hand. Never had a second orgasm the same night been more intense than the first.

Diana struggled to catch her breath as aftershocks rippled through her muscles. Victoria bent over her, kissed her lips, her nose, her eyelids.

A loud groan issued from the phone. Merrick's release triggered a round of giggles between the two women. Maybe they sounded like perverse schoolgirls, but Diana didn't care. She hadn't felt this boneless, this relaxed, since . . . well, never.

She looked into Victoria's eyes. "You haven't—" A tiny wave of embarrassment filled her at her selfishness.

Victoria cupped her cheek with her bare hand. "I told you this was for you."

"I—" Diana swallowed the guilt. "I want to give back to you."

"Oh, you will." Merrick chuckled through the phone's speaker. "On Friday."

Victoria's lips tilted in a sly smile that had anticipation for the weekend racing through Diana's blood.

The next morning over coffee and croissants, Diana finally developed the nerve to ask a question that had been plaguing her since Kat first gave her Victoria's number. "Do you . . . have you and Merrick ever played with another man?"

Victoria smiled, a knowing, wicked one. "Just one. Daniel, an old friend of Merrick's. He's—" Her grin became even more devilish. "He's one of those people you have to experience to appreciate."

"Do you two still see him?"

Victoria sighed. "Not *see* him. Not since he got married. He followed his wife to a job in New York. The bitch left him for her boss." Disgust filled her voice. "He didn't deserve that crap. The last I heard he was trying to move back to D.C., but he wasn't sure if he could get his old job back. I really hope he does move back though."

"Oh, really." Diana had no clue of how to follow that proclamation. *This is just supposed to be a fling, remember?* She settled for picking at the last half of her croissant.

"Is two men one of your fantasies?"

Diana glanced up to find Victoria watching her over the rim of her coffee cup. Air whistled between her teeth before she nodded. For some reason, this morning was an odd mix of the comfortableness of a long-time relationship mixed with a bad case of first-time, morning-after jitters.

Victoria laid her hand over Diana's. "Honesty in this type of relationship is the best policy, dear. If there's something in particular you would like us to do, or if there's something you absolutely abhor, tell us. In fact, make a list. We'll discuss it over dinner on Friday. Set our parameters before we play."

Diana managed to swallow the dry hunk of croissant in her throat without choking. Victoria's forthright attitude was such a difference compared to her past lovers. "Sounds good."

Victoria glanced at the clock on the microwave. "Damn. I don't normally ask someone to leave this early." She shot Diana a mock lecherous expression complete with waggling eyebrows. "I'd prefer a little morning sex, but I have a pre-interview for this week's taping scheduled at nine, and I really need to review my notes."

"Of course." Diana stood, her hand sliding from under Victoria's. Now, she was officially getting kicked to the curb. A sense of relief washed through her that she didn't have to make an excuse.

"Diana?"

When she turned, Victoria grabbed her wrist and pulled Diana between her legs. "You will be here on Friday at seven p.m." Blue eyes stared at her, drilling into her soul.

It was a statement, not a question. Diana resisted the urge to grin. "Yes, ma'am."

A kiss, this one as intense as Victoria's gaze. Her hands slid down and cupped Diana's ass cheeks. Their breasts pressed together, and Diana could feel Victoria's nipples matching her own state of arousal.

She broke the kiss with an effort. Both of them panted from raw lust. Now, she didn't want to leave quite so badly, but her sense of responsibility took over. "You need to review notes, and I need to get to the office."

"Of course." Victoria favored her with on of her wicked smiles. "See you on Friday. And don't forget your overnight bag this time."

At Victoria's wink, Diana laughed and headed for the front door.

Chapter Four

The rest of Tuesday morning found Diana unable to concentrate. A vague sense of guilt kept intruding in every phone call and every review of paperwork.

Last night had been fun. If she had a change of clothes with her, she might have stayed another hour, talked Victoria into a quickie despite both their schedules.

No, that wasn't quite true. This guilty feeling would have ruined anything they did this morning.

Dammit, what is wrong with me? She stared out the window for a few minutes. The window with the lovely view of the alley between their building and the rear wall of the *Post's* offices. The view made even more lovely when a homeless man wandered into the alley to relieve himself. She turned back to her desk.

It wasn't like she'd cheated on Steve. So why did the stupid feeling nag her?

Disgusted with her own issues, she yanked yesterday's mail out of her purse. She'd grabbed it in the rush to the subway station this morning.

The cream envelope with neat black calligraphy stood out in the stack. A thrill of excitement ran through her at *Winston's* on the return address. She'd dragged Beth to the art gallery over a year ago. Then she spent an hour afterwards trying to talk Beth into arranging a show of her paintings.

Diana ripped open the flap, pulled out the card and smiled as she read it. *Good for you, Beth.*

That's when the reason for the guilt hit her. It wasn't about Steve at all.

Diana waited in the lobby of Beth's office building, resisting the urge to pace while the guard eyed her. Everyone in D.C. had gotten more security conscious since 9-11, but the civilian tech companies with DoD contracts were especially cautious. Even though Beth didn't work on any of those projects, no visitors entered the main offices without a coded card.

Diana couldn't help grinning like an idiot when Beth bounced out of the elevator, chestnut ponytail swinging.

Beth's own grin melted from embarrassed to crazy. "You got it."

"Why didn't you say something, bitch?" Diana pulled her into a hug. "I'm still buying you lunch, even if you are a rude *puta*."

During the walk to Chinatown, they talked about Beth's show.

"My work's paired with a sculptor, Paolo Ceranos. It's not like I've got the whole place to myself."

"Still, this is great. When did you talk to the owner?"

Beth stilled. The rigid posture reminded Diana too much of the scared teenager she had been that last year of high school.

"I went back the day after you and I visited."

Diana stopped on the sidewalk. "That long ago? What the hell was wrong with him?"

Beth shook her head, a hesitant expression on her face. "It was another six months before I got up the nerve to let Aaron see my paintings. And it was only a few weeks ago I finally relented and let him schedule a showing."

Diana tilted her head. "Aaron? Do I detect a little attraction to Mr. Aaron Winston?"

Beth turned on her heel and arrowed for the restaurant.

Even though Diana was three inches taller, trying to catch someone in athletic shoes while she was in heels nearly broke her ankle. She managed and grabbed Beth's arm. "Hey, I'm sorry for teasing you."

Beth paused, her attention somewhere near her toes. For a second, Diana thought she'd turn around and flee back to the glass cage that was her office.

"I'm sorry. It's—" Beth sucked in a deep breath and looked at Diana. "I'm pissed at myself for not standing up to Alicia when she started her boytoy shit at our last lunch. I'm sorry I'm taking it out on you."

"No problem. If it makes you feel better, Micki tried to kick her under the table."

"How do you know that?"

Diana grinned. "She connected with my shin instead."

They made it through sweet and sour pork and chicken lo mein before Beth said, "What's really going on?"

"Can't I want to celebrate the fact you quit hiding your talent?"

Beth reached for the fortune cookies and tossed one to Diana before she cracked hers open. "Hmm . . . Says here that Monkey plays tricks with friends." She stared at Diana over the rim of her glasses.

"No, it doesn't." But Diana could feel heat spreading through her cheeks.

Beth snickered. "Girl, if you were white, your face would be as red as Alicia's hair." She waggled her fingers. "Come on. Spill."

Crap. Beth had always been able to read her, ever since second grade. Diana took a sip of tea for reinforcement. "I met someone."

Beth was silent for a long time. "And?"

"Another woman."

"Okay, you're losing me. You like screwing both sides. What's the problem?"

"She's married."

"Oh." Beth toyed with her own cup. "And she's not willing to leave her husband, I take it?"

"It's not that." Diana stared a couple of lonely noodles on her plate. She'd promised Victoria she'd be discrete, but dammit, she needed some advice. "Her husband knows about me, and she wants him to join us."

"And?"

Diana blinked. "There's no 'and' here."

"Wow." Beth's expression was unreadable.

God, she wished she could take it all back. She shouldn't have said anything. None of her friends would ever speak to her again.

Beth broke out in laughter. "I can't believe you're *finally* letting your freaky side loose."

"I am *not* letting my freaky side loose." Diana crumbled her cookie between her fingers. "I just . . . I can't get rid of this guilty feeling. It's stupid, I know, but—"

Beth sobered so fast it was like someone had flipped a switch in her brain. "Hold it right there. You owe Steve nothing." She slashed her hand across the table. "The bastard left *you.*"

"I feel like I'm betraying you."

The deep breath Beth took to continue her tirade escaped so fast the candle on their table danced wildly. "Me? I thought we settled things between us years ago."

Her eyes widened and she leaned back in her chair. "Are you trying to say you're *in love* with me?"

Diana's blood froze. "No! Oh, God, no."

Beth rolled her eyes. "You didn't have to blurt out the disclaimer that fast."

"I mean, I do love you, I'm just not in love—" Diana buried her face in her hands. How'd this conversation turn into such a fiasco?

A soft touch on her wrist made her look up. Beth's eyes shone with concern. "Hey, I'm sorry. I was just teasing. Personally, I think it's great you've met someone. That's better than wallowing like Alicia and Micki, which you *know* is why Alicia's started this whole stupid challenge." A slim eyebrow arched over the rim of her glasses. "Or did you pick up this lady in a bar *because of* Alicia's bullshit?"

Beth's disgusted expression drew a laugh from Diana. "Actually, this whole thing happened because I told Kat and Steffi the real deal with Hank over dinner Friday night. Next thing I know, Steffi's in the john and Kat's handing me this woman's phone number."

"Wait a minute. You just met her?"

Diana nodded.

"And you had sex with her?"

Diana nodded again.

Beth sat back with a huff. "Now, I am insulted. How many *years* did it take before you made a move on me?"

"It's not the same thing."

Beth tried to hide her grin behind her own teacup. "So who is this woman who's got you turned upside down?"

"I can't tell you." Diana played with her napkin. "There's . . . repercussions. You know what this city's like."

After glancing around to make sure no one was paying them any attention, Beth leaned across the table. "It's not the First Lady, is it?"

Diana laughed and shook her head. "Good grief, girl. You are warped."

Beth turned serious. "So what is the problem? Are you scared about the three of you together?"

"Yeah." Bits of napkin lay around her plate. "I've never done a threesome before, much less . . ."

"Much less a scene with more than one other person." Beth blew out a breath. "Look, not everyone is as fucked up as that Jack nutcase you dated."

"But—"

"Kat wouldn't have set you up with anyone who couldn't control themselves. Did this woman do anything after you told her to stop? Ever do anything that made you feel you were in danger? I'm not talking about pushing you a little further than you wanted."

"No. In fact, she was super gentle since Kat had told her about Steve. Just a little bondage and a feather." Diana took a sip of her tea. Talking things out with Beth made her realize how stupid her fears were.

Beth's face scrunched, and her expression almost made Diana laugh again. "That's it?"

"Sorry my sex life isn't as intense as you like it."

"Wasn't casting judgment here." Beth held up her hands, then a mischievous grin lit her face. "When are you getting together with both of them?"

"Friday."

"I can't go shopping tonight, but tomorrow, I know just the place over by Du-Pont Circle."

"But—"

Beth jabbed a finger at her. "No arguing. You're going to knock their socks off this weekend."

Chapter Five

Anxiety flittered across Diana's nerves when she pressed the intercom button on Victoria and Merrick's gate. Unlike last Friday's stormy weather, the air was warmer and smelled of spring. There were also more people on the street than there had been on Monday. Did the neighbors spy out their windows, keeping track of who went in and out of the Georgetown home?

When the gate buzzed, then clicked open, she sucked in a deep breath. Or she tried to. The white satin corset may have looked terrific in the mirror, but it definitely restricted certain body movements. Even though her flowing, floral-patterned dress covered everything, the lack of panties made her feel distinctly naked.

This time, Victoria greeted her at the door instead of the housekeeper. That small action made Diana feel marginally less nervous until Merrick walked up behind Victoria.

A slight smile curved his lips. "Hello, Diana." His gaze raked across her form, no doubt remembering exactly how she looked naked.

Tall, imposing, altogether masculine. He wore gray trousers and a pale blue button-down shirt. But even with the sleeves rolled up and the throat open, she could see how he could dominate a courtroom. Or a bedroom.

She wiped her damp palm before taking his proffered hand. "A pleasure to meet you in person."

"Yes. It will be."

"Merrick." Victoria jabbed him in the ribs with her elbow. "Behave."

"Don't I always, my love?" He winked at Diana.

Victoria laughed. "You're impossible. Go finish dinner while I take Diana up to the guest room." She threaded her arm through Diana's free one and tugged her toward the staircase.

Instead of taking Diana to the playroom as she half-expected, Victoria guided her in the opposite direction. If the playroom was decorated like a tasteful brothel, then this room could have been an ad for a bed-and-breakfast. Lavender walls matched the floral-patterned comforter on the bed, which was a normal queen-sized four-poster. White lace curtains covered old-fashioned pull blinds. A huge maple chest, a Shaker-style chair and nightstand matched the bed.

A twinge of disappointment hit Diana as she set her overnight case on the mattress. "We won't be sleeping together?"

Victoria's eyes did a slow blink. "Of course. But you'll need some downtime this weekend, dear. Personal space to recover. The first time with Merrick can be . . . intense for a new sub."

Shivers rippled across Diana's skin. Exactly what was she getting herself into?

In a flash, Victoria crossed the space between them. The soft touch of her lips released some of Diana's pent up anxiety.

When they parted, Diana leaned her forehead against Victoria's. "I'm sorry. It's been a . . . long time."

"Since you had a man or been in this kind of relationship?"

"Yes."

They both laughed.

"I promise I won't let him get carried away, but you must promise me to use the safeword if things get too uncomfortable for you."

"Cross my heart." Diana made the appropriate gesture over her chest.

Glee shone in Victoria's eyes. "Now I want a sneak peek at the corset you're wearing."

Of course, she felt the stays when she hugged me. Diana quickly undid the buttons before she lifted her dress up and over her head. It landed on top of her case.

Victoria dropped to her knees in front of Diana. A thin thread of discomfort trailed through her. A mistress shouldn't kneel before a sub. Granted they hadn't officially started their scene, but still . . .

That little thread was chopped to bits when Victoria first ran the pad of her thumb, then tongue, across Diana's slick, open pussy. She had to place her palms on Victoria's shoulders to stay upright. Fingers entered her soaked passage, and she had to clench her jaw muscles to keep from crying out as Victoria played with her.

"Oh, damn." Victoria placed a light kiss on Diana's clit. "Merrick will be pissed at me if we start without him. I already chastised him about playing with subs when they needed time to recover." Victoria brushed her fingers over Diana's slit. "But you are just so damn delectable."

She rose and gave Diana an impish grin. "I love the outfit, but you'd better put your dress back on before we go downstairs." She trailed her fingers down the garters and across the tops of Diana's stockings. "Else we'll never get through dinner, and I want you to have plenty of energy for tonight."

Diana pulled her dress back on, but Victoria closed the distance between them. She brushed Diana's hands away and fastened the buttons, a tantalizing reversal of how she undressed Diana Monday night. Just the memory of being tied to the playroom bed sent a shiver of anticipation through Diana.

"Soon." Victoria's eyes sparkled, and she stroked Diana's cheek. For an instant, Diana was sure Victoria would kiss her again. If she did, neither of them would leave the little bedroom until they both came.

Instead, Victoria pivoted on her heel and headed for the door. Diana swallowed her disappointment and followed.

Over a dinner of filet mignon, steamed green beans and fresh bread, Merrick and Victoria peppered Diana with questions. What she liked in a scene. What she didn't like. Her fears. Her hard limits. Things she'd like to try.

But when they asked about her last dom, she froze.

Victoria's hand slid over Diana's and squeezed. "Like I said the other night, it's best we know so we don't hit any triggers. We want this to be as satisfying for you as it is for us."

Diana swallowed hard and stared at her plate. "I was stupid. I should have paid more attention to how he was acting before the scene. He wanted me to deep throat him. I've got a hair-trigger gag reflex. When I started to choke, he decided he wanted anal sex." She looked up. "With no lube. Then he ignored the safe-word."

Anger crackled like lightning in Victoria's eyes. However, Merrick's face was a mask. "He raped you," he said. The coldness in his voice was worse than the fury in Victoria's expression. Tension rippled through the kitchen.

The wall of stone Diana had built around the incident cracked. *Rape.* For the last several years, she blamed herself for not being more careful, but what the bastard did was no different from what had happened to Beth in high school.

"What about your fiancé?" Merrick's voice was surprisingly gentle, coaxing the truth past her pain.

"Steve is as vanilla as you can get." She smiled at the description. Steve would have a royal fit if he ever heard her call him "vanilla." But then race was never a chip on his shoulder. It had been and always would be a boulder.

Diana cleared her throat. "I think that's why I chose him after Jack. Except I lied to myself about what I really wanted and needed. I let a bad experience color my decisions. I can't blame Steve for leaving. Things between us weren't working."

Victoria's eyes narrowed. "Steffi said he snuck out while you were at work and left a note."

Diana met her stare. "Oh, I blame him for being a candy-assed wuss, but not for our relationship crashing."

Merrick laughed, and the tension in the room shattered. He raised his glass. "May you find your fulfillment, madam."

Once they all clinked their glasses, Diana took a healthy sip of wine. "Do you mind if I ask you two a very personal question?"

Merrick gestured for her to continue.

"How did you two end up together? Everyone I know, well, the doms want . . ." The alcohol-fueled bravery faded. She wasn't sure how to say it without insulting one or both of them.

Merrick shook his head and chuckled. "Honestly, I don't understand the full-timers. I would be absolutely bored if my only conversation with a sub con-sisted of commands."

"It comes back to being honest with yourself and your partner or partners about what you really need." Victoria's elbows were propped on the table, and her chin rested on her folded hands. "For the most part, we have a conventional marriage." Her secretive smile sent a wave of desire through Diana. "But just like Merrick hates the idea of a twenty-four-seven slave, I need to be with a woman once in a while."

Diana digested the information. "But you said you two played with Merrick's friend Daniel."

Merrick snapped his fingers and turned to Victoria. "I knew there was something I meant to tell you. I got a text from him today. His request for reinstatement went through. He starts a week from Monday. I was so excited to meet Diana tonight it completely slipped my mind."

Victoria's wicked grin flashed again. "That's wonderful. Does he need help moving or finding a place down here?"

"He said it was already taken care of."

"We'll have to have him over for dinner once he's back in town." A calculating look appeared on Victoria's face as she regarded Diana.

She shivered. Would she be kicked to the curb as soon as this Daniel was back in their lives?

Something must have shown on her face. Victoria rose, stepped behind her and wrapped her arms around Diana's neck. "You are not going anywhere."

Feathery kisses brushed along her skin and sent tingles straight to her pussy.

Merrick watched her as Victoria nuzzled the delicate spot behind her ear. "As for our rules, when you enter the playroom, you are to remove all clothing except your garter, stockings and shoes if you are wearing such items. From now on, you do not wear panties or any other undergarment that would cover that beautiful pussy of yours. You will then kneel next to the chair, hands clasped behind your back and eyes down, to show us you are ready to begin."

"Tonight will be the exception on clothing." Humor and excitement laced Victoria's voice. "She dressed to please us tonight, darling. I think you will be delighted."

A frown tilted Merrick's mouth. "One exception for tonight only. Otherwise, you will be punished. Do you understand, Diana?"

"Yes, Sir." Her heart raced. And surely, Victoria felt the rapid beating too from the way she played with the low neckline of Diana's dress.

"Rule number two is that if you speak without being asked or after being told to remain silent, we will ball-gag you."

"Yes, Sir." She was having a hard time concentrating with Victoria's fingers under the fabric of her dress and caressing the curve of her breasts.

"If you are instructed to move, you will crawl on your hands and knees unless we tell you otherwise."

"Yes, Sir."

"In general, we all sleep together in the playroom after a scene. The next morning after everyone's awake, your sole responsibility in the playroom is to make the bed."

"Yes, Sir."

"The last and most important rule. No sex or games in any other room of the house except the playroom. The rest of the house, garden, garage, etc. is neutral territory. Victoria does not tolerate anyone, including me, breaking that rule."

"Yes, Sir." So far, Merrick hadn't told her anything she couldn't handle.

"Do you have any questions?"

"No, Sir."

From the way his eyes darkened, he was sporting a healthy erection under the table. "Do I still get to spank you tonight?"

Any coherent thought sizzled when Victoria's hands moved to Diana's breasts and squeezed them through the corset. Somehow, she managed to nod.

"Good." His smile was predatory, an alpha wolf letting the lamb know how much danger she was in. "The safeword is 'pumpernickel.' Shall we, ladies?"

Another shiver of trepidation hit Diana as she stood. This wasn't going to be anything like Victoria's gentle initiation earlier in the week. She could leave now if she wanted. But she was too aroused, needed a release, any kind of release, which was probably the reason Victoria toyed with her the instant Diana entered the house.

At least, she understood why Victoria stopped herself in the guest bedroom. Rule number three must be very important because Diana already knew Victoria was the type who claimed exactly what she desired.

Swallowing her anxiety, Diana followed Merrick to the playroom. Once the three of them were inside, he locked the door. At the *snick*, she jumped.

"Don't worry, little girl." He shook his head. "It's a precaution on weeknights after Consuela accidentally left a present for her granddaughter at the house one time."

Victoria's silvery laugh followed. "She nearly walked in here while we were entertaining. And I forgot to lock the door Monday night. Oops." She didn't look the least bit repentant.

A sliver of relief pierced Diana at Victoria's humor. She suspected Victoria had left the door open to make her more comfortable. If she had been with just Merrick in a locked room, every instinct would have screamed at her to leave.

Per their instructions earlier, she quickly stripped off her dress and knelt next to the chair with her fingers twined behind her back. Though she kept her head down, she peered up through her lashes.

She'd hoped the corset and the lack of panties would please Merrick as it had Victoria, but the severe expression was still plastered to his face. In fact, the couple seemed to be having a wordless conversation. His eyebrow twitched. She released a heavy sigh and said, "It would be best if it was dealt with now."

Merrick undressed, taking the time to hang his shirt and trousers in the little closet next to the bathroom door. He walked around the bed, and Diana wanted to whistle in appreciation.

Most men his age had a little extra pudge around their middle, but Merrick obviously took care of himself. Long, muscled legs meant he did some kind of endurance sport to stay in shape.

Her eyes worked their way up his thighs to take in his erection. The length of his cock would put some porn actors to shame.

The hairs on the back of her neck rose, and she realized Victoria was watching her examine Merrick. She played with a single-tail whip. At Victoria's sly half-smile, Diana quickly lowered her gaze again.

"Over here, little girl." He snapped his fingers and pointed at the floor in front of him. Diana started to climb to her feet when the whip snapped her ass. She jerked and cried out.

"On your hands and knees," Victoria said.

Heat flooded Diana's face. She wasn't sure what was worse, the condemnation in Victoria's voice or the fact that she already forgot one of their rules. The sting on her ass was nothing in comparison. When she reached Merrick, she kissed each of his feet and knelt again with her hands behind her.

When he didn't react, she released her held breath. Good. They weren't going to micromanage the scene as long as she showed proper respect.

His cock bobbed millimeters from her lips. Worry wiggled through her brain. She'd been honest about her past when they'd asked her downstairs at dinner. He said he wanted to spank her. Surely, he hadn't changed his mind.

Merrick palmed the back of her head. New terror hit her. She wanted to fight, wanted to cry. No, they wouldn't be this cruel this first time.

"Open wide for me." His voice was gentle, coaxing.

She looked up at him. "No, please don't make me—"

The thin whistle of air warned her, but the bite of the whip on her ass still drew a sound of pain from her.

Merrick's fingers threaded through her short hair, tilting her head back and guiding her to his cock. "Open wide," he repeated.

"Please, don't," she whispered. He was too damn long. She'd choke for sure. It wasn't just the gag reflex. She had been suffocating in her own vomit, and her dom didn't care.

He stared deep in her eyes. "Then you know what you need to do."

Say the safeword. Her inner voice only stated common sense. Say "pumpernickel," get dressed and walk out of this house forever. Except . . .

She would be right back in the same ugly, lonely place she had been before she called Victoria.

Diana opened her mouth. The head of his cock brushed past her lips and withdrew.

"Good girl." Victoria's soft encouragement helped.

Merrick pushed a little farther the second time. Diana flicked her tongue around the tip. The slightly salty pre-come met her taste buds. Again, he withdrew.

Victoria knelt behind Diana and straddled her calves, one hand on Diana's wrists, the other cupping her mound. "Tilt your head back and relax your throat, dear."

He plunged half of his cock into her mouth, while Victoria massaged her pussy. The intellectual part of her understood the positive reinforcement technique. When Victoria slid a finger inside her passage, a moan rolled across Diana's tongue and triggered an answering sound of pleasure from Merrick.

He kept to the same pace, but his erection went a little farther into her mouth with each pump. She tried to keep Victoria's instructions at the forefront of her mind, but it was so damn hard to concentrate on the dick in her mouth when someone played with her pussy.

Merrick thrust his cock, past her tongue and down her throat. Diana gagged. All the panic from the last time with a dom flooded her. She struggled, tried to buck Merrick's tight two-handed hold on her head, Victoria's on her wrists.

"Breathe, Diana," Victoria murmured. "Through your nose. In. Out."

Diana tried to concentrate on Victoria's voice, but the panic overwhelmed her. She couldn't move, couldn't fight them. Nothing in her body seemed to work. Her chest ached from the need for oxygen. If she didn't run now, she'd suffocate.

She screamed.

"Diana!" Merrick's sharp voice cut through the terror. His dark blue eyes stared into hers. Only then did Diana realize she wasn't suffocating, that his cock wasn't blocking her air, that he knelt in front of her.

He palmed her cheeks, projecting authority, but she couldn't stop shaking. The safeword lay on the tip of her tongue, if she could just get her mouth to work and say it.

"You are strong enough to get past this. You will service me as a proper sub should. And you *will* suck my cock until I come or I tell you to stop. Do you understand me?"

The panic attack eased at his commanding presence. Then she realized something. He wasn't going to hurt her. He'd stopped to give her a chance to say the safeword. Part of her wanted to use the out he'd given her. But if she did, if she allowed her fear to rule her, how could she ever be a proper sub to anyone?

She lowered her gaze and nodded.

"Say the words, little girl."

"Yes, Sir."

"Are you ready to continue?"

Was she? She took a deep breath and released it. Underneath the receding fear, she wanted to stay. "Yes, Sir."

Merrick stood and placed his hand at the back of her head again. "Open."

She obeyed, but couldn't help a wince as he eased his cock into her mouth once again. He pressed a steady rhythm, going a little deeper each time.

Victoria no longer toyed with her pussy, just stroked her thighs and calves. The effect calmed her, but it didn't banish the terror gibbering at the edges of her mind.

Instead, Diana focused on keeping her throat relaxed, her lips tight around Merrick's cock to produce the most friction. She swirled her tongue around the head each time he pulled back. The sooner she pleased him, the sooner it would be over, right?

She moaned again, deliberately vibrating the length of him along her tongue and throat. His fingertips dug into her scalp, a welcome pain-pleasure. The familiar feeling kept the panic at bay. She repeated the technique as he withdrew.

His sac pulled tight against his body. Merrick was so close. Her tongue circled around the head of his cock. Hips pumped faster, using her until one last deep thrust.

Come hit the back of her throat and set off a second of blind panic again.

"Breathe, Diana," Victoria whispered in her ear.

A mixture of relief, sadness and anger flooded her. She did as Victoria instructed, kept her throat relaxed and swallowed every drop of his come. But when Merrick pulled out of her mouth, she couldn't stop herself. The tears came in great racking coughs.

Merrick lifted her onto the bed while she sobbed. He climbed onto the bed behind her and sat. She wanted to curl into a ball, but he pulled her between his legs and pressed her back against his chest.

He hugged her. "Shhh. You did very well, Diana."

"I'm sorry," she repeated between each gulping breath. She was dimly aware of Victoria at her feet, removing the strappy stilettos. Only now did she see that Victoria was naked as well, laying on her stomach between Diana's spread legs.

Diana shook her head. "No, I don't deserve—"

"Shush." Merrick's command brooked no argument. "You got past your fear, and you will accept your reward, just as you would have accepted your punishment if you had failed."

Diana wanted to say something, but her mind didn't work right. Besides, she'd just been praised by one of her doms, hadn't she?

Victoria's mouth descended on Diana, and her fingers plunged into her passage. She couldn't stop her hips from bucking as Victoria sucked hard on her clit and finger-fucked her. Didn't have time for a coherent thought.

The orgasm erupted, shaking her body hard. So hard, she couldn't make a sound. Her pussy spasmed around Victoria's fingers, almost on the edge of pain.

Merrick said something in her ear, but his voice sounded very far away. She couldn't think, like her climax had shattered her mind as well as her body.

"Is she all right?" Worry threaded through Victoria's words.

Who's all right? Diana lifted her head to see who had joined them, or tried to. Nothing seemed to work right.

"We were a little too much for her. Diana, I need you to answer me." That was Merrick, deep and compelling.

"What was the question?" Her own speech slurred, but that didn't make sense. She only had a half glass of wine. "Shir," she added.

Merrick chuckled, a vibration under her spine. "One of us needs to take care of Victoria."

A tiny seed of an emotion travelled through the fog in her brain, but Diana couldn't identify it. Something to do with the other night. "I can eat her, Sir." That was it. Guilt. Victoria didn't have an orgasm during their first session either.

More laughter rippled across Merrick's chest. "Your spirit is admirable, little girl, but you need to rest. Can you cuddle up next to Victoria for me?"

Despite her blurred vision, Diana could see Victoria now lying next to her and Merrick. Her quicksilver hair spread across the blood-red pillow case. Merrick shifted out from under her, and Diana settled in the crook of Victoria's arm.

Her eyes met Victoria's brilliant blue ones. "Whash wrong with me?"

"You're in subspace, dear." Victoria kissed her forehead and stroked her hair. "You did so well. I'm proud of you."

"Oh." Diana contemplated the answer while she traced the outline of Victoria's areolas with a fingernail. She'd heard of the drug-like concept from other subs, had actually wondered if there was something wrong with her because she'd never experienced it. She giggled. "I feel like I'm on nitrous at the dentist."

"Well, then we definitely won't let you operate heavy machinery." Humor danced in Victoria's eyes.

While being held was nice, Diana needed more. She cupped Victoria's cheek and kissed her. She tasted fruity and tart from the red zinfandel from dinner. Diana's tongue invaded, demanding more than a sub should, but she couldn't stop. She craved the touch, the reassurance that she could please her domme. Her tongue caressed Victoria's before flicking the sensitive spot on the inside of her upper lip.

Victoria sighed into Diana's mouth. Their lips parted as Victoria arched her back. Diana's attention was drawn to Merrick, his head nestled between Victoria's thighs, her legs over his shoulders, as he ate her out.

The sight made Diana's mouth water. Things seemed a little clearer in her head. She scooted down the bed until her mouth was level with Victoria's chest and climbed to her hands and knees. Her lips latched onto Victoria's closest erect nipple, sucking it hard before taking a gentle bite.

"Yes," Victoria hissed. She stroked Diana's back, fingers trailing down to her bare ass. Nails dug into her skin still tender from the whip.

Diana switched to Victoria's other breast, lavishing the same affection on it she'd given to its twin. Between her ministrations and Merrick's noisy attention, Victoria writhed.

She stiffened. "Ohgodohgodohgod!" Her body shook and trembled.

A sense of pride hit Diana. She'd made it through her first serious scene in a very long time. Everybody involved seemed content. Or at least, it appeared so from the soft mewling sounds Victoria made as Merrick licked her pussy clean. Diana wrapped her arms around Victoria and cuddled next to her once again.

Victoria pulled her close for another kiss. "You did very, very well, dear."

Merrick climbed to the head of the bed. The length of his hard masculinity molded against Diana's back. His arm wrapped around both women. "Pumpernickel."

Whatever tension was left in Diana's body fled at Merrick signaling the official end of their session.

"I must say you did much better than I expected," he added.

She laughed, a pathetic, sad sound. "You mean, beside the panic attack." Wetness filled her eyes at her own weakness.

"You needed to face what happened with your last dom," Victoria whispered.

The implication of what she said wasn't lost on Diana. "You'll fuck my ass." For some reason, the prospect wasn't as scary as it might have been a couple of hours ago.

"Yes." Merrick nuzzled her neck before he continued. "But not at the moment. You need your rest." He sat, reached down and pulled the blanket tucked at the foot of the bed over the three of them.

Exhaustion and coziness dragged on her eyelids. For the second time in months, sleep didn't elude her. And for the first time in years, Diana felt secure and content tucked between their bodies.

Chapter Six

Diana woke to the absence of sound. Pale sunlight filtered through a crack in the heavy drapes. Not her bedroom. Not her apartment.

The playroom.

She rolled over. Victoria's light floral perfume lingered on the pillow next to her. She reached behind her and dragged the third pillow next to the others. The clean woodsy smell of Merrick. She inhaled their scents deeply and released the air. The same contented feeling as last night filled her. Despite her misgivings and her stupid-ass panic attack, playing with them hadn't been such a bad thing after all.

She looked around the room. They must have awoken and decided to let her sleep. But with no clocks in the room, she had no idea what time it was.

A low rumble came from her stomach, and she smiled. *Definitely past breakfast.*

Diana pulled on her dress in the dim light and retrieved her shoes. The door wasn't locked when she tried it. Footwear in hand, she padded down the hall to her guest bedroom. Brilliant sunshine filled the tiny lavender space. Her case was on the bed where she left it.

She took a quick shower, combed her hair and brushed her teeth. Her reflection caught her attention. Her skin no longer had the ashy hue from the constant stress over the past few months. The lines etched around her eyes weren't quite as obvious. Despite the emotional intensity of last night's scene, she almost looked like herself again.

Kat and Beth were right. I just needed a good, kinky fuck.

After donning jeans and a turquoise blouse, she headed for the stairs. The homey aroma of bacon and eggs met her before she reached the second step. She jogged the rest of the way down and strode to the kitchen.

Merrick stood at the stove, a smile on his face when he glanced up. "Good morning, sleepyhead. Your omelet's almost ready." Like her, he wore jeans and his feet were bare. A pale purple oxford covered his chest.

Now, that was weird. Did they have cameras in the room? "How did you know I was up?"

His smile turned wry. "With a house this old, the pipes announce every time someone flushes."

"Oh." A little wave of relief filled her. She was doing it again, jumping on every little thing with assumptions and suspicions. The clock on the microwave blinked from 12:03 to 12:04. "I'm sorry. I didn't realize how late it was."

"Last night was rather intense for you. I'm not surprised you needed the sleep." He flipped the omelet.

She looked around the kitchen. It was just him, his wife nowhere in sight. Nervousness brushed Diana's skin. "Where's Victoria?"

"She had a Daughters of the American Revolution luncheon this afternoon, so it's just you and me."

"Oh." She stopped on the opposite side of the island, unsure of what to do.

He slid the omelet onto a plate before running the small skillet under the faucet. "You sound disappointed."

Heat rushed to her face. "I'm sorry. I didn't mean . . ." Oh, god, could she have fucked this up any more?

The toaster dinged. He set the pan in the sink and turned off the water, then he reached for the slices. "Between what happened with your last dom and your fiancé, you're leery of my gender." Another smile took the sting out of his statement. "I don't blame you."

She rubbed her toes of her right foot against the hardwood. "Yeah. I'm sorry. It's nothing personal."

"I didn't take it as such." He gestured to the kitchen table. "Why don't you eat while we talk? I don't want Victoria berating me for not taking good care of you when she returns."

Her stomach chose that moment to gurgle.

They both laughed, and the pressure inside Diana's chest eased a little.

Merrick sat the plate and the napkin-wrapped silverware in front of her. He poured them both coffee before claiming the opposite seat. "I must admit I had an ulterior motive in encouraging Victoria to attend her luncheon."

"Really?" Her fork paused in mid-air.

Merrick's eyes were a darker blue than Victoria's, almost gray, but they shone with the same sensual intensity. "I wanted a little time alone with you as well."

"I see." She set the fork down without eating the bite of omelet. Anger rose out of her anxiety. "And why should I trust you?"

He sat back in his chair. "I understand your feelings, but last night was necessary for you to face your fears."

She folded her arms over her chest. "And how do I know you won't ass-rape me to get me over *that* fear?"

"Right now, you don't." He shrugged. "It's up to you to make the choice to trust me. However, I would like to make last night up to you by sticking to our original agreement."

She raised an eyebrow. "Spanking only?"

Another charming smile. "Well, I would like to bury my dick in that pretty little pussy of yours. And Victoria would be vexed if I didn't record the encounter for her private viewing later."

"Whoa." Diana held up her hands. She knew there was something she forgot to bring up when they had been discussing limits, but she needed to put it in a way he'd understand. "Victoria was adamant about discretion. Filming you two with anyone, not just me, would be an invitation to disaster. What if Consuela decides she absolutely has to clean what she thinks is an office? What if you piss her off, and she takes one of your recordings? Hell, what if you lose your goddamn phone?"

He laughed. "Is that a 'yes' or a 'no?'"

Diana pursed her lips. Deep down, the thought of Victoria watching Merrick fucking her sent a perverse little thrill through her. Besides, was it any different than Merrick masturbating while watching Victoria eat her out? "All right." She unclenched her arms long enough to shake an index finger at him. "But if this ends up on an internet porn site, I know a cop who'll shoot you for betraying me."

"I promise, no porn sites. But to make sure we're clear, I can record me spanking and pussy-fucking you for my wife's viewing pleasure. Once she's finished, the recording will be erased."

The way he said it made her feel wicked, sexy and incredibly turned on. So much for the clean, dry panties she had put on after her shower. Her juices soaked the cotton and dampened her jeans. But she couldn't give in too easily. "Fine, but touch a whip and I'm out of here."

"Agreed. Eat your breakfast before it gets cold."

Merrick changed the subject, didn't so much as make a sexual innuendo. They spent the rest of the meal debating the current push for photo identification at the polls. On an intellectual level, he was fascinating. She could understand why Victoria fell for him and why their relationship had lasted so long. He was a wonderful mix of smarts and kinky sex appeal.

He cleared her plate and refreshed her coffee before she worked up the courage to ask something that had been troubling her. "How do you deal with jealousy?"

He finished refilling his cup before he met her gaze. "What do you mean? Am I jealous of Victoria getting to eat you out first? Maybe a little."

"No." She took a sip of coffee to cover her discomfort. "I've never been involved with multiple partners before because I was worried about the dynamics."

"Ah." He set the glass pot back on the coffee maker before he rejoined her at the table. "As in, am I or is Victoria jealous when one of us is with a third party?"

She nodded.

He grinned. "Victoria's bi, like you. I've always liked the fact that my wife looks at females the same way I do. I don't have to hide my appreciation of other women from my significant other like so many of my fellow males."

She waved a hand. "But still . . ."

He took a drink of his own coffee. "We talk. About our needs, our fears, our desires. That's more than a lot of co-called normal couples do. Of course, it's helped that Victoria would rather bring a woman into our relationship than a man."

Diana's shoulders tightened at her real question. "What about your friend Daniel?"

Merrick shrugged. "It was curiosity on my part. When we were in school eons ago, we . . . discussed the possibility of one of our girlfriends wanting to do two men at once. He stated that I'd be the only one he trusted in that sort of a situation. So when Victoria asked about trying another man in our games—"

Diana laid a hand over Merrick's. "I'm sorry. I—" She looked out the window for a moment. "According to Victoria, you have, *had* a long-term thing with him before he moved to New York. I guess I'm projecting my own insecurities."

She tried to pull away, but Merrick grasped her hand and held it tight. "You have nothing to be jealous of, Diana. He may rejoin us. He may no longer be interested in this type of play. I haven't had a chance to talk to him yet."

A weak laugh burbled from her throat. "Except Victoria's already planning on bringing him into our situation."

Merrick laughed as well. "And as you've deduced, Victoria usually gets what Victoria wants." His expression sobered. "Do you really want our next scene just between you and me? Or would you rather wait for Victoria?"

Diana hesitated. A half hour ago, she would have said no. Without Victoria in the playroom, she wouldn't have trusted him. His rich white-man bearing made her nervous. But human Merrick who laid his marriage and his feelings on the table before her . . .

"Yes, I would like to play with just you."

He stood and tugged on her hand. "Shall we?"

She inhaled a deep, relaxing breath and nodded. "Same safeword?"

He smiled. "'Pumpernickel', it is. Do you remember the rules?"

"Yes, Sir."

He led the way up to the playroom. When she saw the messy covers, she knew immediately she faced an additional punishment. The frown on Merrick's face as he eyed the rumpled sheets and bedspread confirmed her suspicions.

A shiver of excitement rippled through her body as she stripped off her shirt and bra. Had she subconsciously left the bed unmade, hoping for exactly this?

Once she removed her jeans and panties, she folded everything then knelt beside the chair and clasped her hands behind her back.

The irony between the previous session and now hit her. She felt less naked than she had last night with her corset and stockings. Her nipples budded from her excitement and Merrick's attention.

He folded his arms over his chest. She quickly lowered her eyes as his intense gaze burned through her skull. "Did I ask you if you remembered all of our rules while we were downstairs?"

"Yes, Sir."

"What was the rule concerning the bed in the playroom?"

She swallowed her excitement. "That I was to make the bed once everyone was awake, Sir."

"And your reason for not doing so?"

"I . . . forgot, Sir."

His exhale said more about his exasperation than any words. "You realize I will have to add a punishment for this transgression?"

"Yes, Sir," she whispered.

"And do you understand it will be a punishment of my choosing?" Once again, he left the proverbial door wide open for her to get out of the situation.

Except curiosity gnawed to learn just how far he would go. "Yes, Sir."

He sauntered to the racks, rubbing his chin as he examined each implement.

Diana's breath hitched. He had every right now to use a whip, despite his earlier promise. She'd been the one who broke a rule first.

It took everything she had not to sigh in relief when he finally walked away from the racks and over to the boudoir.

"What makes you think that I won't pull something out of a drawer that's worse than the whips, little girl?" He didn't look at her, but amusement threaded through his voice.

Apparently, her control wasn't as good as she thought. Heat flamed in her cheeks. "I-I don't, Sir."

He pulled out a rectangular wooden box from one of the top drawers. "Stand."

She obeyed, though the maneuver was hampered by her hands behind her back. He opened the box and removed what looked to be several strands of pearls. Or it did until he unwound them. She shuddered when she saw the three nasty alligator clips.

The soft material that covered the teeth was a small relief when he attached the clamps to her erect nipples. She quelled a whimper at the painful pressure.

"Spread you legs for me," Merrick murmured.

The husky quality of his voice made her pussy throb. She did as she was told, and he crouched in front of her where he could see just how wet she was already. Her skin flamed even hotter.

His fingertip stroked her parted pussy lips, spreading her moisture, teasing her. When he attached the clip to her clit, she cried out.

He rose, once again rubbing his chin as he contemplated what to do with her. Some instinct said he was only mind-fucking her, that he already knew exactly what punishments he would inflict before he would let her come. Her body, on the other hand, trembled in anticipation of what he would do next.

As if he'd read her mind, Merrick reached out and flicked the clip on her left breast. The pleasure-pain drew a sound, half fear and half desire, from deep in her throat, but otherwise, she didn't move. A satisfied look appeared on his face, and he crossed to the closet.

She watched from the corner of her eye as he pulled out a body length pillow of the same deep red color as the sheets. It was huge and cut in the shape of a half cylinder. Perfect to raise someone's ass in the air if she were laying on top of it. Her ass.

He yanked all the covers off the bed and laid the pillow horizontally across the mattress. "Get on the bed, and lay with your hips at the apex. You may walk." He patted the pillow.

"Yes, Sir." She scrambled to obey, more out of anticipation than fear. Then she understood why he didn't make her crawl. Every movement yanked on one or more of the damn clamps. Despite their padding, the metal clips dug into her flesh and added a new dimension to the pain. Once she was properly positioned, he paced around the bed and studied her body from every angle.

"Lift your head." When she did so, he slipped a pillow under her cheek. "Cross your arms underneath the pillow and rest your head. Once she obeyed, he said, "Can you breathe properly?"

"Yes, Sir," she whispered.

Merrick stepped back out of sight. "You may not have an orgasm until I give you permission. Do you understand?"

Worry and anticipation mixed in her stomach. He would push her as hard as he could. "Yes, Sir." Her voice sounded tremulous and uncertain to her own ears.

Could she stop herself from coming? She certainly hadn't been able to when Victoria ate her out.

"Spread your legs."

Like before, that simple statement made her wet, her pussy pulse. Her clit throbbed in time to her heart, making the attached clip even more torturous. She eased her knees apart as far as she could manage.

He touched her, petting her damp curls, stroking the slick flesh between her thighs. She closed her eyes and reveled in the sensation.

Smack.

The first blow made her jerk. The alligator clip on her clit pinched. The flat of his palm landed three more times. There was no pattern, no way to keep the pain in her clit from growing worse as her body swelled from the stimulation.

Smack. Smack.

Diana couldn't help it. She squirmed, which only made the agony between her legs worse.

"Are you trying to relieve yourself, little girl?" Merrick's tone was perturbed.

"No, Sir."

Another *thwack* filled the room. Her ass stung, and tears formed in her eyes.

"I think you're lying to me." *Thwack.*

"No, Sir!"

"Did I ask you a question?" He didn't wait for an answer. Another stinging slap landed on her raised buttocks. Her nipples were engorged, so hard and tight as the clips rubbed against the mattress from every little movement.

She wanted him to stop. She wanted him to spank her until she came.

Smack.

A moan crawled from her throat. She shuddered as her body hit the turning point, where the pinches on her breasts and clit felt so damn good she could stay like this forever.

Thwack!

The pressure in her body built, the delicious edge right before she came. But Merrick hadn't given her permission. She bit her lip, hard. Anything to distract her, keep her body from exploding.

Just when she didn't think she could halt her orgasm, Merrick stopped spanking her. The absence was too profound. She wanted to move, needed to, but the slightest wiggle would shoot her into ecstasy.

She could hear Merrick behind her, the heavy inhale and gusty exhale like he fought for control of himself. He was as close as she was from the sound of it.

She panted while she hung on the edge for the longest time. No doubt he waited, to see if she could master her body or if she'd twitch and let herself cascade out of control. She didn't dare move a toenail, but each breath only emphasized the exquisite pleasure-pain of her nipples.

The rasp of his jeans signaled his approach. His warm hand stroked her spine. "Very well done. Do you know how rare it is for an improperly trained sub to curb her reactions?"

"No, Sir."

He laughed. "That's a good thing. I wouldn't want your head to get as swollen as your pretty little pussy." His fingers trailed down her back, skimmed the crevice of her ass and lightly touched her open folds.

Her breath hitched. Her body revved into overdrive. *Can't come. Can't come.* She dug her fingernails into the mattress. Despite the silent chant, her nerves screamed, wanting, *needing* a release while she struggled to tame her rebellious body. She tried to think of something, anything else, but all she could picture was Merrick's long cock inside her.

Tears trickled across her cheeks as she fought her own body. Thankfully, his fingers withdrew before she embarrassed herself by totally losing it.

"Yes, excellent." His hand, wet from her own juices, massaged her sore ass. Her nose grew stuffy from the emotional turmoil, and she sniffed.

Merrick paused. "Are you crying, Diana?"

God. Saved from one embarrassment only to fall into another. "Yes, Sir."

"If the spanking was too much, why didn't you say the safeword?"

"It-it wasn't that. I—" She swallowed the large lump in her throat. If he'd been looking into her eyes, she wouldn't have been able to be that honest. "I was afraid I would displease you by losing control." Another sniff. "Sir."

His hand caressed her ass again. The stinging faded. Would he start spanking her again or would he fuck her?

Cloth rustled behind her. Then came the shift and sway of Merrick climbing onto the mattress. Crisp hair and hard muscle brushed the backs of her thighs as he positioned himself. He removed the alligator clip from her clit. The relief triggered a fresh wave of tears.

His cock touched her puckered hole. Her edgy arousal drowned under a tide of panic. Every muscle in her body tensed.

"Shhh." Merrick stroked her back, her ass, her thighs. "Discipline, little girl."

Her body trembled. The adrenaline on top of her endorphins did funky things to her head. He could push the issue since she disobeyed one of their rules. She found herself thrusting her ass against him. "I'm yours, Sir. To do with as you will."

"Yes, you are." But she could detect the undercurrent of pleased pride in his tone. "You may come now."

Instead of taking her ass as she expected, he shifted his cock lower and rammed into her pussy. Nor was he going to let her come that quickly. His withdrawal was slow, easy. She thrust back again, only for him to pull out of her completely.

"Please," she whimpered.

A sharp slap landed on her ass. "What do you say to me?"

"Will you please fuck me, Sir?"

This time, he took her harder, faster, ramming her pussy like he was hammering a nail. The clamps dug into her nipples every time his thrust shoved her into the mattress. And it felt so damn good. So good she couldn't have stopped herself from coming no matter how hard she tried this time.

Every neuron in her body fired at once. Her body convulsed and shook. And in the middle of it all, she felt the pulse of his cock deep inside her, hot come filling her.

His body sagged against hers, though one hand propped him up to keep most of his weight off her back. Otherwise, he didn't move except for sucking in deep lungfuls of air, his cock still inside her.

She couldn't move either. Didn't want to.

So this was what proper domination felt like. Merrick, even Victoria, made every other experience in Diana's past pale by comparison. If their friend Daniel was as commanding, intense, then maybe bringing him into the mix wouldn't be so bad. Would Merrick and his friend take her separately or both at once? Her body shuddered at the thought of two men fucking her at the same time Merrick's cock slipped from her.

"Pumpernickel." His voice was hoarse. She vaguely remembered him shouting near the end. When she still didn't move, he asked, "Diana? Are you okay?"

She looked over her shoulder and smiled. "Yeah."

He reached out and wiped the wetness from her cheeks with his thumb. "You sure?"

She took a deep breath and evaluated everything. The clamps reminded her they still clung to her nipples, and there was a little soreness from the spanking. "I'm fine."

Merrick rocked back on his heels and tugged the cylindrical pillow from underneath her. It landed silently on the floor. "Roll over, sweetheart."

Once she did, he removed the alligator clips from her nipples and laid the string of pearls on the nightstand. He lay next to her and pulled her close.

She tried to remember the last time she felt this relaxed cuddled next to a man. The trouble was she could never remember being relaxed with any man. It always seemed there was some unspoken expectation between her and every guy she had been with. Until now. A dry laugh shook her.

"What's so funny?" Merrick stroked her arm in idle affection.

She hesitated at telling him the truth, but Merrick and Victoria had been totally honest with her. "It's amusing and a little weird that the first time I'm comfortable in bed with a man after sex is with someone else's husband."

His hand paused in mid-stroke. "Diana, this can't be more than it is."

"No." She rose up on an elbow to look him in the eye. "Don't misunderstand me. I think I'm content here with you because there's *not* any assumptions or presumptions about what I want or what you want. It is what it is—two people having fun." She grinned. "And it'll be three people when Victoria gets home."

He laughed. Then he palmed the back of her head and pulled her down for a friendly kiss. A kiss that promised friends with benefits for as long as they wanted.

Chapter Seven

Pleasant soreness accompanied Diana into the office Monday morning. She'd barely changed out of her athletic shoes and into her heels when her cell phone buzzed.

"Hello?"

"What are your plans for this evening?"

It was too damn early in the morning for games. Diana glanced at the caller ID before she said, "And good morning to you too, Victoria."

"Oooo, you are so getting whipped for talking back." Humor in Victoria's voice belied her threat. "Seriously though, do you have plans?"

"I'd love to, but I need to be looking for an apartment." Diana stood and glanced out her office before she closed the door. That she actually had an office with a door was one of the few advantages of this job. "I have to be out of my place in a couple of weeks."

"Actually, that's part of what we wanted to discuss with you over dinner."

Concern niggled her brain as she sat down again. "I'm not moving in with you and Merrick."

"Who said anything about you moving in? You said you were looking for a place, and Merrick has a lead on a decent condo in Alexandria close to the Blue Line."

"Uh-huh, and why did you really call?"

A sigh huffed through the receiver. "Daniel's in town. He's already moved into his apartment, but since he doesn't start his job until next Monday, he's bored."

"And?"

"He's having dinner with us."

Diana leaned back in her chair and stared at the ceiling. "Why are you pushing this, Victoria?"

"Because I love you both, and I think you'll get along famously. We'll meet at a restaurant, not at our house. No pressure, I promise."

Diana laughed. "Why do I have the feeling you'll have an open tab, hoping we both get drunk and come home with you?"

Despite kinky sex all weekend or maybe because of it, Victoria's throaty chuckle made Diana's pussy clench with desire. "A woman can hope, can't she?"

Against her better judgment, Diana found herself changing platforms at Metro Center and heading north on the Red Line. Raw curiosity drove her. Victoria was obviously devoted to Merrick, yet she just as obviously thought highly of Daniel. And Victoria was not the type to impress easily.

Diana found the restaurant easily enough, another snobby establishment along Connecticut Avenue. What surprised her was that the maitre d' didn't blink when she gave him Merrick's name. Instead, he pivoted on his shiny black shoes and beckoned her to follow.

He led her to a tiny table tucked in an alcove. For a split second, she hesitated. The setting was too cozy, too . . . intimate.

All three people at the table rose as she approached. Merrick and Victoria made a show of kissing her on the cheek. Merrick gestured at the third person. "Diana, this is our friend, Daniel Myers. Daniel, Diana Traynor."

To her relief, Daniel only held out his hand. "Pleasure to meet you." He definitely wasn't what she expected. A little shorter than Merrick, maybe five-ten or five-eleven. His dirty blond hair tended toward unruly compared to Merrick's precision cut. Their suits had the same fitted, expensive look, and probably cost more than her rent. But where Merrick had classic rich white boy good looks, Daniel's face could be considered rugged at best.

It was his eyes that unnerved her. Sharp, piercing. Living sapphires that seemed to see right through her.

"Same here," she managed. The maitre d' seated her, then prattled about the wines available until Merrick picked something that sounded very pricey.

After the gentleman trotted off to get the bottle, Daniel leaned a little closer to her. "Don't sweat it. I never know what he's talking about either."

The comment made her feel a little better. She smiled. "I figured wine lessons were included in law school."

"Now, why do you think I'd ever be stupid enough to go to law school?" He grinned. The brilliant expression lit the little alcove. Her stomach twisted. That smile could be her undoing.

"I'm sorry." She glanced at Merrick, who also wore an amused expression. Oh, she'd definitely stepped into something here. "When Merrick said he knew you in school, I, well, made an assumption."

Daniel leaned back in his seat, a cocky look on his face. "You know what they say about assumptions."

Her smile turned wry. "I'm pretty sure I've only made an ass of myself. So where did you two meet?"

"Private school." His gaze turned analytical. "Now, you're making the assumption I'm a rich snob like him."

"No, I—" Dammit. He could read her mind. She'd like to make it through one evening with these people where she didn't totally embarrass herself.

"Hey!" Merrick protested.

Victoria covered her mouth, no doubt trying to stifle a laugh.

One of Daniel's eyebrows lifted. "That's like me assuming you're a crack whore because you're a black woman."

Diana's eyes narrowed. "Well, now I know for sure you're a racist dick."

Once again, Daniel's expression broke into a wide, endearing grin. "I thought that was expected of white cops."

Cop? Diana blinked. He actually had a normal job?

"I like you." He turned to Merrick. "You always pick subs with backbone." His sharp gaze met hers again. "If we want to slap labels on ourselves, mine would be 'white trash.' I was a scholarship case. On my first day of high school, a couple of jerks tried to make an example of me."

She couldn't see him as a victim. "And you beat the shit out of them?"

His attention flicked to Merrick and back. "Not without help."

Diana faced Merrick. "Let me guess. The bullies wanted revenge?"

He nodded. "We watched each other's back for four very long years."

Their admission hit a chord. It'd only been one year, but the crap the students put her and the rest of the defunct cheerleading squad through stood out in her mind. She stroked the stem of her wine glass to keep a handle on her emotions. "Believe it or not, I do understand."

Victoria clapped her hands. "Enough with our morbid pasts." She changed the subject to the zoo's latest panda acquisition, and dinner proceeded with studied politeness.

As Diana suspected, Merrick and Victoria kept the wine flowing during dinner, and then they insisted on dessert. She wasn't sure if it was the alcohol or Daniel's efforts to keep the conversation light, but she found herself relaxing.

Once the waiter placed the dishes of vanilla ice cream, each topped with a different liquor, Daniel leaned close to her once again. "You do know they're trying to get us both drunk and in bed with them tonight."

She grinned in return. "Victoria already let the plan slip on the phone this morning."

On the other side of the table, Victoria pouted. "You two are such spoilsports."

Daniel ignored her. "Would you like to go out tomorrow night? Just the two of us. Have a chance to get to know each other better before they talk us into something?"

Acceptance lay on the tip of Diana's tongue, which shocked her, but she shook her head. "I'd love to, but I've got two weeks to find an apartment, and someone keeps distracting me." She glared at Victoria, who pasted an innocent expression on her face.

"That reminds me." Merrick dug into his suit pocket and pulled out a business card. "A client was recently appointed to an ambassadorship. He's looking for someone to housesit while he and his wife are overseas, and he asked for a recommendation. They have a condo in Alexandria. It'll be a little longer commute for you unfortunately, but I think you'd enjoy the neighborhood."

Diana took the proffered card and glanced at the hand-written home address on the back. Her stomach lurched. That area was way more expensive than her current apartment in Rosslyn, the one she couldn't manage now. "How much do they want in rent?" she asked, knowing deep in her heart she couldn't possibly afford it.

Merrick laid his hand over hers. "Diana, sweetheart, they want to *hire* you to watch the place, and they'll pay each year in advance."

"Wait a minute!" Daniel glared at Merrick. "A client wants a house sitter and you didn't suggest someone with twenty years of law enforcement experience?"

"They wanted someone responsible," Merrick said. He managed to keep a straight face, but Victoria broke into a giggling fit.

"Thanks, buddy." Daniel turned to Diana and snatched the card out of her hand. "Let me know when your appointment is, and I'll meet you out there. I know a little hole-in-the-wall Italian place. Best food on the Virginia side of the Potomac." He waggled fingers of his other hand in Victoria's direction. "Pen."

"Demanding, isn't he?" Victoria shot Diana a wicked smile before she faced Daniel. "You know you'd get farther if you'd say 'please.'" But she had already pulled out something that looked more like a work of art than a ballpoint and handed it to him.

"Really? I've never had to say 'please' with you before. In fact, you like it when I take what I want."

Tingles rippled up Diana's spine. She'd never pictured Victoria as submissive, but the byplay between her and Daniel left no doubt that their roles had been interchangeable in the playroom. And she couldn't help wondering what it would be like if Daniel decided to take what he wanted from her.

He scribbled a number on the back of the card, under the first address. "Here's my cell."

Their fingers brushed when he returned the card. The wary touch from earlier was gone. Her eyes met his. Sensual curiosity lay in their crystal depths.

Diana tried to suppress the shiver of desire as she tucked the card in her purse. "Thank you, Merrick. I'll call him tomorrow."

"And?" Daniel prompted.

She shook her head in amused exasperation. "You won't take 'no' for an answer, will you?"

"No." He grinned.

She laughed. "All right. I'll call you when I have the appointment."

"Now you don't have an excuse for not coming home with us tonight." Lust sparkled in Victoria's eyes, her look eager.

"Stop pushing her, Vicki." Daniel scowled at Victoria. "Give her a chance to know me without you two hovering."

"Friday, then?" Victoria took a sip of her wine.

Daniel opened his mouth, but Diana laid a hand on his arm. "Let it go. She won't give up until we agree to something."

He eyed her. "You sure?"

She nodded.

He turned back to Victoria. "You chase this one away, and so help me, I *will* whip you black and blue."

She smiled behind her wine glass. "Promises, promises."

Except deep down, Diana knew it was more than a promise. It was a fact. And her pussy dampened at the idea of Daniel Myers whipping her own ass.

Chapter Eight

Diana couldn't contain her giddiness as she rode down the elevator on Thursday afternoon. The meeting with Ambassador and Mrs. Stanfield went far better than she expected. In fact, they'd already written her a check for the first year. All she had to do was save the money, and her niece or nephew could have a real backyard to play in. It was too freakin' much to imagine.

When she bounded down the steps of the condo building, she found Daniel leaning against a car in front of the main doors. From the nasty looks the doorman gave him, he'd been parked there for some time.

She stopped in shock. The car was a mint-condition blue '67 Mustang. "Wow! Where'd you get this? She's beautiful."

He shook his head, an amused expression on his face. "If I'd known this is what it took to impress you, I'd have driven it Monday night."

Diana circled the vehicle, then looked at him. "Did you restore her yourself?"

"How'd you figure out she's restored?" He walked over to where she stood by the driver side.

"You mean besides the age. Here." She pointed. "See the faint ripple in the paint? Down here where the body panel curves under the car. The bondo wasn't sanded properly."

Daniel laughed. "I've taken her to a couple of car shows, and none of the judges of noticed. Where'd you learn?"

She shrugged and crossed her arms. "From the Major."

Something dark glinted in his eyes. "The Major? An ex?"

"No. Foster father." She mentally kicked herself for opening her mouth. Why did she feel the need to confess everything to everyone lately? Better to take the offense. "And if Victoria didn't already tell you, I'm bi. So if you're going to get jealous of every person over the age of eighteen in my life, you're going to give yourself an aneurysm."

Daniel looked away. "Sorry. I . . ." He blew out a deep breath, then smiled at her. "My own demons are getting in the way."

Diana bit her tongue. Damn, his ex-wife had seriously done a number on him. As much as her past had done to her.

"Why don't you drive?" He tossed the keys in her direction, and she snagged them in mid-air.

"Seriously?"

"Why not?"

"Most men I know are particular about their cars and don't want X-chromosome cooties on the steering wheel."

He took a couple of steps closer to her. Victoria was right about one thing. His presence filled her personal space, but not in an intimidating way. More like . . . being protected and cherished.

Now where the hell did that come from?

He stared into her eyes. "Driving my vehicle all depends on how well you take directions."

She shivered at his insinuation. Victoria hadn't been joking when she said he was someone Diana would have to experience. If she got this excited just bantering with him, could she handle a scene with him?

His fingertips stroked her cheek. "Let's get dinner. I'm starving."

Somehow, she didn't think for a minute he was referring to food.

By the end of dinner, Diana had to admit Daniel knew how to handle people. He'd managed to get her to talk about the 'ugly time'.

"A mechanic?" He grinned. "I can't see someone like you with grease under her fingernails."

"Now you're stepping into sexist territory, Officer Myers." She wagged her index finger. "My job earned me enough money to get both Steffi and me through college." She leaned back in her chair. "So what's your story? Beside the fact that you earned a scholarship to a private school?"

He leaned forward, chin resting on his fist. "Let's face it. A modeling career was not in my future."

She laughed. "Fishing for compliments?"

"Maybe." He turned serious. "When a brain is all you've got going for you, you learn to use it. The only reason I managed to afford college was thanks to academic scholarships. My parents didn't have a dime to their names most of their lives. Mom got knocked up with me when she was fifteen. Her parents kicked her out, and Dad's parents wouldn't have anything to do with her either. Dad dropped out of high school to take care of her. You know how far a person can get without a high school diploma or GED in today's world."

Diana reached across the table to touch his arm. "I'm sorry."

His palm covered her hand. "I'm just saying you're not the only one in the world to get the shaft. I think it's pretty damn remarkable how far you and Steffi have come."

He shifted closer, and for an instant, it seemed like he'd kiss her. Even though she told herself over and over nothing would happen between them tonight, her lips parted in anticipation.

Hesitation flicked across his face, and he stood abruptly. "It's late. Let's get you home since you have to be at your office bright and early."

She couldn't stop the flood of disappointment, but she rose as well. "Are you still joining us tomorrow night?" As soon as the words spilled out, she wanted to slap a hand over her mouth. Talk about sounding desperate.

His roguish grin appeared again. "Wouldn't miss it."

Friday afternoon found Diana staring at numbers on a spreadsheet. The same spreadsheet she'd clicked open after lunch. The one she couldn't concentrate on because she couldn't get a certain blond cop out of her head.

He'd been a perfect gentleman. He drove her straight to her apartment. He walked her to her door. Once again, he acted as if he wanted to kiss her. Instead, he said, "Good night," and peeled out of the parking lot before her addled brain could offer him a nightcap.

This was so not good. She hadn't obsessed over Victoria or Merrick this way. As she'd told Merrick while they were in bed last Saturday, the lack of expectations made things comfortable between the three of them.

So what exactly was she expecting from Daniel? Or had Victoria built him up too much, and she had no right to expect anything other than a good time?

Diana sighed in relief when her smart phone saved her from more pathetic mulling. "Hey, Beth. What's up?"

"Have you heard from Alicia?"

"Not since we had lunch together." She frowned. "Is something wrong?"

"She hasn't responded to the invitation to my show, and she's not answering my calls. Her office said she left early today, too."

Diana sat straighter. "Miss Prim and Proper? That's not like her. Have you checked with Micki?"

"Yeah, I just got off the phone with her. Other than a two-second blow-off call a week ago, she hasn't heard from Alicia either."

Diana winced. "Ouch, Micki called me that same night. Is she okay?"

A sigh whistled through the receiver. "I don't know. She got pissed at me when I asked her if she was bringing a guest to the show. And she called me last Friday, too. I think she misses Lee, and Alicia's stupid-ass challenge is getting to her."

Diana froze. Micki's partner on the D.C. police force had died in the line of duty a year ago. The thought of the same thing happening to Daniel made her chest ache.

"Okay, deep breath, girl," Diana said, as much to herself as to Beth. She tapped her pencil, trying to think things through. "Since Alicia brought up her whole boytoy idea, I'm guessing she's found someone and had to come up with a cocka-mamie reason to date him. You know how fixated she gets when she's got someone new in her life."

"I suppose so." Beth didn't sound quite so reassured.

"I'll lay the bill for our next group lunch on it. As for Micki . . ." Diana stared at the spreadsheet. It wasn't like she was getting anywhere on these numbers. "I owe her a call anyway. If anything's really wrong, I'll let you know."

"Okay." Another deep sigh sounded through the receiver. "I'm sorry. I guess I'm stressed about the show, and I'm making shit worse than it is."

"So what's new?"

"Bitch."

"I love you, too." After she thumbed the "End Call" icon, Diana glanced at the clock on her phone. One more hour to go before this insane day was done.

She pulled up Micki's number. Maybe Micki could make some discreet inquiries about Daniel for her. It was always good to have an independent source to corroborate any information, right? Her thumb hovered for the "Call" icon. But did she really want to deal with the shit Micki would dish out if she knew Diana was interest in a fellow cop? Even worse, Micki would blab to her dad, and then the Major would call Diana and want her to bring Daniel to dinner . . .

And she was right back to obsessing about a certain blond police officer.

At the knock on her door, she looked up. One of the interns poked his head in. "Ms. Traynor, your car's here."

"What car?"

"The one from Ambassador Stanfield." The intern grinned. "Running with the big dogs, Ms Traynor?"

Her heart sank. Had his assignment fallen through? Did he and Mrs. Stanfield want their money back? Goddammit! She'd already given her notice, and now she was back to square one on finding a place to live.

She shut down her computer and grabbed her bags. By the time she reached the lobby, her lunch was holding a vote on whether to make a reappearance.

A limo sat in front of the building. The driver, in a traditional suit and cap, stood next to the rear door, his fingers wrapped around the handle. "Good evening, Ms. Traynor."

"What's going on?"

He didn't answer, just opened the door. Ambassador Stanfield poked his head out and waved her forward. "There you are. Come along, Diana. I can't be late."

She hesitated for the briefest of moments. Things couldn't be that bad, could they? She climbed in and found herself sitting next to Merrick, who had an amused expression. The partition was up, so she couldn't see the driver, but the limo smoothly pulled into the beginnings of D.C. rush hour.

Ambassador Stanfield pulled out his wallet. "Sorry for the rush, Ms. Traynor, but my wife and I are leaving sooner than expected." He handed her a key card and a black American Express card. "Here's the key for accessing the elevator and the condo. The card is for any emergencies regarding the property that might arise. Make sure you give copies of your receipts to Merrick. If the vendor for the situation refuses to accept the card, call Merrick and let him deal with it. It's what I pay him for."

"I told you, Diana's very organized. Things will be fine."

She shivered. Merrick's voice held the same soothing quality he used the night he forced her to deep throat him. And dammit if it didn't make her pussy wet at the sound.

"I know, I know." Ambassador Stanfield waved a hand. "I hate these state functions. They make me nauseated."

"If you hate them, why do you want to be an ambassador, sir?" As soon as the question popped out, heat flooded Diana's face.

Stanfield's expression had the same intense look as Merrick's or Victoria's or Daniel's. "Because one can find great pleasure in things she is sure she will dislike."

Diana's heart skipped a beat. He knew. Without a doubt from his expression, Stanfield perceived the real relationship between her and Merrick. That he wondered what it would be like to have her kneel before him. That he regretted leaving the country before he could find out.

The limo slowed and the passenger window rolled down. A Marine with a machine gun looked into the compartment. "Good evening, Mr. Ambassador. I need to see picture identification for your companions."

"They aren't staying," Stanfield replied.

"I'm aware of that, sir. However, I still need to see I.D."

Diana glanced out the window. *Oh, my god! I'm in front of the White House!* She pulled out her driver license and handed it to Merrick, who gave their IDs to the Marine.

A few minutes later, he handed back their licenses and the window rolled up. Their driver guided the limo through the second set of barricades and up the main drive.

When the vehicle halted, Stanfield grasped Diana's right palm. "Thank you again for house-sitting. I hope we can meet under more enjoyable circumstances the next time." He kissed the back of her hand and slid out of the limo.

Moments later, the car pulled back into normal D.C. traffic.

"He knows," she stated.

"Yes."

She had to give Merrick credit for not denying it. She twisted in the seat to face him. "What happened to all that crap I was given about discretion?"

He smiled, and his fingers stroked the gap between her skirt and knee. "I didn't say anything to him if that's your concern." He pushed her skirt up, gaining access to her inner thighs. His attentions spurred the edginess she'd felt since Daniel left her at her door last night.

"However, Stanfield is not stupid." Merrick shifted so he was kneeling on the limo's floor, his body centered between her open legs. "And he belongs to a club here in town, a club that Victoria and I also belong to. One we'll take you to if you would like. When you're ready."

His words were lost in the anticipation that claimed her mind. She wanted him inside her, anything to relieve her body's neediness.

He reached for her pussy. An annoyed expression appeared on his face. "Did you forget the rule about panties already?"

She met his irritated look with one of her own. "We're not at your home, and you didn't give me a chance to prepare before you showed up at my job."

"Maybe we need to adjust the rules." His fingers slid under the elastic and toyed with her damp passage. "This one time."

Fine. If he was going to mess with her, she could mess right back since this wasn't the playroom. "What exactly are you're intentions, Mr. Davis?" Her eyebrow rose as she regarded him. "If it's a scene, then I don't think it's fair not to include Victoria and Daniel, especially if they are waiting on us at the house."

An evil gleam appeared in his eyes. "What if I just want to fuck you? And what makes you think they aren't already doing the same thing?"

She matched his smile. "If that's the case, I think I can accommodate you."

Merrick had to lean out of the way in order to drag her panties down her legs. Before she could reach for him, he undid his slacks and yanked her body toward him.

There was no teasing, no foreplay this time. His cock rammed into her, hard, furious. And she was so wet, so needy, all she could do was take it. She flailed, tried to find purchase on the slippery leather seat. He simply grabbed her ass to hold her in place as he pumped into her.

She wrapped her arms around his neck and bit the shoulder of Merrick's suit jacket to keep from crying out. The partition may be up, but she didn't know how much noise penetrated the barrier.

Her pussy convulsed around his cock, the orgasm taking her as fast, as fiercely, as Merrick had. She whimpered around the mouthful of coat. Around her, he stiffened. His cock pulsed inside her.

She tried to catch her breath. What had just happened? She'd never come that hard from simple penetration. She usually needed more. Much, much more. "Victoria's not going to be pissed at us, is she?"

Merrick chuckled. "Did you think I was lying about what she and Daniel are doing at the house?"

Diana blinked. "She told you?"

Another laugh, and Merrick nibbled her ear. "We thought it best to take the edge off before dinner. Otherwise, none of us are going to last more than five minutes."

"You mean, like this?" She gestured at their bodies, Merrick's cock still inside her.

"Exactly this." He withdrew, and they both arranged their clothing to a more presentable appearance. However, instead of returning her panties, he shoved them into his suit pocket and winked at her. "So you're legal when we arrive."

She nodded and tried not to think too much about what would follow dinner. Because if she did, she would have to finger herself several more times before they reached Georgetown.

Chapter Nine

Lust sizzled across Diana's nerves all through dinner. From the tension in the kitchen, she wasn't the only one on edge. And contrary to the other night at the restaurant, everyone limited themselves to one glass of wine.

Merrick and Daniel were arguing some fine point of cultural expectation versus legal expectation when Victoria caught Diana's eye and tilted her head toward the staircase. Diana gave a smile and a slight nod.

Both men looked up when she and Victoria rose. Eagerness lit their faces. Victoria laid a hand on Merrick's shoulder. "Give us a little bit to prepare."

He placed his hand over hers. "Not too long, I hope."

Diana didn't say a word as she followed Victoria up the stairs. She didn't think she could if she wanted to. Merrick had been wrong about sex in the limo taking the edge off. If anything, it made her hornier. Her pussy ached at the thought of three people using her, in ways she probably hadn't imagined yet, over the next two days.

Once inside the room, Diana removed her clothes while Victoria examined the racks, her finger tapping her chin. Diana recognized the expression. She would be pushed this weekend. Pushed hard.

For the first time, the hunger for their punishments overrode the terror. She knelt beside the chair, hands behind her back, and kept her eyes focused on a stray piece of lint in front of her.

Victoria's feet crossed the carpet and stopped next to her. "Crawl to the middle of the open area."

Diana obeyed and resumed her position. The leather tip of a riding crop entered her field of vision. Victoria trailed it over her naked breasts, across her stomach and down her pussy lips.

"You fucked my husband in the limo, didn't you?"

"Yes, Ma'am."

Crack. Diana jerked at the stinging blow on her clit. Somehow she managed not to cry out. Victoria prowled around her, a big cat looking for her next meal.

"Did I give you direct permission to fuck him?"

"No, Ma'am."

The second blow on her clit drove pain through her body.

"Did you like it?"

"Yes, Ma'am."

Crack. This one landed on the tip of her left breast. Her own juices dampened the leather tip and made the sting of the crop worse. A glimmer of fear entered her mind. Was Victoria really that upset about her having sex with Merrick outside of the playroom?

"What are you going to do to atone for not seeking my permission?"

"I don't know, Ma'am."

Crack, crack. Her right breast burned from the double hit. Diana struggled to stay in position.

"That answer's not good enough, little girl."

"I'm sorry, Ma'am."

The crop landed on her ass and she jerked, as much from the relief as the pain. A whipping on her ass she could handle.

"Did I ask you a question?"

"No, Ma'am. I'm sorry, Ma'am."

Four more smacks landed on Diana's ass, the pain almost welcome. She waited for another question, another landing of the crop, but there was nothing but faint rustling behind her. Not daring to look, she concentrated on evening out her breathing.

Victoria walked in front of her again, naked, and grabbed her by the hair. "Eat me, you little bitch."

Finally. Diana didn't need to be forced. She eagerly surged forward and licked Victoria's shaved pussy. Salt and musk, with a hint of sweetness, hit her tongue.

Victoria released her hair and stroked Diana's face, head and shoulders. Her thighs trembled as Diana focused on her domme's task.

A flick of her tongue. A long, slow sweep. A circle around Victoria's engorged clit before lightly sucking on the tiny bud. Diana alternated, changed the order at random, until Victoria's nails dug into her bare shoulders. The low moan that filled the room drove a spike of pleasure through Diana, but it wasn't enough. She wanted Victoria screaming. She arrowed her tongue and plunged it into Victoria's passage.

Her plan worked splendidly until Victoria's knees started to buckle. For a split second, Diana panicked. Did she break the scene to break Victoria's fall? She opened her eyes and reached up to catch Victoria.

Merrick was there, standing behind Victoria supporting her. Daniel leaned against the door, his arms crossed. Diana had been so intent on her task she didn't realize the men had come into the playroom. Merrick made *tsk*ing sounds.

He stared down at her, the stern mask on his face. "Did Victoria tell you to stop?"

Fear rose, made Diana's throat dry. "No, Sir."

"Did I tell you to stop?"

"No, Sir." She peered at them through her lowered eyelashes.

He tugged his wife back a couple of paces. His hand replaced Diana's mouth in playing with Victoria's pussy. Both his and Victoria's eyes glittered as they watched Diana.

"On your hands and knees, little girl," he ordered.

Daniel crossed behind her. Then she heard the sharp whistle of the crop. Her body tensed. But the snap didn't land on her.

"Excellent quality, Vicki. Where did you get it?" Diana shivered at the deep timbre of his voice.

"A lovely little tack shop down in Manassas." She sighed and rubbed her ass against Merrick's trousers as he continued to finger-fuck her.

The sight only set Diana's libido on high, but this game had barely started. None of them would let her come anytime soon. Tears of sheer frustration blurred her vision. Another whistle and snap made her flinch, even though the blow landed on something behind her.

"How many strikes have you given her, Vicki?"

"Only ten."

Merrick chuckled. "What was that lecture you gave me about being gentle with her?"

"She's ready for more."

Daniel swung the crop between Diana's legs. She jerked at the sting on her pussy and bit her lip to keep from making a sound.

"Not very vocal, is she?" Daniel remarked.

Another laugh from Merrick. "She nearly chewed my suit jacket apart to keep the driver from knowing what I was doing to her in the limo."

Fingers trailed along Diana's spine and she shuddered. Part of her wanted to run out the door. As Merrick constantly repeated, all she had to do was say the safeword. But what would they say if she quit this scene?

This is nothing. And I'll never have Daniel's cock if I stop now.

The crop landed on her ass. Her body shook, more from the realization of what she really wanted than the strike.

"Do I have to order you to make a sound, little girl?" Daniel's voice rasped in her ear. Why did his use of the term bother her?

"I'll do what my master commands, Sir."

He rubbed the hardened tips of her breasts with the riding crop. "And who is your master here?"

Shit! A logic question with no right answer. No matter who she said, the other two would be offended. And if she said all three, then they'd mock her for not understanding what she'd gotten herself into. Blood pounded in her ears.

"Answer me." Daniel's voice was calm, reasonable, but her muscles tensed at what she knew came next.

Crack. His blow landed on her ass, but it was so much harder than Victoria's. Tears welled in her eyes.

"All of you, Sir."

The leather tip of the crop touched her chin and tilted her head up until she faced Daniel. He crouched in front of her. "If you have three masters, and if you service one master orally, what must you do for the others?"

She blinked the tears away and sniffed. "Service the others equally, Sir."

"Good girl." He patted her head and stood. "On your knees."

She obeyed, but when she placed her hands behind her back, he slapped her left upper arm with the crop. "I want your hands as well as your mouth on my dick."

"Yes, Sir." A frisson of pleasure traveled down her spine and between her legs. Wetness trickled down her thigh at the thought of touching him.

He unbuttoned and unzipped his jeans, and his cock sprang from his shorts.

Surprisingly, he didn't palm the back of her head and shove his erection down her throat. He simply stood there waiting for her to start. Part of her was thankful for that small favor. Gagging on his thick cock would have embarrassed her to no end.

She reached out with the tip of her tongue and flicked it between the head and the rod. He still didn't move. Emboldened, she swept her tongue around the head. His taste was earthy, wholly male. She took as much of him as she could into her mouth while grasping the root with both hands.

He touched her then, ran his fingers through her short hair, caressed her neck. His callused hands felt so good on her skin. His strokes broke her concentration, and she nearly choked.

I'm not losing it here. Diana eased back until her lips molded the head again. She breathed through her nose while her tongue tickled his delicate frenulum. Once the reflex died and she was assured she wouldn't throw up, she sucked more of him again.

With one hand, she played with his sac. The other followed her lips up and down his cock. She enjoyed pleasuring with him so much that his sharp shove startled her.

It took a second to regain her balance. Disappointment hit her hard. His pre-come had leaked into her mouth. He was so close to coming. She was sure of it.

Diana looked up at him, trying to find what she had done wrong. His chest heaved. His sac was tight and wrinkled. But she didn't dare ask why he'd stopped her. She lowered her gaze to the carpet. Tears from physical agony she didn't mind, but the last thing she wanted was for him to see tears from her emotional pain.

And that's what it was. She'd known him only five days, and she liked him. Not "fun playmate" liked him. "Liked him" liked him. Oh, god, was she in trouble.

Chapter Ten

Diana swallowed the lump in her throat and pushed the idea out of her head. She couldn't possibly be attached to Daniel already. She barely knew him.

Focus on something else. Like the fact they weren't allowing her to bring them to climax. A new emotion infiltrated her. Shame. Why wouldn't they let her please them?

No, there had to be more to the delays than that. Victoria wouldn't let Diana service her to prove her power that first night. Last weekend, Merrick delayed to teach Diana self-control.

So what exactly were they planning? Just how long were they continuing this game of deprivation tonight? Until she collapsed from exhaustion?

Someone else stepped in front of her. A quick glance showed Merrick. He'd taken the time to undress.

He lifted her chin to meet his gaze. "What's wrong, little girl?"

"Why won't you let me pleasure you? Have I done something wrong?" The words tumbled out before she could stop them.

His palm cupped her face. "Is that what you think?"

"I don't know what to think." The tears came despite her best effort. Dammit, it was like she was a child again, trying desperately to please her parents. She wanted to cuss, use every swear word she could think of. She wanted someone to tell her she was doing fine.

"You're not supposed to think in this room. You're only supposed to feel. And trust us to make sure everyone's satisfied. Can you do that for me?"

She swallowed hard before she whispered, "Yes, Sir."

His palm shifted from her cheek to the back of her head. "You know how I like it."

She swallowed again, then opened her mouth wide. No gentle penetration this time. He took her mouth as hard and fast as he'd taken her pussy in the limo.

Diana tilted her head, concentrated on her breathing, and kept her lips tight.

This is how servicing a dom should be. Letting him take her any which way he felt like and her accepting his control.

One last slow thrust, and Merrick withdrew from her. No semen coated her lips or throat. He hadn't come either. Nor had he whipped her.

"On the bed. Lay on your back on the half closest to us."

"Yes, Sir." She scrambled to obey his order. Victoria had turned down the bed-covers while she'd sucked Daniel and Merrick's cocks. The new crisp, white sheets felt wonderful on her burning ass.

Victoria climbed onto the mattress too. She positioned herself next to Diana, except she was on her knees and elbows, her ass high in the air.

She looked over her shoulder. "You know how I like it, Danny." She wiggled her hips.

"Why, certainly, Miss Vicki." Daniel had lost his clothes as well. He climbed onto the bed, positioned himself and rammed his cock into her. She made encouraging noises as he doggy-fucked her.

"Show-offs. Spread your legs, little girl." Humor glinted in Merrick's eyes as he knelt between Diana's knees. "Sometimes, the old stand-bys are the best, aren't they?" He winked.

Diana couldn't help it. She smiled. "Yes, Sir."

He grabbed her ass. She whimpered at the fresh pain from her tender flesh. It was forgotten when he hoisted her and impaled her on his engorged cock. This time, he fucked her slow and easy.

Fingers twined with hers. She looked at the woman beside her. Ecstasy etched itself on Victoria's face, and she squeezed Diana's hand. Diana clutched Victoria as if she were a lifeline on this whirlpool of sensation.

Diana closed her eyes at the delicious friction in her pussy. Now, she understood what Merrick meant about taking the edge off earlier. She wouldn't have lasted this long without the quickie in the limo. Hell, she would've come from sucking Daniel's cock.

Merrick released one ass cheek and toyed with her clit. Or she thought it was Merrick. Her mind was too immersed in its hormonal cocktail to force her eyes open to see for sure. The pressure built inside her, layers added by hearing Daniel fuck Victoria, smelling the musky scent of raw lust from all of them.

"Diana, look at me."

Her eyelids fluttered open at Merrick's husky murmur.

He picked up the pace, hammering into her. "Let it go, little girl. Come for me."

His permission was all she needed. Her tentative control shattered, and every muscle contracted, sending waves of bliss through her. Merrick stiffened, and his hoarse shout followed the throb of his cock as he pumped his come into her.

Victoria's familiar chant of "Oh god" launched on the heels of Merrick collapsing next to Diana.

"Last one wins," Daniel declared. He grinned at her, a wicked promise as he pumped Victoria's pussy once. Twice. On the third, his eyes closed and serenity filled his rugged features.

Victoria fell to her side and sidled closer to Diana. "Pumpernickel." With a contented sigh, Victoria placed the sweetest kiss on Diana's mouth. "That wasn't so bad, was it?"

"No," she whispered. "Not bad at all."

The men cuddled against hers and Victoria's backs until everyone was touching. In that warm, contented huddle, Diana realized this was the happiest she'd been in her life.

Except the last time she'd felt this good, everything had turned to shit in a heartbeat. A tremor rippled through her. Victoria purred something in a comforting tone and stroked her thigh. But Diana was awake long after the breathing of her lovers stilled.

When Diana awoke, the bed was still full, the other three sound asleep. Daniel snored softly, and she covered her mouth to stifle a giggle. A small patch of light trickled past the fringe on the drapes.

As much as she wanted to stay in bed and go back to sleep, her bladder reminded her why she woke up in the first place.

She managed to slide from under Victoria's arm around her waist, but Merrick's possessive leg over her calves proved more problematic. She eased it up. He snorted, jerked and rolled over. Thankfully, they all stayed unconscious.

After a quick trip to her room and the adjoining bathroom, she debated on whether to return to the big bed in the playroom. While she desired the closeness, she needed a little time to process everything that happened yesterday. She donned her bathrobe and headed for the kitchen.

Within minutes, a pot of coffee brewed while she retrieved the morning's *Post*. She smiled as she spread the sections across the table. Merrick and Victoria were such a contradiction. Very modern in terms of relationships, yet so old-fashioned in other ways. Like reading newspapers.

"Good morning."

Daniel stood in the doorway, naked. So much for a little alone time. "Morning. Coffee's almost ready." She pulled another cup out of the cupboard.

The silence stretched as he watched her. His scrutiny set off warning bells in her head, but she couldn't decide which kind of warning they were giving her.

He crossed the kitchen. For something to do, she turned to retrieve the cream from the refrigerator. When she pivoted, he was inches from her.

"Do I make you nervous?"

She straightened her back. "A little. Yes."

"Why?" Crystal eyes stared into hers.

Honesty seemed her best option. "I'm not sure. I guess because I don't know what to expect. You acted like you wanted to kiss me the other night, but you didn't. Then last night during the scene, you had no problem with me sucking your cock . . ." She shrugged as her voice trailed off.

Tilting his head, he regarded her. "Is that what you want? A kiss?"

His incredulous attitude ignited her temper. "Victoria and Merrick have no problem kissing me."

For several seconds, she didn't dare breathe. Waited to see what he would do.

His hand rose and rested on the back of her neck. He moved cautiously, like someone not wanting to scare a small child or an animal. His head dipped.

It was the lightest brush of his lips, but she wanted, needed more. Her lips parted, an invitation.

His tongue swept her bottom lip, tested and tasted, before a gentle bite on the fleshy middle. It was a slow, seductive invasion.

She reached for him, but he tugged her wrists behind her back. His tongue teased hers, explored her thoroughly. Her nipples beaded until bittersweet pain filled them, and no doubt he could feel the hard tips when he pulled her tight against his body.

His cock swelled and pressed against her, just above her mound. Not where she needed it. She shifted, wanting him to fill her. Her pussy throbbed, impatient, willing to explode from his mouth on hers.

When they parted, she couldn't seem to find her breath. She stared at him, amazed. No one had ever kissed her that thoroughly. Nearly made her come just by that simple act. And she wanted more.

Before she could kiss him again, he spun her around and jerked her arm into some kind of locking hold. A cry of pain escaped from her. She tried to move, but even a twitch made her shoulder feel like he would rip it from the socket.

"Demanding little sub, aren't you? I don't think it's a kiss you really want." His breath was hot on her neck.

"Let me go." She tried to fight, but it hurt too damn much.

He nuzzled her neck though he kept a tight grip on the arm he'd twisted behind her back. "You can scream for Vicki and Merrick if you want. They would come running and rescue you." A nip on her ear lobe sent an arrow of lust straight to her pussy. "Do you want to be rescued?"

"No." The word came out more of a gasp than coherent language. Part of her wanted to weep because he could push her buttons so easily.

A soft chuckle. "I didn't think so the way you were watching us last night. Did you like the way I fucked Vicki from behind?"

When she didn't answer, he twisted her arm a little more. She bit her tongue to keep from crying out.

"Answer me."

"Yes." The pressure on her shoulder eased.

"Did you imagine yourself in her place?"

"Oh, yes." The words slipped out before she could stop them. She bit her tongue again to keep from adding she'd imagined him fucking her in every position since their dinner on Thursday.

His cock pressed against her hip. Before she realized what was happening, he shoved her face down onto the tabletop, her breasts smashed against the wood. One huge hand grasped both of her wrists behind her back. He yanked her bathrobe out of the way. Cool air caressed her ass, her exposed pussy.

She swallowed a sob. No doubt he could see her parted pussy lips, the liquid glistening. He would know how much her body wanted him. This was so out of bounds, violated all of Victoria's rules. And yet, she wanted him to take her. Here. Now. Hard.

Respect for their hostess overrode the lust threatening to consume her. "W-we shouldn't do this in here."

"Do what?" His cock probed her slick opening, teased her clit.

Desperation raised its head. As much as she found Daniel fascinating, the last thing she wanted was to ruin her relationship with Victoria and Merrick. "You know her rules. Sex in the playroom only."

A slap landed on her ass. "Are you talking back to me?"

"No, I—" Her train of thought disappeared when he pushed into her. Despite Merrick fucking her twice yesterday, despite her wetness, Daniel stretched her body to the point of pain. She cried out, and he stopped.

He said nothing, let her catch her breath, before he pushed further into her. In spite of his attitude and his words, he took his time, letting her pussy adjust to him. Then just as carefully, he pulled out.

"What were you saying, little girl?"

"I—" She was disturbed and titillated by his use of Merrick and Victoria's nickname for her. Why the hell was she bothered by that and not by his forced fucking? "Nothing."

He eased that huge cock into her again. God, she didn't want this to stop. Didn't want *him* to stop.

"Good girl," he said softly. With his free hand, he found her clit and massaged the hard little bud as he slid out and back in.

A moan built in her throat and escaped. Her knees wobbled. If she wasn't trapped against the table, she would have collapsed to the floor. She wished he would speed up, pump into her hard and fast. Instead, he kept to that agonizing pace.

The soft shushing of bare feet on hard wood brought her head up.

Victoria stood in the doorway in her own bathrobe, her fists propped on her hips. "Really, Daniel? What have I said about using my kitchen table?"

Heat flooded Diana's face at Victoria's perturbed expression. She wanted to run to her room and hide, but she couldn't, not with Daniel pinning her to the wood. *With his wood, you mean*, said her insane inner voice followed by its mocking giggle. She closed her eyes.

"I think she's a little jealous." His warm breath caressed Diana's ear. His cock made another slow slide into her pussy.

"Who's jealous?" Merrick's voice. Now her embarrassment was complete. Would they blame her for this? Ban her from their bed?

"Really, love? What's the point of having rules if you and Daniel continue to flaunt them?" Victoria asked her husband.

"Us?" Merrick's tone held mock annoyance. "Who was fondling Diana in the guest bedroom before dinner last week? Or did you think I couldn't smell her sweet scent on you?"

"I didn't fuck her on my kitchen table."

Diana squeezed her lids and clamped down on her mortification. Or tried to. Daniel said nothing, just continued his slow fucking of her.

"Do you really want to stop him?" Merrick's voice sounded on the edge of laughter. "Diana looks like she's very close to coming. Would you do that to the poor girl?" Wood scraped against wood. "Why don't you sit on my lap, and we'll watch? You can punish them for violating your rules later."

Something rustled nearby. Diana jerked, struggled, but Daniel had her firmly pinned. There wasn't a damn thing she could do to stop him from fucking her.

Except say the safeword.

So why don't you? her inner voice asked.

Because deep down, she liked what he was doing to her. Liked him kissing her. Liked him.

What disturbed her more was their audience. But Merrick had watched Victoria eat her out more than once, just as Victoria had watched her husband take Diana in every imaginable position. So why did the thought of the two of them treating Daniel and her as entertainment trouble her?

"Diana, open your eyes and watch us."

She couldn't resist Merrick's sharp command. Her lids flickered, and her gaze settled on them. She forced her eyes to stay open even though she wanted to savor Daniel's cock pushing into her.

Slightly to her right, Merrick sat on one of the kitchen chairs. Not only did he position his seat to get a good view of Daniel fucking her, the placement allowed her to watch Merrick and Victoria as well without twisting her neck into an uncomfortable position.

Victoria had shed her robe. She faced Daniel and Diana, straddled her husband's lap, and impaled herself on his cock. A dreamy look filled her eyes as she leaned against his chest and he tweaked her nipples.

Diana didn't think she could be any more aroused, but watching them sent her libido over the moon. Her internal muscles squeezed around Daniel.

He stopped moving. His erection filled her, felt so good, but dammit, she needed some friction. She wiggled her hips.

In return, Daniel withdrew from her completely. She whimpered at the loss.

"You two might want to catch up. My little girl here is about to explode," he said.

Not *little girl*, but *my little girl*. The idea sent a warmth through her that had nothing to do with the sex or the domination.

Diana wriggled, wanting that magnificent cock, wanting him back inside her. An evil chuckle sounded above her ear. "Or we could bind her in the playroom and leave her all fired up for the rest of the morning."

"You wouldn't," she squealed. Her reward for the outburst was another slap on the ass.

"What did I tell you about talking back?"

"I'm sorry, Sir." Every muscle tensed in frustration.

Instead of her usual amused seductiveness, another expression filled Victoria's features. One that made Diana very nervous. "Actually, punishing you both in the playroom is an excellent idea."

"Now?" Daniel tried to sound bored, but Diana could hear the current of excitement in his voice.

"*Casa mea, regulae meae.*" Victoria's smile was pure evil. "My house, my rules."

Oh, god. Diana's body trembled at the thought of what Victoria might do to them.

"We must obey our hostess." Daniel released Diana's wrists and gently pulled her upright. She swayed for a moment, her knees threatening to rebel and give out.

"Upstairs. Now." Victoria's already throaty voice dropped an octave.

Diana scurried to obey. Once inside the playroom, she shed her bathrobe and knelt next to the chair in the appropriate position.

Victoria tossed the huge half-circle pillow on the mattress. "Daniel, on the bed, face down over the pillow. Merrick, please secure him."

Daniel sauntered to the bed, his cock jutting proudly. The man actually had the audacity to wink at her in front of Merrick and Victoria before he climbed onto the huge mattress and positioned himself.

Diana swallowed hard. It was her fault for not stopping Daniel. Victoria wouldn't actually hurt him, would she? The dominatrix in her was out in full-force.

Merrick said nothing. Instead of his usual stern expression, he looked amused as he pulled the leather and velvet restraints from their compartments and fastened the cuffs to Daniel's wrists and ankles.

Victoria stalked over to the bureau and yanked open the bottom drawer. She pulled out something with straps. A larger-than-life, anatomically correct purple dildo hung from the leather.

Diana swallowed hard. No one had used a strap-on on her before, but Jesus! The size of the thing. She could barely handle Daniel's cock. A tiny bit of relief swept through her when she saw the tubes of lubricant in Victoria's hand as well.

Victoria stepped into the device, pulled it up her long legs, and buckled it in place. She sauntered over to the racks, giving both Daniel and Diana a good view of the device.

Daniel smirked and rolled his eyes. "You think that's going to scare me? It's not exactly like I'm an ass virgin here."

Shut up, Daniel. Please shut up. Diana tried to plead with her eyes, but he ignored her.

"You know how much I like it when you peg me, Vicki," he mocked.

Victoria picked up the single tail whip. She trailed it over Diana's back as she crossed back to the bed. "Oh, Danny, sweetie." She shook her head and patted his cheek. "You're not getting pegged. At least, not by me."

For the first time this morning, he actually looked worried.

"Did I give you permission to play with my sub this morning?"

"No, Ma'am," he ground out through clenched teeth.

The whip snapped his ass. Victoria circled the bed. "Did I give you permission to do a scene this morning?"

"No, Ma'am."

Crack.

Fury filled his eyes.

Diana stared at him. This was all her fault. She should have stopped him in the kitchen. *I'm sorry*, she mouthed.

He gave her a half smile and a slight shake of the head. A little part of her was relieved. So he wasn't angry with her.

"Did you forget the rules regarding sex in my house?" Victoria continued

"No, Ma'am."

Crack.

"He's yours, Merrick." Victoria stroked Daniel's cheek with the whip. "I hope you'll remember this the next time you're a guest in my home." She leaned close to his ear. "While Merrick teaches you a lesson, you are not allowed to come. If you do, we will leave you strapped to the bed and repeat the procedure until you can control yourself."

Merrick ripped open a foil packet and rolled a condom over his erection. Diana shuddered. He was going to ass fuck Daniel for disobedience. Maybe repeatedly. Her anal muscles squeezed together at the memory of the pain inflicted on her years ago.

She couldn't let this happen. "Miss Victoria, please don't do this! I knew your rules. I screwed up. I didn't say the safeword or call for you. Please don't punish him for my mistakes."

Victoria's pale eyes turned on her. "You're totally correct in all of your points, little girl. And while it's admirable you feel compassion for him, what you should have done was accept your punishment instead of breaking yet another rule."

Horror punched Diana in the stomach. God, how she hated ball-gags. And she had issued the proverbial engraved invitation to Victoria to use one.

Merrick reached into a drawer and pulled out a harness with a bright red ball. He tossed it to Victoria, who set her whip on the chair.

"Open wide." She deliberately used Merrick's words in a mocking tone.

Indecision tore at Diana. *Say the safeword. Don't say it.* She closed her eyes to try to calm herself and took a deep steadying breath.

She opened her mouth.

Victoria was surprisingly gentle as she strapped the gag in place. "Diana, open your eyes."

She obeyed and a couple of tears escaped.

Victoria cupped Diana's wet cheeks. "Since you cannot speak, slap the floor three times for the safe signal. From now on, for any questions I ask you, slap the carpet once for 'yes' or twice for 'no.' Do you understand me?"

Diana smacked her hand on the floor once and resumed her subservient position.

"Good girl." Victoria stroked her hair. She took a few steps away from the chair. "Come over here so we both have an excellent view of the boys."

Diana crawled to the spot Victoria indicated. When neither she or Merrick were looking, Daniel winked again.

What was he trying to tell her? That he'd been punished this way before?

Things clicked in Diana's brain. Daniel was a switch.

Before she had time to mull that realization, Merrick climbed on the bed. The tube of lubricant he held would be a small mercy.

"On you hands and knees too, little girl," Victoria ordered.

When Diana hesitated for a fraction of an instant, the whip bit her ass cheek.

Once in position, Victoria gave her the same three lashes she'd given Daniel. She asked no questions because Diana had already confessed her transgressions.

"Spread your legs wider."

Diana did so. Victoria's body heat caressed her ass and thighs, but she didn't touch Diana.

"Watch."

She didn't want to be a witness to Daniel's humiliation. Last night had been so much easier when she was the one used.

Merrick smeared the thick lube over his fingers. Old terror reared up in Diana when he started playing with Daniel's ass. His other hand fondled Daniel's balls and cock.

Daniel buried his face in the sheets. She couldn't blame him. In his position, she would have done the same.

"Daniel, look at us," Victoria commanded.

Instead of rage or fear or humiliation in his eyes, Diana saw the same thing she'd seen in the kitchen. Lust. He was enjoying this?

"Since Diana must watch Merrick fuck you, it's only fair that you watch me fuck her."

Diana wanted to die at Victoria's pronouncement. The thought of multiple partners had been intriguing last week, but now?

She nearly jumped out of her skin when Victoria's warm, wet fingers touched her puckered hole, rimming her. The other hand played with her slick folds, encouraging her to keep her thighs apart.

And she wanted to. Victoria's ministrations felt amazingly . . . good.

One finger pushed past the ring of muscle and penetrated her ass while the other hand thrust into her passage. No one had ever done two holes at once, not until Victoria. The sensation was as incredible as the last time. Diana couldn't help herself. She moaned.

Daniel smiled at her and pushed back against Merrick's hand. All the new sights and sounds swirled in a heady mix. Watching them excited her as much as Victoria's manipulations of her body.

Merrick stopped for a moment and slathered lube over his condom. Victoria's touch disappeared. Given the couple's tandem attentions until now, Diana could guess what would happen next. Her body tensed. Victoria's fingers messing with her ass were one thing. That gigantic dildo was another.

Anticipation sparkled in Daniel's eyes. Merrick pressed his cock against Daniel, who jerked and moaned as it slid home.

Something cool and wet that could only be Victoria's strap-on ran over her clit and probed her passage. The ball-gag muffled her whimper as the huge purple thing pushed into her. Despite the uncomfortable stretching, relief flooded Diana.

The tandem fucking took on a dual rhythm. As Victoria shoved into her, Merrick would pull out of Daniel. Any emotional discomfort Diana had fled at watching two men. They looked gorgeous together.

The tempo increased. The excitement had her so close to the edge when Victoria abruptly withdrew the dildo.

A faint cry of protest sounded in the back of Diana's throat. That earned her another crack of the whip.

"Merrick."

He closed his eyes at Victoria's warning tone, fighting for control of himself. Very carefully, he pulled out of Daniel's ass.

"Vicki . . ." The harsh plea broke the quiet. Daniel wouldn't say it, but the begging was evident in his eyes.

Victoria strode past Diana, the whip in her hand. She no longer wore the strap-on. Daniel flinched, but the whip snapped his right ass cheek, not anything more sensitive. "Did I give you permission to come?"

"No, Ma'am." His answer was almost guttural.

Diana wanted to cry at the frustration. Victoria had taken Daniel's suggestion in the kitchen literally. She would leave them both restrained and on edge the entire day.

She glanced at her husband. "Come, Merrick."

He climbed down from the bed, his sac tight against his body. With the same excruciating care, he peeled off the condom and tossed it in the small waste can by the bureau. Diana blinked in surprise when Victoria dropped to the floor, rolled on her back and spread her knees wide less than a foot from Diana's face.

Her husband was on Victoria in a flash, ramming her hard. The slap of his thighs against hers filled the room. Less than five seconds, he stiffened and what could only be described as a low roar came out of his mouth.

Beneath his body, Victoria jerked and shook as her own orgasm claimed her.

They lay there, stroking each other, panting until their trembling subsided.

Diana wasn't sure how long it was before they parted and climbed to their feet. Her own muscles quivered with deprived need.

Victoria contemplated Daniel for several seconds, her index finger tapping her chin, before she shook her head. "Delayed gratification will be sufficient for you I believe." She pivoted to look at Diana. "For you, the belt will do."

The belt? What fresh torture was that going to inflict?

Once again, Merrick crossed to the bureau and pulled something with black straps from a drawer. The only comforting thing was that the two protruding blue rods weren't a huge as the purple dildo.

Two rods?

Diana's heart sank. What was worse? That Victoria and Merrick were going to make sure she was on the sexual edge the rest of the day? Or that she was going to get ass-fucked after all?

Chapter Eleven

Diana tried not to wince as Merrick and Victoria fitted the butt plug and the dildo portions of the belt into their respective holes. At least, they used plenty of lube. They secured the belt with locks on each hip.

"That's a lovely little chastity belt," Daniel quipped. "Are you afraid I'm going to escape my bonds and ravish your precious sub?"

"After your performance in my kitchen, I wouldn't put it past you," Victoria replied. "You may stand up, Diana."

The damn belt made what should have been a simple process excruciating. The plugs stimulated her body in ways she'd never imagined. Plus, the section of the belt covering her pussy forced her thighs apart.

Once she was on her feet, Victoria removed the ball gag. "I hope you learned your lesson."

"Yes, Ma'am."

"Good. Pull the chair over here."

The belt teased her ass and pussy as she struggled to move the chair where Victoria indicated. The damn thing was heavier than it looked.

"Sit down."

Diana obeyed, but bit her lower lip as the plugs were shoved deeper from her weight on them. She found out why the chair was so heavy. Merrick popped a secret compartment on the arm. A metal band swung out, and he locked the device securely over her wrist. He repeated the process with her ankles and other wrist. She was effectively plugged and trapped.

Victoria crossed her arms. "You two can sit in here for a while and contemplate your misbehavior. And Daniel, I'd better not see any semen on my sheets when I return."

"Yes, Ma'am." From the grin on his mug, he found the whole situation terribly funny.

When the door closed behind them, his smile faded and he muttered, "Well, this is a nice mess we got ourselves into."

"We?" Game or no game, ire spiked through Diana. "There is no 'we.' *You* pinned me to the kitchen table and started fucking me."

A wicked grin lit his face. "*You* could have said the safeword at any time. I think you enjoyed my dick inside you too much to say no."

"Cocky bastard, aren't you?"

His grin broadened. "Why, yes, I am. In fact, I'm one cocky bastard getting a major case of blue balls here." He tugged at the restraint on his right wrist.

An electric buzz from the plug inside her pussy made her jump. "Shit!"

Daniel looked at her. Concern filled his eyes. "What's wrong?" He shifted on the bed.

Another vibration teased her ass, and she gasped at the exquisite sensation. "What the hell is that?"

"Diana? Tell me what's wrong." He yanked on his arm restraints.

Both the plugs went off, and she cried out.

"Diana?"

"Stop moving," she ordered through gritted teeth.

He didn't listen to her. He kept tugging on his cuffs, struggling to get free. The continuous vibration coupled with the mild electric charge sent her body into overload. The first orgasm ripped through her, and she screamed.

"Victoria!" Daniel roared. "Merrick! Get your asses in here!"

No one came to the door.

The pause while he yelled gave her a respite from the stimulation.

"Stop moving, dammit." Diana gasped for breath while her body continued to twitch.

Daniel wrestled with the restraints again, and his struggles set off the plugs. The second orgasm took even less time than the first. Her body convulsed, unable to resist, much less escape from the belt or Daniel setting it off. Her back arched. If it wasn't for the weight of the chair, she would have fallen over and pulled it on top of her.

"Goddammit! Hold still, Daniel!" Her words devolved into another scream as the third orgasm shook her.

"Okay, okay, I'm not moving. I'm holding perfectly still." He raised his right hand. Her pussy twitched at another shock and vibration.

"When I say don't move, I *mean* don't fucking move," she ground out.

"I'm sorry," he murmured. His blue eyes really did look contrite. "What's wrong?"

"Ever have a dom apply electric shocks to your nipples or privates?"

"No."

"Well, now I have." She glared at him.

"I don't—" He flicked a couple of fingers, but it was enough to put tension on the restraint.

A sound that was half pain, half pleasure tore from her throat at the stimulation from the pussy plug. Once it passed, she shot him a furious look. "How the hell have you remained a cop this long when you totally ignore orders?"

Daniel stared up at the bed posts. "They must have some wireless control system inside the frame."

"No shit, Sherlock," she muttered.

"I can't believe Victoria would be stupid and unsafe doing something like this." Daniel's eyes scanned the room, or as much as he could from his position. He accidentally moved his left ankle, and the butt plug vibrated. Diana hissed at the erotic sensation running up her spine.

She wasn't sure what pissed her off more. That Victoria and Merrick left her alone with someone so clueless. Or that she was seriously enjoying what the belt did to her. Especially the ass plug.

"Victoria's big on safety." Daniel watched Diana as she maneuvered back into a normal sitting position. "She and Merrick must be watching us from a webcam or something."

"Well, we've definitely given them a hell of a show then."

His forehead wrinkled. "Or she could have a remote in her hand while she's watching the camera, trying to make us think I'm triggering the belt. Diana, do you trust me?"

"The answer to that is, 'Hell, no.'" So why was she hoping he'd move so she could feel the intense pleasure again?

He chuckled. "Don't blame you. We can figure out the limits of their system before you have a heart attack."

"A heart attack isn't going to kill me."

Another laugh. "I don't think someone can die of pleasure."

She shook her head. "The problem is asphyxia. I read somewhere that if you tickle someone too long the diaphragm goes into seizures and they suffocate. A continuous orgasm through electro-stimulation can do something similar."

Daniel frowned. "Bullshit."

"It's what I read." The condescension in his voice scraped her already raw nerves, but the defensiveness in her own rubbed in the salt.

"On some half-assed sex website? Or were your previous doms so fucking stupid they couldn't train a dog?"

Diana clamped her mouth shut and stared at the huge chest of drawers. How long were Victoria and Merrick going to leave her in here with this asshole? Even better, what exactly did she think she saw in him earlier?

Thankfully, he kept his mouth shut as well. The silence echoed in the playroom. She'd give anything for a clock. How long had they left her in here? She wished she'd grabbed some toast or an apple. The few sips of coffee ate her gut like acid.

As if on cue, her stomach growled.

"You hungry?"

Her stomach gurgled again. She refused to look at the asshole.

"Hey, I'm sorry. I shouldn't have insulted your dom."

She ignored him. Or she did until he tugged on his right arm strap. She shrieked at the shock and vibration.

"So which plug did I set off?"

Her eyes narrowed. Focusing her anger at him didn't stop the aroused tingling along her skin.

"I'll yank it again if you don't answer me."

She should have been enraged by his threat. He wasn't her dom. But her nipples budded in anticipation. She simply smiled.

He jerked the cuff, and her body exploded in the most marvelous orgasm. She leaned her head against the back of the chair and panted as the tremors subsided.

"Hmmm, so the right wrist cuff activates the vaginal plug. I wonder what the right leg cuff does?"

Her head jerked up at the evil tone in his question. His grin was equally wicked. "You going to talk to me?"

They stared at each other. Diana counted to twenty in Spanish before he deliberately raised his right ankle.

The vibrator in her pussy delivered its shock. She wanted to scream, but she couldn't. Nothing seemed to work right. The orgasm rippled and ricocheted through all her muscles. It went on and on . . .

When it finally stopped, she desperately sucked in air.

"Continuous tension keeps the current going." When she didn't answer, he said, "Diana?"

The black spots danced with the colored ones in front of her eyeballs. Every muscle in her body ached like she'd been gangbanged by the Redskins. All fifty-three of them. Plus the coaching staff.

When the spots faded, her head lolled to the right, enough for her gaze to meet his. She pressed her lips together. This was all his fault, and if he was going to insult her, she wasn't giving him the satisfaction of talking to him.

He tugged on the left ankle restraint. Her back arched again at the delicious shock inside her ass, and she moaned. Who knew there were that many nerve endings in that part of the body?

"So that's the butt plug, huh?" He watched her, his wicked grin spread wide. "If you don't speak, you know I'll do it."

Diana hoped he'd do just that. They continued their stare-down. The fingers on his right hand twitched. But in the end, he stayed perfectly still.

The wicked grin faded to a scowl. "I can't believe this. I've been topped by a bottom." He buried his face in the mattress.

"Serves you right, switch" She snickered. "Thanks to you I'm not suffering from blue balls. Or the female equivalent, anyway." She arched her back and stretched as much as she could while manacled to the chair.

His head shifted enough that one blue eye peeked above the sheet. A muffled word came from the mattress that sounded suspiciously like "bitch."

It never occurred to her to play the part of tease with another sub. But before she could figure out how to put her new-found power to good use, the playroom door swung open.

Victoria's eyes gleamed as she tapped the whip handle against her thigh. "Since our little girl is having too much fun with her punishment, it's time for something else."

Chapter Twelve

Diana shivered when Merrick appeared behind Victoria. His cock was already erect again, and from the amused twist to his mouth, she knew exactly what was coming next.

Victoria stalked to the bed and examined the sheets. "I trust you won't defy my rules again?"

Daniel merely grinned at her and inclined his head toward Diana. "No guarantees if she's here."

The whip cracked across his ass. The smile faded, and he sighed. "No, Ma'am. I will not break any of your rules again."

Satisfied, Victoria crossed to the chair and bent over Diana. The whip caressed her cheek. "You liked what the anal plug did to you?"

Why couldn't they ask her this in private? Why in front of Daniel? Diana stared at the carpet. "Yes, Ma'am," she whispered.

Victoria leaned closer. Her index finger pressed Diana's chin up until their eyes met. "You were enjoying yourself in the kitchen before I walked in. After all the punishments, do you still want Daniel to fuck you?"

It was a trick question. She knew what the price would be to have Daniel's magnificent cock inside her. And she definitely wouldn't have a choice of where she could have it. Shame coated her skin because deep down she would have done just about anything for the opportunity to be with him.

Despite the edge of fear nudging her mind, Diana whispered, "Yes, Ma'am."

At the bed, Merrick unbuckled the cuffs that held Daniel. Yet, she could feel both men's attention on her. Part of her was flattered and aroused. The other part, the one that remembered the helplessness and the pain screamed at her to say the safeword and leave now.

"You told me you wanted to have two men fuck you at once." Victoria murmured.

The air froze in Diana's lungs. Victoria wasn't suggesting what she thought, was she? Diana nodded.

Victoria leaned even closer to Diana's ear and whispered, "I've had them both. Trust me, you won't forget the experience." She straightened and sauntered to the door. "Be gentle with her, boys." She winked at Diana before she left, pulling the door closed behind her.

Daniel rolled off the bed and stretched. His mouth widened in that wicked smile of his. He pulled the half-cylinder pillow he'd been draped over off the mattress and propped it in the corner.

Merrick knelt in front of her and unlatched the manacles. His hands ran over her legs and feet. "Stand up."

Her limbs still shook from the multiple orgasms. Every muscle felt like cherry Jell-o. The belt forcing her thighs apart made the simple process of getting up from the chair even more difficult. Merrick stood, held out his hands and helped her upright.

Again, he knelt before her and unbuckled the belt. She had to rest her hands on his shoulders to stay upright, but he didn't object.

"Do I get front or back?" Daniel tossed the small pillows back on the bed.

Merrick looked up at Diana and smirked. "Didn't Victoria say not to scare her?"

She knew Merrick was trying to be reassuring. Her ass muscles clenched around the plug at the thought of Daniel's cock penetrating her there. He was too freaking big.

Merrick tugged at the belt. "Relax, little girl."

Anxiety made letting go so damn hard. Diana concentrated on breathing and loosening the tension. With a liquid sound, Merrick pulled the plugs from her. Her face heated from her obvious pleasure in the device.

His head dipped, and his tongue licked her juices. She closed her eyes. The gentle touch intensified her arousal. The belt's vibrations and electric charges hadn't left her drained. They'd merely been the appetizer.

"Climb on the bed and lay on your right side facing Daniel."

Her eyes fluttered open at Merrick's instructions. He stood next to her. Daniel already lay on the mattress, his head propped on his fist. Daniel's smile didn't have the same wicked glint. Instead, it was steady, reassuring. The flat of Merrick's hand smacked her ass when she didn't move fast enough.

She wanted them both so bad she could feel her own liquid trickling down her thigh. But she didn't know if she could handle someone fucking her ass. The pain of her old dom's rape was too sharp in her mind years later. Not that Merrick would give her a choice.

Unless she said the safeword and walked out.

The need to experience two men won over the fear. She climbed the steps and positioned herself as ordered.

Daniel chuckled. "You're going to have to get closer if you expect this to be any fun."

He stroked her cheek, then laid the most delicate of kisses on her mouth. His touch was soft, sensual, not the demand to submit as it had been that first time in the kitchen. This one totally promised a pleasure she wouldn't forget.

She returned his attention, her free fingers drifting along the crisp hair of his arm, the hard edge of his hip.

Merrick nudged her still stinging ass. "Left leg over his hip, little girl. Assuming you can control yourself long enough, Daniel."

He snorted. "Better than you can, old man."

"Usual bet?" Merrick said.

"What bet?" Diana glanced wildly between the two men. Daniel's huge hand grasped the back of her thigh and guided her leg over his. His cock nudged her slick flesh.

"How many times we can make you come before we let go." Apparently, Merrick hadn't noticed or didn't care about her failure to remain silent. Behind her, the mattress shifted and dipped. His familiar body molded to her back, and his cock pressed against the cleft of her ass. He trailed kisses along her shoulder. "And who comes last."

Daniel's cock pushed into her. Not on the edge of pain like before, but still tight. She whimpered in disappointment at his shallow entry. He toyed with her left breast. "Greedy little thing, isn't she?"

"Very." Humor laced Merrick's voice. His fingers traced her puckered hole. Maybe not so puckered since he easily penetrated her.

Diana jerked and her nails dug into Daniel's arm. The plug was one thing. The thought of someone's cock actually fucking her ass triggered all her internal alarms. She couldn't do it. Not again. She twisted her head, the safeword on the tip of her tongue.

Daniel's palm pressed against her cheek, forcing her attention back to him. "No, honey, look at me. We won't hurt you." He sealed the promise with the most delicious kiss.

The pressure on her hole grew. She wiggled, fear mixing with lust as he played her breast, her mouth, like a master. He pinched the hard tip. Her back arched at the pleasure-pain, and Merrick thrust inside her ass.

"Breathe, Diana," Daniel whispered into her mouth.

Gradually, the fear released her. Merrick's cock didn't hurt. In fact, it felt . . . pretty damn good.

Daniel started a slow, easy rhythm, just as he had in the kitchen. Merrick alternated his thrusts with Daniel's. And the total experience put the belt to shame.

The men's tempo increased, and she moaned from the delectable tension ricocheting between her pussy and ass. Their cocks rubbed against each other through the thin membrane of her flesh. The first warning contraction tightened her muscles.

Daniel and Merrick slowed their pace. A low protest sounded in her throat.

"Something wrong, honey?" That damn wicked grin on Daniel's face said he knew exactly what was wrong.

"Please." The breathless pleading didn't sound like her at all. "Please don't stop."

As if on cue, the men stopped. *Rat bastards.* This was her real punishment, not Daniel's manipulation of the plugs.

Daniel chuckled. "I think we're just too much for our little girl."

"Should we stop and put the belt back on her?"

"No!" Her mouth expelled the word before she could stop it.

Merrick reached around and pinched her nipple. Hard. Diana cried out.

"Any more backtalk and I'll put you in a different belt. One that is more painful than the first one you wore. One that definitely will not give you any release. Do you understand me?"

"Yes, Sir."

Merrick started the rhythm again, and Daniel followed his lead. Their hands roamed over her skin. Each caress added to the sensuous electricity between the three of them. Her lips met Daniel's. Her free hand reached behind and grabbed Merrick's ass cheek, urging him deeper.

The delicious friction built to a fever pitch. Daniel eased his hand between them and thumbed her clit.

"Don't. I can't—"

"You may come," Merrick whispered in her ear.

His permission meant nothing. Her body had a mind of its own. Her hips rocked between the men, seeking them, needing them. The thin line of discipline fractured and collapsed. She shrieked as every muscle spasmed at once. Her pussy and ass convulsed around the cocks embedded in them.

"Shit," Daniel murmured. His eyes closed. He pumped once, twice, then hot come flooded her still quivering pussy.

Behind her, Merrick laughed. "I win." His hand claimed her hip, and he pumped her hard and furious. And it felt so damn good, tension built in her body as he ground into her ass.

Daniel's eyes blinked open and he stared into hers. His cock slid from her pussy. His fingers dipped and spread her juices around her clit, teasing it back to life while Merrick fucked her ass.

The second orgasm took her and splintered her body into a million pieces. She was vaguely aware of Merrick's growl, but the pulse of his cock as he shot his load into her ass extended the tremors that shook her.

Everything felt so good. *This is the way sex should be.* The tears started and she couldn't stop them. Daniel and Merrick held and stroked her as all the old rage and pain poured out.

Chapter Thirteen

After Diana changed the sheets and straightened the playroom, the rest of the day passed in a blur of weirdly normal suburban weekend entertainment. Once everyone took showers and dressed, the four of them went to a little bistro two blocks from the house for brunch.

They spent the afternoon playing various card games, ordered in from a Japanese restaurant for dinner, and watched a sitcom. What surprised Diana most of all was when Victoria declared an early night since everyone had been up at daybreak.

No games. No sex. No cuddling in the big bed.

Despite everything that had happened earlier, it was a little disappointing.

Not sleepy at all, Diana changed into her nightclothes, curled up in her bed and tried to focus on the novel she'd downloaded to her smart phone.

The knock on her door was so quiet she thought she imagined it. The vagaries of a two-century-old house she concluded until it sounded again. Then Daniel's equally quiet, "Diana?" She crawled out of bed and opened the door to find him standing there in his pajama bottoms.

Blood roared in her ears as it drained from her head and filled other body parts. Her breasts swelled when his gaze swept them. It wasn't like her baby doll hid a whole lot. It wasn't like he hadn't seen them, touched them, earlier.

His smile was almost self-deprecating. "May I come in?"

She couldn't speak, her mouth was so dry. In contrast, liquid flooded her pussy. She nodded and stepped back.

Daniel closed the door behind him. His presence filled the little bedroom, but it wasn't intimidating. More like this morning, when his cock stretched her . . .

She clamped down on that train of thought. "Did you need something?"

"I . . ." He ran a hand over his head, like his fingers tried to find the words in his brain for his tongue to use. "I know I have no right to ask this, especially after I got you in trouble this morning, but I—" The words came out in a rush. He stepped closer, raised a hand, then dropped it. "I want you."

She froze at the hoarse emotion in his voice. "You mean you want to play? Just the two of us?"

"No." He stared at the wall behind her bed. "I'm sorry. This isn't coming out right. I just want to have sex with you. No games. No playing."

"Plain, old vanilla sex?" Somehow that prospect was scarier than him pinning her to the kitchen table and fucking her from behind.

"Well . . ." He ran his hands up her bare arms, leaving goose bumps in their wake. "I was thinking more chocolate with sprinkles."

She laughed at his impish grin. She couldn't help it. "Do you have any idea how racist that was?"

"But my charming personality and huge dick will make you forgive me, right?" He pulled her tight against him. Her pussy clenched at his cock pressing against her belly. But the vulnerable look in his eyes latched onto her soul.

She needed answers more. "Why didn't you kiss me after you took me home Thursday?"

His eyes dropped, but his hold on her shoulders tightened. "Because—" His hard swallow was audible. "Because if I had, I wouldn't have been able to leave. I . . . like you too much to be that much of an asshole."

She pulled away from his grasp and crossed her arms. "So you decided to be an asshole during the scene this morning?"

Again, the wickedly charming smile appeared on his face. "I rather got the impression you wanted to be punished. You craved it. It's like you not saying the safeword while we were in the kitchen. All you had to do was say something when you were manacled to the chair."

"I was pissed at you."

"Because I insulted your previous dom." He twitched and she half-expected him to touch her. Instead, he ran his hand over his hair. "I get it, and I'm sorry." He huffed out a breath. "I was jealous."

Then everything coalesced. "Victoria told you."

A wry smile tilted his mouth. "Apparently, their webcam has audio as well as video." He shrugged. "She only told me because she was concerned about your wellbeing. That what I said may have unintended consequences."

Diana stared at the blinds. Everything was so messed up in her life. Why wouldn't her attempt to enjoy herself with no strings get messed up, too?

He sighed. "Look, I said what I came to say. If you don't feel the same, I'll leave you alone." He turned toward the door.

Diana let her arms fall to her sides. "Who says I want you to leave?" She reached down, hooked the hem of her nightie with her thumbs, and pulled it over her head. Daniel's sharp intake of breath when he saw she didn't wear any bottoms aroused her more than any of the games in the last twenty-four hours.

Daniel slowly pulled on the drawstring of his pajamas. He eased the material over his cock, his hips, and stepped out of the bundle on the floor.

It was probably a good thing she didn't wear panties. They'd already be soaked.

He pulled her into his arms. Raw need filled his kiss. His hands caressed her back and drifted down. They molded her ass and lifted her so his cock pressed against her pussy. His touch was sensual, no pain, only pleasure.

She twined her arms around his neck and played with the short hair at the base of his skull. His tongue swept hers, searching, demanding.

He broke their kiss with a ragged gasp and bent his head. His lips toyed with the hard bead of one nipple. The tiny licks and bites could only be called worship. He gave equal time to her other breast before he knelt and nibbled his way down her stomach.

Diana couldn't remember a time where she was this turned on by a man performing the most basic acts. Was it because she knew what else he could be capable of? Would she be disappointed if he didn't dominate her here? If he didn't try to break Victoria's rules?

Any contemplation disappeared when he ran his finger over her pussy. Her very slick, very needy pussy.

His tongue followed his fingers. The flick of the tip against her clit nearly shot her out of her skin. She grabbed his shoulders to stay upright. Fingertips probed her passage, testing her readiness.

This wasn't like the games or the punishments. Or even Daniel and Merrick fucking her simultaneously. She'd lost count of the number of orgasms she'd had with the belt this morning. But nothing compared to the sweetness of him touching her now.

"Daniel." His name turned into a moan.

He plunged his fingers into her, working her, stretching her. Her nails dug into his skin at the pressure. She whimpered at the light sucking on her clit.

"Daniel," she whispered. "If you don't stop, I'll come before you're inside me."

He looked up at her and raised an eyebrow. "And that's a bad thing?"

She stroked his cheek, his stubble rough on her palm. "This time I want you inside me when I come for you."

His eyes darkened. No longer crystal, but the severe blue-gray of storm clouds. "Then you're on top."

"Why?"

He stood and kissed her again. "Because I want to see all of you when your pussy is squeezing my dick."

She shivered at his tone, his words. Even Merrick's unfailing stern politeness didn't have this effect on her. All she could do was nod.

Daniel shoved her rumpled covers to the foot of her bed and lay down in the middle. His cock rose straight up, hard and thick, in invitation.

She climbed onto the mattress and straddled his hips. His cock brushed her folds though she was up on her knees. With one hand on his chest for balance, she used her other hand to center him.

He rested his hand on her thighs. "Take your time." The impish grin indicated his pride over her trepidation at his size. She slid down his cock.

Taking him wasn't as uncomfortable as this morning. Maybe it was the psychological aspect of choosing him instead of Daniel dominating her. Maybe it was the fact that everyone in the house had fucked her over the last twenty-four hours.

Maybe she simply wanted him as much as he said he wanted her.

She began a slow rocking rhythm. He reached up and cupped her breasts, his thumbs tracing circles around her nipples. She grabbed one hand and kissed the palm before pressing it back.

Daniel tweaked both hard peaks. Their nerve endings seemed to be connected to her pussy. It contracted around his cock.

She reached behind her and stroked his balls. His eyes closed and his jaw muscles clenched. His sac was tight and wrinkled. A delighted smile tugged her lips. Good to know how close he was. That she had that kind of effect on him.

His hands dropped from her breasts. One thumb found her clit. Retaliation shone in his eyes.

Fine. Two could play that game. She rode him harder. Faster. The pressure built along her nerves, centered in her pussy.

Daniel massaged her clit, trying to make her come first. It turned into a test of willpower. His body bucked, matching her rhythm, driving his cock deep into her.

She had to give up on playing with his balls and braced her hands on his chest to keep her balance. He grabbed her hips to keep her in place.

Their tempo was wild and wanton, but at the same time, very . . . domestic. He was someone who could walk both the vanilla and kinky side of the trail. Her heart lurched at the realization.

She lost her concentration at the shock. Her body took advantage of her brain's distraction. Daniel pulled her to him just in time. His kiss swallowed her cries as she convulsed around his cock.

Diana still trembled from the aftershocks when he broke the kiss and whispered, "I win."

He rammed into her one more time, and his muscles stiffened beneath her thighs. The feeling of him pumping come into her triggered a pleasant coda of twitches inside her.

She lay on top of him for a very long time, content to listen as his heartbeat slowed to a steady rhythm again. Time seemed to fade from awareness. There was only this moment.

He shifted, and she half-expected him to get out of the bed. Instead he rolled her to the side and pulled the covers over both of them before pulling her tight against his chest.

Afraid of breaking the spell wrapped in the silence, Diana lay quietly until his breathing deepened and sleep claimed him.

This hadn't been just sex. At least, not for her. This was supposed to be fun and games only. Now what the hell was she supposed to do?

She still hadn't moved when the first fingers of dawn peeked around the curtains.

Chapter Fourteen

"Shit."

The muttered curse word jerked Diana out of a restless half-sleep. "Wha . . ." She lifted her head and peered through blurry eyes.

Daniel scrambled out from under the covers. "I'm sorry. I didn't mean to spend the entire night and get you in trouble again." He snatched his pajama bottoms from the floor and shoved a foot into the cotton.

"It's only—" She tried blink away grainy stuff. The digital clock on the nightstand winked from 9:59 to 10.00.

A firm knock sounded on her door. "Breakfast," Victoria's voice rang out.

Diana jumped out of the bed, the delicious ache in her muscles reminding her of everything they'd done. It was like she couldn't get enough of him.

She glanced at Daniel, and his expression mirrored her resignation. She pulled on her robe before she said, "Come in."

Victoria walked in with a tray. She didn't look half as surprised as Diana expected. Instead, a silver eyebrow rose, and a smirk tilted her full lips. "You've had more than your share, Myers. It's my turn."

A sheepish grin filled Daniel's face. "Yes, Ma'am." He looked at Diana, and his mouth opened. But whatever he was about to say, he thought better of it in Victoria's presence. Instead, he pivoted and charged out the door.

Victoria inclined her head toward the bed. "Sit. Eat." Once Diana was settled, Victoria set the tray over her lap. "When you're done, jump in the shower. You have fifteen minutes before I expect you in the playroom." She headed for the door.

"Victoria, I'm sor—"

She whirled, an intense look in her eyes. "Did I ask for an explanation?"

Diana lowered her eyes. "No, Ma'am."

"Fourteen minutes. I'd hurry if I were you. You're going to need your strength."

The riding crop burned when it landed on her ass again. Even though Victoria's droning voice marked them, Diana had lost count of the blows Lost track of how long she'd been on her knees and elbows in the playroom. Despite the thick carpet, pain radiated from her joints. She focused on that ache as an equally naked Victoria stalked around her.

"It's the second time you've broken my rules in less than twenty-four hours." Victoria smacked her breasts this time.

"Yes, Ma'am." Diana blinked at the tears of shame. With the spreader clamped to her ankles, Victoria could see her excitement. Was she disobeying Victoria deliberately? Did she need the punishment so badly that she screwed up in order to be whipped? Was sex with Daniel that great she'd endure anything for it?

A shudder rippled through her. Her pussy spasmed at the memory of his cock filling her, stroking her body into orgasm after orgasm.

Dammit, she had a good thing with Victoria and Merrick. They fulfilled her sexual needs. They found her a new home, even if it was temporary. And she'd thrown everything away because of the instant, insatiable attraction to Daniel Myers. Even in her mixed-up head, it made no sense.

"Am I your master, Diana?"

"Yes, Ma'am." Her answer was more sob than word.

"Is Daniel your master?"

She couldn't lie to Victoria. "Yes, Ma'am."

There was a long silence broken only by Diana's quiet sobs. Victoria finally said, "A sub can't serve two masters, Diana."

"I know." The truth hit her hard. So hard she blurted the words before she could stop them. "I think I l—" She choked on the syllable. "I think I l—" It couldn't be true.

And every time she'd said the word in the past, things had gotten even more fucked up.

"Oh, honey." The riding crop made a quiet *huff* when it hit the carpet. Victoria dropped to the floor next to her. "Pumpernickel."

Once Victoria released the spreaders on ankles and wrists, Diana collapsed to the carpet and pulled her body into a ball. Victoria curled around her, one arm around her waist and the other stroked her hair, the touch comforting.

They lay on the floor for a long time before Victoria said, "You've only known him for a week." Her breath tickled the fine hairs on Diana's neck.

She swiped at her nose with the back of her hand. "I know. I don't want you to think I don't care about you and Merrick—"

A soft laugh tickled her ear. "Oh, I'm not surprised that you fell for him, dear. I'm surprised at how fast it happened."

Diana rolled over and stared at her. "Are you saying that this was all more than a game fix-up?"

Victoria shrugged and smiled one of her secretive smiles. "What was the harm? You were both lonely. You've obviously hit it off."

"What about . . ." She couldn't meet Victoria's gaze. "Us," she whispered.

Victoria wrapped a possessive leg over Diana's. "I think we could be very good friends for a long time. If you intend to be Daniel's though, you need to ask his permission."

Could she give up Victoria if Daniel ordered her to? She looked at Victoria. "What if he says no?"

Her sly smile stretched into a wicked grin. "I don't think we'll have any problem convincing him." Her hand slipped between Diana's thighs and caressed her open folds.

Her hips thrust to meet Victoria's touch. How could she possibly give this up?

Victoria pulled her closer for a kiss. The contact was light, reassuring, forgiving. Not dominating, but the melding of equals.

The change between them was unnerving and comforting at the same time. But deep down, Diana knew Victoria could flip the switch and become her domme again. If she needed her. If she asked. If she submitted.

Fingers slid into her passage. Her internal muscles clenched around the teasing digits. "Come for me, little girl," Victoria murmured into her mouth.

"No." Diana smiled to sooth the abruptness of her negation. "Not yet." She gently pushed Victoria onto her back. "Spread your legs for me, Ma'am."

With an amused expression, Victoria complied. Pale, silver and full of joy, she really was beautiful.

Diana descended on Victoria and gave back everything she'd been given over the last couple of weeks. Everything to make Victoria cry out in passion as her back arched and she shook under Diana's touch.

Diana spent Monday evening packing boxes. She'd left the Georgetown house after Sunday brunch, needing the space to try to get her head straight. But when the phone rang, she didn't need Caller ID to know who it was.

"You know stalking is illegal."

Daniel chuckled. "Can't a man invite a lady to dinner and not be called names?"

She sighed. "Nothing personal. But I've got to be out of this place in less than two weeks, and I've barely started packing."

"Have dinner with me, Vicki and Merrick tomorrow, and Wednesday night I'll come over and help you."

She laughed. "Sure you will. And then nothing will get done."

"You supply the pizza and beer, and I swear on my badge I will behave myself."

Diana tucked the phone between her shoulder and ear and grabbed a piece of bubble wrap. Talking with him was so comfortable she didn't want to end the call. "How was your first day?"

"Not bad. They assigned my partner and me to a high school for the last six weeks of the term. After that, we'll be given a regular patrol."

She laughed again as she wrapped a framed photo of Steffi and Kat. "Great. Two men ogling a bunch of high school girls."

"First of all, I prefer women, not girls. And I especially prefer women with curves."

Something about his tone made her want to tease him more. "So your new partner is a woman severely lacking in curves?"

"I am *not* going there. You know the saying about not dipping your pen in the company ink?"

"Or sticking your baton in a fellow blue?"

"Stop. Right. There. I am not discussing this. My work life and my personal life are very separate. And I do my damnedest to keep it that way."

The edge in his voice surprised her. She blew out a deep breath. "I'm sorry I crossed a line."

His voice softened. "It's . . . okay. My ex—"

The silence stretched. She almost expected him to hang up. "Daniel, I'm really sorry."

"It's not you. Back in New York, she used to accuse me of sleeping with female officers. Misdirection to cover up her own affair. I don't want my old shit to come between us."

"Noted." She set the wrapped frame in the box at her feet. "So what do we talk about?"

"We could have phone sex."

Another laugh. Damn, it'd been so long since she laughed this much with a man. She thought about it. No, she had never laughed this much with any male. "You're crazy. How's that any different than you coming over?"

"I'm hoping you'll tell me why bother and to come over anyway."

"I'll agree to dinner tomorrow night."

"And after dinner?"

Her breasts grew full and heavy at the image of him bending her over her own kitchen table and fucking her senseless. "We'll see."

"Tease." But there was no animosity in his voice. Just a promise to try to change her mind.

And no doubt, she would once she saw him, felt the warmth of his skin on hers. Already, her pussy soaked her panties at the sound of his voice. "I'll see you tomorrow night."

"Sweet dreams," he murmured.

She'd have the same dreams she had last night, but she wasn't about to increase his ego by telling him he starred in all of them. "Good night."

Sure enough, Daniel's warm palm against the small of her back sent tingles straight to Diana's pussy, even through the pale pink linen dress she wore, as he guided her to their table.

Both Daniel and Victoria aimed to drive her arousal higher through dinner. They used any excuse to touch her, and touched her under the table without any excuse. Their competitive attention would have embarrassed her under any other circumstances, but Merrick took the whole thing as great fun and subtly encouraged her to do the same.

She laughed at the story Daniel and Merrick related about some prank they pulled in school when someone laid a hand on her shoulder. "Diana?"

She looked up. *Steve.* Her heart stopped. Her lungs froze. She hadn't called him, texted him, wrote to him since he'd walked out on her ten months ago. And his last contact had been the ugly note he'd left on the refrigerator the day he'd cleaned out his belongings.

"Hello." She couldn't wrap her tongue around his name. She glanced at the woman beside him. The bitch's skin was several shades lighter than hers. Of course. He didn't realize she was on a date, and he wanted to make sure she knew he was seeing someone. Old insecurity and anger, emotions she thought she'd laid to rest months ago, rose along with the bile in her throat.

Steve's gaze flicked to Merrick, then Victoria. Recognition. No, he wasn't just showing off his new girlfriend. He hoped to parlay his approach into a political advantage. But his assessment settled on Daniel when she didn't introduce Steve to the group.

Daniel, who made a point of knocking Steve's hand away from Diana's shoulder and pulled her closer to him.

Something ugly shone behind Steve's eyes. She could see the pride override the calculating side of him. A familiar sneer twisted his lips. "You always were a little too oreo for my taste."

Before her rage at the insult burned the ice from her lungs, Daniel burst out of his chair. He twisted Steve's arm and slammed him into the pillar behind Victoria before the rest of the people at the table were out of their seats. Everyone in the restaurant stared.

Diana couldn't breathe. Old memories she'd buried years ago came racing back. Mom beating on Steffi. Dad slamming her into the wall when she tried to pull Mom off her baby sister who cowered on the floor, sobbing.

"Apologize." The one word came out of Daniel as an animalistic growl.

Instead, Steve did what he always did when cornered. He threatened. "This is racial harassment. I'll sue your ass—"

"You called my date a racial slur in front of witnesses. Apologize and I won't arrest you for a hate crime." Daniel's voice was low, dangerous. Just like Dad's had been when he told her to leave his house and not come back.

"I'll have your badge then." Steve's voice rose. "Do you know who I am?"

"You're the city councilman stupid enough to call my dining companion an ugly name." Victoria's words dropped, diamond-hard, into the quiet air. "I suggest you leave quietly. Now."

"Come on, baby." Steve's arm candy glared at Diana. "She isn't worth it."

"Fine." Steve shrugged out of Daniel's hold, only because the cop let him.

No apology came, but Diana didn't really expect one. The maitre d' hovered nearby as Steve stalked out of the main dining room, his date tottering on her heels as she tried to keep up with him. Merrick pulled the anxious-looking maitre d' aside and spoke quietly with him.

Daniel reached for her arm. "Are you—"

Diana jerked out of his grip. Old rage and new rage mixed and exploded, but in the wrong damn direction. She couldn't stop it. "What the hell were you thinking! He'll pull strings to get you fired."

Victoria stepped closer. "No, he won't—"

"Stay out of this," Diana hissed. "I've had enough of your meddling with my life." She whirled to face Daniel, and her index finger jabbed his chest. "I don't need a fucking white knight to fight my battles."

She grabbed her clutch from the table and threw down a couple of twenties. "I don't need your fucking charity either." Tears threatened. She was not crying in front of a bunch of jerks with more money than they knew what to do with, who got their kicks from sex games with a middle-class woman. The walls and ceiling seemed to contract around her. She needed to get out.

Diana aimed for the main entrance, but Daniel kept pace. "Diana, dammit, stop and listen to me."

She charged past the doorman and was on the street when Daniel grabbed her arm again. "Would you stop for two seconds—"

"Let go!" Her left fist curled and swung, but he ducked. She used the momentum to pull free.

"Diana—"

"Shut up! You—" She tried to push the words past the red blurring her vision, the lump in her throat. "You're no different than him. Than any man in my life. It's all about controlling me!"

"That's not true—"

"Games are one thing, but you can't keep them contained to the bedroom. You can't. Roughing up my ex *in public* proves you can't."

"I'm not going to let some asshole walk up and insult the woman I care about!"

She threw up her arms. "The only thing you care about is whatever you can stick your dick into! Here's one for you! Yank that huge white cock of yours between your legs and fuck yourself in the ass!"

She pivoted and for once, luck was on her side. A cab pulled to the curb. She hopped in and slammed the door.

"Where to, lady?"

"The Smithsonian Metro station." It was the closest one her burning brain could think of.

The driver pulled into traffic. "I don't think your boyfriend's going to follow."

"He's not my boyfriend." The automatic words didn't stop her from glancing back. Daniel stood on the sidewalk, his hands loose at his sides and a sad look on his face.

It's for the best, the rational portion of her brain said. But if that were true, why the hell was she crying?

Chapter Fifteen

Staring at her bathroom mirror, Diana stroked concealer over the bruise-like circles under her eyes. The cucumber slices had helped a bit with the swelling from the last two sleep-deprived, weepy nights, but she still looked like she went a couple of rounds with Tatyana Ali. Regardless of her own fucked up life, Beth needed her support. And dammit, she was not missing Beth's first showing.

Except she didn't want to go by herself.

She picked up her smart phone and thumbed the quick dial icon for Micki.

"Well, if it isn't Ms. Traynor. Nice to know I finally rate a call back."

Of course Micki would give her shit. *What were you expecting?* "I'm sorry. Things have been a little crazy. Would you like to meet for breakfast this morning?"

"I'd love to, but I can't. I'm on duty in five minutes."

Maybe the lack of sleep and obsessing over another cop had damaged more brain cells than she thought. "Duty? But you don't have to be at the station until eight-thirty."

"That would be true if I was still confined to a desk."

Diana sat down on the toilet. "You're back on street duty?"

"Yep." Pride filled Micki's voice, but something else lay under her words, a strong hint of sadness. Understandable since the anniversary of Lee's death was last month. Reinstatement to street duty would only remind Micki of her loss.

"I'm so happy for you." And Diana meant it. "Why didn't you say something?"

Micki laughed. "You sound just like Beth and Alicia. Maybe if one of you three would return my goddamn calls once in a while, you'd have known before this week."

Despite Micki's good-natured teasing, another wave of guilt swept through Diana. "You're right. I've sucked as a friend, and I have no right to ask, but I need a couple of favors."

"You know I will if I can. Shoot."

"Can I meet you at your station and catch a ride to Georgetown for Beth's show?"

"As long as you don't mind riding in the back."

Diana's heart skipped a beat. "You're seeing someone?"

Micki sighed. "Yeah. Sort of. It's a long story. I'll tell you tonight. What's the second?"

Hopefully her bad luck wouldn't spread to her friends again. Diana sucked in a deep breath. "I'm moving next weekend."

"Good. It's about time."

It took Diana a second to find her voice. "It is?"

"Steve's an asshole. I'm glad you're moving on."

"Isn't that the pot calling the kettle black?"

Micki laughed. "If you're going to throw racial slurs, I'm hanging up."

For the first time in over a year, a sense of normality settled over Diana. Maybe her love life was fucked up, but she still had her friends. "Thanks, Micki."

"No prob. See you at the station."

Diana thumbed the "End Call" icon. She was truly happy for Micki, and she needed to concentrate on that. Otherwise, she'd start crying again and totally ruin the excellent cover-up she'd applied.

Diana checked her phone as she pulled open the police station's door. It was a few minutes after six. She showed her ID to the desk sergeant, who buzzed her into the back offices.

"Donovan should be out in a couple of minutes, ma'am, if you want to take a seat." He pointed to some benches along the wall.

A thin thread of satisfaction ran through her when the sergeant surreptitiously checked her out. She hadn't worn the lavender silk sheath in ages. Not since Steve said it made her look like a slut.

Tuesday replayed in her mind. Deep down, a tiny hint of vindictiveness dwelled, and it had enjoyed itself immensely when Daniel defended her by roughing up Steve. It still didn't make Daniel abusing his authority or treating her like a possession right.

What would he think of this dress? Her mind conjured him walking down the hall, pushing her against the wall and having his way with her.

She blinked. It was her imagination, right? He couldn't possibly be walking down the hall with Micki and talking.

Those crystal blue eyes met hers and he stopped. Micki strode forward, smiled and waved. She realized Diana was staring past her and did a slow pivot.

Daniel took a tentative step forward. "Diana."

Something that sounded like a strangled cat came from her throat. She whirled and raced into the ladies' room.

Chapter Sixteen

Diana charged past a couple of women at the sinks, dove into a stall and slammed the door shut. *He can't be here. He can't be here.* Of all the satellite police stations in the District, why the hell would he be at Micki's? And why was he wearing a suit?

Oh, my god, was he Micki's plus-one?

She leaned her forehead against the stall door. Her chest heaved, threatening to launch her into full hyper-ventilation.

The pneumatic door cylinder hissed. Micki's voice rang out. "Ladies, would you please exit? This is a police matter."

Amid some grumbling came footsteps, then silence except for the blood roaring in Diana's ears. Did Micki leave too?

No, the slow click of heels approached the stall she hid in. "I hear you told my new partner that he could, and I quote, 'Wrap his huge white cock between his legs and fuck himself in the ass.'"

Her new partner? Diana couldn't move. Could this night get any worse?

There was a light knock on the door. "C'mon, girl. Talk to me."

Diana tried to swallow, but her tongue felt like it was glued to the roof of her mouth.

"Diana, Daniel told me what happened at the restaurant with Steve. You do realize I would have done the same thing." There was a bump against the door, and Micki continued. "No, that's not true. I would have done worse. You know I can. And Steve's a wimp compared to Rick Allen."

For the first time since junior prom, one of them actually said the name of Beth's rapist aloud. Diana squeezed her eyes shut at the old ache. "If you had, you definitely would've ended up in prison this time."

"Maybe. But I won't stand by and let someone hurt a person I love. Daniel's not that way either."

"I-It's not like that."

"You may think you're fuck buddies, but trust me, he's got the bug for you. Bad."

"He's going to Beth's show with you."

"I'm just his wingman because his ladylove, who advocated painful self-abuse, was going to be at the show, and he was hoping to talk to her. I never dreamed it was you." Micki chuckled. "You know, when I first met him I thought about setting you two up."

"That's not funny."

"What? Your creative suggestions for sex or that I thought you were meant for each other."

"Neither one."

"Are you coming out?"

"No."

A deep sigh. "You're going to really hurt Beth. You two are the only exes I know who've managed to stay friends after—"

Diana jerked the stall door opened. "What?"

Micki had been leaning on it. She wobbled but managed to stay on her heels. She turned to face Diana. "Don't sweat it. Everyone knows."

"Wh-what do you mean everyone knows?"

"My family, Steffi, Kat, Alicia. Taneka." She folded her arms over her white blouse and shrugged. "We figured you two never said anything because it didn't work out."

Diana sagged against the stall frame. "That's why Kat . . ." It explained the entire set-up with Victoria.

Micki's dark blonde eyebrows wrinkled. "Why Kat what?"

"Never mind." She shook her head.

The pneumatic cylinder hissed again, and Daniel stepped inside. Micki's head swiveled between him and Diana. "You two need to kiss and make up, but make it snappy." She checked her watch. "We are *not* going to be late to Beth's showing." She glared at them both as she strode past Daniel and out the bathroom door. It swung closed behind her.

Diana stared at Daniel. He took one step and stopped. The silence dragged through the restroom.

"I'm not sorry for what I did," he blurted.

"Then that just puts us back to square one." Wetness welled beneath her lids. *I am not crying in front of him.* "I'm not submitting to someone who can't control himself in public."

Suddenly, he was moving, practically carrying her across the bathroom until he pressed her against the wall. "Is this what you prefer? Someone treating you like a thing to be used in private?"

Her breath caught in her throat. For some strange reason, she wasn't scared. With anyone else, she would have been terrified or pissed. Not totally turned on like she was now.

"Is it?" he growled. He pinned her wrists to the wall, and her clutch fell to the floor.

"Yes. Sometimes I want to be tied up. Whipped. Punished. But not always," she murmured. "Sometimes, I want the flowers and the door opened for me and someone to cook for me."

He pulled back a smidgeon, but not enough to release her. "And what do you want me for?"

"Both," she whispered.

"You have no idea of what you're asking."

"Yes, I do."

His breath grew ragged. Through his slacks, his erect cock pressed against her mound. "I can't do both."

"Then what's with the Jeckyll and Hyde shit?"

"What?"

"You were the super gentleman on our first date. We've had vanilla sex."

"With chocolate sprinkles." A tired smile flared and faded. His gaze dipped toward the floor. "But I can't do vanilla relationships. I tried." The ache in his voice sounded so familiar. He was just as hurt, confused, by his ex as she was by hers.

But she couldn't deal with anything deep either. Not yet. "What about a vanilla relationship with chocolate sauce and sprinkles?" She kept her tone light, teasing.

His head rose. Crystal eyes stared into hers. "What are you proposing?"

"That we start slow. That we date. That you stop beating up my exes."

"Now where's the fun if I can't do that?"

She glared at him. "Whose show do you think I'm going to tonight?"

"You dated the sculptor?"

Her eyes narrowed. "No, the painter."

His expression turned confused for an instant as he worked it out. "Oh." He pressed closer. "Dating, huh?"

She shrugged, or tried to with her wrists trapped. All she managed to do was hike her classic sheath dress up a couple of inches. And she could tell by the look in his eyes he was very aware that a millimeter or two of fabric further and her pussy would be exposed. "If those dates happen to include Victoria and Merrick, so be it. Other couples do things with married friends all the time."

"You're insane."

"Why?"

"For wanting things both ways. Life doesn't work that way."

"Says who? My baby sister is a lesbian who wants the white picket fence, the two-point-two kids and the puppy. She just happens to want it with her girlfriend. Life isn't always black and white."

Humor gleamed in his eyes though his expression remained stern. "Really? You're going to use that phrase here? Now? After what you accused me of?"

"I insinuated that you were sexist, not that you were racist."

"But you screaming at me still came down to your current white boyfriend roughing up your black ex-boyfriend."

"Maybe."

"Maybe?"

She shrugged again. He looked down at her now-exposed lace panties and looked up at her. Behind the humor, lust smoldered.

"Then this will help you decide." Daniel didn't hesitate. His mouth claimed hers with a ferociousness that left her breathless. He released her wrists and yanked at her underwear. The sound of the delicate seams ripping echoed against the cold tile.

Ruining her expensive panties would have normally pissed her off. Instead, all she wanted was him. Inside. Now.

Gasping, she broke the kiss and fumbled with his belt before he brushed her hands away. His motions were a blur. His cock surged forward, and he grabbed her ass and lifted.

Out of sheer instinct, she wrapped her legs around his waist and her arms around his neck. He rammed into her pussy. Stretching her. Filling her.

Daniel pumped into her. His fingers dug into her ass cheeks and spread them, driving his cock even deeper into her. She needed this, needed him to take her with a passion that went beyond games, beyond society's limits.

Her breath became sobs. "I need you."

He stopped. She blinked, shifted on his cock, but he pinned her against the wall. Crystal eyes bore into hers. "Say it."

She wanted to tell him to shut up and fuck her. "Say what?"

"I don't want to hear you *need* me." Anger flickered behind his gaze. "Say what you really feel."

"I-I can't," she choked out.

"Yes, you can." His voice grew more gruff. His cock did a slow slide out and in, and she wanted to cry. "Say it."

"I can't. It'll ruin everything." Her voice rose to a wail. "*I'll* ruin everything."

He leaned his forehead against hers. "If you want the vanilla and the kink from me, I need to *hear* it," he whispered. "Please."

There was so much pain in that one word. Her heart cracked. Or maybe it was the ice around it. "I love you."

He closed his eyes and exhaled. "Good girl."

His rhythm started again, wild and uncontained. He simply took her until she shattered with a scream. An instant later, he moaned in her ear and his come filled her.

As they both gasped for air, someone rapped loudly on the bathroom door. "Hurry up, you two! We're going to be late." Micki sounded very irritated.

Heat filled Diana's cheeks as Daniel withdrew and set her on the floor. "Oh, god, do you think she heard us?"

"I'm pretty sure the entire station heard *you*." The wicked grin plastered itself on his face.

"Pull up your pants," she ground out while she tugged her dress back in place.

He chuckled. "Yes, ma'am."

She snatched her clutch and the ruined panties off the floor. The little bit of lace looked sad, and she shoved it into the trashcan.

As she fixed her hair and checked her make-up in the mirror, a put-together Daniel wrapped his arms around her and pulled her against his chest. He leaned close to her ear and whispered, "I love you, too."

His admission sent a wave of longing through her. She pivoted and sealed the proclamation with a kiss.

Micki banged on the door. "Get the fuck out, or I'm coming in!"

They broke apart, laughing.

Diana trailed fingers along his tie. "Come home with me tonight."

"You couldn't stop me."

She returned his smile. For the first time in a very long time, things in her life were very right.

ENSLAVED BY LOVE

Beth's Story

Chapter One

The first drops hit the pavement when Beth Winslow turned the key in the front door. A flash of lightning lit the dark sky and thunder rumbled less than a second later. And of course, the stupid lock stuck again because of the April storm's humidity.

Dammit, Paolo was supposed to fix this. She rattled the key until the tumblers finally gave. Light exploded, followed immediately by a massive *crack* overhead as she stumbled inside. Rain pounded the sidewalk before she slammed the door shut.

The entryway and front parlor of the Georgetown row house was dark, but delicious smells came from the kitchen. She smiled. It was Friday, Aaron's turn to cook. He always came up with these delicious dishes she couldn't replicate in a lifetime.

For one instant, satisfaction overwhelmed her irritation. Her girlfriends may be looking for someone to warm their beds, and she had not one, but two gorgeous men in hers. Tonight's play date made mincemeat of Alicia's snide jibes at lunch last week.

"I'm home," Beth called out. They had to be somewhere in here.

"In the bedroom, Elizabeth."

Shit. If the use of her full name wasn't bad enough, she recognized the tone in Aaron's voice all too well. And she had no one to blame but herself.

She set her messenger bag by the umbrella stand and jogged up the stairs.

The sight that greeted her in the master bedroom set her breasts straining against her bra. Aaron stood near the foot of their bed. The dim lamp turned his magnificent nude body into a sculpture of sharp planes and deep shadows. Paolo knelt before Aaron, his mouth worshipping their master's cock.

Aaron stared at her through slitted eyes. She quickly removed her clothes and glasses and neatly placed them on the dresser before she assumed the appropriate kneeling position near the men. It was so very hard to keep her hands clasped behind her back when she wanted nothing more than to join them.

"Did you finish your guest list for the showing?" Aaron's voice only carried his irritation with her. No hint of a reaction from what Paolo was doing with his lips, his tongue. But then, that level of control was part of the reason she chose him as her dom.

"No, Sir," she whispered.

He exhaled, not quite a sigh but the sound definitely carried his disappointment. "You know you will have to be punished."

"Yes, Sir." Her pussy quivered at his statement. Aaron always came up with the most delicious punishments.

"If your disobedience wasn't such a rarity, I would be concerned." His fingers threaded through Paolo's dark curls, subtle encouragement of the other sub's excellent oral skills. Skills she had been at the receiving end of. Her nipples tightened from the excitement of watching them.

Aaron closed his eyes. His body stiffened. His moan penetrated the quiet of the room. He was so beautiful when he came.

Once Paolo licked Aaron's cock clean, he looked up with adoring eyes. Aaron murmured soft words of approval, and Paolo beamed. But Aaron did not gesture her to join them.

Her heart lurched. No doubt, Aaron wouldn't let her climax because she failed to do her task in the proper timeframe. That she could deal with, but from the stern look he shot her, she would not be allowed to touch him, please him, either.

Aaron helped Paolo to his feet and positioned him in front of her. Pre-come glistened at the tip of Paolo's cock. His sac hugged his body, tight and wrinkled.

"Your task, my disobedient little slave, is to suck Paolo's dick."

Beth couldn't help a little smile. This task was more pleasure than punishment.

"You cannot let him come in less than five minutes," Aaron continued. He paced around her.

Oh, crap. If Paolo wasn't already so close to the edge, the challenge would be easy. But Aaron knew her better than she knew herself. Knew she'd stall putting together the mailing list. Knew the perfect punishment.

"But you must make him come in less than ten minutes," Aaron said. She heard a drawer open and close. "That's when I need to baste my roast. You are not allowed to come or touch yourself. You may start."

"May I use my hands as well as my mouth to pleasure Paolo, Sir?" she whispered.

"Yes."

Something black slithered over her right breast and teased the nipple. Aaron's favorite whip.

Trying to ignore what was coming, Beth wrapped her hands around the base of Paolo's straining erection. Her tongue swirled around the head. His hiss of pleasure sent a tremor through her.

From the corner of her eye, the single-tail whip flashed. Her mouth released Paolo, and she cried out at the stinging *crack* on her ass.

"You're not sucking him, Elizabeth." The tip of the whip snapped her left nipple.

She swallowed the exquisite pain. Aaron specifically forbade her to come. Paolo said nothing since he hadn't been given permission to speak, but he stroked her hair, reassuring her, encouraging her.

She ran her tongue along the length of Paolo's cock. Her hands followed her mouth up and down his shaft. She focused on his cock and counted her heartbeats between Aaron's whip strokes. Approximately thirty seconds between each.

It became harder and harder to concentrate. Her internal muscles quivered with each strike, needing the release if only she'd relax and let it come. The leather landed on her ass for the tenth time, and Aaron stopped.

She wanted to sigh in relief at obtaining one of the goals he assigned her, but she didn't dare. Paolo's huge hands moved from her hair to her shoulders. Despite keeping his nails super-short between his construction job and his sculpting, the edges dug into her skin. The discomfort only added to the liquid pooled between her thighs.

Heat caressed her back. Powerful calves cradled hers, Aaron kneeling right behind her. His hands cupped and stroked her stinging buttocks. He gently parted her ass cheeks and played with her puckered hole.

She couldn't stop her body from tensing under his touch. *Please, don't touch my pussy. I'll never keep it together if you touch my pussy.*

As if he read her mind, his other hand brushed her abdomen and glided down to her soaked and open slit. She whimpered around the cock filling her throat while he teased and tormented her. His fingers danced around her clit, never touching it.

Panic jarred her mind when she realize she'd lost track of her count. He deliberately distracted her. Not that he tried to make her fail, but to force her to discipline herself. To confirm her suspicion, two digits thrust into her needy passage, stroking her to the verge of insanity. God, how she wanted to grind against his hand.

For an instant that seemed to stretch for an eternity, Beth was torn. Complete her task like a good little sub and hope that he'd take mercy by filling her pussy later. Or let herself come on his fingers and take whatever twisted punishment Aaron would come up with next.

The feeling of someone watching her made her peer up. Paolo's rich brown eyes stared into hers. The subtle jerk of his hips sent his message. *Don't push, Aaron. Not now.*

He was right of course. They were all on edge about the upcoming show. Acting like a selfish scaredy-bitch only exacerbated the tension. And not in a good way.

She squeezed her internal muscles, acknowledging Aaron's efforts and his dominance. Paolo's pleasure was her task, doing what she knew he loved. Circling the head of his cock with the tip of her tongue. The lightest of flicks across the frenulum. Then swallowing the length of him until her lips met the root. Tickling the delicate spot between his sac and his ass.

Paolo exploded in her mouth with a roar. His cock pumped hot, salty come, and she swallowed every drop before she gently licked him clean.

His orgasm only made her more desperate for release. But she couldn't. Not without permission.

Aaron withdrew his dripping fingers as she sat back on her heels and resumed the proper position. "Very good, little slave." He nuzzled her neck as he continued to play with her ass. "But back up and spread those knees."

The tip of a finger inserted itself into her puckered hole as she complied.

"Paolo, kneel. Touch her pussy. Play with it."

"Yes, Sir." Evil humor lit his dark eyes.

Dammit, she could barely keep her body in control as Aaron toyed with her ass.

Paolo stroked her slit. Beth closed her eyes. Her whole body shuddered under the men's sensual manipulation. Once again, fingers entered her pussy and caressed the sweetest of spots.

"Feel how wet she is?"

"Yes, Sir." Paolo added another finger, filling her, bringing her so close to the edge. A wretched whimper forced its way from her throat.

"Do you need completion, Elizabeth?" Aaron murmured in her ear.

"Yes, Sir." Her voice sounded eager, yet depraved, to her own ears.

"Hmmm. If you can get your list together and the mailing labels printed before dinner, I'll see about rewarding you."

"And if I can't, Sir?" She struggled to keep her voice under control as he nibbled the join of her neck and shoulder. He must have signaled Paolo because all of the fingers in her holes left, with nothing else to fill the emptiness.

"Do you really want to go another twenty-four hours without a dick between those sweet legs of yours?" Aaron's breath was warm against her skin.

"No, Sir."

"Then you'll get the list done before dinner. But since you desire an incentive . . ."

Sharp clamps dug into her nipples, and she cried out. In comparison, the chain connecting them lay cool against her skin. From the kitchen, a buzzer went off.

She blinked her eyes open. Aaron was gone. Paolo already had donned jeans and pulled a forest green Henley over his broad shoulders.

A white, toothy grin gleamed against his dark skin. "I'd move it if I were you."

Chapter Two

Beth hit "Save" and "Print" on her laptop. *Yes! Done!* From the study came the distinctive *whirr* of the laser printer.

Paolo nudged her with his elbow since his hands were full of plates and silverware. "No computers on the table during dinner."

"I'm moving." She pressed the lid closed on the machine and slid it back into her messenger bag before rising and carrying everything back to the study. The printer hummed as it spit out the last sheet. She tucked her bag in its spot and grabbed the stack of address labels.

Every little movement drove new sparks of agony into her breasts as her t-shirt caught and tugged on the alligator clips clamped to her nipples. That was welcome.

More agonizing was the pressure Aaron placed on her to show her paintings. In all fairness, this was a joint exhibit with Paolo and his sculptures, but resentment nibbled on her soul. Why the hell couldn't Aaron just let things stay the way they were? Dammit, she liked things the way they were.

She shuffled back to the kitchen. When Aaron caught sight of her in the doorway, he laid his carving knife and fork on the counter and held out his hand. She gave the stack to him. The weight of guilt, not appropriate sub behavior, kept her from meeting his eyes.

The heavy sheets rattled as he flipped through them. "There's a few more here than you originally indicated."

"Yes, Sir."

He was silent for a long moment, and she peeked at him through her eyelashes. She couldn't decipher the expression on his face. He almost looked sad.

It didn't make sense. He had chastised her a few weeks ago about how few people she planned to invite when he'd ask for a prospective headcount. She had added more, which should have pleased him, and she knew he'd ordered plenty of extra announcements. Usually, she could decipher his temperament, but this time she was stumped.

"Put them next to the box of invitations and stamps on the buffet. Once Paolo has the table cleared off after dinner, you can ready them for mailing," Aaron finally said.

"Yes, Sir." She accepted the sheaf and returned to the dining room.

She glanced at the pass-thru before she whispered to Paolo, "What did I do?"

He snorted as he folded napkins and placed them under the forks. "It's what you didn't do."

"His mood is about more than my procrastination over my mailing list."

Paolo's full lips pressed together. "Then you need to discuss your concerns with Aaron. Not me."

He was right, of course, but a clue would have been nice. Aaron's behavior went far beyond his normal perfectionistic streak when it came to his gallery.

Before she could question Paolo further, Aaron walked in with the platter of sliced roast, little red potatoes and green beans and set it in the center of the table. The entire thing looked like a five-star restaurant's presentation. He indicated Paolo and she should be seated. Once they were settled, Aaron served the food.

No one said anything during the meal, the tension suffocating. The roast tasted like cardboard. After a few bites, she placed her fork on her plate.

"I'm very sorry for disappointing you—"

The intense look Aaron gave her nipped the rest of the words in her throat. "Did I request an apology?"

She bowed her head and stared at her hands folded in her lap. "No, Sir."

The rest of the meal passed in agonizing silence.

Three hours later, Beth placed the last stamped and sealed envelope on her makeshift tray. The house was quiet except for the soft strains of Mozart coming from the study. Stretching eased the kinks in her shoulders and neck, but it also tugged the tight, swollen flesh of her breasts. She rose and carried the tray to the table next to the front door. She'd take the invitations to the post office in the morning.

Turning off the lights as she passed each room, she headed for the study. Aaron's blond head bent over the desktop's screen, and his fingers danced across the keyboard. Eyes on the floor, she knelt with her hands behind her back and waited for his acknowledgment.

In this position, her nipples burned at the pressure of her t-shirt on the clamps. Her knees ached by the time he saved his spreadsheet.

He swiveled toward her. "Are your invitations done?"

"Yes, Sir."

"All of them?"

Her face burned at his doubt. "Yes, Sir," she whispered.

The silence dragged for a long time before he said, "Friday nights are our play nights."

It was a statement, not a question. She clamped her jaw shut to keep from saying anything, from trying to defend herself. He never delivered any admonishment that wasn't deserved.

"I told Paolo to sleep in the guest room tonight. He needs his rest. Exhaustion invites mistakes, and I don't want him injured at work because he stayed up most of the night as a result of your procrastination." Aaron rose from his chair and circled his desk before leaning on the front edge. "So now, I find myself in the difficult position where one of my subs feels he's being punished due to the misdeeds of my other sub."

Beth swallowed the lump in her throat. Her eyes burned. She'd really screwed up this time. Paolo must be pissed with her for spoiling the evening.

"Look at me, Elizabeth."

She quickly blinked away the threatening tears and faced Aaron. He had the same odd, sad expression as he had in the master bedroom earlier. He wasn't about to dismiss her, was he?

"What were the terms I gave you when I accepted you into my household?"

A shiver rippled across her skin. "That I follow your proscribed positions and behavior unless told otherwise. That I do not speak unless asked a specific question or acknowledge a specific command. That I address you as "Sir" at all times within the house." Her voice caught on the last one. "Th-that I follow your commands without fail, Sir." The last word came out more as a sob than a coherent syllable.

"What are you afraid of, Beth?" The gentleness of his tone hurt worse than his earlier scolding.

She bowed her head. "Y-you will dismiss me for disobedience, Sir."

His fingers tilted her chin until she faced him again. "You're lying, but my question is why are you lying to yourself?"

Aaron's touch sent a wave of lust straight to her pussy. She forced herself to focus on his question, but no matter how she reframed it in her mind, the query still didn't make sense. "I-I don't understand, Sir."

His sharp blue gaze penetrated her soul, but whatever he saw, he didn't share. Instead, he said, "I promised a reward for completing your task this evening."

Liquid warmth spilled onto her already damp panties, but she didn't dare move.

"Go to the master bedroom and prepare yourself."

"Yes, Sir."

She rose and strode from the room. Her body trembled as she climbed the stairs. Whatever lesson Aaron tried to impart set her mind at odds with her body.

She'd confessed her painful history to him long before their first play session. That ugliness was over and done with. Submitting to Aaron gave her a freedom she never thought possible. She wasn't afraid of being with him, letting him use her any way he pleased.

Dammit, she'd spent too many hours with her shrink sorting out her fucking issues. From her parents ignoring her to her own naiveté when comprehending the difference between abusive codependence and a power exchange relationship.

You're lying, but my question is why are you lying to yourself?

Beth rolled Aaron's strange question around in her head as she removed and folded her clothing. She admitted her fear that her screw-up would result in Aaron's dismissing her. She had been very straightforward when she said she wasn't ready to show her paintings. How could he say she was lying?

She knelt at the foot of the bed. Without her t-shirt holding the chain still against her skin, it swung with each rise and fall of her chest and tickled the sides of her breasts.

He didn't make her wait. By the time she'd taken ten deep breaths to calm her anticipation, he appeared in the doorway.

She didn't dare raise her head, but every other sense was aware of his presence.

The whisper of his soles on the carpet. His spicy scent. Her body shuddered at his fingers stroking her hair.

And she wanted to weep when he withdrew.

What the hell was wrong with her? Her emotions jumped all over the place, which wasn't like her. *Nerves. Just nerves over this stupid show.*

Goosebumps rose along her skin as she forced herself to refocus on the now. What kind of reward did he have planned? Would he use the riding crop or simply place her over his knee and spank her? Maybe tie her up and take her from behind?

Dammit, girl! That's the future! Just breathe . . .

The exercise helped. A little.

She nearly jumped out of her skin when a strong masculine hand appeared under her nose. "Stand up, Beth."

She grasped Aaron's palm, and he drew her to her feet. When he released the alligator clamps, the surge of blood through the tips of her breasts forced a gasp from her.

His head dipped, his mouth on her tortured flesh an odd counterpoint to the pins and needles under her skin. Without thinking, she placed her hands on his shoulders to remain upright as his tongue coaxed her to respond.

A different type of tingling replaced the ache of the clamps, one that tugged all her nerves to life before centering in her pussy. When she thought she'd come from his lips on her breasts, he straightened. His hands cupped her face, his gaze burning into her soul. Once again, she felt like he searched for something in her, but she didn't know what. If only she could figure it out, she would give him whatever he wanted. Freely. Without any thought.

His mouth descended on hers, the kiss demanding her surrender. A surrender she willingly gave. He pressed her backward until her thighs hit the edge of the mattress.

Aaron broke the kiss. "Turn around. I want you facedown with your legs spread."

Beth obeyed. He'd already positioned a pillow to raise her ass so that when she bent forward, only her toes touched the floor. Excitement raced through her.

He tugged her right arm behind her back. The zip of Velcro ripped the air before he wrapped soft velvet around her wrist. He repeated the motion with her left arm. "You're not allowed to come until I give you permission."

Always the same terms, yet he knew how to drive her insane with desire.

"Yes, Sir," she whispered. Cool air wafted between her thighs and caressed her open pussy lips. She shivered. Between the men's erotic torture earlier and her own anticipation, she wasn't sure how long she could last.

Keep it together, girl.

The snap of the riding crop on her left ass cheek made her jump. The familiar sting penetrated her body as if he'd actually thrust his cock inside her.

"Are you going to continue to defy my orders?" Another snap of the crop landed on her right buttock.

"No, Sir."

Crack. She welcomed the pain. It was so much better than his disapproval.

"Do you understand that I decide what you will wear at your opening?"

"Yes, Sir." Her clit pulsed in time to the throb of her ass.

A whistle and snap of the crop. She squirmed against the bedspread. She couldn't help it.

"There will be other members of my club at the opening. I will not have you embarrass me."

His club. He'd promised he'd take her when he thought she was ready, but after a year, she wondered if she would ever be. Was the showing at the gallery a test?

A smack of the crop distracted her from analyzing Aaron's purpose. Another and she whimpered. Not from the pain. She grasped at the threads of her self-control. He hadn't given her permission yet.

He tossed the riding crop next to her before he grabbed her stinging ass cheeks and spread them wide. She swallowed another whimper. He shoved his cock deep into her. Her precarious balance wobbled at his force. If she hadn't been so damn wet already, his roughness would have hurt like hell. Instead, his claiming of her body nearly sent her over the edge.

"Will you defy me any more?" How could he speak in such a normal voice while he pumped into her?

It was all she could do to ignore the friction of the comforter against her tender nipples, her clit. "I-I'll try not to, Sir."

He paused in mid-thrust. "That's not good enough, Elizabeth."

The old shame flooded her. Nothing she'd done had been good enough for her parents either.

As if he could read her mind, Aaron stroked her skin, her hair. "I never would have accepted you into my service if I believed you would fail." He resumed fucking her, but this time his rhythm was gentle, loving.

And that was worse than if he started whipping her again.

"Please, don't, Sir," she whispered. She could take his punishments, but his tenderness threatened whatever security she'd obtained by serving him.

"'Please, don't' what?"

"Don't be gentle with me, Sir. I don't deserve it." The urge to struggle, to flee, consumed her, but in this position, on her toes and her arms bound, it would be impossible.

He withdrew from her. She suppressed the sob that threatened. Had she pushed him too far in her stupid self-doubts?

A jerk on her wrists, and they were free. Ice filled her veins. He was going to ban her from the bedroom tonight.

He helped her to her feet. She turned and stared up at him. The sad expression tilted his eyes and mouth.

"What am I going to do with you, Elizabeth?"

Her gaze dropped. She couldn't bear that look on his face any more.

His fingertips tilted her chin, and he lowered his mouth to hers. The kiss was soft, caring.

She wrenched away. "Don't. Please don't."

"Turn out the lights when you leave." There was no admonishment or recrimination in his tone. It was simple, matter of fact. He turned down the covers and climbed into the bed. Lying on his back, he closed his eyes. His cock rose straight from his body. Proud. Just like him.

"But—" Heat flamed across her skin. She knew the terms. She wanted the closeness, the warmth. What the hell was wrong with her? Why couldn't she accept his love?

Her issues had been the very same thing that had driven Diana away years ago.

Or was she looking at things in the wrong way?

You're lying, but my question is why are you lying to yourself? Aaron's question earlier hung in her mind.

She crossed to the switch and flicked the lights off. As she stood there, something alien rose in her.

Anger.

How dare he kick her out when she'd done exactly what he wanted? If he couldn't be clear in his demands or his questions, then that was his problem as the dominant.

She marched back to the bed and crawled in the opposite side.

Before she settled under the covers, Aaron was on top of her, his thighs forcing hers apart. Years ago, his actions would have triggered violent flashbacks. Now . . .

Now, the press of his cock against the opening of her pussy caused her internal muscles to clench, demanding to be filled. She needed him inside of her. Wrapping her legs around him, she arched her back to meet him, but he pulled away.

"If you stay, you submit to doing this my way. You do not dictate terms." It was the first time she heard any lack of control in him, his voice hoarse, even if she didn't understand the emotion or the reason for it.

"Yes, Sir."

"Lie perfectly still." He kissed her, a slow, passionate proclamation of exactly what he would do to her. Not take her and use her, but make love to her. While her body had its own ideas on accepting his terms, her soul screamed in rebellion.

He reached behind his back, grabbed her ankles and planted her feet on the mattress. His mouth trailed down her neck and lingered at the base of her throat. She couldn't help squirming underneath him.

His chuckle vibrated against her stomach. "Patience."

A test. That was all it was. Obedience while physically restrained was easy.

But remaining absolutely stationary of her own volition, especially as he worked his way down to her pussy—

At the first flick of his tongue across her clit, Beth dug her fingertips into the comforter. She barely restrained her hips from thrusting toward him. After everything he'd done to her since she walked through the front door tonight, her body ached with the need for release.

Instead, he continued his leisurely torture of her swollen clit. He'd bring her to the brink, then pause to see if she could keep control of herself before he would torment her again.

She tried counting to ten. He nibbled on her inner thigh as he slid first one, then two fingers into her drenched pussy.

She switched to silently reciting the squares of integers. He broke her concentration by rimming her ass. Dammit. He knew how ticklish she was there. Her muscles trembled at the effort not to come. Or laugh.

Aaron rose up on his knees. His cock probed her, and her lids fluttered shut in relief.

The mattress shifted around her. "Open your eyes, Beth."

As much as she didn't want to, she forced herself to look at him. His forearms braced on each side of her, his nose millimeters from her.

"Please chain me—"

Even though shadows hid his face, he delivered the impression of arching his eyebrow. "Did I give you permission to speak?"

"No, Sir."

"Who decides what we do in bed?"

"You do, Sir."

Time seemed to stretch and drag. She clenched her jaw to keep from saying or doing anything. He wouldn't tolerate any more disobedience tonight, and she couldn't bear to be banished to the couch.

"You may touch me."

Beth wrapped her legs around his waist, twined her arms around his neck.

"You may come now." He entered her deliberately, exquisitely. Making love to her was the cruelest thing he'd ever done to her.

She erupted in a full-body orgasm that took her sight, her voice, her mind.

Dim awareness informed her that he only thrust in her twice more before he stiffened.

When their shudders faded, they remained tangled together for a very long time.

"I love you, Beth, whether you accept it or not."

It was a statement, not a question or a command. It brooked no answer.

He pulled out of her and rolled to the side. Drawing the covers round them, he curled around her. Protective, like she was the most precious thing in the world.

This was the type of master she told her shrink she wanted, so why was she fighting Aaron? Fighting herself?

You're lying, but my question is why are you lying to yourself?

She lay awake long after Aaron's breathing fell into the slow, steady rhythm of sleep, his words rolling over and over in her mind.

Chapter Three

On Tuesday morning, Beth's smart phone rang as she flipped the last of the pancakes on the skillet. The caller ID read "Katherine Donovan." Micki's mom. As much as she wished this was a purely social call, she knew the embarrassing deluge was just beginning. "Hey, Mrs. D."

A squeal of delight from the speaker forced her to hold the phone away from her ear. "Congratulations! We're so proud of you, Beth."

"Thanks."

Mrs. D. rattled off a zillion questions, but before Beth could answer one, the Major demanded the phone. "Is this why you didn't come over for Easter dinner?"

The neurons in Beth's brain refused to fire. The Major and Mrs. D. were closer to her than her own parents. They'd supported her through the ugly times even though her stupidity was the reason their own daughter nearly went to prison.

She wanted to admit that she and Aaron had gone to Easter Mass with Paolo and his mother, but fear wrapped itself around her heart. From the pass thru, she could see the odd look Paolo shot her. Aaron stared at the news feed on his pad, but no doubt, he listened to her conversation as well.

"Yeah," she finally said. "I was on a deadline."

Mrs. D. must have wrestled her phone back from her husband because she said, "We'll definitely be there, dear."

After their good-byes, Beth set the phone so that any more calls went straight to voice-mail. She couldn't deal with the drama over her show this early in the morning. Neither Aaron or Paolo said anything when she brought their breakfast to them.

Beth sat at the table and stared at the pancakes on her own plate. She'd followed Aaron's recipe to the letter, but the yellow disks were flat in comparison to his, but her lack of culinary skills wasn't the real reason for the queasiness in the pit of her stomach.

Their lack of fluffiness didn't stop Paolo from inhaling his portion and most of the sausage links, then eyeing her uneaten stack.

At his wistful expression, she laughed and handed him the plate. "They're yours."

"You need to eat something, Beth," Aaron said without looking up from whatever he was pretending to read.

Her stomach did another nauseating flip when she took a cluster of grapes from the bowl in the center of the table. The truck would be here any minute to load her paintings. It wasn't just her work. The crew would pick up Paolo's sculptures as well.

Part of her wanted to grab a can of paint thinner, splash it all over the converted carriage house they used as their joint studio, and burn the place to the ground.

Aaron set his pad on the table and looked at her. He must have sensed her mood. "Go to work, Beth. I'll take care of everything."

"But, Sir—" Her protest died at his frown. "Yes, Sir."

"I'll be late tonight. Paolo is in charge, and he has my permission to use you as compensation for last Friday. You are to be home on time. No side trips. No stalling."

Her breath caught at the twinkle in Paolo's eyes. *That bastard.* Not only had she apologized, but she'd done his chores for the last three days.

And yet, her body shivered in anticipation. It was so rare for the two of them to play alone.

Aaron studied her, as if he waited for a protest or outburst.

She bowed her head. "Yes, Sir. I understand. I will be home on time."

Beth walked through the front door exactly at five-thirty. "Paolo?"

Silence echoed through the house. Had he been caught at the construction site after all?

His absence gave her a chance to think about lunch with Diana. Her reluctance to confess when her ex suspected Beth was seeing Aaron opened a can of worms she'd rather not look at. It wasn't a matter of talking about her current relationship with Diana either.

Shoving aside the disquieting thoughts, she placed her laptop in the study before returning to the kitchen for a soda. A note in Paolo's neat script was pinned to the stainless steel fridge door with one of his stylized copper magnets. She yanked it loose and read it.

I'm in the carriage house.

She smiled and pulled the fridge door open. Now that the bulk of his finished sculptures had been removed, he'd have plenty of room to create. With two cans in hand, she headed for the back door and crossed the tiny garden.

But when she entered the old carriage house, Paolo was nowhere in sight. The sharp buzz of an electrical tool above her head told her exactly where he was. But why was he working in her studio upstairs?

She climbed the steps to find him in the middle of the room on top of a ladder, shirtless. Sweat gleamed on his bronze skin, highlighting the shift of his muscles.

His silky black hair hung loose. She was so busy admiring the delicious view it took her a moment to realize what he'd done.

He clicked off the power drill.

"Why are you hanging chains from my ceiling?"

Paolo grinned. "You needed the appropriate frame for your painting." He pointed behind her.

Beth pivoted to find a twisted metal square leaning against her supply table. The edges of what appeared to be a frame were deliberately rough, but the images were unmistakable. Each side depicted a couple in the throes of passion.

"It's gorgeous." She stepped closer and ran her fingertips over the polished copper that formed the locks of the top woman. She shot Paolo a sly smile. "Should I ask what inspired this?"

He climbed down the ladder. "You did."

A little shiver rippled up her spine. Two cuffs dangled from the ends of the chains. Beth glanced at the frame again. The cuffs would be collars for the man and woman on the top edge.

But what if a person hung from the cuffs? Open. Vulnerable. Available for anyone who wanted to take her.

She mentally shook herself out of her fantasy. "Wh-what do you mean?"

He crossed to her stack of blank canvases leaning against the corner by the ancient fireplace. Oh, no, he wasn't—

He dragged out the one painting she'd hidden from Aaron. "This one needed a special frame for such an erotic piece."

"Put that back." The heat she tried to force in her voice was flooded by her mortification. "Put it back right now, Paolo."

Instead, he pulled the protective sheet from the canvas and set the painting by itself against the bare wall. "It's the three of us, isn't it? That's why you threw such a fit about including this one in the show."

Despite the abstract design, a person didn't have to look very hard to see two men fucking the woman between them. Not one man taking her ass, but both men penetrating the oil woman's pussy.

Blood roared in her ears. "Yes."

Paolo walked over to her, behind her. His strong arms wrapped around her waist. "I'd be worried about hurting you if we both took you at once."

She leaned back against him, her embarrassment dying at the feel of his hard chest against her back, his erect cock poking her ass. Wood and ozone clung to him, spicing his own enticing scent.

"Not if . . ." She forgot whatever she'd been about to say as his warm, rough palms slid under her t-shirt and stroked her abdomen.

"Not if what?" His voice rumbled with desire. His fingertips edged beneath her bra and brushed the sensitive undersides of her breasts.

Beth swallowed hard, trying to find the words. "Not if you took your time." An odd little sound escaped from her as he pushed the bra out of the way and cupped her. "Not if I was fully aroused."

"Like this?" He rolled her nipples between the pads of his thumbs and forefingers before pinching them.

"Mmm-hmmm." She shifted, pressed against him, grinding her ass against his cock.

"Let's go into the house," he murmured against the curve of her ear.

"Why?"

"Because I stink like a pig farm after working at the construction site all day, and I wouldn't subject a lady to my stench."

She turned and placed her palms on his chest. "Don't. Please. I like the way you smell."

He laughed, a hearty, living thing that echoed against the high timbers that formed the roof. "You are one *loca chica*."

Her lips tilted in what she hoped was a pleading smile. "Please. I'll let you do whatever you want to me. Just don't take a shower first."

He grabbed her ass and lifted her. The hard ridge of his erection pressed against her pussy. "I can do whatever I want to you anyway."

"I know." She dipped her gaze. "Please grant this one little request. Sir."

He eased her back to the floor. "Not in here though. It's too chilly tonight." He snatched his shirt from where it hung on his ladder before he took her hand and led her back to the house. They paused long enough in the mudroom for Paolo to ditch his work boots and socks before climbing the back staircase.

She tried to control her trembling as they entered the main bedroom. With Aaron, she always knew where she stood. But Paolo took pride in surprising her, just to see what kind of reaction he could wring from her. She accepted that was part of his personality as a switch. But after she'd screwed up on Friday and ruined their play date, she had no doubt he'd wreak some kind of revenge.

He released her hand. She set aside her glasses and undressed. From the weight in her jeans, she'd forgotten to unload her keys and phone earlier.

Damn it.

She couldn't ask for a time-out since she'd already entered the bedroom. It was suppertime for most people. No one should be calling her for the next hour or two, right?

Paolo stalked over to the closet and pulled out a heavy steel rod. The ankle spreaders.

Beth suppressed a smile. Maybe they'd have a simple play session after all.

Once naked, she knelt at the foot of the bed. Paolo padded to the toy drawer. She couldn't see what all he took out, but the rattle of handcuffs was unmistakable.

"On the bed. Hands and knees."

She scrambled to obey his commands. Paolo didn't believe in whipping a sub for punishment. No, his idea of a punishment was far worse.

After driving her insane, he wouldn't let her come.

It had only taken once for that lesson to penetrate. And she sure as hell didn't want to be wearing the chastity belt for the rest of the night.

Paolo threaded the handcuffs around the middle slat of the headboard. He jerked her wrists forward and locked the cuffs in place.

He walked out of sight and the mattress shifted behind her. "Spread your knees."

She complied, but apparently, it wasn't enough. He thrust his thick, muscular thigh between hers and nudged her legs further apart, making sure to rub her pussy in the process.

A tremor rippled through her at his touch. With a series of clicks, the ankle cuffs locked into place. The mattress shifted again, followed by his deep laugh.

"Wet and ready before we even start?"

"Yes, Sir."

He slapped her ass cheek. Not a proper spank, but an attention-getter. Her lungs ached before she realized she was holding her breath in anticipation of another smack.

Soft padding around the bed, then his head dipped close to hers, his scent intoxicating. "I prefer your hair loose." Another shiver rippled across her skin as he undid her ponytail and raked his fingers through her locks.

"I'm sorry, Sir," she whispered. How could she forget that little detail? *No orgasms for you, Beth.*

The bitter thought must have shown on her face. Paolo made a low sound in his throat. "We don't play enough together, so I'll forgive your lapse. I have something more interesting in mind. Do you want to know what it is?"

His silky whisper aroused her more than his index finger tracing the curve of her ear. "Yes, Sir."

"You didn't say 'please.'"

Beth licked her lips. "Please, tell me, Sir."

"Unlike our Master, I want to see how many times I can make you come." His thumb brushed her damp lower lip before he tilted her chin, forcing her to meet his eyes. "Shall we make a wager, Beth?"

His repayment for Friday night's banishment from the bedroom. She should have known better. She wouldn't be able to walk once he was through with her.

It took a couple of tries to unlock her tongue from the roof of her mouth. Paolo was much better than Aaron at pushing certain of her buttons. "Wh-what kind of wager, Sir?"

Fingertips trailed lightly from the nape of her neck, along her spine, to the crevice of her ass. "Making a small bet as to how many—"

The rhythmic throb of dance music shattered the erotic tension between them. Cold sweat beaded along her forehead and back.

Oh, fuck! My phone!

"Did you forget the rules, *mi amor*?" Paolo's wicked smile sent shivers through her. "This is even better than what I had planned."

He rose and stalked over to her neatly folded clothes.

"Paolo, please. No."

He wagged a finger at her, and fire replaced the cold as he pulled her phone from her jeans pocket.

Real terror gripped her. What if the caller was a client? Paolo wouldn't do this to her, would he?

He walked back to the bed and set the device next to her head. The caller ID read "Michaela Donovan."

Shit. Micki. Probably calling to RSVP.

Paolo pinched Beth's nipples, hard enough to elicit a whimper at the pleasure-pain before he tapped the speaker phone icon. Dammit, the bastard was going to listen to every word.

"Hello, Micki." Curses filled her head. She couldn't get her breathing under control, and she sounded like a really bad porn actress.

"Why the hell didn't you say you had a showing when we met for lunch, you bitch?"

Beth tried to focus on Micki's words, but Paolo had disappeared from her vision. The mattress dipped behind her. *Oh, sweet Jesu, he's going to fuck me while I'm on the phone.*

"The, uh, the details weren't finalized until last week." She tried to look over her shoulder, then between her legs. There was a flash of neon plastic before he placed a pillow under her abdomen to block her view.

"Congratulations! Definitely put me down on your RSVP list."

"Will-will—" Rational thought fled her mind when Paolo gently worked an ass plug into her puckered hole. Her muscles clenched around the bit of silicon, but that only encouraged him to move the toy in and out. More heat filled her face as she realized the little noises she was making.

"Are you all right?" Concern filled Micki's tinny voice.

Paolo chose that moment to slide his cock inside her. The lube on his fingers added another dimension to the sensual onslaught as he toyed with her clit.

"Yesss," Beth hissed. She could hear the tension in her own voice. No wonder Micki thought she was nuts. She swallowed hard and tried to focus on the next appropriate question. "Should I put you down for plus one?"

Only harsh breathing and the faint crackle of static indicated the signal hadn't been dropped.

The urge to curl up and die overrode Paolo's slow fucking of her pussy. How could she be so stupid? Micki was still mourning over Lee, still blamed herself for his death in an undercover operation that had gone terribly wrong. She hadn't admitted to any of their little circle that she and Lee had been a romantic item.

Beth couldn't blame her for that. It had been a year and she hadn't come clean about Aaron and Paolo. She didn't know which of the two of them would have the worse consequences if the truth of their love lives became common knowledge.

Beth grabbed the first excuse she could think of. "I'm sorry. I thought you had someone lined up already the way you jumped on Alicia's challenge."

As if realizing he'd lost her attention, Paolo switched to a new tactic. He pulled his cock from her pussy. When his tongue replaced his fingers, a full-body shudder took her. Familiar threads tightened in her abdomen. She couldn't come. Not while she was on the phone.

"Are you sure you're all right?" Suspicion replaced Micki's earlier concern. *Damn her cop instincts!*

"Just an aerobics video." Beth buried her face in the comforter. Oh, god, that sounded so lame, but it was the only thing she could think of to account for the noises.

It wasn't his sounds that were the problem. It was his talented mouth inducing her moans. She couldn't stop the building climax. Another sweep of his tongue over her clit sent her body into convulsions. She shook, biting into the covers to keep from crying out.

"You know what? Put me down for two. I'll see you in a couple of weeks," Micki snapped. The harsh buzz of a disconnected call filled the room.

"You are a fucking bastard, Paolo Ceranos!" Beth yanked at the cuffs, but all they did was rattle.

"I'm not the one who brought a forbidden device into a play session." He remained behind her, his fingers smearing her juices over her sensitive, still quivering flesh.

She wasn't sure which pissed her off more, Paolo or her body's response to him. "You still shouldn't have answered it."

Before she knew it, he jumped off the bed and grabbed her chin. This time the gleam in his eyes was pure evil. "I think you're forgetting who's in charge here. Or are you deliberately trying to push me into striking you?"

The rage she experienced Friday night with Aaron rose its ugly head. "So what if I am?" she snarled.

An odd, icy calm blanked his expression. "I see."

He disappeared from her view again, but she could hear him shuffling through the toy drawer again.

The sharp yank on her hair took her by surprise. She opened her mouth to protest, only for Paolo to shove a ball gag in place.

"Since you cannot keep your mouth shut when commanded like a proper sub, then we'll keep it open for the duration." His motions were jerky as he buckled the device into place. He palmed her phone.

On the plus side, he obviously didn't intend to force her to answer more calls since he'd gagged her. He wouldn't whip her. And he'd already made her come once, so his usual punishment was out.

What would he do now? The unknown stabbed through her soul, and she shivered. Things were always so carefully planned in her life. The clockwork assurance was why she loved her job. Loved being with Aaron and Paolo.

And yet, here she was. Deliberately fucking things up on purpose.

Paolo climbed onto the bed, behind her once again, and yanked out the ass plug. "Like I said, I plan on seeing how many times I can make you come. And there's nothing more beautiful than making an angry sub come against her will."

She closed her eyes. *Beth, you are such a dumbass.*

Paolo wasn't truly angry. Neither he nor Aaron were foolish enough to discipline a sub when their emotions were compromised.

And as much as it pissed her off to admit it, he was correct. She had broken the rules. She would be punished right this minute.

Something pressed against her tender pussy. Not him. It penetrated her. The sudden vibration inside her drew a muffled sound from her throat. Her heart raced at the familiar, hated buzz. The electric pulse hit her clit and she jerked. The contact was less than a second, but her pussy was on fire.

Paolo directed the vibrator against her nipples. She could feel him judging her reactions as he applied the device to various body parts. Pathetic whimpering filled the air.

Hers.

She hated vibrators with a passion. Her erogenous zones were too sensitive for the electronic toys. She'd rather have an unpadded alligator clip on her clit than endure a vibrator. And they buzzed like the paper wasps whose nest she accidentally knocked down the summer she turned eight.

The ball gag blocked her curses. She yanked at the cuffs. Their rattle mocked her. She lurched to her right, a desperate attempt considering the ankle spreaders firmly locked in place.

He looped an arm around her waist and laid the plastic against her clit. She shrieked, or tried to as her body erupted in another orgasm.

Somewhere amidst the sensory overload, the straps of the ball gag loosened. She gasped, the deep lungfuls of air a relief. The ankle spreaders landed with a muffled *clunk* on the carpet. Grateful that small favor, she collapsed on the comforter and carefully straightened her legs.

Paolo stretched out beside her. "Are you finished with your back talk? With fighting me, Beth?"

"Yes, Sir." Her whisper was hoarse to her own ears.

"Good." He brushed her sweat-damp hair away from her face. The look in his eyes had the same emotional intensity as Aaron's did Friday night.

It was too much. She rested her chin on the pillow and stared through the slats of the headboard at the wall. Surely, Paolo wouldn't proclaim his love, too, or some other stupid bullshit, would he?

Instead, he exhaled loudly. "Tell me why you don't want your friends to know about the three of us."

She whipped her head back to face him. "Wh-what are you talking about?" He remained silent, the question in his solemn expression. "Sir," she added belatedly. Another round with the vibrator was out of the question.

He stared up at the ceiling. "You and Master Aaron have put me in a very awkward position, Beth. Neither of you are telling each other your real feelings, and I don't appreciate being forced into the role of Switzerland because of his pride and your fear."

"I said I was sorry about Friday night—"

"Friday night is only part of the problem. And you are trying to avoid my command. Tell me why don't you want your friends to know about your relationship with us."

The bastard. He deliberately fried her brain cells, manipulated her into this conversation. "I-I never said—"

His gaze returned to her and he rolled onto his side, his head propped on his fist. "It's been a year. Are you that ashamed of us?"

Her conscience squirmed uncomfortably inside her mind. "Not . . . ashamed."

"We've had Sunday dinners with my mother." His hand idly stroked her back. "We've spent numerous weekends with Master Aaron's sister and her family at their beach house. Considering your lack of relationship with your parents, I'm not surprised we haven't met them, but your friends?"

"It's complicated."

"How?"

Paolo really wasn't going to let this go. She sucked in a harsh breath. "I don't think they would understand. Not after . . ."

With a start, she realized that while she'd confessed to Aaron, Paolo didn't know the whole story. "You know what happened to me in high school?"

He nodded. "I think it's incredible that we've gotten to the point that you're comfortable enough that we rarely need to use safe words."

The old, familiar ache started in her stomach. "The rape itself wasn't all that happened. Micki? The call you made me answer? She came looking for me along with our friends Alicia, Diana and Taneka. When they—" Spots appeared in front of Beth's eyes. She'd forgotten to breathe.

Paolo ran his fingers through her hair. "Take your time, *mi amor*."

After a couple of gulps of air, the ancient, bitter humor returned. "Rick was so busy raping and choking me, he didn't realize Micki was behind him. By the time Alicia and Taneka could pull her off him, he had a concussion, two cracked ribs, and some internal injuries."

"She was one of your cheerleader friends?" The look on Paolo's face showed his doubt to the damages she listed.

"Micki's dad, Major Donovan, is, was Army special forces. And her brother's a marine. Trust me, she definitely knows how to fight."

"And now she's a suburban mom with two-point-three kids and a labradoodle?" Paolo's attempt at humor didn't cover the anger and sadness in his eyes.

She smiled, a small one to show she appreciated his attempt. "She's a D.C. cop with black belts in a couple of different martial arts."

Her humor was short-lived. The ache in her stomach spread. "They put everything on the line for me. Everything that was important to them."

"And what is so important to a group of cheerleaders?"

He wasn't mocking her, but the rage at the unfairness of it all returned with a vengeance. "You don't get it. When the principal tried to cover up my rape, our coach LaShaun quit as the school's cheerleading coach. In retaliation, they fired her from her teaching job for breach of contract. The entire team quit in support of her and me. Some of the girls lost scholarships because of the fall-out. We all were constantly harassed, and it wasn't just the name-calling and the ugly snickering in the hallways. Slashed tires. Things stolen. Crank calls at all hours of the night.

"Worst of all, Micki could have spent years in jail. Because of me." She couldn't talk. Her throat ached too much.

"I'm sorry, Beth." His fingertips stroked her cheek.

They were both silent for a long time before he said, "Do you realize that Master Aaron and I would do the same thing in the same circumstance?"

She closed her eyes against the uncomfortable emotions swirling through her.

"No, I'm lying." Paolo's voice had turned into an animalistic growl. "I wouldn't settle with beating the shit out of the bastard. I would kill him."

Beth's eyes popped open. "Don't say that. Don't ever say that again." She didn't deserve that kind of devotion.

"Why?"

"I'm not going to be responsible for anybody else's pain."

"Did you inflict the pain?"

"I—" Her mind twisted around his logic, sensing the trap. "You don't understand."

"What?" Now, he did mock her. "You think you're the only newbie sub in history who mistook an abusive asshole for a dom."

"That's not—"

"It *is* the reason you're afraid to tell your friends about your current relationship." He looked up at the ceiling for an instant before he regarded her again. "What about your ex-girlfriend Diana? She's one of your high school friends, isn't she? She knows about your kinky streak."

Heat flooded Beth's skin at yet another personal failure. "Yes, but my needs scared her. It's the reason we broke up."

His chuckle was rueful. "From your description of her, you tried to force a sub into a dominant role in a desperate stab at self-protection. Of course, she found it uncomfortable."

Oh, shit. Beth buried her face in the pillow. Paolo was totally right. Her own needs had blinded her. How the hell were she and Diana even still friends after what she'd done?

A smack on her ass jerked her out of her self-recrimination. Her eyes shot to Paolo.

This time, humor quirked his mouth. "Back on your knees."

She glanced down at his erection. Yeah, she was definitely wallowing. How else could she forget her dom's needs?

Since he left her handcuffed to the headboard, she knew what he wanted from her. The thought alone reignited the spark of her lust.

Not that it really left. Not with Paolo constantly touching her as they talked.

"Yes, Sir." She propped herself on knees and forearms, which left her ass high in the air. Vulnerable. Needy once again.

He continued to run his hands over her skin. His touch comforted and aroused at the same time. He rose to his knees, and his light caress focused on the most sensitive skin along her crevice. A shiver rippled across her flesh.

Paolo positioned himself behind her again. Rough hair and hard muscle pressed against the backs of her thighs. His fingers traced their way to her puckered hole.

When he began working the cool lube into her, she shuddered. He took his time, deliberately prolonging the anticipation.

This was what she needed. To be taken. Used. Filled. Until they both came.

The exquisite pressure grew as his cock pushed against her, her body reluctant to make things easy despite the plug from earlier in their play.

He penetrated her ass slowly, carefully. Easing out a bit before pushing in a millimeter further. The vague discomfort disappeared as her flesh surrendered to his demands.

She couldn't stop herself from rocking against him, wanting, needing more. With a grunt, he spread her ass cheeks wider and embedded his cock to the hilt.

His fingers sought her pussy. Some part of her was surprised how wet she still was. A mewl of pleasure purred from her throat as he gave her the lightest of caresses.

She ground her ass against him. Wordless begging sounds filled the bedroom.

He withdrew until only the head of his cock remained inside, then eased forward. Oh, so careful not to hurt, to draw out the pleasure.

"Please, Sir," she whispered.

Her answer was a low-pitched laugh. This was the Paolo she knew. The one who would draw out the experience until she was a sobbing heap, pleading for release.

And she reveled in every minute of the sweet agony.

He continued his torturous penetration and withdrawal. His fingers stroked her parted pussy lips, careful not to touch her clit.

Her breathing turned to rapid pants as she struggled to control her reactions. He hadn't forbidden her from coming. He had claimed he wanted to see how many times he could make her climax. But for some strange reason, it seemed more important not to let go until he did.

"Beth," he murmured.

A fingertip flicked across her clit. She cried out as the explosion of bliss hit her. Carried her away. Dimly, she was aware of Paolo jerking, pumping hot come deep in her ass. All part of the ride into peaceful oblivion.

Chapter Four

Over breakfast the next morning, Beth announced. "I'm going to be late tonight, Sir. I promised to help my friend Diana with picking out a new outfit"

Aaron looked at her over his reading glasses. "Where are you going?"

Under the table, she squeezed her hands together. It wasn't her place to spill Diana's secrets, but his question seemed innocent enough. "Hidden Pleasures."

He set down his pad, leaned back and pulled his money clip from his pocket. "Since you'll be there anyway, I have two packages I need picked up, please." He handed her several large bills.

"Yes, Sir."

"Is there anything else?"

Shit, had Paolo said something? She glanced across the table, but his face was impassive.

He was right that she needed to talk to Aaron about her issues. Going public with their ménage had ramifications. But she wanted time to process her own feelings before they talked. And it promised to be a long, intense conversation.

She licked her dry lips. "Yes, Sir." Pressure grew in her chest. Her heart tried to pound its way through her ribs. "We need to talk about our relationship."

Aaron's wide, slow blink told her that Paolo hadn't narced on her. "This sounds serious."

"It is."

"Now?"

Beth twisted her fingers together. "This may take longer than the fifteen minutes before I need to leave for work."

Aaron frowned. "And you've already said you'll be late tonight. I have a dinner with two buyers. Can we do this Thursday night? I dislike cutting into our Friday evening for the second week in a row. It's not fair to Paolo."

"I'm cool with it." Paolo held up his hands.

"Tomorrow night is fine." She glanced at Paolo before returning her attention to Aaron. "This involves him as well."

His gaze flicked between her and Paolo. "All right. A house meeting tomorrow night."

Beth released the breath she held. They would talk. The question was would the three of them be together at the end of the evening.

When the elevator doors parted at five-oh-five p.m., Beth spotted Diana across the lobby. A nervous smile lit her friend's face.

"Thanks for doing this," Diana said as she hugged Beth.

"No problem. Do you want to grab some dinner tonight after our expedition?" Beth pushed the glass door open, and they stepped into early evening sunshine. The sidewalk bustled with folks headed for home.

Diana shook her head. "Can't. I've got some calls to make. I need to be out of my place by the end of the next month."

Beth paused on the sidewalk. "Hey, if you need to borrow some money for rent—"

Diana wrapped a hand around Beth's elbow and tugged. "I'm not a moocher, and you know it."

Dammit. She'd stepped on Diana's pride. Since their senior year in high school, Diana had taken care of herself and her baby sister after they'd been tossed out by their parents. Granted, Micki's parents had taken them in, but Diana had insisted on paying back every penny.

Diana continued walking to the subway station. Beth had to jog to keep up with Diana's longer stride and keep her arm.

"I'm sorry. I didn't mean—"

Bright red nails flicked Beth's attempted apology away. "I didn't want to stay there anyway. Too many bad memories." Diana shot her a sly smile. "I could bunk with you—"

"No." The denial shot out before Beth could stop it.

"Uh-huh. That's what I thought." A knowing expression spread Diana's smile even wider.

Beth's heart raced. "Just what do you think?" she retorted.

"Nothing, girl. Absolutely nothing." But Diana's shit-ass grin didn't fade until they boarded the Metro.

The subway ride to DuPont Circle was thankfully short. Beth led the two blocks to Hidden Pleasures.

The store wasn't joking about the hidden part. The front entrance didn't face the street. Instead, it was tucked in an alcove after going through a side courtyard. Discreet and classy, but well lit at the same time.

A little chime above the door tinkled as they entered the shop.

"Darling! Long time, no see." The owner Clarice rushed over from the counter and kissed both of Beth's cheeks. She turned to Diana. "And who is this adorable creature?"

Beth couldn't help grinning. "My friend Diana needs something special."

Clarice cocked a perfectly drawn eyebrow. "Friend or *friend*?"

From one of the other rooms, Beth could hear Sonya with another customer. She lowered her voice. "It's her first ménage scene, and she wants to impress the couple."

"I see." Clarice tapped her chin with a neon blue fingernail as she circled Diana.

"Anything new in leather—" Beth started.

"No, no, no." Clarice waggled her index finger. She smiled at Diana. "You are too beautiful, and we want something that pops." Clarice clicked her tongue. "This is a classy couple, right?"

Diana tilted her head. "Yes."

Clarice looped her arm around Diana's. "I know just the thing." She tugged Diana toward another private room.

Diana shot a desperate glance over her shoulder at Beth. "Aren't you coming?"

Laughter burbled out. "Relax. Clarice has impeccable taste."

After the other two disappeared, she drifted around the shop. It had been too long since she'd bought anything for herself. Maybe something sedate, but sheer.

Sonya's voice drifted down the short hallway. "Well?"

"I'll definitely take this." A familiar voice, but not Diana's.

Beth ducked down behind the rack and peered between the feathered peignoirs. If the pronounced East Coast enunciation hadn't tipped her off, the auburn hair of the woman approaching the counter was a dead giveaway.

Alicia.

What the hell was Miss Prim-And-Proper doing at a kink store? Had she actually taken her own challenge, found a "boytoy" as she termed it at lunch two weeks ago, and tried something new?

Beth cocked her head as Sonya suggested matching stockings to go with the black leather one-piece. Confusion mixed with a smidgeon of jealousy. With Alicia's super-pale skin, C-cup boobs and long legs, she'd look gorgeous in that outfit. The ultimate dominatrix.

"Do you have a pair of black or red stilettos?" Sonya asked.

Alicia shook her head before she gave a self-deprecating laugh. "I'd be afraid I'd break an ankle."

"A pair of black pumps will do in a pinch, but you might want to think about buying a pair." Sonya wrapped the purchasing in the store's signature black and purple tissue.

"So all I have to do is kneel when he gets home?"

Beth couldn't see Alicia's face, but the nervous tremor in her voice wasn't like the self-assured CFO. But then, Beth never would have pictured Alicia as a submissive in a million years.

"Trust me. It will drive him insane. Good luck." Sonya winked.

"Thanks." Alicia turned to leave.

Beth sagged in relief when the little bell above the door tinkled. She wasn't sure which of them would've been more embarrassed if Alicia knew she was here.

Sonya walked around the rack. She gazed at Beth, still crouching on the floor, with an amused half-smile. The hoop in her bottom lip reflected the overhead light. "Co-worker, neighbor, or a member of your church?"

"What?"

Sonya snickered. "The previous customer. I'm assuming that's why you're hiding back here and not because you're planning to shoplift."

Beth straightened. "She's someone from high school." And here she was, acting like an idiot teenager.

"Lemme guess. Snotty cheerleader who made you do her homework?" Sonya fingered the series of hoops decorating her right ear.

A rueful smile tilted the corners of Beth's mouth. "Actually, we were both on the cheerleading squad. And while I did tutor her, I made her do her own damn homework." She shot a look at the shop door. "I didn't know she even wanted to be a sub."

Sonya laughed. "So that's why you were hiding. Well, if I had a dom as hot as Aaron, I wouldn't be advertising it either."

Crap, she forgot after the shock of seeing Alicia here. Beth reached into her messenger bag. "Thanks for reminding me. I'm supposed to pick up a couple of packages for him."

Sonya waggled her pierced eyebrows. "You are going to look so cute in the schoolgirl uniform."

Beth stiffened. "What?" She seemed to be repeating that word an awful lot today.

"Uh-oh." Sonya winced. "I didn't mean to ruin the surprise."

"It's okay." Except it wasn't. She tried really hard not to compare her body against Alicia's, or even Diana's classic hour-glass figure. Is that how Master Aaron saw her? As a girl, not a woman?

"Yo, Beth! Get your ass down here!" Diana's demand cracked her bout of insecurity. She handed the bills Aaron had given her this morning to Sonya.

"Go." She waved. "I'll have everything ready for you."

Beth strode down the short hallway. Clarice leaned against the wall outside of the changing room, her lips pursed.

"What's wrong?"

Clarice waved at the slated door. "Your friend insists I have too much of a dick to give her an honest opinion."

Beth rolled her eyes. "Diana . . ."

The door opened and her dark head poked out. Ire flashed in her eyes. "That's not what I said, you self-conceited bitch. I said it needed to appeal to both a man and a woman." She turned to Beth. "Get in here."

Beth stepped inside the changing room and stopped short. Diana wore a strapless snow-white corset in satin that stood out against her dark chocolate skin. She looked like a freaking BDSM Disney princess. "Wow."

"So it looks okay?" Diana twisted to look at the back in the mirror.

"It looks incredible."

Diana turned back to Beth. "Should I get the matching panties? I feel a little naked."

"No." Beth shook her head. "I'd go with white stockings."

"That's what I said," Clarice called out. They ignored her.

"Wear your lavender floral dress over it," Beth added. "The one with the flowing skirt."

Diana frowned. "I'll look like a little girl on Easter Sunday."

"No, you won't. Not with your Amazon height," Clarice yelled.

Beth grinned. "She's right. You'll be sin wrapped in primness and knock their socks off."

Diana smoothed non-existent wrinkles on the hip-length piece. "You sure?"

"Yes." Beth could have kicked herself. Diana was worried about the cost. Money had been tight since her asshole fiancé had walked out on her. But she looked so damn good in the outfit, and she deserved a little fun. "Happy early birthday."

"No." Diana's glare matched her shaking index finger. "My birthday's not until July, and it's too freaking much. I'm not borrowing any money—"

"Tough shit. It's a present, not a loan." Beth grinned. "Did you hear Clarice?"

"Cash or on your AmEx, hon."

"AmEx."

Diana looked away, but the mirrors caught the combination of gratitude and ire on her face. "You are a bitch, Beth Winslow."

Beth leaned against the doorjamb. "So this is what it feels like to be the dom. I think I like it."

Diana's reflection glared at her. "Are you going to help me out of this thing? Or just stand there with that self-satisfied look?"

Beth stepped forward to tackle the hooks. "I want you to be happy, Di. I really do want you to be happy with your mystery couple."

Diana's teeth clicked.

Beth gritted her own teeth at the all-too-familiar sound. The last time she'd heard it had been when Diana dragged her into Aaron's gallery that first time. The time she'd chickened out of approaching him about her paintings. "What?"

"Nothing, girl." Diana carefully folded the corset and grabbed her bra from the bench. "Thanks for the early birthday present."

Beth's steps slowed a couple of blocks from the townhouse. Aaron wouldn't be home yet. If she waited another couple of hours, Paolo would already be in bed when she got home. She stepped into the little French-style café. It had been over seven hours since she grabbed a turkey and cheddar sandwich from the deli in her office building, and she didn't feel like leftovers at home.

No, you want to avoid your problems again, the little voice inside her chided.

Like every other time she needed to think, she ordered a chef salad and two chocolate croissants. The very items she'd been eating when Aaron and Paolo had come into the café a year ago.

She sat down and poked at the eggs, greens and guilt. The story she'd told Diana wasn't entirely truthful. Yes, she had gone back to Aaron's gallery the day after Diana had dragged her inside. But the second he had approached her, she'd squeaked a "No, thank you," and bolted out the door.

After wandering through Georgetown shops for the next few hours, she'd stopped here for something to eat. When the guys had walked in, Aaron had come to her table and asked if they could join her. Her mortification urged her to say no. Instead, the artist inside of her said, "Yes."

Within minutes, a lively conversation over the pros of different mediums had her enthralled. When Paolo showed her the tag he'd made and wore, she relaxed even more. They were a couple.

Until they exchanged a look and Aaron asked if they could see her again.

They.

Saying yes had been the biggest chance she'd taken in her life.

And this last year had been the best year of her entire existence. Even she had to admit, her painting had new life.

Because she was living again.

Paolo was right. She was letting her fear destroy everything.

Enough. She grabbed her bag from Hidden Pleasures, went to the counter and requested three chocolate croissants to go. Her brisk pace brought her the last three blocks in record time.

When Beth unlocked the front door, only the light in the entryway and the one over the kitchen stove were on. Aaron wasn't back from his meeting yet. She set the croissants on the table before she carried the shopping bag to the study and set it on his chair.

The second tread of the staircase squeaked as she climbed it. Paolo was supposed to fix that, too. Her heart gave a little flip. She took him for granted, and she really needed her ass kicked for that.

When she crept into the master bedroom, his soft snores greeted her. She stripped off her clothes, folded and placed them in the chair by the bureau, but then she stood for a moment, watching him. The play of the streetlight enhanced across his proud nose and strong jaw.

She was on the verge of retrieving a pad and her pencils when he murmured, "Come to bed, *chica.*" He patted the mattress.

"I'm sorry I woke you." She padded to the other side of the bed and crawled under the covers.

He started to roll over, but she laid a hand on his shoulder. "Don't move."

His back vibrated with his laughter. "I can't hold you if you're behind me."

"Maybe I want to hold you." She pressed against him, wrapped her arm around his waist and inhaled. The faint scent of ozone clung to him. He must have been working on a new piece earlier this evening.

"Beth?" His huge hand engulfed hers. "Is everything okay?"

"Almost perfect," she whispered.

She wasn't sure how long she'd been asleep when the mattress shifted. First, body heat caressed her spine, then hard muscle molded against her back. Her arm was still snug around Paolo's waist.

Aaron's hand stroked Paolo's hip before dropping to encircle her. Warm breath fluttered her hair.

"Perfect," she whispered.

"Go back to sleep, Beth." Aaron's quiet voice was filled with amusement. He placed a kiss on her shoulder.

"Yes, Sir." She snuggled in her cocoon of male bodies and did as she was told.

The guys were gone when Beth's alarm went off the next morning. She wasn't sure what would have been more uncomfortable: dealing with Aaron and Paolo before their formal talk or the dread of real communication that would plague her all day.

Focusing on her guest list for the show was more productive she decided on the bus ride to the office. As she tapped through the list on her smart phone, she realized she'd received calls, texts or e-mails from nearly everyone.

Everyone except for Alicia.

Guilt tweaked Beth for spying on her friend last night. She tapped the call icon for Alicia's home number and left a message.

Guilt yanked a little harder on her conscience. Leaving a message on Alicia's home voice-mail was a chicken shit move.

Beth tapped Alicia's cell number. She sighed when it rolled over to voice-mail as well and left another message.

Funny how neither Micki or Diana had heard from Alicia since their lunch nearly two weeks ago. Despite her speech at lunch, it wasn't like Alicia to take chances with men. Exhibit A was her ex, Hank the total dweeb. Maybe she should have approached Alicia last night at the Hidden Pleasures. Maybe she had gotten in over her head with whoever she was secretly dating.

Beth slipped her phone in its holster on her belt. Should she borrow Aaron's car, drive over to Alicia's place in Chevy Chase, and check on her?

No, she was being ridiculous. God, the crap her mind came up with to avoid her own issues.

One thing at a time, girl. You need to clean your own house before you start on your friends.'

Chapter Five

Beth's hand shook, and it took three tries to shove her key into the lock. Of all nights for the office bully to dump his workload on her.

Or he tried to.

The four-fifty-five stunt had been the proverbial last straw. She surprised herself and her boss by ripping the bully a new asshole.

But then her boss spent twenty minutes trying to make sure Beth was okay. How it wasn't like her to blow up at the office. So instead of catching the five-oh-seven bus, she was almost an hour late getting home.

Beth kicked the door shut behind her. "I'm home!"

Paolo jogged downstairs, his dark hair still damp from the shower, but one look at her and his greeting smile faded. "What's wrong?"

"What's wrong? Get in the kitchen. Where's Aaron?"

Paolo's eyes widened at her blatant rudeness and lack of proper address.

"In the kitchen making tea for us," came the other masculine voice.

She turned to find Aaron leaning against the doorjamb between the foyer and the dining room.

One dark blond eyebrow rose in askance. "Want to tell us what crawled up your ass and died?" he continued.

Beth sucked in a deep breath. This was not how she wanted to start this conversation, but since he asked . . .

"I'm tired of everyone making assumptions. About what I should want. What I should do. How I should feel."

She stomped past Aaron and set her messenger bag down on the table. Tried to collect herself before she faced him again.

When she looked up, his expression was a mask. Concern filled Paolo's eyes as he watched her over Aaron's shoulder.

"Painting was the one thing that was *mine*. Mine alone. Something that wasn't touched by the other crap in my life. And you took that from me, Aaron." Her voice softened. "I know you were doing what you think you should as a master. Pushing me to be my best. But this is incredibly personal, and you didn't even ask."

"Why did you come to the gallery two days in a row if you didn't want to show your work?"

"That first day I let Diana drag me in. My friends are like you. Doing what they think is best for me, regardless of what I really want."

"And the second day?" Once again, he had that odd expression.

Understanding hit her hard. Aaron was afraid of losing her.

"There was something else I wanted. Someone else." She gave him a rueful smile. "Part of me was thankful I hadn't made a fool of myself when I saw Paolo's tag at the café later that night." She reached for her own medallion through her t-shirt and wrapped her fingers around it. "And then when you both asked me to join you—" She blinked the wetness from her eyes.

"I can cancel the showing, Beth." Aaron murmured.

"No." She shook her head. "In a lot of ways, you were right. I have been scared of revealing too much of myself."

Aaron looked out the window for a moment before his gaze returned to her. "Are you ashamed of our relationship?"

"No. It's more—" She grasped desperately for the right words. "After what happened to me in high school, my friends were, are, rather overprotective. I didn't want to hear their accusations that I was doing something stupid with you two." She shrugged. "Let's face it. This isn't exactly a conventional relationship. The showing is a . . . safe environment to get them used to the idea."

"What made you change your mind?" Too much seemed to be riding on Aaron's words. Even Paolo's expression said he sat on the edge of a precipice.

"Diana already suspects I'm secretly seeing you. And I found out this week neither she nor Alicia are in conventional relationships either." She couldn't help the self-deprecating laugh. "It made me realize how much of an idiot I'd been. And how much I love both of you."

Before she could react, she was enveloped in both of their embraces. Having two men tell her over an over again how much they loved her thawed the ice she didn't even realize surrounded her heart.

Beth, Paolo and Aaron spent the next few hours hashing out new soft and hard limits in their day-to-day lives over tea and Chinese take-out.

"I have a confession to make," she said as she broke her fortune cookie.

The guys exchanged a look before Paolo shrugged and said, "At least, we know it's not, 'Hey, I'm really a dude.'"

She threw half her cookie at him. He neatly snagged the treat out of the air and popped it in his mouth.

"Sonya accidentally told me about the schoolgirl outfit." Beth broke apart the remainder of her cookie before she looked at Aaron. "Is that how you think of me? A little girl?"

A wicked smile tilted the corners of his mouth. "I think of you in a lot of ways, Elizabeth. That particular outfit was for a game I planned. If you feel up to it tomorrow night."

He leaned forward on the couch and picked up a piece of her cookie that had fallen on the table surface. At his silent command, she opened her mouth. He placed the bit on her tongue, brushing her lower lip in the process. "Did she tell you about the other outfit?"

Beth shook her head while she chewed the almond goodness.

"Your dress for the showing is on the bed. I'd like you to try it on."

"Yes, Sir." She climbed to her feet and jogged up the stairs. A tiny nugget of worry nipped at her heels. It wasn't that she questioned Aaron's taste, but what would she do if the outfit wasn't *her*?

One of the huge white boxes she'd brought from Hidden Pleasures sat at the foot of the bed. She tentatively approached and traced her fingertips over the pristine cardboard.

This was a business function. Surely, he'd kept his selection tasteful.

She eased the top off and set aside. Sucking in a harsh breath, she unfolded the crisp black and purple tissue.

The shiny braided medallion caught her eye first. She gently lifted the black leather choker it hung from. Gold, silver and copper twined around each other in an intricate design. A metalwork version of her painting of the three of them.

Heat flooded her cheeks. Paolo had to have been studying her canvas for weeks to produce this. She ran her fingers over the design. Its intimacy wasn't obvious unless the person knew what to look for.

Since the choker and its medallion were custom-made, she had no doubt the dress was as well. She carefully lifted the black leather bodice.

Strapless. The leather skirt panels split with volumes of deep purple satin inset between the multitude of slits.

It was gorgeous.

What the hell was Aaron thinking? She'd look like a preteen dressing in her mother's clothes.

"I swear you are the only woman I've ever known who would hold a brand-new dress like it's a rattlesnake about to bite her."

Beth jumped at Aaron's voice. The leather fell from her nerveless fingers. Both men stood in the doorway, watching her.

"It's also not nice to sneak up on someone," she snapped.

"Oooo, I like this new, aggressive Beth." Paolo grinned and winked at her.

Aaron made a hurry-up motion with his hand. "Come on, Beth. I need to make sure this fits before the show."

"I-I can't wear this." She bent to retrieve the dress from the carpet.

"Why not?" Aaron demanded. He started ticking off fingers, mocking her in a falsetto voice. "It's too expensive. It's too hot. It's too cold. It's too revealing. It isn't my style."

Paolo elbowed Aaron. "You forgot 'My boobs are too small.'"

He cocked his head and pretended to examine Paolo's chest. "What are you talking about? Your boobs are bigger than mine and Beth's put together."

She laughed and shook her head. They would harass her until she put on the damn dress. She laid the garment on the bed and started to strip. "I hope you two are proud of yourselves."

"Always," Aaron said.

She stepped into the dress and pulled it up over her hips. Aaron was behind her in an instant to zip her in. Paolo gave a low wolf whistle.

"Look," Aaron murmured. He guided her to the full-length antique mirror that stood in the corner.

Air turned to ice in her lungs. Her whole body started shaking. She hadn't worn any gown since the night of her junior prom. The realization hit her harder than she imagined.

"Breathe, Elizabeth. We're right here with you. No one's going to hurt you." Aaron knew or suspected the dress would trigger an anxiety attack. He released her shoulders. "We won't let them. Either Paolo or I will be with you the entire night."

She clenched her fists and forced her lungs to expand. It had been seven years since her last episode. Sixteen since the rape. Dammit, she was not letting anything ruin this show for all of their sakes. She took another gulp of oxygen before she said, "It's okay. I'm okay."

Turning to face Aaron, she smiled and took his hand. "Thank you for the dress. It's beautiful."

Concern marred his usual stern look. "You sure you're all right?"

She nodded. "I will be."

Paolo approached them, the choker in his hand. "Do you feel up to trying this on? I'd like to see the full effect."

"Of course," she said. A twinge yanked on her nerves as he gently fastened the Velcro, but she managed to keep the shaking to a minimum.

"I've made appointments to have your hair and make-up done, or are you going to fight me on those issues as well?" Aaron added dryly.

"No more disobedience, Sir." She had to bite her lower lip to keep from laughing.

He turned her to face the mirror again. "Something like this." He undid her ponytail before he gathered her hair and piled it on top of her head. A few tendrils hung loose about her face.

If Diana had looked like a BDSM version of a Disney princess last night, then her outfit took it to a whole new level. She was a princess who needed to be ravished by her knights.

She turned back to Aaron. Her hair spilled to her shoulders, and her lips parted. Anxiety had nothing to do with her inability to catch her breath.

He chuckled. "Not tonight, my dear." His warm palm cupped her cheek. "We've all had too much emotional bullshit to deal with this evening. That's an invitation for disaster."

"But—" She closed her eyes and swallowed her disappointment and desire. He was right. "Yes, Sir."

He leaned closer, and her heart raced at his body heat. "Do you really want us both at the same time?"

Her eyes fluttered open, and she met his intense gaze. Her tongue swept her dry lips. "Yes, please," she whispered.

"Tomorrow night, but only if you follow my directions." The corner of his mouth quirked.

"I will, Sir," Beth promised.

Aaron and Paolo helped her out of her new dress. She hung it carefully in the closet while the guys prepared for bed. From the glances she stole, she wasn't the only one excited about tomorrow night's game.

No matter how much she ached for their mouths, their fingers, their cocks, she needed patience. Soft, chaste kisses were the only thing she received as they cuddled under the covers.

And for once she felt comfortable enough with them, and with herself, not to press the issue.

When Beth entered the kitchen the next morning, Paolo was spooning scrambled eggs and fried potatoes into cornmeal tortillas. She tried not to wince as she pulled the grapefruit juice carton out of the refrigerator.

"You need a solid meal to start your day." Paolo frowned at her.

Apparently, she hadn't been careful enough. "Solid is great for you. You do manual labor, Mr. Welder. I, on the other hand, sit on my ass in front of a computer most of the day, which is exactly where your grandmama's *huevos rancheros* will end up. On my ass."

"You could use a little more meat on your bones, *chica*." He slapped her buttocks.

"He's right, Beth." Aaron stalked into the kitchen and headed straight for the coffee. "You will take your backpack today. There's an envelope with instructions and money." He poured his cup and faced her. "Make sure you eat lunch today. Plenty of protein and complex carbs."

Her mouth opened. Lunch money? Seriously? He was treating her like a child. Her pulse throbbed. What the hell had happened to last night's talk?

Paolo leaned close and said in a mock whisper, "You'll need the energy. We plan to put you through your paces, little sub."

Her jaw snapped shut at the gleam in Aaron's eyes, the gentle kiss Paolo placed on her neck. She shivered. Damn, she was on the edge of coming just from the combination of their words and her imagination.

"Yes, Sir." She lowered her gaze. "Do you have any other instructions, Sir?"

"Just one." Aaron crossed the kitchen and cupped the back of her head. His mouth seduced and demanded at the same time, and she willingly surrendered. His cock pressed against her abdomen through their clothes. Liquid heat filled her, except that even the one little part of her mind, which tried to stay rational, suggested she call in sick. That she should spend the day letting Aaron and Paolo do whatever they wanted to her.

When Aaron withdrew, he leaned his forehead against hers. "Remember I love you."

"Y-yes, Sir. I suppose I should get to work." How was she going to make it to the bus stop the way her knees quivered?

"Don't I get a kiss?" Paolo's baritone rumbled with amusement.

"Sorry." She twined her arms around his neck. His claiming was gentler, sweeter. A reminder that no matter how hard Aaron pushed her, he would be there to catch her. Their lips parted, and she couldn't catch her breath.

"I love you," he whispered before he released her.

She grabbed his hand and Aaron's and squeezed. "I love you both. I'll see you later."

Beth pivoted and raced from the kitchen before she jumped them and totally forgot about work.

At six-oh-seven p.m., Beth walked out of the Four Seasons public bathroom, feeling slightly ridiculous. The pigtails with bright red ribbons and the black necktie she wore were the least of her concerns.

The black push-up bra Aaron had provided stood out like a beacon through the sheer white blouse. The red and black plaid skirt was so short a stiff breeze would display the matching lace thong. To finish off the ensemble, he'd provided her with white bobby socks and saddle shoes.

Nearly everyone in the lobby stared at her as she crossed the marble floor. And those who didn't were nudged by their companions.

Public humiliation had never been on her BDSM menu. This was no more than Aaron testing her limits and proving his power. Honestly, it wasn't like she traipsed through the lobby totally naked and in a dog collar, but it didn't stop her from checking for trouble in her peripheral vision.

From their expressions, every man in the lobby undressed her in their imaginations. A couple of women did as well. Instead of embarrassment, heat seeped into her pussy.

The surge of power lengthened her stride. Everyone could wish to their hearts' desire, but she only spread her legs for two men.

From the corner of her eye, she spotted someone moving to intercept her. The dark suit, close-clipped hair and earpiece were a dead giveaway.

Shit. She was steps away from the front doors. If he dragged her back to the hotel's security area, Aaron and Paolo would have the sense to come in here looking for her. She hoped.

Beth turned and smiled. "Is there a problem, sir?"

The dark-haired guard returned her smile, but there was no warmth behind his eyes. "Are you a guest here, miss?"

"No, sir. I'm on my way to a costume party, and I used the public restroom to change."

"Costume party?" His once-over indicated exactly what he felt, disgust and lust at the same time.

"Maybe Brittany Spears was a little before your time."

At his frown over her slam, she reached into the side pocket of her backpack and pulled out her driver license and her work ID. "Here." She deliberately raised her voice. Nothing like a scene to get someone to back down. "If you don't believe that I'm not a prostitute, radio your office and have them check the last eight minutes of the recordings for those cameras—" She jabbed an index finger at the one over the front door, then the one over the check-in desk. Working for a defense contractor was its own education. "And the one in the back hallway leading to the ladies' room." She planted her fists on her hips. "Oh, and if I were a prostitute, I doubt if any of your *guests* will appreciate being called a quick draw."

Several people nearby snickered at her last comment.

The guard pressed his finger against his earpiece. "Did you hear that?"

Beth clenched her toes to keep from tapping her saddle shoe against the marble floor. She'd been wet and needy when she exited the bus, but this delay was seriously spoiling her mood.

The security guard's face turned the proverbial beet red. He forced his frown into a neutral expression. "I'm sorry for the delay, Ms. Winslow." He handed her IDs back to her. "Have a good evening?"

"Thank you," she said and slipped the cards back into their pocket. Odds were that Aaron was already outside. The stupid guard destroyed the spontaneity of their scenario.

Maybe not. Maybe this would be funny later. The whole point of tonight was some relaxing play time because they wouldn't get another chance before the show. But how to resuscitate the scene?

She contemplated her options. The hotel bar was a possibility, but only if she wore another outfit. Her work jeans and sweatshirt weren't classy enough for the

Four Seasons. In this schoolgirl outfit? Forget it. She didn't have the patience to deal with the men in the bar.

Sucking in her frustration, Beth headed through one of the multitude of glass doors. Surely, Aaron wouldn't get pissy over her tardiness. No, he wouldn't. She was the one acting like a spoiled brat. The guard had only been doing his job. Maybe that was the point of Aaron's outfit and place selection. A little humiliation to get her head in the game.

Chill air from the scattered showers earlier cut through the thin clothes she wore. Goosebumps rose along all her skin, not just the exposed areas. Gray clouds threatened to dump more rain.

She scanned the guest arrival area, but no navy Jaguar sat at the curb. Maybe Aaron was late as well thanks to rush hour traffic. Another blast of wind hardened her nipples into painful points, and not in the good way.

Just as she decided to go back inside the hotel, a sleek black town car pulled up in front of her, and the rear passenger window slid down. Aaron peered out. "Do you need a ride, miss?"

Repressing the urge to giggle, she approached the car. "My mother told me never to get into a stranger's automobile."

His expression was calm, but desire shone in his eyes, which soaked her miniscule thong. "It's threatening to rain. You'll be drenched before you get home. Surely, your mother wouldn't want you to catch pneumonia, would she?"

As if he'd cued the weather, a gust slashed through her costume. "No." She lowered her eyes. "I don't think she would."

The driver's door popped open, and Paolo climbed out. His black curls were pulled into a queue beneath the cap that topped his chauffer costume. His dark eyes twinkled as he rounded the vehicle. Beth stifled another giggle.

Aaron's head disappeared inside the vehicle.

Paolo opened the rear passenger door with a gallant sweep of his arm. "Miss, I can put your backpack in the trunk if you'd like."

She slid the straps from her shoulder and handed him the pack. His fingers brushed her wrist when he took the burden from her, no lingering longer than necessary. Every action was solicitous, polite.

Somehow, that made what they did more enticing. Even though the security guard had dampened her mood, anticipation built inside her again.

Beth climbed into the car, deliberately flashing the length of her thigh and her naked buttock. "Thank you very much for the ride, Sir." She carefully watched him from the corner of her eye.

"You're welcome." His face remained impassive. However, his trousers told another story.

Paolo slid into the driver's seat, and the sedan pulled away from the curb. Within moments, they merged into the heavy traffic. The backseat felt dark. And just dangerous enough to set her nerves on fire.

"I-I live at 2714 Kent Circle." Her old address. She fiddled with her fingers as if she were the nervous schoolgirl.

Aaron laid a palm over her twitching digits. "Do you have to be home right away?"

"My mother's expecting me for dinner."

"I'm sure she won't mind if you're a little late." He turned over her left palm and brought it to his lips. The light kiss fired her pulse.

She pulled her hand from his grip. "I don't think that would be a good idea." Despite any initial reservations about this game, she tried to guess what he'd do next. She pressed herself in the corner between the seat and the door.

He didn't pursue. Instead, he leaned back into the soft leather. "Where do you think you're going?"

"Nowhere." The tension added a dimension to her edgy need.

"Good. I'd hate to see you hurt yourself."

She tugged at the door handle. Paolo's dark eyes flashed in the rearview mirror. The bastard had engaged the child proof locks. His safety streak struck again. If she and Aaron mock wrestled in the back seat, neither of them would accidentally fall into traffic.

Aaron laid his palm on her bare knee, jerking her back to the scene. "Don't you think we deserve something for giving you a ride?"

Beth played with one of the pigtails. "Like what?"

"A kiss." His expression held a hint of amusement.

She wasn't quite sure if it was part of his act, or if her performance was that bad. Pissed at her own stupid insecurity, she ran her tongue over her bottom lip. Aaron watched the pink tip as if mesmerized. The sensation of power she'd experienced in the hotel lobby surged through her.

"What kind of kiss?" she said.

"I'll show you." He scooted closer. Cupping the back of her head, he drew her to him. The touch of his lips was tender, sweet even. She hadn't been kissed like that in a very long time.

When he pulled back, he said, "Was that so bad?"

"No." She dropped her gaze. "No, it wasn't."

"Would you like another?"

"I-I guess." Squeezing her legs together didn't alleviate the growing ache. This delicate seduction was harder to endure than riding crops and handcuffs.

Don't jump to conclusions. Those can always come in later.

Aaron slid a hair closer. His mouth caressed hers, ending with a gentle tug on her lower lip.

She stared into his eyes, which was against the normal play rules, but he didn't move to punish her. Instead, he was perfectly still. His intense blue eyes bore into her soul. His hand resting on her knee was their only physical connection. Yet, it felt as if she were falling into something from which there was no escape.

Their purpose penetrated her. This was the careful, poignant introduction to sex she should have had. Their intent triggered a sentimental wave. Whatever their differences or issues, Aaron and Paolo left their stamp on her with this act of sheer romanticism.

In the slightest of whispers, she breathed, "May I have another kiss, Sir?"

He tilted her chin with his free hand. She surrendered to the increased insistency of his mouth and parted her lips. As much as she wanted to sink into that kiss, she knew she couldn't give in just yet. He seduced her into his invasion.

She jerked back. "Ewww! That was your tongue!" She swiped the back of her hand over her mouth.

A faint snicker came from the front seat. As much as she wanted to whack the back of Paolo's head, she was determined to remain in character.

Aaron had a wicked grin on his face as well. "Haven't you ever been French-kissed by one of the boys at your school?"

Beth looked down at her clasped hands. "N-n-no. I mean, I've heard about it."

He twirled the closest of her pigtails around his index finger. "You're a very pretty girl. Wouldn't you like to learn so some other boy doesn't catch you by surprise?"

"I don't know. I-I guess." The change in her breathing didn't have to be feigned. She was horny as hell so it was no stretch to act like a hormone-addled teenage girl.

He framed her face with his palms. His foray was delicate, careful. On the other hand, she couldn't check her response. Her tongue tangled with his before she tickled the left corner of his mouth.

Aaron unbuckled her seatbelt and pulled her onto his lap, all without breaking contact. One hand cupped the back of her head. The other slid up her skirt.

She wrenched her mouth free from his and grabbed his wrist, the one about to disappear under her hem. "Hey! What do you think you're doing?"

In a swift move, he encircled both of her wrists in one of his hands. "You said I could have a kiss for giving you a ride home. Then you asked for more. You didn't say where I could kiss you." He pointedly looked at her mound before giving her a wicked smile.

Beth wriggled, but all she succeeded in doing was to make his cock under her hip even harder. Her panting filled the backseat. "That's all you'll do, right? Just kiss me? You promise?"

"I promise. Paolo and I will only kiss you." His lips brushed her ear. "Unless you beg us to do other things to you."

She couldn't stop the shudder that took her. The parameters of the game. Drive her insane until she pleaded with them to fuck her. Except she wasn't sure how long she could hold out, especially once Paolo joined in the play.

A jolt shook the chassis. She peered out the window to find Paolo turning into the alley that ran behind their house.

A flicker of disappointment danced through her arousal. She had half-expected the guys to parade her in front of the neighbors in this outfit, and the idea of people watching her thrilled her just like it had at the hotel.

Maybe that was the real reason she worked so hard at being a wallflower. Fear of what she'd do, what she'd want to do, if she had an audience. Was that the real reason Aaron had never taken her to his private club? That he knew her better than she knew herself? Knew she would lose all inhibitions in front of a captive, appreciative crowd?

Paolo guided the sedan under the carport attached to their workshop. He turned off the ignition and climbed out of the driver's seat.

Aaron didn't move. He locked eyes with her as if waiting for another outburst or question.

Beth couldn't think of a damn thing to say. For their special Fridays, he sometimes reserved a hotel room for a change of pace. She'd half-expected him to have one at the Four Seasons when his instructions said to meet him there. Home seemed a little bit of a let down after the costume and the rental car.

The rear door opened. Paolo reached for her. Before his actions registered, he picked her up and slung her over his shoulder. He turned to hold the car door for Aaron.

She cocked her head to look at their master. Again, that amused, confident expression appeared on his face. He climbed out of the backseat and headed for the workshop.

After locking the car, Paolo followed Aaron through the back door and across the first floor. Wire, metal bars and other odds and ends covered the two tables. Otherwise the place was immaculate. It didn't look like he'd started anything new over the last couple of days either. But he'd smelled like ozone the other night, and he was always working on *something*.

Maybe she wasn't the only one experiencing a major case of nerves over the show. Maybe she had been that much of a selfish bitch not to realize he was as anxious as she was about showing his work for the first time.

The steps to her studio creaked under Aaron's feet. Paolo climbed the stairs with her body still hanging over his shoulder.

Irritation gathered in her stomach. What had these two done to her studio? The frame Paolo created for her was one thing. Messing with her supplies was another.

At the landing, Paolo waited with her. She couldn't see a damn thing inside her workspace.

She had a terrific view of Paolo's fine ass though. Part of her wanted to beat it and demand he put her down. But the rest wanted to see how this played out.

"Bring her in."

At Aaron's words, Paolo carried her into her own damn studio and set her on her saddle shoes. Her jaw dropped.

Flames crackled in the ancient fireplace. The easels and the table with her supplies had been moved to the far wall with the blank canvases, well out of the way of the huge plush scarlet rug that covered the bare wooden planks of the floor.

The sweet scent of vanilla filled her studio. A multitude of white candles took up a couple of smaller tables and the windowsills on the rug side of the room. Their flickering flashed off the cuffs that had held the oil painting of the three of them.

The cuffs hung loose and empty, the painting gone. A large, low black box sat on the floor between them. Red fabric, the same shade as the rug, cushioned the flat top.

Beth shivered as she realized the dual purpose of the cuffs hanging from her ceiling, the height of the box. She hadn't been the only one imagining her as a prisoner at the mercy of two men.

Paolo held her wrists behind her back as Aaron approached. His fingers undid the black necktie. "So, are you a virgin?"

The question felt like the same punch to the gut that had driven her to the ground long ago. *It's just a game.* Beth swallowed hard. *All you have to do is say the safe word.* "Yes." The sixteen-year-old lump in her stomach wasn't what made her thong damp, but the mix threatened to engulf her.

Say the safe word.

Instead, she licked her lips. "You said all you would do is kiss me." She lifted her chin a notch. "You promised for both of you."

His stern expression was back. "Are you saying you don't believe I'll keep my word?"

"I-I, um, no."

He pulled the necktie free and tossed it on the rug. His fingertips traced the buttons on her white blouse, down to the waistband of her plaid skirt. "The real question is what should I kiss first."

"May I make a suggestion, Sir?" Paolo's chest rumbled against her back.

Aaron cocked an eyebrow as he looked over her shoulder. "What?"

"Remove the young lady's glasses. I would hate for them to be broken while we are . . . kissing her."

"Of course," Aaron murmured. He gently lifted her frames and set them on the fireplace's mantel before he returned to her.

He undid the top button of the blouse. His fingertips caressed the tiny "V" of exposed skin before he placed a kiss at the base of her throat.

Her breath froze. Despite all the things she'd done with both men, the gesture was too intimate.

"Don't," she whispered. "Please, don't." She shook so hard she knew she would've collapsed if it weren't for Paolo's firm grip.

Neither were the safe word, so Aaron ignored her and loosened the next button. Another delicate press of his lips to her skin. Her flesh prickled under his kiss. She needed pain, not love-making.

This was his real punishment. Had she learned nothing over the last week? *I love you, Beth, whether you accept it or not.* Tonight, he planned to make her accept it.

Not just him. Paolo nibbled where her neck curved into her shoulder. He planned to convert her to his will as well. Their intentions fostered a whole different slant to her surrender. It meant accepting them as her soul mates, not just her lovers. The dichotomy threatened her emotional stability. She swallowed the lump in her throat.

Aaron tugged her blouse from the waistband of her skirt and finished unbuttoning it before he brushed the thin cotton from her shoulders. "You are so beautiful. I can't decide what I should kiss next."

When she said nothing, he reached for her skirt's zipper. "When we're done kissing you, you'll be ours, body and spirit."

His statement, not his action, smashed through whatever barrier lay across her psyche. The words themselves were so innocuous.

And therein lay the problem. She had no hesitation surrendering her body, but she hadn't let anyone touch her soul. Not even Diana. The emotional wounds were far harder to cope with than the physical ones.

It wasn't just Rick's cruelty to her that made her so damn self-protective. It was her parents' constant disapproval and their rejection when she needed them the most. And by letting those experiences force her to withdraw from real living, she'd done far more damage to herself and others than those three had to her.

Raw regret tore a sob from her. So much wasted time. So much unintentional pain she'd inflicted on people she loved.

"Yellow," Paolo said. Aaron paused in undressing her. She could feel them both watching her, analyzing what they saw, questioning whether to halt their play.

Beth shook her head through the tears. "Green." *It's not an anxiety attack.* Damn it, she didn't want to stop this scene. If she did, the wall around her psyche would grow back, stronger than ever, and she'd be truly lost.

They must have sensed her silent plea. Aaron cupped her chin. His expression asked, *Are you sure?*

She smiled past the wetness trickling down her face and mouthed, *Yes.*

He stepped closer and palmed her cheeks. His mouth met hers in a soul-scorching kiss, but it wasn't a kiss as much as an acknowledgment of her total capitulation to his emotions and desires.

Aaron tore his lips from hers and spun her around. Her hands shot out for balance and landed on Paolo's broad shoulders. Only then did Beth realize he had released her wrists.

He grabbed her chin and his tongue invaded her, layering his desire on top of Aaron's. His body pressed against hers, his cock just as hard.

Beth whimpered when first one of her hands, then the other, was pulled from Paolo. The gauzy blouse brushed her skin as Aaron removed it. A click and her breasts sprang free from the black lace imprisoning them.

More kisses trailed down her spine. Paolo's dark hair tickled her as butterfly touches peppered her jaw, her throat. She couldn't seem to catch her breath under the dual onslaught,

Her skirt was lifted. Cool air and smoldering kisses caressed her ass.

"Hey!" This was supposed to be a game. She needed to stay in character.

Except she no longer wanted to play. She wanted them to fuck her, but it was too soon to give in, no matter how much she needed to be filled with their cocks.

"You didn't say I had to take off my clothes." Her protest didn't sound very convincing, even to her.

"No, we didn't, but you're not taking them off, are you?" Lust burned bright in Paolo's brown eyes. "You should have demanded that you remained dressed as part of your conditions." He deliberately stared down at her very naked, very swollen breasts. "A little late to complain now, isn't it?"

Beneath her skirt, Aaron hooked her thong with his fingers. She struggled, but Paolo's arms encircled her and effectively trapped her. The lace was soft, but it rasped against her skin as Aaron dragged the wisp of fabric down her thighs, her calves.

He lifted her right foot. She felt her saddle shoe loosen, then it and the bobby sock slid off. He repeated the removal of her left shoe and sock. Lace lay between her bare feet and the plush rug.

Beth strained against Paolo's grip, but even if she hadn't been mock-fighting, she doubted she could break his hold. Her breasts rubbed against the wool blend covering his chest.

Behind her, Aaron chuckled. "She's feisty, isn't she? Maybe we need to chain her up to get our payment."

Paolo grinned, a deliciously wicked promise. "I think you're right." Shadows from the flames danced over his face now that night had fallen. His appearance was sinister and seductive at the same time.

"If you don't let me go, I'll scream."

"Please do. It makes everything that much more interesting."

She opened her mouth and sucked in a deep breath. Before she could release the sound, his lips consumed hers. His tongue teased and tantalized. His hands cupped her ass and pulled her snug against the hard length of his body. She automatically wrapped her legs around his powerful thighs. He took a few steps, set her down and tore away from her.

Aaron snagged one of her wrists. Paolo grabbed the other. With two loud snaps, Beth found herself hanging from the ceiling of her workshop and balanced on the balls of her feet on top of the box.

"Let me go!"

The men ignored her.

"Get the windows," Aaron ordered. He proceeded to strip off his clothes while Paolo circled the room, unfolding the antique shutters over the equally antique glass.

A sliver of disappointment slid inside Beth's arousal. The nineteenth century panes wouldn't have given an outside observer a clear view of their faces, but there wouldn't have been any question what the three of them were doing in her studio. No sense having the neighbors mistaking their play with real trouble and calling the cops, but a little thrill rippled through her at the idea of someone watching them.

Aaron approached her, naked. His cock jutted nearly upright. He examined her for a moment before he reached for her hair. His touch was gentle as he undid the ribbons and the elastic bands underneath them.

He tossed them aside and ran his fingers through her hair. The locks had curled slightly from the humidity. He grabbed a handful and buried his face in the tresses.

"Do you have any idea how good you smell?" he murmured.

"You said you would only kiss me," she reminded him.

"How do I avoid inhaling your scent?" His head tilted until his nose rested against her neck. The whisper of air on her skin tickled when he breathed in deeply.

His simple act was far more sensual than she could have imagined. She bent her head to give him better access.

He pressed against her. The crisp hair of his chest teased her nipples. His cock poked her slit, begging for entrance.

God, how she wanted to give in. *Bastard.* This was too easy. All she had to do was ask.

And the guys would win their little game.

She may be the bottom, but that didn't mean she couldn't make this harder on them. A tiny giggle burbled from her throat at her plan to even the odds.

Aaron lifted his head. He examined her through slitted lids. "What's so funny?"

Before she could answer, hot skin and hard muscle enveloped her from behind. "I think she's challenging your authority, Sir." Leave it to a switch to stir the pot.

"I wasn't. Honest." She watched Aaron through her lowered lashes. "Your thingy rubbed against my private parts."

Both of Aaron's eyebrows rose. "My thingy?"

Beth could feel Paolo shake as he laughed silently. "I'm trying to stay in character here."

Aaron stepped back. "Then maybe we should drop the role-playing portion of this evening's entertainment."

"You're going to unchain me?" The pit of her stomach lurched. This wasn't what she meant. Or wanted.

"Now, why would I do that?" Aaron's smile promised pure mischief.

She took a deep breath. Good, she didn't want to ruin play night two weeks in a row.

"It just means all previous rules are off."

"No rules?" she squeaked.

"Let me put it this way, darling Elizabeth—" His eased close to her once again. "If I'm not limited to my mouth—" He shoved his fingers into her passage. "Do you really think you can outlast us, my dear?"

She gasped as he touched that delicate circle inside her, massaged it. Her body arced and the chains groaned. Every cell erupted in naked pleasure.

He continued thrusting his fingers into her. Behind her, Paolo parted her ass cheeks and rubbed his cock along her cleft.

The orgasm brought only a brief moment of release. Aaron slid his fingers out of her passage. Using her own juices, he stroked her clit until it was harder than before they started this game.

Paolo's hands reached around her and palmed her breasts. He tweaked and rolled her nipples until they were as hard as her clit.

The muscles in her thighs shook, and the arches of her feet ached. What would happen if her legs gave out? How long could she hang by her arms?

She needed a focus. Counting. Counting was good. Counting in Japanese even better. *Ichi, ni, san, shi, go, roku—*

Aaron must have sensed her mental exercises to keep from coming again. He stopped playing with her clit, and he smeared her cream over her lips. The musk of her arousal distracted her.

"Lick," he ordered.

She sucked the three digits into her mouth and wiped them clean with her tongue. By the time she finished, Aaron's chest heaved.

He looked over her shoulder. "Take care of her."

She couldn't help the twinge of gratification that she had such an effect on Aaron.

While he disappeared behind her, Paolo circled around and knelt before her. A slow sweep of his tongue across her slit made her want to scream. Her pussy was ultra-sensitive from the first orgasm.

"Please, god, please, don't do that."

He peered up at her, a smirk on his face. "It's just a kiss, *chica*."

"No, it wasn't." The words came out in short bursts as she tried to calm her pulse. "Technically, it was a lick."

His dark eyes twinkled in the candlelight. "Technically, all bets are off, but since you said 'please,' I'll be sure I only use my lips."

True to his word, his lips surrounded her clit. The sensual massage drove her into a frenzy. Her hips thrust against his face, and he grabbed her thighs in his large hands to still her motion.

He teased and tormented her, always pausing when she was on the verge of exploding. True to his promise, he tortured her with only his lips.

Aaron's hands caressed her neck, her arms, her back. His soft kisses at the sensitive spot at the base of her spine tingled, a lighter counterpoint to the jagged sparks Paolo produced.

The men's gentleness spurred her closer to insanity than she thought possible. "Please." She moaned the word.

"Please what?" Aaron's hot breath warmed her shoulder as he nipped her skin.

Winning this game didn't matter anymore. She needed them. Needed them so bad.

"Please fuck me," she whispered.

With a final lick of her clit, Paolo stood. "Promise you will say the safe word?"

Beth nodded. She couldn't imagine not being able to handle them both. Her juices slicked her inner thighs.

Aaron nudged her feet further apart and spread her ass cheeks. His cock sank into her wet heat. Her lids closed at the relief of him filling her.

"Open your eyes, *chica*."

She forced them open. Paolo's dark eyes watched her while he slid a finger into her. Aaron growled behind her as Paolo slowly stroked both of them. Then he gently tugged on her, stretched her, prepared her.

His cock nudged, invaded until he was as buried in her pussy as Aaron. She wanted to scream. Not in pain. She was so gloriously full.

Paolo smiled. She could only imagine what expressions crossed her face. "Ready?" he murmured.

"Yes," she hissed. "Oh, yes."

They began to move. A slow alternating of cocks sliding into and out of her. She wished she could make the beauty of this moment last forever.

But in their efforts to prepare her, to groom her body to accept both of them at once, she wasn't going to last. The warning tightness through her pussy had already started.

"I'm sorry—I can't—"

"Let it go, Elizabeth."

She wasn't sure if it were Aaron's permission or the simple fact she couldn't take anymore. Her mouth opened, but her cry was soundless as the convulsions took her.

Internal muscles squeezed the cocks inside of her. Through the post-orgasm haze, she recognized the blissful expression on Paolo's face.

But it was Aaron who erupted inside her first with a wild cry. Before his cock finished pulsing, Paolo stiffened and shot his hot come.

She could feel the three of them mingling inside her as the men held her tight between them.

Chapter Six

Nearly two weeks later, Beth drifted through the gallery in her new gown. Handshakes and air kisses abounded, but a little part of her still felt on edge, and not because the guys were out of sight. Their hovering had driven her crazy during the first half hour of the show. She pulled them aside and told them to lay off, or she would sic Micki on them. They both laughed before they split off to work the crowd.

Her crack about Micki aside, Beth worried just a little. Everyone she had invited had come. Everyone but the three she needed the most.

Katherine Donovan rushed up and wrapped her arms around Beth. "We're so proud of you, honey!"

Even the Major, standing behind Mrs. Donovan, was grinning from ear to ear. "'Bout damn time, Elizabeth."

"Thank you." The words rushed out before she could stop them. "Have you talked to Micki? She said she was coming, but I haven't seen her."

The Major and Mrs. Donovan exchanged a worried look before Mrs. Donovan pasted a bright, and totally fake, smile on her face. "When was the last time you spoke with her?"

A frisson of unease rippled up Beth's spine. "Yesterday. She—" Crap, she didn't want to scare the Donovans about Alicia, even if the problem had turned out to be a false alarm. "I'm sorry. It's my own nerves. I talked to her on the phone. She said she'd be here."

"I *am* here, doofus."

Beth pivoted to find Micki, Diana and a man she didn't know. But the way his arm firmly encircled Diana's waist, there was more than a casual connection between the two.

"You look incredible, girl. Sorry, we're late," Micki said as she hugged Beth. She turned and glared at Diana. "I had trouble getting people out of the bathroom." She jabbed a finger at the blond man. "This is my new street partner and Diana's current fuck buddy, Daniel Myers."

"Micki!" Diana punched Micki's arm in outrage.

"Michaela Donovan, you do not use that kind of language in public." Mrs. Donovan's expression was positively mortified.

Just like the Major, Beth covered her mouth to keep from laughing as Micki made more appropriate introductions of her parents, but she examined this Daniel. Diana had said there were repercussions if people knew the couple she was seeing. She must have talked Micki in setting her up, but Micki's statement about their relationship wasn't a joke. The way Daniel touched Diana definitely said they were an item.

Holy crap! Was Diana now with Micki and her new partner? That would explain the repercussions part.

"Is your young man coming tonight, dear?" Mrs. Donovan asked Micki.

Micki's pale skin flared brilliant crimson. "Ryan's meeting me here." She cleared her throat. "He called saying he was late getting out of the office."

Okay, wrong assumption about Micki. Beth shot a look at Diana, who frowned and gave a slight shake of her head. Wow, so neither of them knew what was going on.

"You mean Colonel Jeffries kept him late?" The Major rubbed his chin. "Must have something to do with the current crisis in Asia."

"Dad!" Micki wailed. "You were checking up on him?"

Mrs. Donovan elbowed her husband in the ribs. "Quit giving her a hard time." She reached over and squeezed Beth's hand. "We'll catch up with you later. Obviously, my daughter's been holding out on her friends." She leaned closer. "I saw his picture. He's adorable."

Micki slapped her hand over her eyes.

"Hey, I'm adorable, too," the Major protested.

"Of course, you are, dear." Mrs. Donovan pulled him toward Paolo's work.

In unison with Diana and Daniel, Beth turned back to Micki. "You've been holding out. I want to hear about this Ryan."

Micki waggled an index finger. "Oh, no. If anyone gets picked on tonight, it's these two."

"What did we do?" Daniel shot back.

Micki scowled. "Everybody in the station house could hear your make-up sex in the public ladies' room."

Diana buried her head in Daniel's jacket, and her shoulders quivered.

A self-satisfied expression appeared on his face. "Sorry." He didn't sound a bit sorry.

"Make-up sex?" Beth's gaze bounced between Micki and Diana before settling on the latter. "Is Daniel the one I was helping you shop for two weeks ago?"

Diana's head rose. "Can we talk about this later?" she hissed.

Micki folded her arms over her chest. "No, we're talking about it now. It was bad enough I had to see Alicia post-fuck and hear Beth doing it over the phone—"

Diana started laughing again. "I knew it! You're seeing Aaron Winston."

Beth wanted to sink into the floor. This was not how she imagined this conversation. The loss of control threatened to spawn a panic attack. "I-It's not what you think—" She tugged at the choker strangling her.

"Lay off her," Daniel growled at the other two women. He stepped closer. "Are you all right, Beth?" Real concern lay behind his eyes. Diana sobered at the sound of his voice.

However, Micki continued her tirade. She rolled her eyes. "All I can tell you is when I RSVPed for the showing I definitely heard what sounded like sex noises over the phone."

Understanding clicked in Beth's mind. This had nothing to do with any judgment of her. Micki was trying to cover her guilt at finding someone new.

God, I need to be smacked. Maybe this had been the whole damn problem all along. She'd been so busy worrying about her own issues that her friends' problems barely registered on her radar.

"That was my fault." At Paolo's reassuring voice behind her, the urge to collapse left her. His strong arms wrapped around her, supporting her physically and emotionally. Under that strength and love, the last bits of her anxiety washed away.

"I knew she was trying to talk on the phone, and I was doing my best to tear her away," he finished.

Micki's jaw dropped, and Diana mouthed, *Whoa.*

Beth didn't have to turn around to know how sexy he looked. His silk shirt was the same shade of purple as the satin insets on her dress. His black leather tie and pants matched the rest of her outfit. The medallions he'd created for himself and Aaron had been turned into tie clips.

Like a typical male, Daniel's expression said he was sizing up Paolo.

Beth sucked in a deep breath. The moment she'd anticipated, dreaded, had finally arrived. "This is my boyfriend Paolo."

He released her long enough to kiss the backs of Micki and Diana's hands. Daniel's lips quirked when the men's palms met and they shook. Beth sensed some understanding had passed between the two, but for the life of her, she wasn't sure what it could be. She'd have to question Paolo later.

"You're not leaving me out, are you?"

Beth didn't have to look. At Aaron's smooth tenor, she automatically reached out for him and pulled him close. "And this is my boyfriend, Aaron."

With his purple silk tie, black suit and black dress shirt, the three of them looked like a matched set. No doubt that had been Aaron's plan all along. This was their official "coming out" party.

With a crazy grin, Daniel had the decency to shake hands. Micki and Diana stood staring with their mouths hanging open.

One heartbeat. Two. Five. Beth waited, but neither of her friends said anything.

Diana shook her head and muttered. "That explains the Pakistani family at her apartment."

Micki's attention switched from Beth to Diana and back to Beth. "Am I the only one out of the four of us who only fucks one guy at a time?"

"You'd better be. I told you I don't share." A tall, imposing man in a military dress uniform stepped to Micki's side and laid a long, deep kiss on her. "Sorry, I'm late, honey."

"No problem." She proceeded to make introductions.

Beth observed Micki. This was the most relaxed she'd been since Lee's death. However she met this Ryan didn't matter. She beamed looking up at him.

"Can I pull you away from your friends for a moment, Beth?" Aaron murmured. "There are some buyers who'd like to meet you."

She loathed leaving Paolo at Micki and Diana's mercy, but Daniel winked at her and said, "Ryan and I will keep them from tearing Boyfriend Number One apart."

Aaron wrapped Beth's arm around his, and together they crossed the gallery. A couple stood near one set of her paintings, the Sun and Moon Quartet. Beth didn't recognize the man, but the silver-haired woman they approached she would know anywhere. Victoria Butler, the star of the political commentary show, *Inside the Beltway*.

"So you're the young lady Aaron has been gushing about?" A brilliant smile lit Victoria's face, but this one seemed much more genuine than the one she wore on television.

Aaron gestured at the paintings. "Victoria and Merrick bought the set."

Pleasure danced with shock along Beth's nerves. Sure enough, bright gold stars were affixed to each of the plaques. "Have you decided where to hang them?"

"In our playroom." A not-so-coy expression tilted Victoria's mouth.

The couple's assessing looks now made sense. They were good friends of Aaron, and they were both doms. But if Victoria Butler expected to intimidate her, she would be sadly surprised.

Beth tilted her chin as she pretended to examine the canvases. "A playroom? With no or limited natural light sources, you'll want an underlight for each canvas. That will set off the metallic paints to their best effect."

Victoria inclined her head. "Thank you for the advice."

There was more underlying the acknowledgment. Before Beth could sort it out, an excited squeal ripped through the air behind her.

She pivoted in time for Alicia to engulf her in a bear hug. In contrast to the weepy mess she'd been yesterday afternoon, Alicia looked happier than she had before she married the dweeb.

No, Beth corrected herself. *Before her dad had died in that stupid car accident the summer between our junior and senior years.*

She eyed Richard Brand standing behind Alicia. Billionaire. Philanthropist. Genius. The jury was still out on his asshole status.

"I'm so happy for you," Alicia said as she released Beth.

"Thanks, girl." She glared at Brand. "Is he being nice to you?"

Instead of pretending to be serious, he smirked and turned to Aaron. "Be careful with this one. She threatened to electrocute my balls yesterday."

"I'm sure you deserved it," Victoria said dryly.

Merrick stroked his chin and gave Beth a look that made her feel more vulnerable than if she'd been naked and in chains. "You can bring her to the club if she needs additional training, Aaron."

Before she could retort, Victoria jammed an elbow into her husband's side. "Use your company manners while Beth and I have a heart-to-heart." She looped her arm around Beth's free one and tugged her away from Aaron.

He gave Beth a reassuring smile, and she let Victoria lead her out the side door to the small patio-garden.

Victoria sighed. "I apologize for Merrick. He likes power games, but he'd never touch someone else's sub without permission."

"He and Brand belong to the same club as Aaron."

"Yes." Victoria laughed. "I can see why Aaron keeps you to himself."

"You didn't drag me out here to talk about our men," Beth prompted.

Victoria sagged and released Beth's arm. She took a few steps away before she turned back and hugged herself. Her blue blood poise evaporated. "I know I have no right to ask you for anything, but I'm worried about a mutual friend of ours. Diana Traynor?"

"She's here tonight if you need to talk to her," Beth offered.

A wistful smile appeared on Victoria's face. "It's not me I'm worried about. She's become quite close with a fourth member of our little group. They had a major fight while the four of us were at dinner two nights ago—"

"You mean, Daniel?"

"She's mentioned him?"

"I wouldn't worry." Beth grinned. "I heard they had very loud make-up sex in a Metro PD substation bathroom this evening. I think they're okay."

"Good," Victoria murmured. "Good. He's become quite smitten with her."

From the tone of Victoria's voice, Daniel wasn't the only one. *Holy crap! Victoria and Merrick are the married couple Diana is having a threesome with.* Repercussions wouldn't begin to cover the situation. Not when Diana's sister Steffi worked as an assistant producer at *Inside the Beltway.* Beth struggled to keep her voice and expression neutral. "It's hard not to be."

"Do you still love her?"

The question hung between them for what seemed like an eternity.

"I'll always love her," Beth said quietly. "But I'm not in love with her if that's what you're worried about. I'm very much committed to Aaron and Paolo."

"Good." Victoria nodded sharply. "I don't want to see Daniel getting hurt."

Her concern touched a spot deep in Beth. Maybe, just maybe, everything would work out for her friends. "You like playing matchmaker, don't you?"

Victoria laughed lightly. "Whatever makes you say that?"

Beth shrugged. "I heard you introduced Steffi to her girlfriend. Now, Diana and Daniel."

"I like seeing the people I love happy." Victoria waved her hand. "We're both getting too maudlin. Shall we return to the party, my dear?"

Not maudlin. Sentimental, maybe. Beth led the way back inside the gallery. Was there any way to guarantee her friends' happiness?

Probably not. She scanned the gallery. The evening was starting to wind down so she spotted them easily. Alicia, Micki and Diana were standing near the Sun and Moon Quartet with their men. *And woman* as Victoria joined the group. It was nice to know there were people in their lives that wanted them to be happy, too.

"Are you okay, Beth?"

"Everything's fine." She turned and wrapped her arms around Aaron's neck. "Thank you for making me do this show."

His eyebrows rose. "I didn't think I'd ever hear that from you."

"There's a lot of things you should hear from me." She stared into his eyes. "I love you."

His fingers stroked her cheek. "I love you, too." His kiss sealed that promise.

Chapter Seven

Night had fallen on a very long Saturday when Beth handed the delivery woman a wad of cash and accepted the two large pizzas. "Keep the change." She nodded to the security guard and headed back to the elevator with the food. Her stomach growled in response to the odor of tomato sauce and pepperoni seeping through the cardboard boxes.

After the girls and their significant others had unloaded the U-Haul truck, Victoria had insisted Diana and her friends needed their privacy, and she'd ordered all the guys to a barbeque place she knew in downtown Alexandria. Beth hated to admit it, but after the drama of the last month, she appreciated a little downtime with her girlfriends.

And Victoria would bask in the presence of six men.

Aches in her muscles from carrying boxes made themselves known on the ride back up to Diana's new place. Well, not totally new. Diana was condo-sitting for a freaking ambassador.

The more Beth thought about the odd mix of people who helped Diana move today the more absurd the whole scene seemed. The cop and the construction worker she could get, but it was watching a billionaire like Richard Brand or a TV personality like Victoria Butler haul belongings from one side of the city to the other that sent the day over the edge.

By the time she exited the elevator, she had a full-blown case of the giggles. By the time she reached the door of Diana's unit, she laughed so hard she could barely keep a grip on the pizzas.

Micki must have heard the hysterics because she opened the front door, an odd expression on her face. "What the hell is your problem?" She rescued the boxes from Beth who collapsed on a Queen Anne chair.

Alicia and Diana also looked at Beth as if she'd lost her last marble. Maybe she had.

When Beth caught her breath, she grinned at her friends. "I owe all of you an apology."

"For what? Smoking pot without sharing?" Micki said as she carried the boxes to the coffee table. Alicia jumped to clear the unpacked books cluttering the surface.

Sobriety hit Beth hard and fast. "No. For not trusting you."

"No," Alicia said. "If anything, I owe you an apology. It's been pointed out—" She glared at Micki. "I was a bit of a bitch to you at our last lunch."

"Yeah, you were," Diana added. She set the pitcher of margaritas she'd mixed on the low table. "I had the bruise on my shin from someone's sucky aim to prove it."

Micki dropped to her knees and held up her hands in surrender. "I said I was sorry for kicking you!"

Diana held up a single middle finger before she headed back to the kitchen.

Warmth flooded Beth when she sat on the floor across the table from Micki. Why the hell had she doubted her friendship with these women? After everything they'd been through together over the last sixteen years, they were closer to her than her own family. Her only relationship that remotely compared was the one she had with Aaron and Paolo, which led to another consideration.

Diana returned from the kitchen with glasses and settled on the carpet beside Beth. Alicia knelt on the other side of the coffee table and began pouring margaritas.

Beth caught Diana's attention and inclined her head toward Alicia. Diana pursed her lips before she nodded. Micki watched them with a perplexed expression.

Beth cleared her throat. "Alicia, you heard Richard talking with Aaron and Merrick about the club the three of them belong to?"

Alicia handed the full glass to Beth. "Yeah."

"Do you know what kind of place Club Noir is?"

Red crawled up Alicia's neck and over her pale face until it met her hairline.

"Oh, my god!" Diana shrieked. "You've been there!"

Beth's jaw dropped. A wave of jealousy swept through her. Aaron told her she wasn't ready, but Alicia had known Richard less than a month.

"Wait a minute." Micki's gaze flitted from face to face. "What club?"

"I'm not allowed to talk about it," Alicia whispered. She bowed her head, and her auburn hair curtained her blush.

"Shit," Beth muttered. "I thought I was warning you. I can't believe your dom has already taken you there."

"Dom?" Micki looked at Alicia, shock on her face.

Diana turned to Beth. "You haven't been there?"

She shook her head. "You?"

"Just once. With the asshole." Diana sipped her margarita before she continued. "I like my kink private." She grinned. "I'm not the exhibitionist that Red is."

"What club?" Micki shouted.

Beth took pity on her. "You've got to swear this doesn't leave the room."

Micki's blue eyes narrowed. "As long as it's not illegal."

Beth crossed herself. "It's not. Club Noir is a private BDSM club. They cater to people who can't afford to let their preferences become public knowledge."

Micki's eyes hardened. "They chain you up and whip you?"

Diana giggled and leaned closer to Beth. "I think she's jealous we have new doms."

Pink swept across Micki's cheeks. "I am not."

"So you're telling us that you don't handcuff that big, hot switch of yours to the bed frame and have your way with him?" Beth grinned. Apparently, even Micki had a few secrets she hadn't admitted. Alicia raised her head and stared as Micki's cheeks flared hot pink.

"There's nothing wrong with having a little fun in bed." She tucked a loose strand of blond hair behind her ear.

"Uh-huh." Beth couldn't resist teasing her. "And what do you do with your nightstick?"

"It-it wasn't my nightstick."

"Then what was it?" Diana needled.

Micki looked up at the ceiling. "A banana,"

Beth leaned on Diana as they both roared. Even Alicia was slapping the carpet while she laughed her ass off.

Micki's gaze dropped to the pizza box, and she opened it before she cleared her throat. "There's something I need to get off my chest. My former partner Lee and I were lovers."

At her pained tone, the other three sobered.

Beth reached for Micki's hand. "You don't owe us an explanation."

"Yeah, I do." Micki blinked a couple of times. "I failed him, just like I failed you—"

Beth squeezed Micki's hand. "You didn't fail me." Her voice sounded fierce to her own ears. "I was too young, inexperienced and naïve to understand myself. None of what happened with Rick Allen was your fault."

Something loosened in Beth's chest. It was the first time she'd said the name of her high school rapist aloud in front of the other three women since the last time the police questioned her that godawful night.

The corner of her mouth quirked. "If anything, I felt guilty that you almost went to jail for beating the crap out of him."

"Dammit, you shouldn't have dropped the charges!" Old anger flared in Micki's eyes.

"I didn't. I was sixteen at the time, remember? A minor. And frankly, cutting the deal with the DA was the one thing my parents ever did right in their lives." Beth squeezed Micki's hand again. "That bastard was not worth your future."

"Besides—" Alicia took a sip of her margarita before she continued. "There's more than one way to get revenge."

Unease niggled the back of Beth's skull. "What did you do?"

Alicia and Diana shared guilty looks.

"Out with it," Micki demanded.

"Alicia talked me out of cutting his brake line." Diana grimaced.

"And?" Beth's attention flicked between the two women.

"Remember Jimmy Thompson?" Alicia said.

"The football team's center?" Beth's unease turned into confusion.

"Yeah." Diana grinned. "Turned out Rick wasn't only a rapist, he was a racist bigot as well. He'd grab Jimmy's ass or his jockstrap before the ball was hiked. Did other shit to him as well. So Jimmy filmed Rick in the locker room and gave me the recording."

"How? Any camera back then would have been obvious," Beth said.

"Not unless you have friends with access to spy cameras." Alicia smiled and both she and Diana looked pointedly at Micki.

"What? This is the first I've heard about this." Micki looked as confused as Beth felt.

The realization of the one person they knew who did have access to that kind of technology hit Beth. "The Major gave you the camera."

"Actually Butch did." Diana's grin turned to pure evil at the mention of their cheerleader advisor's husband, who also was a member of Major Donovan's spec ops team. "The Major made sure the nude recordings were uploaded to an escort website along with Rick's contact information. His *real* contact information."

Micki shook her head. "I can't believe Dad would do that."

"Seriously?" Alicia asked. "You're his baby girl. But that night you were sitting in a holding cell, looking at five years in prison for beating the shit out of Rick. You did not see how mad he was. How proud he was of you."

"How much he wanted to shoot both Mr. Allen and Beth's dad between the eyes," Diana added.

"And that's why Chandler Rickard Allen has a criminal record for solicitation," Alicia finished.

"What?" Beth stared at Alicia. She'd made a point over the years not to dwell on the asshole. Not to let him ruin her life. Apparently, her friends weren't quite so . . . well . . . "forgiving" wasn't the right word.

Diana snickered. "There was a sting operation on the site after the FBI received an—" She made bunny ears with her index fingers. "—anonymous tip. The idiot was dumb enough to try to charge the undercover officer who contacted him for a date."

Beth shook her head. "How do you know all this?"

"You mean the stuff the Major and Butch didn't tell us?" Diana shrugged. "Because Special Agent James Thompson of the FBI keeps me updated. If it's any consolation, Rick the asshole is doing time in Joliet right now for sexual assault."

Beth had never doubted her friends' loyalty, but after the shit had hit the fan at school and turned them into pariahs their senior year, the extent to which they, and people she never expected, had gone . . .

It simply blew her mind.

She ran a finger around the rim of her glass. "Do you guys think things would be different—"

"Don't even go there, bitch." Micki glared at Beth across the table.

"Yeah," Diana chimed in. "If things were different, Alicia would still be in denial over her submissive tendencies."

"Right . . ." Micki drawled. "And that's coming from someone covering up her affair with another cheerleader."

Beth's head whipped toward Diana. "You told them?"

"We already knew," Alicia said. "You two aren't as subtle as you'd like to think." She drew in a deep breath and turned to Micki. "Neither are you. We all knew about you and Lee."

Beth reached for a slice of pizza. "God, we are a pathetic bunch."

"Excuse me?" Alicia glared across the table.

"We're all so worried about our little secrets. Turns out none of them really matter, do they?"

"No, they don't." Alicia smiled, a mischievous one that made her look like a teenager again. "Want to hear another secret?"

"Always," Diana mumbled around a mouthful of pizza.

"This cannot leave this room either, or I'll get my ass whipped and not in the fun way." Alicia met each of their gazes.

Beth nodded along with Diana and Micki.

"I found this out last weekend. Hank had cleaned out all our accounts as well as embezzled from Richard's company to pay for his prostitutes."

They all stared at Alicia in shock.

"Why isn't he in prison—" Micki started.

"You can stay here—" Diana blurted.

"You'll have funds from my sales on Monday—" Beth shouted over the other two.

Alicia held up her hands. "Whoa. I'm fine. Richard replaced the funds in the personal accounts before the divorce was filed—"

"Wait a minute." Micki drop her slice on the cardboard lid. "The funds going in and out would have shown up on the bank statements."

Beth's blood boiled. "That skeezy little dweeb! He scanned the statements and changed the numbers."

Alicia took a drink of her margarita before she said, "Yeah. Richard gave Hank a choice. Repay all the money by working for a friend of Richard's overseas, or go to jail in the U.S."

Diana rolled her eyes. "Quit dragging this out. Who's Hank working for, and why would anyone want a known thief?"

Alicia's smile grew downright devious. "He's working for Sheik Abdul ben Hassein as a janitor now."

Beth grinned back. This punishment was devilishly delightful. She'd have to revise her opinion of Richard Brand.

"Who?" Micki asked.

Diana worked her jaw a couple of times before she managed to say, "Are you seriously telling us that Hank is working for the Emir of Kutom?"

Micki choked on her bite of pizza. "Fuck! They still cut people's hands off for stealing in that country."

"Oh, my god!" Now, the multitude of presents delivered to Alicia's neighbor when she refused to answer the door made sense. Beth laughed so hard tears rolled down her face. "You're screwing the sheik and his brother, too!"

Once again, scarlet flared on Alicia's cheeks. "I thought we were talking about Hank."

"At the same time!" Beth shrieked.

"Shut up," Alicia muttered. "Just shut up."

Diana shook her head, but her white teeth gleamed in her wide grin. "You weren't joking about getting your freak on last month when we had lunch."

Beth finally caught her breath and looked at Diana. "I can't believe she's doing more men than we are."

Alicia held up her glass. "Can we just toast to a wonderful friendship?"

Diana lifted hers as well. "No more secrets either."

Micki's gaze shifted around the table. "Am I still allowed in the group? I feel sorely lacking by doing only one guy."

"Well," Beth purred the words. "There's always the banana."

They all laughed and clinked glasses.

And for the first time in sixteen years, Beth let contentment roll through her.

CAPTURED BY DEVOTION

Taneka's Story

Chapter One

"To Sarah Phan." Taneka Foster held up her glass of California rosé.

"To Sarah," the other four women answered in unison. It had become a tradition for the surviving former members of their high school cheerleading squad to toast their old friend any time they were all together. Sarah's death in a boating accident had capped a particularly brutal year when they were in high school. At least, Diana's wedding in two days was a happy, glorious occasion.

A bit of Taneka reared its envious head. The two-story condo that Diana was housesitting in Alexandria, Virginia, could have come straight out of *Lifestyles of the Rich and Famous*. Mahogany and rich amethyst velvet composed the living room furniture. The chandelier in the foyer was definitely lead crystal, not some knock-off from Lowe's. And god! The view of the District! The tiny sliver of the Washington Monument stood at attention in the center of the huge floor-to-ceiling windows.

To distract her green-eyed monster, Taneka took a sip of her wine. "It's hard to believe it's been seventeen years since she died."

"It's hard to believe it's been three years since you've come back to D.C." Micki sat next to Taneka on one couch and playfully jabbed Taneka's arm that held her glass. Her wine sloshed but didn't spill.

"Hey, this is not my place, bitches!" Diana glared at them all from where she reigned on the Queen Anne chair between the two couches. "You damage something, you *will* pay for it!"

"Sorry," Micki murmured.

"You try hauling preschoolers through airport security, Officer Donovan, then we'll talk about how often *you* travel." Taneka leaned forward and set her glass on the coffee table.

"Hey, I'm just glad you came back for my wedding." Diana reached over and squeezed Taneka's hand.

"You know I wouldn't miss your special day, girl." Taneka squeezed back before she waved at the ostentatious living room. "I especially wouldn't miss this place. Damn, your next place could be the White House, and it would be a step down."

Diana laughed. "Housesitting for Ambassador and Mrs. Stanfield has been great, but I'm ready for something cozier. I couldn't sleep the first couple of weeks here by myself without imagining I was hearing things."

"So where are you moving to?"

"Daniel has a lead on a rent-controlled place over on Connecticut. It's not too far from Steffi and Kat's place, so we can babysit more often."

Taneka clapped her hands. "Speaking of which, where's the pics of the new baby?"

"You're gonna smell him tomorrow," Alicia grumbled from the other couch where she slouched next to Beth.

"I also want to know how you managed to snag your ex's boss and one of the richest men in the country," Taneka shot back at Alicia as she took the phone Diana handed her. "It sure as hell wasn't your personality."

"Ooooooooo," the other three women chorused.

Alicia's cheeks flamed nearly as red as her hair. "We simply ran into each other at a shareholder's meeting."

"Uh-huh." Taneka turned to Beth. "What's the real story?"

Beth smiled, a wicked, very un-Beth-like smile for the shy, quiet computer consultant. "Can't you tell? He makes her cheeks red."

Diana and Micki snickered. Alicia, on the other hand, looked like she was ready to kill Beth. And Taneka knew she'd missed the joke.

"At least I only need one man to satisfy me," Alicia snapped.

"Not true." Micki raised her hand. "Taneka and I are the only ones who just need one man." She leaned closer to Taneka. "Unless you and Deon are into swapping, then I'm seriously outnumbered here."

Taneka paused in mid-swipe on Diana's phone. "Excuse me?" Her gaze flicked from woman to woman.

She'd known them for years. They all stuck together through the bad times, including when she had almost died from spinal meningitis. When Alicia's dad was killed in a car crash. When Diana and her baby sister were kicked out of their parents' house after they discovered Steffi was a lesbian, and Diana wouldn't let their parents beat on the kid. The awful night Beth was raped. The even worse night when Sarah died.

And Taneka had no clue of what the private joke between them was. It was bad enough she lived clear across the country now. Why had she dragged her family all the way back to D.C. for Diana's wedding to feel like the literal fifth wheel?

"We're not trying to leave you out." Diana patted Taneka's knee. "There's been a lot that's happened over the last year, and we've all been guilty about not sharing our secrets."

"I already know Daniel's white," Taneka teased.

"There's more news than that." Diana grinned.

"I'll go first," Beth blurted. "I wanted to tell you my news in person, not surprise you with it in a text or an e-mail." She sucked in a deep breath. "I'm living with two men, Aaron and Paolo. You'll meet them tomorrow at the wedding rehearsal."

Taneka frowned. "That's not a big deal to have roommates in D.C. This city is so freakin' expensive . . ."

From the looks on everyone else's faces, she realized that's not what Beth meant.

Taneka stared at Beth. "No freakin' way! Seriously?"

Beth nodded.

The context of Micki's comment finally sunk into Taneka's brain. She looked at Diana. "Dee, you do realize the District will only recognize one of your marriages if you've got another guy on the hook besides Daniel?"

"Girl, he and I only mess with one other married couple. And they are the ones who set Daniel and me up." Diana waggled her index finger before she pointed it at Alicia. "That girl and her man has fun with *two* married couples."

"And those couples are literally royalty," Micki said.

"Shut up!" Alicia screeched. "That's supposed to be a secret!"

"Wait a minute." Taneka waved to indicate the other three women. "They can know about your orgies, but I can't?" She laid her offended tone on thick.

Hell, she was *offended!*

Except she wasn't sure if she were upset that her closest friends were keeping secrets from her, or that they all seemed to have a more adventurous love life than she did.

"From what I understand, it's not like they're all together at once. They like to watch each other fuck Alicia," Micki said sotto voce.

"Oh, god." Alisha buried her face in her hands. "I've never been so embarrassed."

"So, taking off your shirt with your sweater at that pep rally wasn't a mistake? Just your exhibitionist streak shining through?" Taneka asked.

Beth, Diana, and Micki howled with laughter.

On the other hand, Alicia's whole body quivered. Taneka wasn't sure if she were crying or—

Alicia raised her head. Tears were running down her face, but she was laughing as hard as the rest. She gulped for air. "There was a time I would have denied that with my last breath, but you're probably right."

"I swear we weren't trying to leave you out of anything," Beth said. "None of us knew about the others until my first showing."

"But that was almost a year ago." The hurt came rolling back through Taneka. Had they all grown that far apart over the years? There was a time Diana or Micki would have told her everything going on back here.

"Like I said, I wanted to tell you in person." Beth rose and squeezed in beside Taneka's left side on the couch before she leaned her head on Taneka's shoulder.

"And I didn't feel right blabbing everybody else's news." Micki wrapped an arm around Taneka from her other side.

"And like Alicia, I promised to keep my relationships quiet." Diana looked almost as hurt as Taneka felt. "There was other people's reputations to consider, not just our own."

"Hey, I'm just being a selfish bitch, and that's not what tonight is about." Taneka hugged both Beth and Micki. "You all don't have kids, and I've been hanging around the mommy brigade too much."

"So you're not mad at us," Beth murmured.

"No." Taneka released the other girls. She leaned forward, handed the phone back to Diana, and picked up her glass of wine. "And I'm sorry for getting into a snit, Dee. This is your week, girlfriend. Here's to your happiness."

The other women repeated the toast, and they all clinked glasses. Taneka plastered on a smile. Like her ex-boss said back in San Jose, sometimes you have to fake it until you make it. And right now, it sounded like her closest friends were making it a lot more often and with a lot more people than she was.

Deon was sound asleep when Taneka tiptoed into their hotel room hours later. He'd left on the overhead light at the entrance. She leaned against the wall and watched the rise and fall of his chest. His muscular arms splayed across the bed. The sheet covered his long legs. Desire and love mixed at the sight of the man she'd chosen.

The clock on the nightstand blinked from twelve-fifty-nine to one a.m., reminding her she had two long days ahead of her. She crossed the thick carpet and peeked into the adjoining room. Sarah cocooned her covers around herself and Miss Violet, her purple teddy bear. Keshon sprawled on top of his sheets, earbuds still in place.

Taneka walked over to his bed and gently removed the buds and laid them on the nightstand next to his phone before she pulled the comforter over his body. He was only nine, but the time seemed to be passing so fast. Maybe she was feeling a little empty-nesting with Sarah starting first grade this fall.

Her jealousy of her friends wasn't warranted. The other girls could have their adventures, but she wasn't about to give up her family for a night of cheap thrills.

She closed the door between the kids' room and hers and readied for bed. As she brushed her teeth, she realized what really bothered her.

There had been a time when she couldn't keep her hands off her husband's body. And Deon had returned every bit of desire in kind. When he had taken the chance and accepted the job at a tech start-up fresh out of college, they both knew there would be sacrifices.

But he'd gotten busier when he was vaulted to the vice-president of development. She'd focused on her own career. Then the kids had come along and she'd been laid off, so she started over by working from home in order to spend more time with Sarah and Keshon. It wasn't anybody's fault their marriage had fallen into a bit of a rut. The last thing she wanted was Deon to think she took him for granted.

Mom and Dad wanted the kids to stay with them for a couple of nights while they were in town. Maybe she should take them up on their offer. Maybe she needed to do a little rekindling of her own relationship before it was too late.

Chapter Two

The next afternoon, Taneka giggled at Mom's odd expression. They stood in the tiny, prim Presbyterian church outside of the District, waiting for the minister to arrive and start the wedding rehearsal. The white clapboard exterior gave way to an equally white interior except for the burgundy carpet and the dark wood pews. A huge gold cross dominated the wall above the altar.

"I know Daniel is Micki's partner in Metro, but why is she on the groom's side?" Mom whispered.

"That's the only thing they argued about when it came to the wedding," Beth murmured. "Victoria stepped in and flipped a coin."

"I still can't believe Diana knows Victoria Butler." Mom shook her head. The celebrity political commentator stood up by the altar and directed the bride and groom like a professional wedding planner.

"Steffi *is* the assistant producer of Victoria's show," Taneka pointed out.

Diana's baby sister stood off to the side. Steffi looked damn good for having a baby eight months ago. Her wife Kat jiggled their son in her arms in an attempt to keep him occupied.

"Mo-o-o-m!" Sarah threw herself at Taneka and clung to her dress. "When are we going to eat? I'm bor-r-r-red!"

"Your fruit candies are still in my purse." Taneka pointed toward Deon who sat with Keshon in one of the middle pews. "Suck on one of those."

When Sarah bounced down the center aisle, Mom turned to Taneka. "You shouldn't bribe her into behaving."

Deon glanced over his shoulder at Taneka when Sarah climbed into the pew with him and Keshon. He raised his right eyebrow in question, and she nodded.

Warmth gathered in Taneka's abdomen and her skin tingled. There had been a time when their silent signals meant something totally different. Like the time, they'd been at his company's party to celebrate a successful business deal that finally put the company in the black. He'd been across the huge backyard deck at Adam's place, the company's CEO, and Deon given her that same raised eyebrow.

The quickie in one of the upstairs bathrooms had been the start of a particularly erotic weekend. Yeah, she definitely needed to make use of their private time while they had someone to watch the kids.

"Taneka, did you hear me?" Mom said.

"Yes, I did. Do you really want the kids for the weekend?" Taneka deliberately gave Mom the side-eye.

"Not if they're hopped up on sugar," Mom grumbled.

"I carry some sugar-free, fruit-flavored candies to suck on so the kids can equalize air pressure in their ears," Taneka said. "Which is a trick you would know if you and Dad would bother to come out and visit your grandchildren once in a while."

"Someone's got to run the diner—" Mom started.

"Mike and Alonso can run the damn diner by themselves if you and Butch would stop micromanaging them," Beth retorted.

Taneka held up her palm, and Beth high-fived her.

Mom shook her head. "You two had better manners as teenagers."

Thankfully, the minister rushed in with a flurry of apologies for his tardiness. Taneka was damn tired of having that same argument with her parents.

And she really wanted to find another bathroom, yank down her husband's pants, and have her way with his body.

Two and a half hours later, the wedding rehearsal dinner was in full swing at a Memphis-style barbeque joint in Alexandria that had been rented out for only them. The restaurant had a rustic feel with pine paneling the walls, scarred hardwood floors, and equally scarred furniture. At least, the decorator picked out nineteenth century replicas of overhead fixtures instead of tacky wagon wheels.

Taneka grinned at the sight of Deon and her brothers teaching the kids how to play pool. The manager had been reluctant to let them play at first until Diana's friend Victoria pulled him aside for a quiet word. His manner abruptly changed when she slipped him something folded with the distinctive green color of U.S. currency. Taneka was pretty sure the bills didn't have any presidents on them.

Dad and the Major were reminiscing about their own youth, again, so Taneka excused herself and headed for the bar. She waited for the bartender to make her bourbon sour when a low feminine voice asked, "Are you okay?"

Taneka looked up to find Victoria standing next to her. Before she could answer, the bartender placed her drink next to her and turned his attention to Diana's friend.

Or was that lover?

"Whiskey neat," Victoria said. The bartender turned away to get her drink.

"I'm fine," Taneka said. "You did a lovely job putting together the rehearsal dinner. What made you decide on a barbeque joint?"

Victoria laughed, a low, throaty sound. "I would have preferred something fancier, but this wasn't about me." She leaned closer. "This is where they had what was essentially their first date."

Once again, envy crawled up Taneka's spine. This woman knew more about one of Taneka's closest friends than she did.

Victoria glanced over her shoulder to where everyone else was talking before she faced Taneka again. "Let's get to know each other."

The bartender handed Victoria the drink she'd ordered. She looped her right arm around Taneka's left and guided her to a smaller table tucked in a niche on the other side of the restaurant's huge bar.

Once they were seated, Victoria blurted, "Do you have a problem with me?"

"What?" The woman's bluntness shook Taneka.

"I noticed you keep staring at me." Victoria brushed back a lock of her silver hair and took a sip of her drink.

Well, if she wanted brutal honesty, Taneka would oblige. "I'm not sure if I think you're using one of my best friends, or if I'm jealous you have a closer relationship with her than I do."

"Well, I did ask." Victoria leaned back in her chair with an appraising look. "She told you? About us?"

Taneka smiled. "It's not going any further than me, and I sure wouldn't tell Deon, much less my parents and siblings. It's just the last time she was in a relationship with a woman, it took her a long time to get over it."

Victoria took another sip of her drink. "I care about her. I wouldn't do anything to hurt her. And Micki has already told the three of us if we do anything to harm Diana, physically or emotionally, no one will find our bodies."

"Then you know what she did to the high school quarterback," Taneka stated.

"Yes." Victoria grinned. "And I also know he owes you his life."

Taneka laughed. "I didn't want Micki to spend the rest of her life in prison."

Victoria sobered and leaned her elbows on the table. "If it means anything, I'm a little envious of how tight the five of you have remained over the years. I've never had that kind of lasting friendship."

The loneliness in the other woman's face hit Taneka. "It's probably hard with your job."

"And the family money." A hint of bitterness flavored Victoria's voice.

"Can I give you some free advice?" Taneka said.

"All right." Victoria's shoulders tensed despite her effort to look relaxed.

"You don't have to control everything." Taneka shook her head at the wistful sensation flooding her. "I had to learn that lesson the hard way."

"May I ask?" One of Victoria's eyebrows rose at her own question.

"Do you know why Alicia was our head cheerleader?" Taneka rested her chin on her fist.

"I rather thought it was her extreme competitive streak," Victoria said.

"You noticed that, huh?" Taneka grinned. "But no. It's because I'm too bossy and because I assumed I should have the position." Taneka smiled. "Mom had to teach me teamwork."

Victoria frowned. "I would have thought with as many siblings you have you would have automatically learned that lesson long before high school."

"I wanted too much to make a mark outside of the family, even though my mother was the coach."

"And your love life?" Victoria's lips quirked. "Do you take control there?"

Taneka laughed. "Not for a very long time. But once the wedding's done . . ."

Victoria glanced around before she leaned over the table. "Do I need to bring you a care package? One domme to another?"

"Why, Ms. Butler? Are you trying to bribe me?"

"It's simply nice to talk to someone who's like me." Victoria shrugged at the admission, but there was an air of honesty about her. "But maybe just a tiny bit."

"Mommy! Mommy!" Sarah spotted them and darted toward their table. "I got a ball in a hole all by myself!" She scooted onto Taneka's lap.

"That's awesome, honey." Tanka looked at Victoria over her daughter's head. "I'll accept your bribe, Ms. Butler, but only to preserve my own sanity."

Chapter Three

The next morning, a package arrived at their hotel room while Taneka helped Sarah button up her brand-new dress.

Deon tipped the bellhop before he carried the box over to her. "Did you order something for the wedding, baby?"

"Not exactly." She smiled up at him. "It's gift from a friend."

"A present?" Sarah jumped up and down. "Can we open it?"

"No, honey, it's a present for Mommy and Daddy."

The gleam in Deon's eyes countered Sarah's disappointed expression. "Well, then I'll put the box up for later." He placed it in the top shelf of the closet.

It had been a long time since they played. The last time they tried was when Keshon was a few months old after he began sleeping through the night. Keshon started crying, and she rushed to his bedroom, leaving Deon handcuffed to the headboard. Keshon proceeded to spew all over her from both ends. She had no choice but to track poop and vomit down the hallway and into the master bedroom and bath. Nobody got any sleep that night.

But tonight?

Tonight, she'd make up for the last eight years.

A couple of hours later, Taneka shoved tissues into Beth's hand as they stood before the altar with Diana. Even her waterproof mascara had difficulty standing up to the tears they both shed. Alicia was doing her fair share of sniffling behind Taneka. But Steffi kept her shit together as matron of honor, trading rings and bouquets at the appropriate times.

The ceremony was simple and lovely. No matching ugly-ass bridesmaid dresses. All Diana wanted them to wear was dresses or suits with knee-length hems, and no one was to wear white or the same color as another bridesmaid.

Micki got out of having to wear heels and hose by being one of the groom's attendants. She wore a burgundy pantsuit with a Mandarin collar.

Keshon and Sarah looked adorable as the ring bearer and flower girl, though Deon had to search their son prior to the start of the ceremony. That kid managed to slip his phone into his suit pocket and his gaming device into his underwear.

But the way Daniel looked at Diana while they were saying their vows? Taneka didn't remember Diana's ex-fiancé ever looking at her friend with such adoration.

The guests didn't go much beyond family and close friends. Micki's dad and Mom acted as Diana's parents. Had either Diana or Steffi contacted their parents about their weddings or the new grandbaby? Or had they tried, only to be rejected again? It was too painful of a subject to even broach with either woman.

Part of Taneka wanted to search out Diana and Steffi's parents and kick their asses to Mars. If Keshon or Sarah came home and said they were interested in the opposite gender, Taneka would do everything in her power to accept and love her child's partner.

Diana and Daniel's vows were a lot more traditional that Taneka expected after her girlfriends' admissions two nights ago. The minister pronounced them husband and wife. The couple turned to the guests and a cheer went up as they retreated down the aisle.

As Taneka watched, Deon caught her eye. His circle beard framed his sly smile, the one that sent shivers across her skin. The wedding dinner could not end soon enough.

Unfortunately, everyone wanted to talk since this was the Fosters first trip back to D.C. in three years. Her baby brother Mike made sure to drag her around to meet her friends' significant others. Apparently, stories about high school had been told in her absence.

This restaurant was much nicer than last night's BBQ joint. Apparently, there was one battle Victoria won when it came to the wedding arrangements.

Diana and Daniel sat at the table with her and Deon while Keshon and Sarah spent time with their cousins. Micki and her boyfriend Ryan joined them. Between the policeman and the Army intelligence officer, Taneka was beginning to feel like she should be in an interrogation chamber.

"Wait a minute," Daniel protested. "I thought you and Mike were twins. Weren't you all in the same graduating class?"

Taneka exchanged looks with her baby brother before she turned back to Diana's new husband. "Mike and I were born nine months apart."

"Whoa!" Ryan leaned back in his chair. "How'd your parents handle two babies in diapers at the same time?"

"Three." Mike held up the appropriate number of fingers. "Alonso's only fifteen months younger than me."

"That's when Mom told Dad enough was enough." Taneka laughed. "According to my sister Jordan, Mom told him to go to the doctor and get a vasectomy, or she'd perform the surgery herself."

"Oh, ouch!" Daniel winced. "No wonder all of her cheerleaders have a kickass attitude." He didn't see Mom approach from behind him.

She leaned over and said in his ear, "And you better remember that. If you hurt Diana, it won't be the major and Butch you have to worry about, young man."

The alarmed look on Daniel's face was so hysterical everyone else at the table cracked up. He twisted in his chair and held up his right hand.

"I solemnly swear I will not harm Diana physically, mentally, financially, or emotionally," he said with all seriousness.

Mom narrowed her eyes. "Are you sassing me, Daniel Myers?"

"No, ma'am."

Mom shook her head and bent to kiss Diana on the cheek. "We need to get the grandkids home. It was a beautiful ceremony."

Both Diana and Daniel rose, hugged Mom, and murmured their thanks. She circled the table. Taneka and Deon stood as well and hugged Mom.

"You two have a good weekend, sweetheart," she whispered in Taneka's ear.

"If the kids get to be too much, call us—"

Mom cupped her cheek. "You remember those weekends you kids spent at the Major's place, or when Micki and Seth stayed with us?"

Taneka's face heated. "Mom, there are certain things you don't want to know about your parents."

"Doesn't mean we don't understand, sweetheart." She winked as Dad, Keshon, and Sarah approached.

After another round of kisses and warnings to listen to grandparents and good-byes, Mom and Dad left with the kids. Deon twined the fingers of his right hand between her fingers and squeezed. She didn't need to be asked twice.

"We're going to head back to the hotel," Taneka said.

"You can't stay a little longer?" Diana appeared wistful.

Taneka wrapped her arms around her friend. "Girl, there's this thing called jet lag. It's real."

Diana laughed and squeezed her back. "It's just been so long."

"You can come visit us, you know." Taneka chuckled before she whispered. "He's a good one. You both need to come out to California."

"We will." Diana sniffed and nodded. "We definitely will."

Once they disengaged, Deon wrapped a muscled arm around Taneka's waist. "Shall we?"

She nodded, her nerves tingling. She wasn't one bit tired despite her little white lie to Diana. Together, they headed for the restaurant's valet station.

Taneka forced herself not to jump Deon the instant they were in the rental. But she was so wet and on edge already, she wondered if she'd ruin the game before they started.

Chapter Four

Deon waved the key card over the lock. It hummed and clicked. Taneka pushed the latch and shoved the door open.

Once the door shut and Deon set the deadbolt, he looked at her expectantly. Not a muscle on his elegant body twitched. None, except his solid length pressing against the zipper of his suit trousers.

She waved toward the foot of the hotel's king-sized bed. "Sit down."

He obeyed without question. They'd discovered this game eased his tension by accident when they were in college.

They'd been in her dorm room at USC three days before March Madness. Taneka was trying to finish a business case study, but Deon had been so jittery about the upcoming tournament. She snapped at him to sit on her bed and not move until she gave him permission. And he didn't for the next two hours.

Oh, she had the paper done in forty-five minutes, but she wanted to see how far she could push him. The power of having one of the toughest men she'd ever known obeying her every word had sent an exciting thrill through her.

And she really wanted to know what goodies Victoria had sent her this morning.

Taneka retrieved the box from the top shelf of the closet and set it on the small desk next to the dresser and large screen TV. It took a moment to retrieve the scissors from her little sewing kit in her luggage. Anticipation surged through her nerves as she sliced through the tape and opened the box. The black velvet restraints were soft against her fingertips.

She held them up to show Deon and smiled at the glimmer in his eyes. "Stand up. Take off your jacket, tie, and shirt, and hang them up."

While he moved to obey her, she slipped the edible cock ring into the top of her corset. Taking her time licking the candy would drive him insane.

Taneka pulled the comforter down so he would be laying on the crisp white sheets. He finished hanging up his clothing and waited for her next command.

Her entire body tingled when she saw he'd replaced his gold nipple hoops with the red barbells she given to him for Valentine's Day. So, she wasn't the only one anticipating a couple of child-free days.

"Shoes and socks off."

As he removed those items, she unrolled the velvet. Long enough for a king-sized bed with Velcro so no bruising would occur, and therefore, no questions asked by the family during the rest of their stay in D.C. Victoria thought of everything. Taneka was beginning to like Diana's friend even more.

She placed one set of the restraints under the top of the mattress and the second set under the bottom.

Deon cleared his throat. "What about my belt?"

She raised an eyebrow. "Do you want a spanking?"

"Whatever you desire, ma'am," he said.

"Take it and your slacks off, hang them up, and don't forget to empty your pockets while you're at it." Taneka chuckled. "Last thing we need is to break your phone. Again."

"Yes, ma'am."

Once Deon was done with his assigned tasks, she realized he hadn't bothered with underwear. He needed a reward for thinking ahead. She slowly slipped off her shoes, unbuttoned her dress, and shimmied it down her body. Underneath the prim summer frock, she'd worn her black satin corset and matching panties. His breath whistled at the sight of her, but he was careful not to say a word.

"Lay down on the bed," she commanded. "Spread your arms and legs."

His massive body took up most of the bed. Her pussy grew damp at the need to mount him and ride his cock until neither of them could speak.

She forced her own breathing to steady while she moved around the bed and fastened his wrists and ankles with the velvet restraints. His pulse throbbed beneath his skin. When she finished, she leaned close to his right ear.

"Close your eyes."

He obeyed, and she ran her tongue around the outer edge of the shell of his ear. She blew on his damp skin, and he shivered.

"You're not allowed to come until two minutes after your cock is inside of me," she whispered.

Deon's throat bobbed before he answered, "Yes, ma'am."

Taneka straightened and raked her nails down his chest. He licked his lips, and his cock bobbed, demanding attention. Instead, she ran her fingertips down the length of his thigh and shin. His skin was hot beneath her touch.

She crawled onto the bed between his legs. His muscles quivered in anticipation. She fished the edible cock ring from between her breasts, tore open the wrapper and carefully slid the candy circle down his length and around his sac. His cock jerked in her hand. She bent over and ran her tongue around the tip and down to the cherry-flavored ring.

Rapid-fire banging rattled their hotel room door. Taneka paused. Her eyes met Deon's, and he groaned.

"If it were about the kids, Mom would have called us," she whispered. She reached up and laid the wrapper on the nightstand.

Someone banged again.

"Please, please go away," Deon muttered.

"Open up," Micki yelled. More banging. "We know you two are in there. I have my badge. If you don't open this door, I'll have management unlock it."

The threat made Taneka wish she had a weapon herself. "I'll get rid of her."

She crawled off the bed, stomped over to the door, and peered through the peephole. Sure enough, Micki was out there. She lifted her fist to beat on the door again.

Taneka yanked the door open.

Except Micki wasn't alone. Beth and Alicia pushed their way into the room along with Micki.

"You and Deon need to pack—" Alicia started. Her eyes widened, and she stared at the bed.

Beth giggled. "Damn, you two didn't waste any time."

Micki shook her head. "Hell, I'm impressed it's only one guy."

Chapter Five

"Taneka!" Deon roared.

She pushed past her friends and flipped the top sheet over her husband.

"That really doesn't help," Micki commented and gestured at the tented cotton.

Taneka glared at her. "Get out."

"Get your dander down, girl." Micki glared right back. "You're being invited to a special adults-only getaway."

"A what?" Taneka propped her hands on her hips.

Alicia's face was turning as bright red as her hair. She whirled away from the bed, but there was a large mirror on the opposite wall over the desk. She closed her eyes. "Um, well, Richard's private plane is leaving soon. This was supposed to be a surprise—"

"Except these two idiots forgot to tell you." Beth folded her arms over her chest. Out of all her friends, Taneka would have laid money that Beth would have been the first one to race out of the hotel room after seeing Deon in all his glory. She'd definitely grown up in the years Taneka had been gone.

"You two need to get packed." Micki headed for the closet and started pulling things out. "The guys are waiting for us in the limo."

"Geez, Micki," Beth chided. "Let them finish."

"All of you need to step outside of our room now," Taneka growled.

"We're headed to a private Caribbean island." Alicia still kept her eyes closed but continued as if she were discussing church.

"Don't worry, Tee," Beth said. "Butch and LaShaun know we're kidnapping you." She took the first handful of hangers from Micki and started folding and packing the clothing.

"Stop!" Taneka shouted.

Everyone paused in mid-action. Well, every one except Alicia who turned her head toward Taneka and cautiously opened one eye.

Taneka inhaled before she began. "This is the first time I thought I had uninterrupted time with my husband, and not one of you has apologized for barging into our hotel room."

"We're sorry," they all murmured.

"We just wanted you to join us," Alicia added. "It's been so long since the last time we got to hang out together."

"I realize that, but—" Taneka growled.

"You really wanted to finish eating that cock ring?" Beth said.

"My wife politely asked you three to step outside." Deon's voice rumbled out of his chest like the call of distant thunder. "I suggest you do so before she whips all of your asses. And not in any pleasurable way."

"But—" Micki said.

"Out!" Taneka pointed at the door.

"Think about coming with us," Alicia pleaded as she trooped after Micki.

"We'll be just outside," Beth said.

Taneka growled.

"Okay, we'll be in the lobby." Beth stepped out of the hotel room.

The door opened again before it closed all the way. Beth stuck her head around the edge. "Text us with your decision."

Taneka reached for one of her discarded shoes on the carpet, grabbed the footwear, and launched it at the doorway. Her shoe struck the fake wood paneling as Beth yanked the door shut with a chuckle.

"I am so sorry, baby," she murmured. Tears stung her eyes. Between the fury and mortification, she wasn't sure what to do.

"Since we're way past our safe word, how about you release me?" He flashed that dazzling smile that made her fall in love with him in the first place. "And we'll talk about it like you promised the girls."

She walk around the bed, pulling the Velcro cuffs free. The edible cock ring cradled Deon's now flaccid penis. She didn't realize how much she'd been looking forward to simply enjoying the evening with him.

He sat up, carefully removed the jellied ring, and laid it on top of its plastic wrapper on the nightstand before he patted the mattress next to him. She lowered herself beside him.

"I'm so sorry," she said again. "This wasn't how I imagined this evening would go."

"I'm not mad at you, baby." He wrapped his right arm around her. "I'm not mad at them either. A little disappointed maybe . . ."

"I'll text them that we're not going," she murmured.

"No." Deon said.

"No?" she looked up at him. "Do you really want to go?"

"When was the last time you got to hang out with your friends without the kids around?" He grinned and pulled her against his chest. "Besides, who turns down an invitation to a private tropical island by one of your closest friend's billionaire boyfriend? Just remember to bring the box that Vicki woman sent you."

Deon winked, and Taneka couldn't help but laugh as she hugged him back.

Chapter Six

The twin engines of the small corporate jet sent a delicious vibration through Taneka's body as the plane left the runway and sped through the night. Or maybe she was still on edge from her aborted play time with Deon.

The guys sat at the front of the plane, talking, while Taneka sat with her girlfriends at a table in the back. Beth practically bounced in the seat beside Taneka and grabbed her hand.

"I'm glad you and Deon decided to come with us."

Taneka couldn't remember the last time she'd seen Beth this happy. "I'm glad, too, but a little warning would have been nice."

Micki held up both hands and glared at Alicia. "My job was to talk to Butch and Coach LaShaun about the kids."

Alicia winced. "I'm sorry! How many times do I have to say it?" She stared out the window for a moment. "I wish Diana had come with us. Who the hell goes to a car race for their honeymoon?"

"Diana," Taneka said in unison with Micki and Beth.

"Besides, who wants to spend their honeymoon with their friends?" Beth added.

"Not everyone wants to get it on with their bridal party watching," Micki teased.

They all laughed, even Alicia, though her face nearly matched her red hair.

Once the captain announced they were at cruising altitude and the seatbelt sign was turned off, the flight attendant Rashida moved through the cabin taking drink requests. Taneka found herself watching the woman. She wore a tight navy skirt and jacket, but her starched white shirt wasn't unbuttoned enough to show cleavage. The attendant was flirty with the five men, but more in a waitress-working-the-tip way.

When she came over to the ladies' seats, her attitude became more professional with everyone except for Alicia. Rashida's manner turned downright sexually predatory, and Alicia squirmed in her seat.

And definitely not because she enjoyed the attention.

Richard may let his bitch get away with this behavior, but Taneka wasn't about to let it slide. She fixed an icy smile to her face, laid her hand over Alicia's, and said, "We'll both take a diet cola."

Rashida obviously got the message. She inclined her head and murmured, "Yes, mistress." She headed to the front to get their orders.

From the expressions on Beth and Alicia's faces, they'd picked up the not-so-subtle message. Micki looked thoroughly confused.

"Mistress?" she whispered. "What the hell?"

"Taneka just went domme on her ass." Beth leaned over the table, her worried attention on Alicia. "Has she been giving you shit?"

"No, um, not exactly." Alicia wouldn't meet anyone's gaze. She simply stared at Taneka's hand on hers.

Taneka withdrew. "I'm sorry if I overstepped, but you looked damned uncomfortable just now."

Alicia released a deep breath. "It's not her. It's me. I'm not comfortable handling sexual interest from a woman."

"Girl, it is okay *not* to switch teams," Micki murmured fiercely.

"Except part of me is curious." Alicia looked on the edge of tears. "And I don't want to make a fool of myself or lead anyone on."

"Or nearly ruin a friendship like I did?" Beth had a rueful smile on her face.

"Wait. What?" Taneka stared at each woman in turn.

No one said a word because Rashida had returned with their drinks. She was especially deferential to Taneka as she set out glasses with ice and plastic bottles, but she wasted no time returning to the tiny galley when she was done.

"Wow," Beth murmured. "You really got to her."

"Huh-uh." Taneka waggled her index finger. "You are not changing the subject."

"Oh, quit acting butt hurt," Micki said as she twisted off the cap of her root beer. "I told you about her and Diana years ago."

"So we're no longer pretending we know nothing?" Taneka turned to Beth.

"It's better everything is in the open." Beth shrugged.

Taneka looked at Alicia. "Are you sure you're okay?"

She nodded though she swiped at her eyes. "Yeah." She smiled weakly. "There just seems to be a huge discrepancy between what I thought I wanted, and what I really am."

Taneka poured her own soda into her glass. She'd been in the same position when she realized what she was. What she really wanted and needed from a relationship. She'd had been a lot younger and smart enough to hit the campus library to find answers to her questions. She couldn't imagine trying to figure everything out at thirty-four.

She eyed Richard Brand over the rim of her glass. If he was taking advantage of Alicia in her confusion and uncertainty, there would definitely be hell to pay.

Chapter Seven

It was near midnight when the private jet landed on Richard's island. Taneka grabbed her overnight bag and followed everyone else off the plane. Any desire for playtime disappeared under a tsunami of exhaustion. The trip to the east coast and all the wedding blitz had finally taken their toll.

Thankfully, Richard's staff had three minivans waiting near the tarmac, one for the plane's crew and two for Richard and his guests. Taneka and Deon rode with Beth and her men. No one spoke much, and their driver wasn't one of those people who felt the need to entertain his boss's guests.

Or maybe their driver was smart enough to realize his passengers were dead on their feet.

The minivan with the plane's crew took off in another direction. Aaron, who rode in the front passenger seat, asked where they were going. Their driver explained the staff lived in cottages on the other side of the island, and there were a couple extra places for any of Mr. Brand's employees to stay overnight.

After a short ride, the minivans pulled in front of a huge house. It was way too big for a simple vacation home, but then Alicia's boyfriend was one of the richest men on the planet. The decorative outdoor lighting highlighted the manicured flowerbeds and the shorter palm trees. Tan stone formed the two-story house. Stainless steel pins held open the wide blue hurricane shutters.

Their little group followed Richard through the front door painted in the same Federal blue as the shutters. The lights inside the house flipped on with their movements.

Taneka tried not to look around in awestruck amazement, though Micki did that for her.

"Man, Richard!" She twirled in the middle of the foyer. "Can't you at least pretend to be normal and furnish this place with IKEA?"

"Ignore her," Ryan said. "I've spent more than enough time sleeping in sand and bugs. I appreciate a clean, soft bed."

The round foyer was painted white, but it gleamed beneath the chandelier hanging two stories above them. The lights themselves were decked out in lead crystals, not cheap glass. A staircase started on their right and curved up to the second floor. From the way Paolo slobbered over a marble sculpture in an alcove beneath the stairs, the art was probably some priceless ancient or medieval original. The tiles beneath their feet were the same Italian style in the condo where Diana housesat.

"The clean, soft beds are in the four guest rooms upstairs." Richard gestured toward the staircase. "Take your pick. All of the rooms have their own attached bathrooms."

"And where are you two going to be?" Beth teased.

"Elizabeth . . ." Aaron chided.

"In the *master* bedroom, of course." Richard smiled. "There's also small refrigerators and coffee makers in each bedroom. Shall we meet for lunch around noon?"

The other three sets of people murmured their assent and their good nights before they trooped upstairs. Everyone stopped at the top of the stairs and stared at the view out the sliding glass door of the sitting room.

"This is unfrickin' believable," Micki muttered.

The sitting room itself was comfortable chic. Again, the plush upholstery of the couches and chairs were the same blue as the exterior accent paint. But it was the nearly full moon gleaming on the beach and waves below that silenced every-one else.

Taneka lowered her carryon to the thick, tan carpet next to her suitcase and strode to the doors. She unlocked it and stepped out onto the balcony. It was easily half the size of the sitting room, but the balcony contained wicker furniture. Of course, the cushions on the chairs and loungers were the same color as the interior upholstery. The beach was roughly fifty yards from the patio below her, but it was a fairly steep incline down to the sand.

"Hell of a view," Deon murmured beside her.

"Yeah, it is." She laughed.

"You know I've always wanted to give this kind of thing to you."

She turned to him and cupped his face. "Baby, you always given me everything and every part of you."

"And if you two don't stop with the lovey-dovey stuff, I'm going to throw up," Micki said from the open doorway.

"That's enough. You are definitely overtired." Ryan stepped up to Micki, wrapped his arm around her waist, and tossed her over his shoulder.

She shrieked. "Put me down!"

"Do you need to be gagged?" Ryan growled. "I'm sure one of your friends has one I can borrowed.

"Ugh! Gross!" she protested. "I don't want a used gag!"

But when Ryan pivoted, Micki had a huge grin on her face. She waved. "See you all in the morning."

They disappeared down the right hallway.

"We should retire, too," Aaron murmured. Beth waved and Paolo winked as they followed their master down the left hallway.

Deon dipped his head and began nibbling along Taneka's neck right above her collar. "Should we go to bed as well?"

"You want to start all over again?" she murmured. Like she was going to say no. Not after being on edge through the entire freaking plane ride. But could she keep her head when she was so exhausted from the last few days?

"Nah, not when you're this tired," he said against her skin. "I just want to show you how much I love you." His hands slid to her ass and squeezed. "Maybe get you to relax a little bit."

"You already showed me how much you love me by agreeing to this insane trip." Her chuckle turned to a gasp when he lifted her and pressed his erection against her pussy. "Maybe I need to slow you down or we aren't going to make it to the bedroom."

He lifted his head and stared at her. "That two and a half hour flight wasn't enough of a discipline exercise?"

"You're making me reconsider," she said archly.

"What ever you wish, my mistress." He set her back on her feet.

She tugged him back inside and closed the sliding glass door. "Which side do you want to listen to?"

Deon had crossed the sitting room and loaded their carry-ons over one huge shoulder before giving her a look. "You don't think Richard put soundproofing between the bedrooms?"

"I'm sure he did." Taneka grinned. "But I can ask Aaron to gag Beth and Paolo if they get too loud. Not that I think Ryan can't handle himself, but you've never had to pull Micki off someone when she's pissed."

"Left it is then." Deon grabbed his suitcase handle and headed in the same direction as Beth's group.

Taneka flipped off the light switch for the sitting room. Richard may be a multi-billionaire with his fancy automated lights, but there was no sense wasting electricity. She grabbed her suitcase handle and followed Deon down the hallway.

Beth's group had taken the first bedroom from the closed door. Deon had turned on the lights for the next bedroom. His low whistle made Taneka pick up her pace.

The so-called bedroom was bigger than their first apartment in San Jose. The custom made bed dominated the room, but there was still space for a table, a desk, and a giant wardrobe. The full bathroom could put a sauna's facilities to shame.

"Check this out, baby." Deon opened the sliding glass door at the opposite end of the room, revealing their own private balcony. The sound of ocean waves murmured a relaxing song.

Taneka smiled. Taking the other room was Beth's way of apologizing for the girls' interruption earlier this evening. She stacked her suitcase with the bags Deon carried in by the wardrobe and turned off the lights.

Even though the moon didn't shine directly into their room, its reflected light was more than enough to see her husband's tall, lanky form. She crossed the room and wrapped her arms around his waist.

"Now, where were we?" she murmured.

He said nothing and lowered his head. His long, slow kiss ignited the fire inside of her that had been simmering all day. Their tongues teased, and their teeth nipped.

When they parted, she murmured. "That's right. I had you tied to my bed."

"Do you really have the patience to start from the beginning?" He slid his hands beneath her shirt, his skin hot against hers. "To take your time licking that candy cock ring before you ride me?" He stroked her waist until he reached the top button of her shorts. His fingers slipped into her panties.

Taneka moaned when he pressed his palm against her lower lips. He knew just how to tease her with his gentle massage.

"You still haven't answered me, baby," he whispered against the skin of her neck. "Do you really want to start your game all over again? When you've been so wet?" Two of his fingers slipped inside of her slick passage. "For so long?"

"You are a bad, bad boy, Deon Foster." Taneka gasped when the pads of his fingers stroked a particularly sensitive spot.

"Does that mean you need to punish me now?" He nibbled the join of her neck and shoulder. "Or do you need to fuck me?"

Her body shuddered at the overload of sensations running through it. He chuckled at his effect on her. His laughter was more of a vibration through his torso than an actual sound.

Part of her knew she needed to take control of the situation. Pulling those threads was nearly impossible though. Her body had its own ideas of what it wanted. Finally, she pressed her palms against his hard muscular chest and pushed.

She drew a shaky breath before she said, "Take off your clothes."

"Yes, ma'am." But he sounded far too pleased with himself as he pushed his pants and underwear to the carpet.

She shifted and slapped his bare ass. "Faster."

He kicked off his shoes and pants as he pulled his polo shirt over his head. Socks flew into a corner before he dove for the bed and rolled over on his back. His teeth gleamed in the ambient moonlight with his presumptuous grin. His long, thick cock stood at attention.

"Mighty full of yourself," she said as she stripped off her own clothes at a more sedate pace.

"I thought you wanted to be full of me," he shot back.

"I am going to have to punish you thoroughly." She stepped out of her own panties. "Tomorrow, when I'll have the rest and patience to do a properly thorough job." She crossed to the bed and climbed on. "Tonight, though—" She straddled him. Wet didn't begin to describe how she felt on the damn plane ride here. "I'm going to fuck you until neither of us can walk."

Taneka rose on her knees and guided him inside of her. His thickness filled her, completed her. He molded her breasts and tweaked her nipples while she ground against his pelvis. She closed her eyes and let the electricity build.

Deon's hand cupped her cheek. "Baby, look at me."

Her eyelids snapped open. It seemed brighter in the bedroom at if the moon drew power from them. She stared into the liquid depths of his dark eyes. She would have sworn she could see his soul staring back.

"I love you, baby," he murmured.

Taneka released herself and joined him in an explosion of pleasure that went on and on and on.

Chapter Eight

Sunlight filtering past the sheer curtains into their bedroom drew Taneka out of a delicious dream. She rolled over to find Deon watching her.

"Good morning."

"Good morning," he replied before he kissed her.

When their lips parted, she asked, "How long have you been awake?"

"Since dawn." He grinned and traced the curve of her shoulder. "I didn't want to disturb you. It looked like you were having a good dream."

She smiled. "It was a replay of last night. The good parts, not the interruption."

"Hmmm. Repeating the good parts is certainly doable." His fingers trailed down her skin before cupping her left breast.

Taneka moaned as his thumb stroked her nipple. Even after thirteen years of marriage, he could arouse her with the simplest of touches. She arched her back, pressing herself against the hard length of his body.

His cock grew and throbbed between her thighs. He kissed her as he rolled her onto her back. He plunged into her, claiming her as his. Her legs curled around his waist. Her heels pressed against his ass. She met each thrust enthusiastically.

There wasn't kids or work deadlines or any other things intruding on their time together. She relished the freedom to be herself with her man.

Her internal muscles gripped and squeezed his cock. She shifted her hips in a wild figure-eight, and her efforts elicited a moan of pleasure from Deon.

"Baby." He panted in her ear. "You keep that up, and I'm not going to last."

His admission only spurred on her efforts. His muscles strained and stiffened. His hot come filled her passage.

That pulsing inside of her was all she needed to let go of her own desire. She squeezed one more time, and her body shuddered with its own release.

They both gasped, trying to catch their breath, when Deon rolled off of her. "Damn, we haven't been this horny—"

Someone banged on their bedroom door, interrupting him. "Hey, west coasters! Wake up! It's lunch time!"

Deon wrapped his right arm and leg around Taneka's body and whispered, "Don't you dare open that door."

Taneka groaned and checked the time on her phone. Damn, it was noon already. So much for sleeping in on a child-free Sunday.

"We're coming!" she yelled. The door latch rattled, but she'd had the presence of mind to lock the door last night.

"I would have thought you'd already came!" Micki yelled back, but she didn't try to enter their room again.

"I suppose we need to get decent and go downstairs." Deon reluctantly released Taneka.

"It would be good manners." She gave him a quick kiss before she rolled off the mattress and stood. She retrieved her suitcase and overnight bag and set them on the table.

Deon chuckled as he placed his suitcase on the bed and opened it. "At least, she waited until we were done this time." He grabbed his toiletry kit and sobered. "What happened on the plane last night? It looked like you had an issue with the flight attendant."

"That woman needs to learn some manners." Taneka shook her head before she cracked open her own suitcase. "I may be wrong, but I think she had her sights set on the boss, and she's trying to make Alicia uncomfortable enough that she'll leave."

"Alicia?" Deon cocked his head. "Trying that kind of crap with Beth I could understand, but Alicia? That woman does not back down from anything."

"Sweetie, a lot of her attitude is a front." Taneka selected clean cotton twill shorts and a matching tank top. "I resented Mom making her head cheerleader back in the day, but she was trying to instill some confidence in Alicia that she was sorely lacking. The crap that dipshit ex-husband of hers put her through seems to have set her back to square one. Part of me wonders if Brand saw her as an easy mark because she was on the rebound from Hank."

Deon tossed his kit on the bed and pulled her into his arms. "Baby, do you really think Brand is taking advantage of her?"

"Yes. No. Maybe." She shrugged. "I don't know. Both Micki and Beth threatened him if he got out of line." She laughed. "So did Alicia's elderly neighbor."

"So what are you worried about?"

"That Richard's pushing Alicia into things she's not ready for. That's she's doing certain things in the bedroom to please him. She admitted as much on the plane."

"Baby." Deon rubbed Taneka's back. "That's between her and her man. The two of you didn't talk for three months because you were brutally honest in your opinion of Hank—"

"But I was right!"

Deon chuckled. "That isn't the point, baby. You could be totally right about Richard, too, and I know you mean well, but she isn't going to listen to someone badmouth her man. Is it worth ruining your friendship with her?"

"No," Taneka muttered sullenly. Damn, she hated it when Deon was right. But he definitely had a higher EQ than she did. It was the whole reason she was an independent writer and publisher. She simply couldn't handle the corporate bullshit with the finesse her husband had. However, when it came to the people she loved, she was totally incapable of backing down.

"Let's go downstairs and play nice because I'm starving." He pecked her on the forehead before he snatched his toiletry kit and headed for the bathroom.

Taneka gritted her teeth while she retrieved her own toiletry kit and cosmetics bag. If only she could figure out whether Richard Brand was a good guy, or just pretending to be one to use her friend.

Richard had his staff serve Sunday brunch on the patio before he dismissed them for the next two days. Everyone was in a good mood, and Taneka did her best to go along with it. Why the hell was she in such a mood? They were on a beautiful tropical island, her closest friends whom she hadn't seen in years were here, and she had a break from the kids for a few days.

Maybe that was the problem. Even with Keshon and Sarah in school, there was so much running around to do with soccer and swim practice plus science club and dance. It'd been a long time since she had the opportunity to sit still for more than five minutes unless it was at her desk.

She pulled her cell phone out of her pocket and frowned. No bars showed on the device.

"Who are you trying to call?" Micki asked.

"Mom." Taneka held up her phone at different angles. "I wanted to check on the kids."

"You're not going to get a cell signal on the island." Richard wiped his mouth with a napkin. "You're more than welcome to use the satellite phone in my office." He stood.

"Tell them I love them." Deon said.

"You could tell them yourself." She whapped his bicep with the back of her hand as she rose.

"I'm trying to enjoy the vacation my wife and my boss insisted I take," he shot back.

She shook her head and laughed before she followed Richard into the house.

"Now that we're alone, may I show you something?" he asked.

"That depends on what it is," she said. Suspicion flared despite her best effort to subdue the ugly beast in her mind.

"It's something I think you would appreciate as a fellow dominant."

"What makes you think I'm a dominant?"

"Besides both Victoria and Rashida mentioning it?"

Well, since he brought up the subject first. "Richard, you need to get that Rashida girl under control," she snapped. "She was out of line with Alicia last night."

"I spoke with her this morning, and a formal warning has already been placed in her employment file." He eyed her as they walked. "I didn't interfere last night because you'd already taken care of the situation, and I didn't want to ruin everyone else's good time. I swear I did apologize to Alicia last night in private, and I wanted to extend apologies to you for both Rashida and Alicia's faux pas as well."

Taneka stopped, and Richard turned to face her.

"Alicia's faux pas?"

"Let me show something you first." He led her to the same downstairs wing where Micki and Ryan's bedroom was upstairs. Richard pulled out an old-fashioned brass key from his front trousers pocket, unlocked the door, and ushered Taneka inside.

Light filtered into the room from very high window. Antique industrial style lighting fixtures lined the ceiling. But it was the décor and furnishings that took her breath away.

Richard had brought her to his very own BDSM dungeon.

Chapter Nine

Taneka stared, trying to take in everything at once. The equipment hanging from the walls was pristine. In fact, none of the whips or paddles looked as if they had been used. The metal of the spanking bench and the wood of the St. Andrews cross was polished to a reflective shine. The cuffs and padding had that fresh virgin leather smell. He even had strategically placed electric outlets near the large set pieces.

"What do you think?" Richard said.

Taneka turned to him and narrowed her eyes. "Why did you bring me in here?"

He smiled. "The use of the room is my way of apologizing for the girls interrupting you at the hotel. If Aaron or I had an inkling, we never would have let Beth or Alicia go up to your hotel room."

Taneka raised an eyebrow. "You really think you have that much control over them?"

Richard chuckled, "Point taken."

"So you two experts couldn't put two and two together, but Victoria could?"

His smile turned rueful. "I can't speak for Aaron, but in my case, I assumed you and your husband would be too tired after all the wedding activities. That you'd be watching TV if you weren't already asleep."

Taneka shook her head. "You obviously don't have children."

Her statement drew a chuckle from Richard. "While I would love to have some, I need to convince Alicia to marry me first."

"You proposed?" This was the first she'd heard about Richard and Alicia being this serious.

"She turned me down." He frowned. "Actually, she answered not yet."

"I'm sorry." Taneka shook her head again. "Her ex-husband Hank did a number on her."

"I know." Richard hesitated. "No one else knows, and she'd be very upset if she thought anyone else did—"

Taneka held up her right palm. "Stop right there. It won't go any farther." She looked around the room again, regretting what she was about to say. "You built this for her. You two should be the first to use it."

He sighed and leaned his shoulder against the door frame. "She's not ready yet."

"You sure about that?"

"Would you risk your marriage by pushing Deon farther than he wanted to go?"

Taneka nodded. "I understand. But what about the other couples, uh—"

This time, Richard laughed outright. "Aaron is rather picky about play time when it comes to his subs, more so than me, so he'd refuse which is why I didn't bother to ask him." He sobered. "From the little I've been told and what I've observed, Micki and Ryan are both still working through their own personal issues. They're not ready for something like this either. I'm not sure they'll ever be."

"But you wanted to show off your new toy room to someone." Taneka grinned at Richard.

"Especially to someone who might appreciate the work I put into it, and someone who would actually get some enjoyment out of it on this trip," he said.

"So what's the catch?" she asked as she fingered a purple leather flogger tipped with jade beads. Real jade, not some fake stones. "You got cameras hidden in here? Your company and Deon's are business rivals."

"Yes, I do have cameras in here, but only if you wish to film yourselves. You can have Deon and Beth check the wiring if you don't believe me." Richard's smile turned self-deprecating. "I'm hoping Alicia will say yes to my marriage proposal this year. She's still pissed at me for loaning money to her ex-husband to cover what he stole from her. Ruining the lives of her closest friends are not going to help my cause one bit."

"True." Taneka looked around the play dungeon one more time. "Are you sure about this?"

"Like I said, it's my way of apologizing for ruining your evening."

She smiled. Maybe she hadn't given Richard enough credit after all. "Well, then, apology accepted, Mr. Brand."

Chapter Ten

Taneka tugged Deon down the hallway to Richard's personal dungeon. She'd already dragged Beth to it to examine the wiring and cameras before they'd gone down to the beach this afternoon. Not that Taneka wanted to film herself and Deon, but neither of them could afford for a sex tape to end up on the internet. Neither of their careers would survive such a scandal.

The fact Beth hadn't blinked at the dungeon's set-up said how far Beth had come from the attack during their junior prom. Plus, she'd given her approval of Richard when Taneka inquired about Alicia's marriage proposal. When Taneka asked why no one had mentioned anything to her about another possible wedding, Beth had shrugged and said there wasn't any point until Alicia accepted.

The whole conversation made Taneka realize how much she missed by living on the opposite coast. Homesickness had swept through her, but she couldn't ask Deon to give up his career, everything he'd worked so hard for, for her high school friends. It simply wasn't right.

Richard decided they would have a hot dog roast replete with s'mores for dinner that night. He was trying very hard to act like a normal, everyday guy. But then, isn't that what she and Deon did? However, the cook-out kept everyone else occupied while she dragged her husband to Richard's play room under the pretense of going to bed early due to jet lag.

"Close your eyes," Taneka murmured when she and Deon stopped at the dungeon door.

"What's going on, baby?" But his eyelids snapped shut despite his question.

She licked her lips. "Do you want to play tonight?"

"All of our stuff is upstairs." A mix of excitement and confusion swept across his face.

"Yes or no, Deon," she said firmly.

He didn't hesitate. "Yes." His Adam's apple bobbed.

"Good." She fished the antique brass key from her shorts pocket and unlocked the door. Grabbing Deon's hand, she led him forward. His pulse throbbed beneath her palm, but then her heart quickened, too, in her anticipation. She flipped on the lights and locked the door. The scent of fresh leather and citrus cleaner filled her head.

"You may open your eyes," she murmured.

He did. Then he blinked again as his jaw dropped open. "What?"

"What do you think?" Taneka murmured.

"May I ask a few questions?" he said.

"Yes, you may."

"Did Brand build this?"

Taneka nodded.

Deon whistled. "Does Alicia know what she's getting into?"

"A little bit." Taneka shrugged. "They've done spanking, obedience, restraints, some other things. But even Richard admits Alicia's not ready for something as hardcore as this."

"I'm not sure I am either," Deon said ruefully.

"Queensryche." Taneka sat on a leather bench with cuffs. "Talk to me, baby. What's wrong? I had Beth help me check the wiring and wi-fi in here if you're worried Richard will use something against us."

"Do I have to say it out loud?"

"Please."

"A black man getting chained up in a white man's dungeon doesn't exactly make me comfortable, Tee."

"I understand if you don't want to." She looked at the equipment with a bit of disappointment. "I admit I wasn't too trustful of him either. But Micki and Beth both said he was a standup guy, and he really loves Alicia."

"Did he build this for her?"

"Technically, yes." Taneka sighed. "But he admitted she's not ready for this level of play. He offered to let us use it as his way of apologizing for the girls interrupting us last night." She looked up at Deon. "But if you don't feel comfortable using it, I don't blame you. We can go upstairs and use the goodies in the box Victoria sent me."

Deon was silent as he circled the room. He stopped next to the same purple leather flogger decorated with jade and fingered the beads. "This is the kind of room I want to build when the kids are out of the house."

"You want to wait until the kids are in college?" she teased. "I thought that was why we were putting my royalty checks aside. So we could build our private play room sooner."

Deon chuckled. "Baby, no one wants to know what their parents do in private. With our luck, Sarah would find the key and be scarred for life."

"Are you saying Keshon wouldn't be?"

Deon laughed harder. "Let's face it, he would only be looking if you stored video games and Cheetos in our personal dungeon."

"Well, the kids aren't here right now." Taneka cocked her head. "Yes or no?"

"Yes, ma'am," he said without hesitation.

"Take off you clothes, fold them and place them on the counter," she ordered. While he undressed, she examined the accoutrements. Heavy steel rods firmly affixed the St. Andrews cross to the wall. The device even had movable cuffs and footrests to accommodate different-sized people and steps built into the rear supports so a smaller person could restrain someone bigger. Maybe Alicia and Richard's relationship wasn't as one-sided as Taneka assumed.

Or maybe Richard planned to bring the other couples they played with here.

Taneka pushed the thought from her mind. It wasn't her business anyway. There was only one person she wanted.

She tried to rattle the cross. It seemed adequately sturdy. She always wanted to try one, but she'd had a hard time finding one that could accommodate someone of Deon's size. Not without having one custom-made, which brought her back to the fact they had no place in their house to store it.

The steel supports were cold beneath her fingertips, but pressing on the leather revealed thick padding between it and the wood. Yes, this would be a good start.

She circled the room, examining the equipment. A thrill had gone through her that he admired the same flogger she had. But they would be on the island two more days. No one else needed to see marks on Deon's body. There was some things she simply couldn't share with her friends.

No, they need something a little more sedate. More sensual. The violet wand would be good, along with the finger talons and the fur mitten. But first, she needed a blindfold.

Taneka selected the royal blue velvet one from the wall. She turned to find Deon in a parade rest position, his feet slightly spread and his hands clasped behind his back. His cock jutted proudly from his dark curls. His clothes were neatly folded on the bench behind him.

Damn. Her mouth watered just by watching him. In so many ways, he looked better now than when they were in college.

She arranged the items in her hands on a small table with wheels. The mobile table made sense. A dominant would want their tools near the bigger pieces of furniture and the immobile ones. She eyed Deon, but he said nothing. Good.

Taneka crossed back to the St. Andrews cross, pushing the table ahead of her. "Come over here."

He stalked over to her, a barely tamed big cat, but one that would obey her commands as long as she kept control of herself and of him. Anticipation ran thick through her veins as she adjusted the footrests. He stepped onto them, and she locked the ankle cuffs in place with solid *clunk*s.

Taneka climbed the two steps behind the cross. She adjusted the restraints for the length of his arms and locked his wrists in place. Anticipation licked her own body as she placed the blindfold over his eyes. Now, he was totally at her mercy. The power sent a shudder through her.

She murmured in his ear, "You can't come until I give you permission. Do you understand?"

"Yes, ma'am."

If they were going to play with electricity, she needed to take some precautions. She carefully removed the sapphire stud earring she'd given to him as a wedding present. After climbing down and placing the stud on the table, she stood in front of the cross, removed his gold nipple hoops, and set them aside, too. It took only a couple of seconds to wiggle out of her own clothes.

She picked up the violet wand and examined it. Solid-state. Good. Richard would literally scare the piss out of Alicia with a Tesla. The woman couldn't stand to be tickled when they were younger.

Taneka tucked the end of the body contact cable in her bustier and checked the contact against her skin. Perfect. She crouched and plugged in the power cord in the outlet at the base of the cross. Nerves assailed her as she slipped on the finger talons. It had been a long time since she'd done this.

Making sure the wand was on its lowest setting, she flipped on the power. She flicked Deon's left nipple and watched him. No reaction. In fact from the way his jaw clenched, he was struggling not to laugh out loud.

All right. If he wanted a good zap.

Taneka turned up the setting on the wand and flicked his right nipple. Electricity sparked. Deon gasped. Much better.

She tapped the talons all over his chest and danced her way down past his belly button. His muscles tensed, anticipating she would be that wicked. Instead, she grabbed his left ass cheek with the talons.

With a yell, he jumped at the concentrated shocks. Well, as far as one could jump while shackled to a St. Andrews cross.

"Had enough?" she murmured.

"No, ma'am."

Taneka started her game again, but this time, she started with his feet. His breath hissed when he couldn't escape her talons. She raked the metal tips up his calf. His thigh.

Once again, his muscles tensed, anticipating she would touch his cock with the talon. Instead, she leaned over and licked the head. Tingles tortured her tongue, and he groaned at the dual sensation of pain and pleasure.

She continued playing with his body, alternately stokes and taps until she used her tongue instead of metal. Finally, she kissed him until her mouth stung and throbbed. Still, his cock remained as stiff as ever.

"You did very good, my big, bad baller," Taneka whispered. She stepped back, turned off the power to the wand, and unplugged it. The next part was more of a torture for Deon than the slight shocks of the wand. She laid the device on the table, stripped off the finger talons and put on the fur mitten.

He moaned when she started stroking the skin she'd been shocking a moment ago. But his moans turned into chuckles as she continued to caress him with the fur. His chuckles turned to laughter, then shrieks and shouts as he tried to evade the tickling of the mitten. The cuffs rattled with his efforts to escape, but they were very sturdy.

"Queensryche! Queensryche!"

Taneka stopped immediately. "You okay, baby?"

"G-give me a chance to catch my breath." His head sagged to his chest, and he panted like he'd ran a marathon.

"That's enough," she murmured.

"No, I don't want to quit—" he started.

"Stop." She pulled off the mitten and laid her index finger across his lips. "We're done for the night." When he didn't argue, she knew she'd made the right decision.

She placed the mitten on the table before she took off the blindfold and un-cuffed Deon from the cross. With one arm around his waist, she led him to the padded bench, sat him, and rubbed his back.

"Better?" she asked.

He nodded, but he was staring at the floor.

"Why'd you let me push you so hard?"

"I wanted to prove myself." He shook his head before he looked at her. "Part of me is wishing I could give you a private island with its very own dungeon."

"What makes you think I want anything or anyone besides you?" Taneka leaned over and kissed him. When they parted, she stood and unhooked her bustier before she shimmied out of her panties.

At the delight in his expression, she straddled his lap. "I love you, baby." She guided him inside of her as she lowered her body. He seized her right nipple between his lips, alternately nibbling and licking it, before he turned his attention to her other breast.

The sensation drove a different kind of electric sparks through her body. She shifted her hips in a steady figure-eight motion and squeezed her internal muscles

Deon grabbed her ass cheeks and spread them like he couldn't get deep enough inside of her. His thrusts met hers. She raked his back with her nails. No, she never would be able to get enough of him.

His legs straightened, and his muscles tensed. He stared into her eyes.

Then they were both falling into the abyss. His cock pulsed and his arms tightened around her as their bodies shuddered.

Deon chuckled as they both tried to catch their breath. "I don't think I could ever get enough of you."

Taneka cupped his face and kissed him. Deeply. Thoroughly. Desperately wanting to make this moment last forever.

Chapter Eleven

After Taneka and Deon cleaned up the dungeon, they managed to get upstairs to their room without anyone seeing them. They lay naked and entwined on the bed. Ambient moonlight filtered past the sheer curtains. They had left the sliding glass door open to the light breeze. The sound of the waves had nearly lulled her to sleep.

"Tee, we need to talk," Deon murmured in the dark.

"About what?" she said. The post-orgasm haziness fled. Her man could only bare his deeper feelings late at night.

When he felt safe in her arms.

"How would you feel about moving back to D.C.?" he said.

She turned on her side to face him and rested her palm on his heart. "We had this talk, baby. A long time ago. You think I'd change my mind about supporting you just because we came back for Diana's wedding?"

"Actually, I was thinking about the kids," he said. "With Mama's death last year, your parents are the only grandparents Sarah and Keshon have left."

"But your company—"

"Richard's corporation is about to make an offer to the partners."

Taneka jerked upright. "He told you this?"

Deon pushed himself into a sitting position as well. "Yes."

Her blood turned to ice. Was Richard's offer to use his dungeon really a set up after all? "Why?" she blurted. "What happened to the IPO plan?"

"Baby, Adam's one of my closest friends. He has the vision, but—" Deon shook his head. "I don't think he has the management skills for a more mature company."

"But the company's been growing—" Taneka started.

"Almost too fast, Tee." Deon grabbed her right hand and stroked it. "Plus, we're losing some quality people because they're getting lured away with signing bonuses. We're only offering stock, and if the IPO goes poorly, I can guarantee a lot more of our people will leave, too."

"What does this have to do with D.C.?" she murmured. "He's planning to move the whole company across the country?"

"No, but he wants to open an east coast division to recruit some talent on this side of the country. The job's mine if I want it."

Taneka couldn't breathe. Too many thoughts whirled through her brain. She'd been in corporate America long enough to know when a buy-out like this occurred, the new owner would make all kinds of promises, but they'd start cleaning house sooner rather than later. If the previous management was naïve, like she knew Adam was and began to fear Deon was as well, they'd find themselves out on their collective asses with nothing to show for it.

Was that what this weekend on Richard's private island was really all about? To interrogate Deon about a software firm he wanted to buy? To butter her up with the private dungeon and the prospect of moving closer to her parents and friends?

She didn't like being used. It was the biggest reason she stayed out of the corporate world after she'd been laid off. She preferred writing fiction. She could make her characters do what she wanted, including making her heroes honorable and forthright. They didn't use her hidden desires against her.

"Tee?" Deon kissed the back of her hand and threaded his fingers between hers. "Taneka? Talk to me, baby. What do you think?"

She swallowed hard. "I think we need to check all our paperwork carefully. And I think you need to get your own business attorney before you sign anything. I don't want you doing anything just because you think it'll make me happy. I can work from anywhere."

"Baby, I swear I'm thinking about all of us. Especially Sarah and Keshon." He smiled, his teeth gleaming. "If I take Richard's offer, they could go to the same private school as the Obama girls."

Taneka swallowed hard again. She couldn't seem to keep that damn lump out of her throat. "What was his offer to you?"

Deon named the figure, but the benefits he mentioned alone were more than they both made now. "So, what do you think?"

"Can I sleep on this before I give you an answer?"

"I wouldn't expect otherwise from you." Deon cupped her face with his free hand and laid a tender kiss on her lips. "I love you, baby."

"I love you, too," she murmured.

They stretched out on the mattress and spooned. Soon, Deon's breathing slowed and deepened. But Taneka watched the shadows shift and grow across the room long after he fell asleep. Part of her wondered what would happen when the shadows finally swallowed her.

Chapter Twelve

Shortly after dawn the next morning, Taneka burst into Richard and Alicia's bedroom. "Is your bullshit offer the real reason for this fabulous trip to paradise?"

"What the hell?" Alicia yelled.

"Taneka!" Richard roared.

From Alicia's knees hiked over Richard's shoulders, they were right in the middle of . . . things.

"Now, you know how I felt," Taneka growled. "And by the way, lock your fucking door if you're going to do the mattress mambo." She jabbed a finger at Richard. "You and I are not done."

"Get out!" he shouted.

When she left, Taneka made a point of slamming their bedroom door. Dammit, she needed some coffee since she'd barely slept a wink last night. She nearly ran into Paolo as she rounded the corner into the kitchen.

"What's going on?" he asked while he wiped his hands on a kitchen towel. The aroma of fresh coffee followed him. "That wasn't a good loud sound."

"It's . . . nothing." Taneka tried to rein in her anger. It wasn't fair to take it out on Beth's boyfriend. "Why are you awake so early?"

"The joys of working construction." He headed back toward the stove. "This time of year I'm usually up at four to beat the traffic to a job site, so seven is me sleeping in. You want some scrambled eggs and toast?"

"Maybe just some toast," she murmured. Her stomach rolled over at the thought of Deon losing everything he worked for. How stupid did Richard think Deon was? The first thing a new owner does is clean house when they make a new purchase. Deon would be one of the first to be let go, not to mention his stock could be worthless after the sale.

Paolo fished two slices of bread out of a bag on the counter and put them into the toaster. Taneka grabbed a couple of mugs from the cupboard. She poured the first cup and handed it to Paolo after he set the carton of eggs on the counter. Micki wandered into the kitchen from the patio as Taneka finished pouring the second cup.

"Was that you two I heard a couple of minutes ago?" Micki asked. She already had a healthy sheen of sweat on her skin and soaking her sports bra and running shorts.

"I was not involved in the yelling." Paolo cracked an egg into a bowl and tossed the shells into the trash.

"You and Deon get into—" Micki started.

"No." Taneka shoved the mug into Micki's hands and stomped back to the cupboard. She didn't miss the look Paolo and Micki exchanged.

"Then who—" Micki started.

"None of your business," Taneka snapped at the same time Paolo said, "Richard."

When Taneka whirled to face Paolo, he shrugged. "I've been with Beth long enough to know there's no secrets between you ladies."

Taneka yanked the cupboard door open and grabbed another mug.

"What's going on, Tee?" Micki said. "It's not like you to pick a fight with someone you just met."

"Well, that's certainly good to know," Richard bit out as he entered the kitchen. He'd dressed in a pair of navy knit exercise shorts and a pale blue t-shirt, but his hair was still in disarray. "Or was this simply revenge for Alicia interrupting you and your husband after the wedding?"

"Why are *you* lying to my husband?" Taneka banged the mug on the counter. "You only invited us here to butter up Deon and get inside information, didn't you?"

"This trip was supposed to be a surprise for all of you." Richard scowled at her. "My girlfriend missed her closest friends and wanted to spend time with you. And I am not lying to Deon." He stared at the tile floor as if collecting his thoughts. "Paolo, Micki, would you mind giving us some privacy for a few minutes?"

"Yes, sir." Paolo placed the bowl of raw eggs in the refrigerator, suggesting he didn't believe the conversation would only be a few minutes, and strode out of the kitchen.

Micki set down her mug and folded her arms across her chest. "No."

"Micki, please—" Richard's face grew redder by the moment.

"Oh, Richard, honey." She smiled sweetly. "You should know by now that if you mess with one Cougar cheerleader, you mess with us all."

Taneka folded her arms over her chest, too. "What's the jail time for fraud, Micki?"

'Five to thirty, depending on the type," Micki answered. Her eyes narrowed. "What stupid thing did you do this time, Dick?" She drawled out the nickname, which Richard clearly despised.

"This isn't any of your business," he snapped.

Micki turned to Taneka. "What stupid thing did he do this time?" Before Taneka could say a word, Micki pivoted to face Richard again. "Please tell me you didn't suggest a swap party."

His mouth fell open, and he stammered a few times before he yelled, "What? No!"

"He brought Deon here because he wants to buy Deon's company," Taneka said.

"Oooo!" Micki grinned. "And he's talking to one of the veeps behind the CEO and board's backs. I see what you mean about fraud."

"It's not fraud to make sure one of the most valuable executives will remain if I buy the company!"

"What the hell's going on down here?" Deon's voice made all three of them in the kitchen jump. He leaned against the doorframe. "Beth took her men for a walk, and Ryan is trying to sooth Alicia, who's in her bedroom crying. So, what the hell has gotten into you three?"

"Does Adam and the board know about this buyout?" Taneka snapped.

"Yes." Deon folded his arms over his chest. "Now, what are you fighting about?"

"Your wife seems to think the reason for this trip is for me to take advantage of you," Richard said.

"Take advantage of me?" Deon stared at Taneka as if she'd lost her damn mind. "No offence, Richard, but you're not my type."

"Ditto," Richard muttered. "Maybe I should check on Alicia." He glared at Taneka. "And you damn well better apologize to her. If you have a problem with me, you take it up with me. You don't take it out on her." He padded out of the kitchen.

"Micki, get the fuck out," Deon murmured.

"Or what?" she snapped.

"I'll report you for police brutality." But Deon didn't look at Micki. Instead, he continued glaring at Taneka.

"You're a bitch, Deon Foster," Micki muttered. However, she stalked out of the kitchen.

"I cannot believe you, Tee." Deon shook his head. "If you had questions, why didn't you ask me?"

"Because you . . ." She needed to pound something, so she unfolded her arms and banged her right fist against the counter. "You want to think the best of everyone. Buyouts like this don't work out for anyone who remains with the new owner."

"Baby, just because you got laid off—"

"I was the best programmer there!" Taneka threw her hands in the air. "But I'm a woman, and Bill had a family to take care of!"

"Dammit, Tee!" Deon held out his hands. "So, some jackass screwed you. You're making more money now as a writer. What he said doesn't matter."

"This isn't about my resentment." Her eyes burned, and she blinked away the wetness. "This is about you thinking you're going to slide by in the same situation. How long have you known about this?"

"Since Adam told me about the possible sale last week." Deon blew out a deep breath. "He's planning on taking the buyout Richard is offering and leaving. You were totally right. He's bored as fuck. The excitement phase is done. And Adam knew Richard called me."

"Why didn't you tell me?" Taneka hugged herself. He'd never lied to her. Not like this.

"Because I didn't want you freaking before we worked things out." He pulled her into his arms, but she couldn't accept his comfort.

"And what happens if you two can't work something out?" she mumbled.

"After you busted in on him having sex, working things out could be questionable right now—"

She jerked from his hold. "This is your fault for not telling me!" Taneka stormed out of the kitchen and raced for the stairs. She wasn't sure which was worse, the fact she made a fool of herself or that fact that Deon didn't think she was capable of dealing with his job change.

<h1 style="text-align:center">Chapter Thirteen</h1>

Taneka sat on a beach towel beneath the shade of a palm tree and watched the waves roll in with a shushing noise. A clean, salty breeze came off the water. Gulls skimmed the crests. Their calls resembled laughter, as if they mocked her. She'd been here long enough the shadows reached for the waves hissing against the white sand. The slap of flip-flops drew her attention.

Beth trudged down the path, two bottles in her hands and a pink towel slung over her left forearm. She reached Taneka and didn't say a word, merely handed her one of the grapefruit-flavored IPAs from Richard's restaurant-sized refrigerator. Beth shook out her towel besides Taneka's, kicked off her flip-flops, and sat down on the borrowed beach towel. She unscrewed the cap and held out her bottle.

Taneka twisted off the cap from her beer and clinked her bottle against Beth's before they both took a long drink. She eyed Beth.

"Aren't you going to tell me how rude I was to our host?"

"Do I have to?" Beth said. She turned and stared at the waves. "Has it occurred to you that you wouldn't have been this pissy if it were mine, Diana's, or Micki's guys wanting to buy Deon's company?"

"Really?" Taneka glared at her. "You think this is all about Alicia?"

"Isn't it?"

"This is about my husband losing his job at the company he helped build from the ground up, and he doesn't see what will happen once Richard has his claws in the business."

"So you'd come stomping into my bedroom, interrupting a scene, because you're pissed I wanted to buy Deon's company?" Beth took another sip of her beer. "Because I'm the one who pointed Richard in Deon's direction."

"Y-you did what?" Taneka stared at Beth. "W-why would you do that?"

"Because my dad was one of the venture capitalist that provided the seed money." Beth shrugged. "With his and Mom's deaths, I own a large chunk of Deon's company."

"Y-you never said anything."

"Dad was supposed to be a silent partner." Beth blew out a deep breath. "I hate to tell you this, but I've been reading the reports. Deon's buddy Adam is not the one to take their company to the next level. Deon, maybe. If he had the right backing."

"Do you have any idea what you're saying?" Beer sloshed out of Taneka's bottle as she gestured wildly.

"I know exactly what I'm saying." Beth frowned. "The question is whether you trust Deon."

"Of course, I trust him," Taneka blurted.

"Do you really?" Beth said. "Because you are seriously questioning his business acumen in front of the man I built Deon up to."

Shit. Taneka clenched her jaw. Beth was right.

"Thank you for not saying it was about Alicia," Taneka murmured.

"Well, you do kind of owe her an apology for busting in on her." Beth smiled ruefully. "And I am really sorry we walked in on you and Deon." She scooted closer and wrapped an arm around Taneka's shoulders. "You know Sarah would be kicking all of our asses if she was still here."

"Yeah." Taneka chuckled. "She definitely would have. I miss her." She sighed. "I miss all of you girls."

"Then why are you fighting so hard not to move back to D.C.?"

"I don't think that's what I'm fighting." Taneka reached up and patted Beth's hand. "I think I broke one of our rules accidentally."

Beth laughed and rested her head on Taneka's shoulder. "Let me guess. Dominating outside of a scene?"

"Yep." Taneka stared at the horizon. White clouds turned pink against the deepening blue.

"Then as his domme, shouldn't you be making it right?" Beth murmured.

"Do you know where they are?"

"In Richard's office talking business." Beth squeezed Taneka once before releasing her. "And Alicia's in the kitchen."

"I don't get why you stand up for her when she was always picking on you." Taneka shook her head.

"The same reason your mom cut her slack back in high school," Beth said. "Because her attitude covers up some major insecurity. You haven't seen how much she's changed over the last year."

Taneka stood up and wobbled before she caught herself.

"And get some crackers," Beth said. "Beer on an empty stomach isn't a good idea when medical help is an hour away by plane."

"Yes, ma'am." Taneka saluted her before she carefully grabbed her towel off the sand and headed up the path to the house.

Chapter Fourteen

After fifteen minutes of apologies, tears, and crackers in the kitchen, Taneka strode down the hallway of the south wing, sucked in a deep breath, and knocked on Richard's office door.

A masculine voice called out, "Come in!"

She pushed the door open. Both Richard and Deon had surprised expressions. She sucked in another deep breath.

"I'm sorry for interrupting, but there's a couple of things I need to say." She looked their host in the eye. "I apologize for entering your bedroom uninvited, Richard. You've been nothing but polite to me, and I let my personal feelings obscure that fact." She turned to Deon. "And I apologize, baby, for breaking one of our cardinal rules. It won't happen again."

"Thank you." Deon smiled.

Richard smiled as well. "And I accept your apology, too, Taneka."

Deon turned to Richard. "Do you mind if we take a break for a couple of minutes so I can talk to Taneka?"

"That's not necessary. I really did think over what you said last night." She approached Deon and took his hand. "My job's portable, so wherever you need to be, that's where we'll go." She squeezed his palm. "Though I admit the D.C. metro area would be my first choice."

"You sure?" he asked.

"Because it does mean he'll be working for me," Richard added.

"I know," she said. "And yes, I'm sure."

Deon looked at Richard. "Then I accept your offer." Both men rose from their chairs and shook hands.

Taneka breathed a little sigh of relief that she hadn't totally ruined things for Deon. And he was right. She shouldn't have let her bad experience color her perception of Richard.

"Is it okay if I tell the girls?" she asked.

"Yes, but I'd appreciate it if the news doesn't leave the island," Richard answered.

"You mean we can't tell my family?" She clamped down on the flicker of disappointment. Secrets caused nothing but trouble.

"Just until we announce the merger." Richard held up his hands. "I have to worry about shit like insider trading if the news gets out before we're ready. It should only be another two weeks."

"All right." Taneka held out her palm. "It's a deal."

Richard took her hand, and they shook. He wasn't the type of asshole who tried to break her bones, so maybe there was some hope for him after all.

Taneka waited until Beth returned from the beach before she said a word. The kitchen erupted with feminine squeals, a lot of jumping, hugs, and more tears.

"We need to call Diana," Micki yelled.

"We are not interrupting her honeymoon!" Taneka yelled right back. "I'll call her with the news when she and Daniel get home."

"So everything's okay between you and Deon?" Beth asked.

"Yes." Taneka hugged her again. "Thanks for being my sounding board."

"Any time."

"Do we need to break up another girl fight?" Ryan called out from the door to the patio. He led Aaron and Paolo into the house. All three men carried a platter of grilled seafood.

"I keep hoping for naked all-girl pillow fight," Aaron said dryly.

All four women glared at him.

"Too soon, man," Paolo pseudo-whispered. "Way too soon."

"How about some champagne instead?" Richard said as he and Deon entered the kitchen.

Of course, Mr. Billionaire had champagne and crystal champagne flutes in his tropical estate. Within minutes, everyone had a glass of bubbly.

"To friends," Alicia said.

Everyone repeated the salute before they dived into the seafood.

Deon wrapped an arm around Taneka's waist. "So we're good?"

"We're awesome." She leaned against his chest. "I am really sorry I almost blew your deal."

"You never break our personal rules so I wasn't sure what was going on," he murmured in her ear. "I'm sorry I didn't realize how angry you were about getting laid off three years ago."

"There's a way you could make it up to me," she said.

"Does it have to do with a brass key?"

"Yep."

Deon chuckled. "Then I guess we're going to bed early tonight. And I'm going to need my energy."

As he stepped away to grab a plate, Alicia wrapped an arm around Taneka's waist. "I'm glad you're moving back."

"You sure about that after this morning?" Taneka teased.

"Yeah." Alicia sobered. "I took all of you for granted."

"All of us?"

"I knew you wanted to be head cheerleader." Alicia shook her head. "I wanted it just as much, but part of me felt like I didn't deserve it. I hate to admit it, but I was never so relieved in my life when we all quit the squad."

"When are you going to stop being so hard on yourself?" Taneka hugged Alicia.

"Once you're back in D.C." Alicia laughed. "Can you imagine all of us together again in the same city? There was a time when we thought we would conquer the world."

"We still will." Taneka clinked her champagne flute against Alicia's. "Here's to good friends."

Chapter Fifteen

Two months later, Taneka pivoted, taking in the empty mother-in-law suite and trying to envision furniture in here, while Deon shooed the real estate agent out the door, telling her he needed to talk with his wife.

Once she was gone, he asked, "Well, what do you think, baby?"

She shook her head. "Do we really need this much space?"

"A bedroom for us and one each for the kids." He ticked each room off on the fingers of his left hand. "We're both going to need home offices—"

"But a mother-in-law suite?" Taneka gestured at the area around her. "You know my mom will end up at Mike or Jordan's if something happens to Dad. And if your dead mother shows up on our doorstep, we have a much bigger problem."

"I was thinking more in terms of a play room." A wicked grin spread across his face as he stepped closer to her.

"For the kids?" she teased.

"I was thinking for us." He pulled her into his arms.

"But how do you plan to get stuff in here without the kids knowing?"

"We can have any workmen come during school hours."

"And where are you going to find these workmen that will only be here for the six or so hours the kids are at school?" She wrapped her arms around his waist and swayed with him.

"Richard gave me some recommendations of people who do discreet work." Deon's expression turned serious. "There's a private club he and Alicia belong to. He asked if we were interested."

Worry ran through Taneka. "What kind of club?"

"The kind where you could learn new ways to torture me."

She frowned. "I'm not sure I want to share you with anybody else."

"Nor do I want to be shared." He looked around the room. "But apparently, both Aaron and Daniel are members, too."

Taneka took a step back. "What?"

"Does it bother you your friends are as much into kink as you are?" Deon raised an eyebrow as if daring her to lie.

"A little," she admitted.

"Well, the sooner we buy a house in the metro area, the sooner you girls can compare notes over wine."

Taneka chuckled. "You know me too well." She took a deep breath and released it. "Let's make an offer on this place."

As they walked hand in hand through the doorway to the main house, Taneka whispered, "So what's this club called?"

"Club Noir."

Club Noir was introduced in the Secrets series with *Tied By Lust* eight years ago, and I've been wanting to revisit the private, exclusive club chapters in the cities around the world. First, we go back to London thirty years ago to when Doctor Johanna Ridgeley meets security specialist Rick Paine in *Domme*. Turn the page for a sneak peek!

Excerpt from

Domme

©2020, Onné Andrews

"May I inquire as to the reason for this meeting, sir?" Rick Paine flicked an uncertain glance at his old friend Jamie before returning his attention to the Emir of Kutom.

"The minister asked you here at my request." The emir leaned against the back of his chair. "I have need of a security expert here in London, Mr. Paine."

"Surely your own people or Minister Wynton-Smythe—"

The emir held up his hand. "It is more complicated than my personal security. I have need of someone with a reputation for discretion to protect an associate here in London."

This was not going to end well. Rick rubbed his right eyebrow. "With all due respect, sir, I'm not the person to watch your mistress."

Jamie gave him the watch-your-manners glare, but Rick really didn't care at this point. The emir, however, seemed amused.

He turned to Jamie. "I like him. It will take a strong-willed person to perform this job." He picked up a manila folder that sat next to his coffee tray. "Please look at these before you make up your mind, Mr. Paine."

Rick flipped through the pages. The first one appeared to be a copy of a standard love letter addressed to "Beloved J". The next made the writer seem desperate and pathetic. The following three grew progressively more threatening and violent. None of them were signed. All of them mentioned the writer knew a devastating secret about this "Beloved J".

He looked up at the emir. "Have you contacted Scotland Yard about these?"

"No." The emir shook his head. "Johanna refuses to do so. She's currently a senior house officer at Tower Hospital. She's concerned the scandal would affect her career."

Rick blinked at that revelation. A doctor? So, she wasn't some bird looking to line her nest. He already respected this Johanna.

He handed the folder back to the emir. "Who is she, and what do you expect me to do?"

"Right now, she's very angry, and she doesn't expect you to do a bloody thing," a woman snapped.

Rick twisted on the couch to find a woman stalking into the living area from one of the suite's bedrooms. She was tall with legs that wouldn't quit, even without her impossibly high heels. Hips curved into a small waist. The prim skirt and blouse couldn't hide her lovely assets on top either. Blue eyes flashed lightning, but all he could think about was how much he wanted to see her chestnut hair flow across her shoulders instead of pinned up.

He belatedly rose when the other two men stood. What was it about her that made all of his manners flee?

She marched to a halt beside the emir's chair and glared at him. "I told you to stay out of this, Faddil. It's not about you. Some idiot has his knickers in a twist over having yet another woman in the medical field."

"No, Doctor," Rick said evenly. "It's about you, and from what I just read, if you don't take this seriously, it will escalate until someone gets hurt. His Majesty doesn't want you to be that person."

"And who might you be?" she said archly.

"This is Mr. Richard Paine," the emir replied. "Rick, may I introduce Doctor Johanna Ridgeley?"

A sly smile crossed her face, one that sent an electric thrill through his entire body. "What an appropriate name."

Domme **is available for preorder!**

Onné Andrews is currently trapped in a tiny Great Lakes town and writes erotic fiction to keep from turning into Stephen King's Carrie. Her men, Pierce and Daniel, feed her cheesecake in bed to calm the monster within her.

For news, sales, and giveaways, join Onne's mailing list or visit Onne's website at www.onneandrews.com. You can also check her out on Twitter or Facebook.

(Your information will not be sold, leased or otherwise given to a third party.)

www.ingramcontent.com/pod-product-compliance
Lightning Source LLC
Chambersburg PA
CBHW070422170726
48291CB00002B/312